DARKNESS DEFINED

S BOLANOS

CHAOTIC NEUTRAL PRESS LLC

SERIES

<u>Paranormal Lines</u>

War on Darkness

Darkness Defined
Order of Light
Knight's of Nyx

Moons of Mystery

Sara's Moon
Charline's Solstice
Diana's Eclipse

<u>Contemporary Lines</u>

iv

Ulwich Preparatory Academy

Fall
Winter
Spring

Oak Haven Romances

One Brave Thing
All the Hype

To my incredible husband, who is literally the only reason this series has a plot.

CONTENTS

"There is always shadow. Where there is light, there is darkness."

CHAPTER 1

SUPERNO HOUSE

MATT

A faded green door with age-spotted glass opened and the jerk that had hauled me out of the half-way house shoved me unceremoniously into an office. "Administrator Smith will see you now."

I ripped my arm free of the unnecessarily tight hold and glared at him as he retreated out the way we'd come. The door snicked shut, then I turned my attention to the room's occupant.

A portly man seated behind a metal desk paused his perusal of open files to give me a once over. His thinning, gray hair was combed over in a vain attempt to hide the balding, and the dark circles under his eyes spoke of a persistent exhaustion. Add to that the frayed edges of his coat and it was clear he cared more about his job than his appearance. Still, his eyes were borderline vacant as he took in my bedraggled appearance.

I fought the urge to shrink as his empty gaze took stock of me from my too small shirt that didn't quite cover my stomach and frayed shorts with more holes than cloth, down to my worn-out shoes.

"Matthew Duncan." Whatever insecurity I'd been nursing vanished with his monotone use of my full name. He gestured at the lone chair across from him. "Have a seat."

I did my best not to sneer and begrudgingly sat. I'd been off of the streets for three hours—max. Immediately stirring up trouble with the guy in charge wouldn't endear me to anyone, not to mention it would guarantee they put me on a shit list.

The administrator grunted at my lack of response and looked back at the page before him. "I see you've had a rough go of things."

Understatement of the year.

He lowered tiny, round spectacles from their perch on his forehead and resumed his inspection of the folder. "Let's see... in the system since you were born. No luck with foster families or adoption agencies. Numerous incidents of running away, disrespecting authority, and physical violence. I guess we should be glad you're not a fire demon with that sort of temper." He sighed and set the folder on his desk. "Still, a demon is a demon."

I waited for the half-hearted laugh to emphasize the sorry joke. Instead, he went on as serious as he had started.

"You'll need to understand that this sort of behavior," he jabbed his index finger onto the hefty folder, "will not be tolerated here. Superno House may be a home for wayward supernaturals, but we run a strict campus."

I frowned, but he either didn't notice or didn't care.

"We have cared for everything from your standard witch with budding powers to demons of the highest carnal class. When I say this will be your last stop, I mean it. However, your stay here can be much more pleasant if you," he peered through his glasses at the report again, then flicked his gaze back up to me, "could enlighten us as to your particular demon class."

I crossed my arms, leaned back in the uncomfortable chair, and propped my feet on the edge of his desk. "I don't know what the hell you're talking about."

"Language, Matthew."

My feet flew off the desk and landed with a thud on the floor... except no one had touched them. I searched for some kind of clue for how he could have done it with no more than a flick of his fingers.

Smith let out a long sigh. "While yours might be the most enigmatic, I've dealt with tough cases before. We will determine what kind of demon you are." He removed his glasses and started cleaning them. "Though with no physical manifestations to provide guidance, the discovery may be less than pleasant."

I bristled. I'd been called a lot of things over the years, and honestly, "demon" wasn't new. Whatever he called me, all I needed was ten months. Ten months until I could no longer be considered a ward of the state. It was the only goal that mattered: freedom. I ignored the bait and simmered in silence, tuning out the nonsense he was spewing about how things were different here. It was all lies. Superno House would be no different from any of the seven orphanages.

Orphans had their own hierarchy. Those that had been around the longest typically occupied the top of the food chain while the newcomers landed on the bottom—or were made to. Funnily enough, it was those attempts that usually resulted in me getting kicked out of whatever place I'd been dropped. I smirked to myself. It wasn't my fault the other boys couldn't hold their own.

"Are you paying attention?" Smith huffed. "Listen here, Matthew-"

"I go by Matt."

His eyes narrowed. "I will not tolerate rudeness. We may not know what kind of demon you are yet, but we will. When we do, this untouchable status you think you've cultivated will be gone. The children here are not the easy pickings you're used to."

My dislike of the man solidified. I was not a bully.

Unexpectedly, the tough teacher act dropped and Smith sagged in his chair, exhaustion pulling him deeper into the dilapidated cushion. "I understand how frustrating being passed around can be. Once we're able to determine how best to help you with your abilities, then the anger will fade. You have my word."

I stared blankly back.

"Has anyone explained why you're here?"

I snorted and crossed my arms. "Got caught after running away from the last place."

Smith shook his head. "That's not quite what I meant. Do you know why you're here specifically?" He tapped his desk for emphasis, and I rolled my shoulders to ease my increasing discomfort. Smith studied me for a moment. "You really don't know, do you?" He paused as if unsure how to proceed, then said slowly, "Superno House is... special."

"Whatever. I've heard that before." If I was anymore disgusted with this ridiculous charade, I might actually spew all over his desk. "As for 'abilities', last time I checked, having a bad temper and being a target for bullies wasn't an ability, it was a nightmare. Not to mention I've been tested for practically everything under the sun... multiple times. So, please, spare me. The results are always either a flat out nope or 'inconclusive'." I tightened my arms across my chest. The tests had been less than pleasant.

"I'll ignore the attitude for now, because I genuinely believe that you do not know about your true heritage. I'd love nothing more than to provide some insight, but without proper testing..." He spread his hands. "Given your—colorful—record, I'd hazard that you belong to the Chaos Class. We have a few of those here. Though, given your obvious anger management issues, it's possible you're a type of elemental. Either way, you are a supernatural, Matt. There's no doubt about that."

I scoffed. "Are you for real? You can stop blowing smoke up my ass. We both know the only reason I'm here is because the age of majority in Nebraska is nineteen. Less than a year, and I'm gone." It didn't take a fantasy to explain why I was angry. Being abandoned at a Catholic church less than a month old then passed from one awful place to another did that to a person.

Smith sighed and leaned back in his chair, rubbing his temples. "It's worse than I suspected." He visually regathered himself and smacked the arm of the chair. "Let's start with a tour of the facilities. That should put things in perspective." Smith stood and walked to the door. He opened it, then waited for me to follow. When I didn't, he added, "You're welcome to stay here, but meals are only served in the cafeteria and that sofa isn't nearly as comfortable as it looks."

I eyed the questionable orange couch that by no means looked comfortable, then pushed myself up from the chair and trailed obediently behind him. I didn't really need a tour; one orphanage was much like another.

Beyond the door, a pair of kids were running full-tilt down the hall. I shook my head. Yep, exactly the same as all the others.

When the kids caught sight of Smith, they ground to a halt just shy of crashing into us. The girl looked to be a few years younger than me and the boy younger still. They looked similar with iridescently dark skin, pinched faces, and decidedly pointed ears.

The girl sneered. "What are you supposed to be?" Her doll-like face twisted into something eerily savage. I half expected to see serrated teeth peeking between her thin lips.

"Now, Mercy, don't be rude. Matt is the newest addition to the home. I expect you and your brother to make him feel welcome," Smith tacked on, his voice stern.

"He doesn't belong here," the boy piped up. His equally delicate features remained perfectly impassive, as if they were carved from black marble.

"Christian!" Smith admonished.

"He's right," Mercy added while her brother's face remained unsettlingly blank. "He's dangerous."

I snarled at her, and she shrank back. Smith gave me a nervous look, but didn't comment. I supposed next to these frail children and with my reputation, I was the bigger threat, but no one would ever peg my five-seven as imposing at first glance.

Smith cleared his throat and angled himself between us. "A specialist will come out next month. She's been recruiting for an exclusive school for... unique demons. It's possible that our recent addition may not be with us long." He gave me a sidelong glance that I was pretty sure I wasn't supposed to notice, and swallowed.

Mercy stepped closer to her brother. "Good riddance."

"Yeah, all demons do is cause trouble. They're just a bunch of bullies," Christian echoed.

I was fully aware that I'd been branded a troublemaker, but that didn't make me a bully. And what the fuck was all this demon shit about?

"That's enough." Smith pointed down the hall. "Off with you, and I better not catch anymore running. We wouldn't want a repeat of last month's incident, now, would we?"

The two shared a menacing look, then continued down the hall. All of two steps later, the peculiar kids vanished from the hallway, leaving two bright points of light where they'd been. I blinked to clear what I assumed was an afterimage, but the glowing balls stayed hovering above the ground. Then, just as suddenly, they zipped down the hall.

I staggered back and looked at Smith, my eyes in danger of falling out of my head. "What the hell was that?"

"Sprites." Smith shook his head. "Intuitive and mischievous to a fault, but they're never wrong." He finished locking his office and took off down the hall. "It's an unfortunate fact that most of the children that end up under our care are Fae or Demonic. There's the occasional elemental, but their own kind keep a closer watch on them."

I remained rooted to the ground, still struggling to make sense of what I'd seen. Except it wasn't possible. No way those creepy kids had turned into tiny balls of light and flew. Was flew even the right word? Whether it was or not didn't matter because it wasn't possible in the first place.

Smith glanced over his shoulder, not really slowing. "I told you these kids would be different. Come on, the cafeteria is this way."

I debated making a break for it, then recalled how Smith had somehow knocked my feet off my desk without touching me. If he could do that, then there was no telling what else the people in this place could do. I shuffled to catch up, equally concerned about being too close to the administrator and not really wanting to be alone.

As we walked, I examined every kid we passed for any signs of weird. Mostly I saw the usual curious faces, a couple more hostile expressions, but other than that, nothing extraordinary, and certainly nothing like I'd seen earlier. A couple of turns later, I was ready to chalk up the whole encounter to low blood-sugar. It was as likely as anything, given I couldn't remember the last time I'd eaten.

Suddenly, Smith stopped and looked over at me. "Do you smell burning?"

I blinked back at him. Now that he mentioned it, there was the faint smell of burnt popcorn, but that shouldn't be unusual in a place full of kids. Suddenly, a stream of fire blasted out into the hall of an adjoining corridor.

"Oliver!" Silence met Smith's bellow. "Oliver, I know that's you. Get out here right now."

A boy about my age stepped out, his shoulders hunched and his vibrant red hair sticking out in every direction as if he'd stuck his finger into an electrical socket.

I wrinkled my nose. The kid reeked of sulfur and had burned sleeves.

"What's your problem? Haven't you ever seen a fire demon before?" He bared his teeth at me. "I suggest you wipe that look off your face before I do it for you."

My hands curled into fists at my sides.

"Oliver." The boy flinched at Mr. Smith's tone. "How many times have we talked about fires inside?"

Oliver tore his angry glare away from me. "It's not my fault! Rufus started it." He gestured behind him and a column of fire shot from his hand.

The fear I'd been doing my best to ignore prickled along the back of my neck. Actual fucking fire had come out of his hand. If he could do that, it was entirely possible the creep twins really had turned into light.

What the hell is this place?

"Shit," Oliver hissed, shaking his smoking hand, which seemed like a terrible idea to me.

"Language," Smith admonished.

"I'm telling you. It was all Rufus." Oliver shot me a glare, and I quickly wiped the panic from my face.

Logically, I realized that getting into a fight with this kid could likely be the end of me, but if he started something, I'd finish it. The fire would be tricky, but I'd gone up against guys twice my size and come out unscathed. I was too close to freedom to let some brat intimidate me.

Smith crossed his arms while a scowl pressed into his full face. "That's enough, Oliver. You and Rufus can go see Miss Mary Ann. I'm sure she'll be able to sort this mess for you and perhaps remind you about the importance of being careful."

Oliver groaned and turned to the open door. "Come on, Rufus, you heard him. Time to go see your girlfriend."

Another kid poked his head out. He was smaller than Oliver, with sun-starved white skin and a dark mop of unkempt hair on top of a spindly frame with a thin neck like some kind of creepy bobble head. The observation was reinforced by the fact that his eyes were abnormally large and couldn't seem to hold still. Together, they trudged down the hall.

Smith rested a hand on my shoulder and I about near jumped out of my skin. "I'm sorry. It's a never-ending battle around here. Adolescence is hard enough. When you add to it budding powers, things can get a bit dicey. Safety is our number one concern, though. Fighting is strictly prohibited," Smith finished pointedly.

I frowned. That was often easier said than done in most cases. Smith nudged me along until the hall opened onto a massive room. Where I'd been expecting the usual sterile white walls, the room was a warm cream decorated with all sorts of art. It made an odd contrast to the standard metal tables with attached benches and the pristine—and currently empty—buffet.

"Meals are promptly at eight, noon, and seven. Though there are snacks available. No junk food, but plenty of fruit." Smith gestured vaguely down a wide corridor. "You'll find the sleeping quarters that way. Girls on the left, boys on the right. A fresh set of clothes should await you on your assigned bunk. Lights out at nine. Now if you'll excuse me, I think I'll be joining Miss Mary Ann in dealing with our fire-starter." He spun on his heel, leaving me standing all alone at the entrance to the cafeteria.

I glanced at the analog clock on the distant wall. Two hours 'til dinner. My stomach growled at the prospect of food and I was half a step away from making a beeline for the snack table. An apple sounded like a fantastic change from the scraps I'd been able to snag over the last couple of weeks. And yet, I hesitated.

A quick glance down the opposite direction Smith had gone showed a hall shockingly devoid of people. I chewed my lip and debated what to do. I could grab some food and even the fresh set of clothes, but that would waste precious time. Both Smith and whoever Mary Ann was were occupied. The path to the main entrance was wide open and after what I'd witnessed, I had no desire to stay here.

I made my way down the hall, careful not to appear rushed or like I was doing something I shouldn't be. The path stayed clear all the way to the remarkably mundane double doors leading to the street and freedom. I smiled to myself and didn't bother looking back as my pace quickened. With any luck, the doors would be unlocked.

I reached for the push bar and suddenly found myself walking back the way I'd come. My worn-out shoes squeaked as I came to an abrupt stop and looked around. With a frown, I spun around and aimed for the exit with more conviction... only to end up even further down the hall instead of outside where I should have been. I growled and tried again... with the same result.

"What. The. Fuck?" I glanced between the door and the hall where I kept ending up. Before I could second guess myself, I sprinted for the door.

"When you've tired yourself out, I'll take you to the showers where you can get cleaned up."

I jumped at the unexpected voice and turned to find an imposing woman leaning against the wall. She had dark hair pulled up into a bun, was easily a head taller than me, had greenish skin, and, yep, those were tusks. I swallowed hard and took a step back.

"You must be Matt."

"What the hell are you?"

She flexed an imposing pair of biceps as she straightened. "Smith mentioned this was new to you. We'll address the impropriety of asking someone 'what' they are later. For now, I'm more concerned with getting you into clothes that don't look like they're going to disintegrate. Come with me." She turned and began walking down the hall toward the cafeteria and the dormitories beyond, clearly expecting me to follow.

Though she hadn't bothered to introduce herself, I had a sneaking suspicion I'd just had my very first run-in with the infamous Mary Ann. She glanced over her shoulder and I hastened to catch up. Maybe I could stay a little longer.

Chapter 2

DANIEL

ALEXI

"I 've already told you, Daniel, I'm not interested." My gaze wandered around the room in search of my suitcase, pointedly avoiding anywhere near my *ex*-boyfriend.

I finally found it hiding behind the cracked door. That was one mercy. At least I wasn't trapped in a closed room with him. That would undoubtedly be trouble if my history with Daniel was anything to go by. Of course, my mother's strict rules about no boys in the room also didn't hurt, not that he was following them. I moved the luggage and opened the door until it touched the wall.

"Don't be like that, Alexi," Daniel said, sitting on the bed and nearly undoing all of my efforts to organize my packing.

I heaved an exasperated sigh and saved a stack of shirts before they could officially topple to the floor, a move that brought me dangerously close to him. Thanks to my absolutely zero self-control, I couldn't help but breathe in the sharp cedar of his cologne.

Getting ahold of myself, I sped up my movements before he could take advantage of my proximity. Sure enough, I caught a sigh of disappointment and looked up just in time to see his fingers pass right *through* my arm. I quickly put more distance between us. Fortunately, while beautiful, Daniel wasn't the brightest. Hopefully, he'd assume that I'd simply been out of reach and not incorporeal.

"Why are you even here?" We hadn't spoken in weeks, not since we'd broken up—again. It had been our lot the last few years to be that notorious on-again-off-again couple.

"Your mum let me in. And I couldn't very well let you go traipsing off to some fancy Uni I've never heard of without a proper goodbye." The wicked gleam in his eye left little doubt what kind of goodbye he had in mind.

Daniel knew he was classically good-looking with his square jaw and dark hair, not to mention a physique that would make Michelangelo drool. He was our small English town of Denham's uncontested resident charmer and my own personal kryptonite. He was also a lying, narcissistic jerk that had never managed to win over my mother, who liked pretty much everyone. Which begged the question: how had he gotten past her in the first place?

A glance back at him showed he was playing with my clothes, most noticeably the underwear. I leaned over and snatched the teetering stack, plopping it into the now open case before he could stop me.

Daniel looked at me with that smug grin, his dark hair falling in his eyes, then seemed to flow up off of the bed. For a human, he was surprisingly graceful, especially since he was even taller than my six feet. Once, it had been nice to be with someone who could literally cocoon me with their embrace. Now it was just suffocating. Daniel stepped forward until he'd invaded my personal space.

My spine stiffened, but I refused to back down. "Like I said before. Not interested," I reiterated in blatant disregard of my already racing heart. This is what Daniel did, what he always did, but I was determined not to make the same mistakes.

"Come on, Alexi, no one knows you like I do. No one can touch you like I can." Daniel's voice was practically a purr.

Desire pulled at me, undermining my resolve. He leaned in just enough so I could feel his breath on my lips. One last hurrah, that's what we would call it. Something to remember him by when I finally left for Arminius and could put all of this behind. But I knew what would really happen. We'd go out, have an amazing night, end up back at his place, and in the morning, I'd wake up feeling used—again.

"I think we could really make the long-distance thing work." His slick words were barely more than a suggestive whisper hovering over my lips.

I barked a laugh. "Are you serious? Long distance? Daniel, we couldn't even make down the street work." This time, the laugh was bitter.

"It'll be different," he argued.

"You mean you *won't* cheat on me?" I fired back.

"Clarke hardly counts, and we were drunk anyway, so it definitely doesn't count."

I looked at him in total disbelief. "Do you even hear what you're saying?" I scoffed to myself. One of us knew better. "You know what? I'm done entertaining your ego. I want you out of my house."

Daniel reached for my arm.

I ripped it out of reach, still not trusting myself if he actually laid a hand on me. "Now."

His arm dropped, and he looked at me entreatingly. "Lexi."

I pointed to the very open door.

"Baby," he cooed.

I stood firm. After what felt like forever, he rolled his eyes and stomped out, every inch the petulant ass who hadn't gotten what he wanted. I waited until he crossed the threshold of my bedroom, then slammed the door shut and locked it for good measure.

I rested my head against the door, still struggling with the contradictory impulse to race after him. It wasn't like I hadn't dated other guys. There was just something about Daniel that kept me coming back like a glutton for punishment. I grabbed a random book off the desk by the door and chucked it at the far wall.

Why am I so weak? How does he still have any hold on me? He cheated on me, for God's sake.

"Honey, are you alright?" a delicate voice asked through the thin wood.

"I'm fine, mom."

"If you're so fine, then open the door."

I stared up at the ceiling in search of divine intervention. When none presented itself, I unlocked and opened the door. On the other side was my mother, a full foot shorter than me, and tapping her foot impatiently.

"Why did you let him in?" I asked heatedly.

She inspected the room before deigning to answer, most likely searching for signs that we'd been fooling around, despite the very clear no fooling around rules. "Frankly, I was hoping it would help you pack faster. Though I see that hope was in vain."

I blinked, taken off guard. "What? I thought you didn't want me to go?"

She let herself into the room and walked over to the bed, where she placed three stacks of clothes in the open suitcase before sitting down in the now empty space. "Oh, sweetie, you know I love you, but truth be told, we both know I can't handle your powers. You need proper schooling with people like yourself. While you've done great blending in with the humans around here, you aren't one. You should be spending more time with your own kind."

I shook my head. "Mom, demons tend to be solitary."

"But not you, Lexi. You're social and vibrant, always have been. Or at least you were until…" Her face twisted as she looked at the door Daniel had walked through shortly before.

I was fully prepared to launch into yet another defense of my decision to continue dating Daniel over the years when she continued.

"This school opening has been the best thing that could have happened. Just think, if we had never joined the Arminius Community Forum, then we wouldn't have even known about the special classes and you would've had to wait another year, maybe even two, before you could enroll. The world hardly knows anything about Shadow Demons. This is your chance."

"The world knows to fear us. Half of the supernatural community here won't go anywhere near me since the Rebellion, and that ended ten years ago. I was eight for crying out loud. What did they expect me to do?" The words tasted as bitter as they sounded.

"I know it hurts, sweetie, but that doesn't mean you shouldn't learn about your powers. You still face the same risks that all untrained demons do. Alexi, if you lose control…" she trailed off. We both knew how dangerous that could be.

"I won't. I'm not some newbie who just learned they had powers. I've been practicing for years." I reached out and gave her hand a quick, reassuring squeeze. "You made sure of that."

She heaved a sigh. "But is it enough? What about your potential? We don't even know what you're fully capable of. What sort of world will open up to you once you start learning more?"

"Honestly, I'm probably close to peaking. I bet I'm years ahead in study from the rest of the class. After all, I've read every resource book on Shadow Demons we could find." Not that there had been many, or that they'd been easy to find, in a world that had no clue supernaturals existed.

"Lexi, I can't help but feel you're making an argument not to go at all."

Her hand settled on mine and I realized I'd steadily been unpacking as we talked. I groaned in despair.

"You were so excited about this last week and now it's like you're dreading it."

I looked over at her, taking in the tight ringlets of sandy blonde hair falling around her petite face that was nothing at all like my own jet black. My heart hurt more at the thought of leaving her here alone than it did at the idea of never seeing Daniel again. My mother was a lovely woman, and it was a shame she'd never remarried. I knew why though. She'd loved my father more than anything, and when he'd left her with nothing more than a swollen belly, she just couldn't move on.

I'd never seen so much as a picture of him before. But from what she said, I was the spitting image of a man that had stolen her heart eighteen years ago. It must be true, because I didn't look a thing like her. Except for my eyes, those were definitely hers—a bright green that shone like spring.

"I'm going to miss you," I finally said.

"I know, honey." She lifted her hand to cup the side of my face. "But I'm only a call away. I'll be fine. My goal has always been to see you succeed, and you can't do that here." She released me and placed another stack in the case, smoothing out the wrinkles on top. "Now, Alexi Roman, I need you to dig deep and be the strong person I know you are." She stood up and gave me a hug.

Her arms wrapped tightly around me, and I carefully returned the embrace. Demonic strength had not been a fun thing adjusting to growing up.

"Enough of this." She pushed me away, surreptitiously wiping a tear. "You need to stop dawdling and finish packing. Orientation is in a week and you still have to collect your things from the community center."

"Yes, mom." With a smile, she patted my cheek and left me to my task. I turned back to my mess of folding.

I don't need much, it's just school after all. It's not like I expect to meet the love of my life.

Now that I was focusing, the suitcase steadily filled. It was hard to believe that, in just a few days, I'd be in Austria at a prestigious university for the supernatural. I briefly considered packing my poster of Arminius University, but dismissed it as childish. After that, it was official. Everything worth packing was.

I flopped onto the bed, causing it to groan in protest and reached to feel beneath. When my fingers brushed a binding, a smile spread across my face. I promptly pulled it out and settled back against the wall. The book was one of the few my mother had found over the years. By some miracle, she'd known what my father was and had known to look out for the same traits in me. That knowledge had saved both of our lives.

As I thumbed through the worn pages, I couldn't help but wonder if Shadow Demon's antisocial nature was a product of our own making or biological. Hopefully, this new school—class really—could finally answer those questions. While I wasn't exactly enthusiastic about Vera Scry being the one to lead it, since she was the reason the supernatural world feared people like us in the first place, it was better than nothing.

I stopped on a page with an illustration of a shadowy woman reaching toward a knight in full armor. The passage on the other side described the scene.

The darkness itself took shape and reached out. Eyes blacker than night drank my soul. Such a creature could put fear into the evilest of man or beast. Would that my Light had not abandoned me. That cursed torch with the power to beat back this monster and preserve my essence.

I felt the darkness encircle me and draw my breath. The Daemon approached, the promise of death in its kiss. Words escaped me as the night stole the very breath from my lungs. My only mercy was that it didn't speak.

A mercy short lived as words like that from a fallen angel poured forth and drew me close, wrapping around me, a lover's embrace. My will was robbed, and I walked forward to fall into oblivion...

The rest of the passage was too obscure to make out. The creature described had all the makings of a terrifying monster and a timeless love. This was where the original owner of the manuscript and I had differed.

Notes in the margins declared the belief that this man was fighting for his immortal soul against some nameless demon and losing. I, on the other hand, believed that while the man had originally set out to slay the creature, he instead had found himself captivated, falling madly in love with his worst nightmare, that the reference to "a lover's embrace" wasn't a typo or poor translation. Even the illustration looked more like a man meeting a secret love than succumbing to pure evil.

I sighed and set the book down. It was pointless to speculate. As far as the rest of the supernatural world was concerned, we *were* evil. Vera Scry had seen to that. I still wasn't sure how I felt about going to a school she'd started. Just because she and the rest of her military unit, self-dubbed the Shadows, had switched allegiances, didn't mean we could automatically trust them.

Who's to say they won't be just as bad or worse than the Regency?

It was a fact that Shadow Demons were rare, just like it was a fact that I'd never met another one, not even the infamous Vera herself. The prospect of meeting her now was simultaneously terrifying and exciting. Not just because of who she was, but because of *what* she was—a level two. Contrary to how most things in the human world were rated, demon classes followed more of a pyramid structure when it came to levels. The lower the number, the higher you were on the general power scale, with level ones, or originals, being right at the top.

I didn't even think it was possible for someone like her to exist so far removed from a direct lineage of power. The stories said that her level was a freak accident, absolutely unprecedented. And yet, the existence of this class at all said that Shadow Demons were primed to make a comeback from the brink of extinction.

I held out my hand and called to the darkness with my essence. As thick fog pooled in my palm, I could feel it straining against my control. My mother had a point. I had no idea what I was really capable of beyond parlor tricks and half-baked theories. What *could* a trained Shadow Demon do?

I guided the substance by force of will across the room to turn off the lights. Instantly, my realm of influence extended. Controlling my tiny bubble of shadow at once became easier and infinitely more difficult. Without the light to destroy it, maintaining the shadow was a piece of cake. However, now that darkness was all around, it echoed my call, reaching for me as much as I reached for it.

It glided along my skin, intimate and gentle, like a lover's caress. That was the main reason I believed the man in the book had been seduced. The night could be full of terrors, but it could also be full of passion. I released the shadow to join its essence—my essence.

I am the darkness, and the darkness is me.

The resonance inside of me intensified as I continued to extend my control. As I reached for the night, the night reached back for me, igniting a longing that went deeper than a mere need to be touched.

I let it go, sinking back to the normal realm of sensation. Someday, I'd find someone who could make me feel as alive as the darkness did, who would understand what I could never hope to explain. I shook off the romantic thought and sighed into the gloom, still struggling with my own mixed feelings. What *would* it be like to meet others like myself? If I was being honest, I was absolutely terrified at the prospect. It was too late to back out now, though. In eight days, I'd meet an entire class full of people just like me.

I smiled into the darkness.

Well, maybe not just like me.

CHAPTER 3

THE NEWCOMER

M

Beneath the strict supervision of Miss Mary Ann, I got cleaned up and into clothes that almost fit. Then I wandered around Superno House while I waited for dinner, doing my best to stay out of the way. The more I saw, the less I understood. Calling these kids different was a nice way to put it. And somehow, somewhere along the line, someone had gotten convinced that I was one of them. A supernatural.

I grabbed a tray and made my way to an empty table by an oil painting of a forest, determined to lie low. If I could stay out of trouble long enough, this place could be my last stop before I was finally free to decide about my own life. A girl sat down at the far end of my previously unoccupied table. I glanced over as she tucked her hair behind her ear. A light smile tipped my lips. She was pretty and there was no reason the wait had to be totally intolerable.

I was about to call over to her when I saw the horns poking up through her straight black hair. Air went down the wrong way and I struggled to cough through it without drawing attention to myself or dying. Thoroughly put off of pursuing anything with someone at Superno House, I focused my attention on my tray. Given how sporadic my meals had been the last few weeks, I didn't care what the food looked like; it smelled edible, and that was good enough.

I took a bite of what I hoped was meatloaf and almost immediately had to smother a moan. Whatever it was, it was good. I fought the urge to shovel all of it into my mouth as fast as possible, already debating about trying to sneak back for a second helping. No amount of going slow would make it last, though. In record time, my plate was clean and the only thing I had left were my thoughts, and boy, did I have plenty of them. Most of the people I'd seen appeared normal enough, but like the girl at my table, I suspected they were all far from it. Even Oliver had looked like any other scruffy orphan and he'd shot fire out of his hand.

I looked down at my hand. He'd called himself a fire demon. I examined both sides of the appendage and imagined what it would be like to do what I'd seen earlier. Unsurprisingly, nothing happened. I scowled, disappointed in my juvenile fantasy, and let out a huff. The way everyone said "demon" made it sound like there was more than one kind. If that was the case, how many kinds were there? Had I met any before? Was it possible Smith was right, and I was a demon? But if I was, then how did he know? And why didn't he know what kind?

I sagged beneath the weight of doubt. Per usual, I had more questions than answers. My stomach gave a small growl, drawing my attention to the more important question right now—could I snag another helping without getting caught? I was about to try my luck when the hairs on the back of my neck stood up.

"I think we should give the new guy a proper Superno House welcome. What do you think, Rufus?" a voice that sounded suspiciously like Oliver said beside me. A quick glance without moving my head confirmed it.

"I think that's perfect," the guy who I assumed was Rufus responded. "Khima?" The girl with the horns looked over.

I blanched as I realized the rest of her was also sporting barbs.

"I'm game," she responded without hesitation.

I swallowed hard. So much for not making waves. Another glance up showed that Rufus was practically on top of the table leering at me. His bug eyes wiggled incessantly, and he smiled, revealing alarmingly pointy teeth. My eyes widened slightly. Behind him, Oliver stood, holding a steady flame in his hand. There was no pretending anymore. These guys definitely weren't human.

Rufus's head cocked to the side and the queer sight of it almost made me lose my dinner. "Carter is coming," he whispered, lowering himself to sit on the bench.

The flame in Oliver's hand disappeared into a closed fist just before a man that looked more like a gorilla than a children's care attendant walked by.

I held my tongue and tried not to look panicked. If I called for help, they'd only find me later and it would be so so much worse. Once he was gone, someone grabbed the back of my shirt and pulled me to my feet, not caring when my legs got tangled between the table and the bench.

Oliver's manic smile filled my vision. "Good, you made it, Scylla."

My optimistic belief that I could take him now seemed stupid and short-sighted. He might be the ringleader, but there was no way I could take four of them on my own.

"Wouldn't want to miss this." The owner of the voice bared a striking resemblance to the kids I'd met in the hall, though she looked meaner and older and was porcelain pale where the others had been dark. Resemblance or no, it didn't make a lick of sense how she could drag me off of the table like it was nothing, not with her light frame.

"Get moving, meat." She shoved me toward a side door. I had no idea where it led. I also didn't have any options, so I walked.

"Meat," Rufus chuckled. "It's funny because he's practically human. I mean, look at him. How did he even get in here?"

"They let in all sorts of weirdos these days," Khima said, pulling up on my left. Who was she calling a weirdo? The girl in the hall had called me dangerous, but compared to this group, I was inclined to agree with Rufus.

Strangely, or maybe not strangely at all, no one seemed interested in five kids working their way to an obviously off-limits metal door. I attempted to drag my feet.

Maybe that gorilla-thing will come back and stop this whole mess before I end up in a pulverized puddle.

The door got closer.

Where did he go? Where are all of the adults?

I intentionally stumbled at the threshold, one last desperate attempt to buy time.

"Hurry up," Scylla hissed, and forced me through the opening.

To my dismay, the door shut with a whispered hiss of air. A quick glance around showed that we were now in some sort of courtyard, or maybe it was a playground, with a high brick wall to our right. I squinted in the darkness and was able to make out basketball hoops and a jungle gym. What I didn't see were witnesses.

My jailer gave me another shove, and I stumbled a forward. I spun around, wanting to keep all four of them in sight. Fat lot of good that did. The group spread out to encircle me, driving me further from the only escape route I knew of.

"He looks scared," Khima snickered, her horns back-lit by distant lamps.

Oliver stepped forward to separate himself from the ring. "He should be." The world took on a sudden light as two pillars of flame shot up from Oliver's hands. I instinctively bent my knees and sank into the ground. I didn't know what to expect, but it didn't take a genius to know that I didn't want to lose my footing.

"Aw, is the little baby crying for his mama?" Scylla crooned to a chorus of cackles.

"I can't hear anything. Maybe I should get closer." Rufus sped toward me as if he wasn't even touching the ground, his teeth glinting in the unnatural light from Oliver's hands. Panic twinged in my chest as the reality of what I was seeing struck home. That freak had wings.

The thought barely had time to form before I had to dodge out of the way. I spun around to search for him, only to be sucker punched by Khima in the gut. The hit ejected all the air from my lungs. I struggled to drag it back in, but it wouldn't come, almost as if someone was simultaneously pulling it back out. I searched my attackers frantically for the source until I saw Scylla's feral smile. She made a pulling motion and I put it together.

Sprite, that's what she is, just like the kids from the hall. Mischievous and what? Intuitive.

Mercy and Christian had called me dangerous, but how could I possibly compare to something that could literally steal the air from your lungs? Then again, Smith had said sprites were never wrong.

I gave up trying to draw air, and the resistance vanished. Scylla stumbled back as if I'd let go of a rope she'd been pulling. I turned to face Oliver. Chances were that if he went down, the others would back off... hopefully.

"What's the matter, Ollie? Too afraid to face me yourself?" I wheezed.

The red-headed demon's face lit with fury. "That's it, step back. I'm going to show this miserable wretch what a real demon can do."

"Hey," Rufus whined.

"Shut up. You're a lower class and you know it." Rufus withered at the onslaught and Oliver turned his attention to the Sprite. "I heard Mercy and Christian talking. He's supposed to be something worth fighting. What do you think, Scylla? Is he worth my time?" Tiny flames licked up and down his fingers while he spoke. It was easy to see how his cuffs had gotten burned. Unlike the fabric, though, his skin didn't seem to react at all.

Her smile looked evil in the lurid light of the flames. "I think all the power in the world doesn't mean shit if you don't know how to use it."

"My thoughts exactly." Oliver's eyes narrowed as his attention returned to me. "You're nothing special. You're just some overgrown toe rag no one wanted, and a coward to boot."

My anger grew as the insults hit me, pulsing like a living thing, eager to escape and tear him apart.

"Scared little chicken shit is what you are."

The world went black.

Where other people saw red, I saw darkness, pure and all-consuming; it was everywhere; it was everything. The first time it had happened, I'd freaked. It had only lasted a moment, but it had been enough to leave me shaking and terrified. That had been a long time ago, and I wasn't the same scared little kid. My focus zeroed in on Oliver. He thought he was tough shit because his hands were made of fire, but he'd have to catch me first. I didn't wait to see if the others would listen to his high-handed command. I rushed him where he was too busy gloating to realize I'd moved.

"What the fu-" Oliver started in disbelief.

Out of the corner of my eye, I saw Rufus flying towards me. He almost sideswiped me, but instead ran into Khima on the other side, who I hadn't even realized was approaching.

Pay attention. This is no time to lose track of people.

Oliver braced himself for impact, the flames on his hands growing into large spheres that encircled his fists. At the last second, I changed my course, heading for Scylla instead. She'd already proved she didn't have to touch me to hurt me. If I even had a chance of taking down Oliver, she'd have to go as well.

Scylla's eyes lit with panicked rage when she finally saw me coming. Before she could react, I was behind her. She seemed genuinely startled, but it was too late. I grabbed her by the arm and flung her back. She soared across the courtyard to slam into the wall back by the door.

For a moment, I almost lost my concentration. I'd never thrown anyone that far before. Then Rufus was bearing down on me again, those unnerving teeth ready to tear me apart. I searched the ground for something to put between me and his mouth of razors.

Then I spied it. In the dark, it looked like only a shadow, but it was definitely club-shaped and that worked for me. It was cool to the touch as I wrapped my fingers around it and fell into a batter's stance. Once Rufus was in range, I swung with all I had. As the miraculous club slammed into his mouth, confusion exploded across his face.

Time stretched as the momentum of his assault met the force of my swing. Then he, too, went flying. I didn't see where he landed. Oliver's head swiveled around like he couldn't believe what was happening while Khima tried to get back to her feet. In the distance, it sounded like Scylla was also recovering. I was running out of time.

I renewed my run for Oliver, my feet pounding on the pavement. He looked far less confident now. Shame it never occurred to him he couldn't see anything with all that fire in his face. Ironic really.

Abruptly, my steps slowed as if I was trudging through molasses instead of open air. That had to be Scylla. I pushed through, determined to finish Oliver before she could finish recovering.

I should've hit her harder.

The resistance vanished as suddenly as it appeared and I sped through. Oliver was thoroughly alarmed now and searching among his fallen friends for help.

Who's the chicken shit now?

When it was clear no help would come, he squared off, his flames growing to outrageous heights. With the fire blinding him, there was no way he could see I wasn't running up the middle anymore. I smiled to myself. This had almost been fun. They'd lasted a lot longer than most.

I couldn't even see Oliver anymore amidst the orange and red plumes, but it didn't matter. A few more feet and this whole thing would be over.

Without warning, the two of us rose off the ground like giant hands had picked us up. I struggled to no avail against the unseen hold. Oliver shouted and his flames went out. The night instantly plunged back into darkness.

I blinked several times to eliminate the afterimage from his inferno. When my vision finally cleared, there were two figures by the door we'd come out of who knew how long ago. As they stepped forward, I saw one was Smith, and the other was a woman.

For a second, I thought she might be another menacing Mary Ann, but something told me she didn't belong at Superno House any more than I did. Whoever she was, she was definitely the reason I was hanging six feet off the ground, unable to move a finger. And she was just like me.

"Smith, what part of 'don't let the demons fight' sounds complicated to you? It's basic preservation." Her words dripped with sarcasm and the barest hint of a Southern accent. "The place may be warded, but all it would take is one curious pedestrian."

"We only sent the missive yesterday when we realized we couldn't identify his race. You weren't supposed to be here for another month," Smith protested.

"I'm a Shadow Demon, Smith. Try to remember that. Not some snot-nosed brat you can tread all over. When I asked for your cooperation, I had no idea I was resigning myself to work with an incompetent, self-righteous, pompous, son of a..." Her tirade snapped off and she took a deep breath. "Let's try this again. Does he know?"

"Know what?"

"For Nyx's sake, Smith. Does he know what he is?" she asked, the essence of put-upon exasperation.

Smith darted an anxious glance toward me and wrung his hands. "According to him, no. I suspected he might be lying, but he seemed genuinely shocked by everything here. Honestly, I don't think he knew about supernaturals at all before this afternoon."

"And yet, he single-handedly took out an Ick Demon, a Sprite, a Spiculo, and a Fire Demon. Impressive." She gave me an appraising look while I tried to parse out what the hell she was talking about. "Do you mind?" She gestured to the air in front of her.

"Mind what?" Smith echoed.

"A light, Smith. As you can imagine, that's not really my forte." I could practically hear her rolling her eyes. "I want to get a better look at my latest recruit."

A sickening tone of subservience replaced Smith's previous combativeness. "Sorry, Miss Scry." He waved a hand and muttered something I didn't catch. Then a bluish light blossomed overhead, illuminating the speakers in high-relief.

To my shock, the woman was much younger than I would have expected for someone commanding so much authority. Old or not, her eyes were sharp and ruthless and she looked meaner than a pissed off copperhead.

I glanced around from my suspended perspective. Now that there was a proper source of light, the damage was clear. Oliver's gang lay strewn about the courtyard. Only Scylla had found her feet while the other two looked comatose.

"Good heavens!" Smith exclaimed, taking in the havoc I'd wrought.

I snickered, and he shot me a look while the woman stared at me as if assessing something I couldn't see. I glared defiantly back, and she cracked a smile. It was gone before I could decide if it was sinister or sincere.

The woman waved a dismissive hand at the apoplectic Smith. "Cool your grits, they'll be fine. The damage is minimal, nothing a healer can't set to right."

"Minimal? He could have caused actual harm! And in case you didn't realize, we don't exactly have the funds to maintain a fully trained healer on staff," Smith snapped as he walked over to help Rufus, the club I'd shoved in his mouth, now gone.

"He's an absolute natural." The woman's smile definitely seemed genuine now. "I dare Gabriel to top this one. He's easily above a ten, maybe even as high as a seven. Hard to tell now, though, with no training."

"Ten!" For a second, it looked like Smith might actually faint. "He could've killed them!"

She rolled her eyes. "Please. Did you miss the part where I stopped them?" She gestured at where Oliver and I hung a few feet apart in the air. "As for a healer, I'll send you mine if you're that worried, but we both know they each got what was coming to them. Besides, the injuries seem mostly superficial."

She tilted her head to the side and Oliver plummeted to the ground. His resulting moan said he was fine, but in pain.

"Miss Scry, I really must protest at your abuse of my wards." Smith marched up to her, wagging his finger.

Her eyes went solid black, and the night seemed to warp around her. Chills crawled up my spine as the darkness tightened around me, causing me to wheeze. The color drained from Smith's face, and he dropped his accusatory finger.

"It's no less than what he deserves. We all know what he intended, dragging my ward out here." Menace laced the low words and goosebumps pimpled my skin. "It's a far cry better than what he would've gotten if I hadn't intervened. Matthew is clearly raw and untrained. If his record is anything to go by, his anger and control are both out of reach."

Without warning, I flew towards her. My eyes widened in panic and I struggled harder. This lady was without a doubt the most dangerous person out here, and after what I'd just felt, I had no desire to be any closer. My flight stopped as abruptly as it had started, leaving me mere inches from where she was standing.

"Do you have any personal effects here?" Vera asked, her eyes still obsidian.

I shook my head vigorously, fear momentarily freezing my tongue.

"Good. Smith, we're leaving. Next time you get even an inkling of a power level like this, you call me sooner rather than later," she ordered, her eyes still boring into me.

I swallowed and fought to keep from shaking uncontrollably.

"Y-yes, of c-course," the cowering administrator stammered.

"And Smith," she finally looked at him, "try to keep this lot under better control. If you need help, I'd be happy to send some... volunteers."

Smith went noticeably paler, an impressive feat considering how washed out everyone already was in the bluish light. Fear once again trickled down my spine.

She turned back to me. "Give me your hand."

I shook my head and tried to shrink away, for all the good it did me.

She rolled her eyes and grabbed my left arm. The world was sucked from around us. There was only darkness. Then I blinked, and we were standing on a sidewalk. A glance behind me revealed a sign with scrolling letters that read Superno House for Wayward Children.

I looked back at the woman, able to see her better in the yellow streetlights. Turned out she was dressed in nothing fancier than blue jeans and a t-shirt with wild red hair that looked like the fire Oliver had been sprouting minutes before.

"Who are you?" I blurted out.

At the question, her entire intimidating demeanor fell like she was dropping a mask. Then she put her hands on her wide hips and smiled. "Sorry about that. Some of these old fogies are still living in the last century. All they know is reputation and fear. Sadly, honey doesn't get you as much as it should these days, but I'm working on that."

She's absolutely certifiable.

"My name is Vera Scry. I'm the expert you were promised. Sorry I didn't find you sooner, but at least you were still here to find. Shadow Demons are a tricky lot, especially if they haven't really manifested. I confess, if I hadn't already been in the states, it might have been another month before I got here." She looked at me expectantly. "You know, you're not restrained anymore."

My leg twitched.

How far could I get?

"But I will say, if you're thinking of running, remember, you were running the last time I caught you."

My eyes widened. Was it possible she could read minds? Was that even a thing?

"Well?" she prompted.

"Well, what?"

She frowned. "Just because I've read your file, doesn't mean you shouldn't introduce yourself. That's just good manners."

Who is this lady?

"I'm Matt and I don't know what I am."

She smiled again and started walking down the sidewalk. When I didn't follow, she glanced back and waited. There was nowhere else for me to go and she'd already proved that running was pointless, so I joined her.

"I figured as much. Well, Matt, I have a proposition for you."

I looked at her out of the corner of my eye. "Proposition makes it sound like a choice." It definitely didn't feel like one.

"Observant, aren't you? I suppose technically it is a choice, though I really hope you say yes and don't make me persuade you."

There was no telling if the persuasion would be a pros and cons argument or torture. Something told me neither would phase her.

"I've started a school to help our kind, Shadow Demons." She glanced at me. "That's what you are, Matt. We're kind of a dying race and I may have created an atmosphere of fear over the last decade, making it especially unsafe for our kind." Her focus shifted to the ground and the loose pebbles she was kicking. "I'm trying to fix that. By bringing together young demons and training them properly, we simultaneously ensure that they embrace their demonic half and that they don't lose control and go on an accidental killing spree." Silence hung for a moment.

"You're insane."

She gave me a crooked smile and shrugged. "So, I've been told."

CHAPTER 4

THE OUTCAST

A

The sun warmed my back as I approached the community center. To my surprise, hardly anyone was around the bleached white building, shining like a beacon in the middle of town. Then again, with it not quite being summer yet, the usual classes and events hadn't started, so that made sense. Of course, that didn't stop the bulletin board from being cluttered with pamphlets.

I chuckled to myself as I spent a few minutes rearranging the multitude of paper. How the heck people expected to get anyone's attention with everything overlapping like that was beyond me. I reached a cream-colored page that was hiding beneath an advert for a dog walker and paused. A small smile tugged at my lips as I freed it from the chaos.

The Denham Agrarian Poets Society has moved meetings to the private residence of Mary Elizabeth Parker. Please reach out directly for updated times and admittance.

I pinned the supposed "update" to a corner where others could see it. When my mother had uprooted us from Greece to this small parish in the UK, I'd never expected to find a community, let alone a community of supernaturals. Luckily, they'd recognized me as one of them and given me the rather vague advice of joining DAPS. Best decision ever.

I gave the board another once over, then dusted my hands and went inside, where I was immediately greeted by an older woman with a faded brown face and graying hair pulled up in a bun.

"Alexi! What brings you here?" Roberta Mannheim may have looked like a quiet old lady, but I was convinced she'd never had a quiet day in her life.

I smiled warmly and rushed to help her with the table she was currently relocating to the side of the room. "Nothing much, Robbie. Came to pick up a few things before mum and I head out."

She paused and straightened up, giving me a beaming smile. "That's right, your kiester got into that fancy early admittance program!"

I shrugged at her enthusiasm. That wasn't quite the case, but it was the story we were going with.

"Come here, squirt." She waved me over, and I obligingly stepped into her warm, grandmotherly embrace, or what I assumed a grandmother's hug would be like. "Ooh, I knew you were too smart for this little old town. But gosh, we're gonna miss you." Robbie suddenly pushed me to arm's length, her wrinkled face now serious. "Now don't you go gettin' yourself into any trouble, Alexi Roman."

I laughed and gave her another big hug. "Wouldn't dream of it."

"I mean it," she said with a sniff. "Mind all them boys."

"Robbie..."

"What? You're a good lookin'-"

I grabbed her hands and quickly cut her off before she gave me the birds and the bees lecture... again. "I'm going to learn, not for romance."

"Well, never say never, dear." She patted my cheek, then put her hands on her hips. "Suppose I better stop dilly dallying and get back to work."

"Anything I can do to help?"

"Oh, no, sweetheart, I've got this. Jerry should be along shortly. You go on about gettin' your things." She gestured toward the back of the room where a hall led to the storage closets and the kitchen. "Be a dear and make an old lady some fresh tea?"

"I'd love to, but how many times do I have to tell you? You're only as old as you feel."

Robbie snorted. "Says the eighteen-year-old. If that's the case, then I feel a hundred and twenty." I was about to offer to help again when the promised Jerry came in. "There you are, you lazy bag of bones. Come, give me a hand."

In the kitchen, I pulled out enough cups for everyone, then rummaged through the cabinets until I found Robbie's favorite tea. While the kettle warmed, I took out my to-do list, crossed off a few items, added a few more.

"Thought I heard you in here."

I swallowed and glanced up to find Nemo Santori leaning against the wall, large arms darkened from spending hours in the sun crossed over his chest. "Hey, what brings you here?"

"Work." Nemo's voice had the unfortunate effect of always sounding like a growl, making it difficult to tell whether or not he was angry. Considering he was a werewolf, it was best not to chance it.

"Yeah? Finally, get roped into helping Marge with the renovations?" I asked with a forced smile and as much positivity as a person could muster. Beside me, the kettle whistled.

He uncrossed his arms and walked over to the counter littered with cups. Then promptly poured himself some tea. "So, the rumors are true. You're headed off to that... school." He took a sip of the scalding liquid, his stern eyes staring at me over the rim. "Is it true that evil bitch is going to be leading it?"

I flinched. By "evil bitch", of course, he meant the notorious Vera Scry, who'd done her part in decimating werewolf packs across Europe. It didn't help that she was also a level two Shadow Demon. Hardly anyone had known about us until she showed up.

"Well? Wolf got your tongue?" Nemo gave me a toothy smile. Most of the town believed his wolf puns to be endearing and quirky. Some of us, however, were in on the truth.

"I... I uh..." I coughed to clear my throat. Vera had done a lot of horrible things while she'd been under the influence of the Regency, but most of them paled compared to the wrongs she'd done the shifter community. "I don't know. I mean, I'm not sure. The forum mentioned her being involved, but not to what degree."

Nemo's lip curled.

"I, uh, should probably finish getting my things." I took a tentative step toward the door, my tea forgotten. Nemo had once been a great mentor, practically a father figure to me, but the second Vera had rudely introduced Shadow Demons to the world, I became persona non grata. It hurt like hell to lose that, but even then, it might not have been so bad if his feelings on the matter hadn't spilled over into the rest of our small community of supernaturals. You'd think I was the one who'd done the Regency's bidding, then switched sides to join the Rebellion.

He grunted. "When do you leave?"

I swallowed and worked diligently to put on a brave front, ironically, something he'd taught me to do. "Our flight leaves in a couple of days. Then I'll be out of your hair for good. Except, of course, for holiday visits and break and... the like..." I trailed off.

Nemo nodded and set down his empty cup. "I best be getting back to work. Thanks for the tea, kid."

"You're welcome," I replied by rote, though I hadn't really made it for him.

He was almost out the door when he paused and glanced over his shoulder. "Alexi?"

"Yeah?" I hated how my voice betrayed my anxiety.

A smile I hadn't seen directed my way in years crinkled his eyes. "Stay true to yourself. You're gonna do great things." With that, he walked out the door, leaving me standing there with my mouth hanging open.

I took a minute to let Nemo's unexpected encouragement sink in. Maybe these last five years of stubbornly attending the secret supernatural community gatherings had paid off. Was it possible I'd really won Nemo back over despite sharing the genetic heritage of the most hated woman to ever wrong wolfkind? Figures it would be the second I was leaving town.

I rolled my eyes and finished organizing the teas. Once I'd delivered steaming cups to the ever-bickering couple, I disappeared into the back with my cup to finish what I'd come to do. The late morning turned to early afternoon as I rummaged through everything to make sure I didn't accidentally leave anything behind. A decision I was grateful for when I found my copy of Demon History sandwiched between dusty board games.

It might not have mattered so much if someone like Nemo found it, but if one of the decidedly human occupants of Denham had stumbled across it, that could have spelled trouble for all of us. Dubious about why I'd been so absent as to have left it here, I wandered over to the box I'd found that was now in serious danger of overflowing. I was finally putting the lid on when another voice called out.

"Alexi? Are you in here?"

My spine stiffened at the soft, timid voice. It took every ounce of decency I had to wipe the scowl from my face. I straightened up, dusted my hands, then turned to meet the second to last person I wanted to see, the last, of course, being Daniel. "What do you want, Clarke?"

They glanced from me to the box and back again. "I heard you were leaving town. Going to some school?" Their light brown eyes looked at me questioningly.

"You heard right." I might have been aiming for laissez-faire, but bitterness ate at my words. And, yet, despite knowing it wasn't entirely Clarke's fault, I couldn't seem to stop myself. "Is that all you wanted?" When they continued to stand there, I reached for the box.

Clarke surged forward, hand in the air. "No! I... uh... I..."

Sweet, merciful night. I did not need this right now. "Spit it out. Why are you here?"

"I was hoping we could clear the air?" They gave me a sheepish look.

I crossed my arms and couldn't help but compare us. Clarke was shorter and about as stereotypically white Protestant as a person could get. Where I was darker and all lean muscles, they were pale and soft. Was that what Daniel had really wanted? Someone he could easily overpower? Had he known that I wasn't human? Was that why he'd cheated on me? With fucking Clarke?

They took another step closer. "Please. I never intended to hurt you. We're friends." That was a loose definition if I'd ever heard one.

"Clarke..." I dropped my arms and scooped up the box.

"He said you were alright with it."

I fought the urge to throw the entire box at Clarke's head. It wouldn't have been hard, even if it was supposed to be heavy. Once my temper was under control, I tightened my grip and met their pitiful gaze. "Newsflash. He lied."

Clarke winced, probably not the least bit surprised.

I rolled my eyes and moved to go past them. Then another thought made me pause. I glanced at them. "Tell me one thing. Were you two even drunk?"

Clarke's face turned a bright shade of red, like they'd been out in the fields all day instead of inside having this awful conversation with me.

"That's what I thought." This time, I made it all the way to the door before I stopped again. Clearly, my conscience didn't care how much being around them hurt my heart. Deep down, I knew Clarke was gullible and naïve. I also knew Daniel was none of those things. "Hey, Clarke, when he comes crawling back—because he will—don't let him."

Clarke's choked sound was all the confirmation that I needed. Daniel had tried to woo me and when he'd struck out, he'd left my place and gone straight to Clarke. What was that saying? Oh right, no good deed goes unpunished.

I finished making my way out of the Community Center, sparing a wave for Robbie and Jerry, who were now enjoying biscuits with fresh cups of tea, and headed toward home at the edge of town. If I had been waffling about going to Arminius before, I wasn't now. I needed away from small town drama and cheating exes. A few years of focusing solely on my studies was the perfect diversion.

CHAPTER 5

THE HOTEL

M

I still had no idea what to expect from this "school" or what on Earth my new warden had done to make everyone so afraid of her. All I knew was that after we'd left the orphanage, we'd walked for what seemed like hours until we reached a hotel.

A man dressed sharply in a red coat, primly pressed with copper buttons, nodded in greeting from behind the counter. "Lovely to see you again, Miss Scry. I trust your visit has been productive?" If he wasn't in charge, he was at least important.

"I've told you before, Jeffery, call me Vera," my kidnapper tsked.

"Whatever you say, Miss Scry. Your usual room?" he asked, completely disregarding her demand. Maybe he didn't know what she was... what we? were.

I glanced at him, a little impressed, considering Administrator Smith had been cowering before her just a few hours ago.

"Yes, but I won't be staying. My adventures this evening have been quite..." her eyebrows lifted, "eventful."

The desk clerk's eyes widened slightly, and his face paled. Nope, he definitely knew. "Not too eventful, I hope." To his credit, his voice didn't shake.

Vera laughed like it was the best joke in the world. If it was, I certainly didn't get it. Then she turned his attention to me. "Jefferey, this young man is Matthew Duncan."

I grimaced at hearing my full name.

"For your sake, though, I strongly recommend you just call him Matt."

"Will Mister Matt be needing special accommodations?"

"Yes, but I'll see to them." Vera gave me a skeptical once over before heaving a sigh and returning her focus to Jefferey. "There's a chance he may try to bolt before I return. Caution the staff." My scowl went unnoticed as she continued. "Other than that, please make sure he's well looked after. I'll be returning for him as soon as I can. There are several other stops I need to make before we can leave, and time is of the essence."

I stared at her in open disbelief. She'd basically kidnapped me and now she was leaving? Maybe I wouldn't have to wait the ten months after all. I could slip out the second I had an opening and that would be that. Fat chance she could find me again after I got lost in the city. Then again, that hadn't worked out so well for me the last time.

"As you say, Miss Scry." To my surprise, Jeffery didn't present her with one of those key-card things, but an honest to goodness key. Fancy and everything.

She rolled her eyes at his dry response and accepted it, then led the way to the elevator. I followed her in silence, soaking in the marble floors and impressionist art decorating the walls. Even the elevator doors were fancy. I glanced at her out of the corner of my eye, even more curious about how someone seemingly so young could just walk into a place like this. The doors slid shut, and I turned on her.

"How old are you? Where are we? Why did he treat you like... like..."

"Like I own the place?" she finished for me, raising an eyebrow.

I deflated a bit. "Well, yeah."

"Because I do. I own several hotels around the world. And to answer your very rude question, I'm twenty-eight. But don't let looks fool you. My husband has been around for a millennium and only looks thirty-five." She cocked her head to the side. "Forty on a bad day. As your powers develop and you truly embrace your demonic side, your aging will slow down dramatically. Trust me, I'm very aware that I only look twenty."

I choked. Like being twenty-eight, magically made it more reasonable that she owned hotels around the world and had men twice her age hopping to her every whim. "Who are you?" I asked once again.

She winced. "You'll learn that soon enough. The school I'm taking you to is actually for all kinds of supernaturals."

Yesterday, or even eight hours ago, I'd have snorted and told her she was off her rocker. Supernaturals weren't real. They were a story, make believe. Except, they weren't...

"Aside from learning how to use your own powers, you'll also learn about magical history, and that includes the history of demons." Vera paused, appearing genuinely anxious for the first time since she'd shown up out of nowhere and carted me off. "It's... not pretty, and you might not like me much once you know more about my role in... uh, recent events."

"You could just tell me now." I shrugged, because really, what did I care? I'd never met her before and she was leaving. It wasn't like who she was had any bearing on my life.

"I could." She stepped off the elevator and walked up to—surprise—another fancy door. A look around revealed very few extra doors, leading me to believe this had to be the suite level. She unlocked the door and stepped inside. "Come on in, Matt. Mi casa es su casa."

I frowned in response to her smile and walked past her into the room. Two steps later, I stopped dead. The nicest place

I'd ever been was the Hiddleston house. They'd been a nice family, but their son had taken issue to sharing his parents' attention. I'd thought they lived in a mansion, that having my own room was the stuff of kings. It didn't hold a candle to this place. To be fair, I'd also never been in a nice hotel, or even a not nice one for that matter, so maybe my expectations were off.

Vera brushed past my shoulder, then walked over to lean against a couch so cushy it looked like it could swallow a person whole. "You'll have to stay here while I run the last of my errands. I apologize that I'll be leaving you on your own for a few days, but I trust Jefferey to take care of you." She gave the room a once over and turned back to me. "I also trust you don't need someone holding your hand to make sure you bathe and eat something decent?"

I finally put my eyeballs back in their sockets and turned to her. "You're really just going to leave me here?"

"Yep." She did a double take at seeing the utter disbelief on my face. "Matt, you're a capable young man. You'll be fine. I'll make sure Jefferey gets you a proper wardrobe and something for dinner."

"I already ate."

"Oh." She looked at her watch. "How the time flies. Well, I'm hungry, at any rate. I'll have something extra sent up, just in case." She hurried toward the door.

"Don't I get a key?" I called after her, causing her to pause in the opening.

Guilt flashed across her face. "You won't need one." She closed the door, and I raced over in time to hear the distinctive sound of a lock sliding home.

"Shit." I could still feel her on the other side, as well as a growing sense of something else. I waited until the sound of retreating steps was long gone, then tried the handle. The damn thing wouldn't turn. Rather than keep failing, I gave it up and wandered around the space.

This was certainly a suite fit for a king. It held two couches and a breakfast table, as well as several pricey looking decorative pieces. The plush beige carpet sank with each step, coating my footfalls in muffled silence. As I explored the rest of the room, I found an equally outrageous bedroom with a matching bath, each gilded to the extreme. If I could pry some of it off, I'd be set for life. But first, I had to get out of here. I glanced over at the sliding glass door.

The door slid open easily, revealing an extensive balcony complete with chairs and a small table. I stepped up to the iron railing. Overall, it was a spectacular view of downtown Omaha. The hotel wasn't overly tall, maybe only ten stories. Looking down at the street below, I immediately nixed any thoughts of getting out that way. It wasn't necessarily that I was afraid of heights, so much that I wanted to live. After taking a cautionary step back, I resumed taking in the sights.

I could just make out the Missouri River between some buildings, and of course, there were the parks. Despite the darkness, or perhaps because of it, the view was stunning. A noise behind me prompted me to look back inside. Room service was rolling in a cart, leaving the door wide open behind them.

Faster than seemed possible, I sprinted across the room towards freedom. The poor attendant looked a little alarmed at my frantic run, but didn't move to stop me. Just in case, I didn't slow down and was going full tilt when I ran into... absolutely nothing. I staggered back and reassessed the opening. It was empty. Nothing was there.

What the hell?

I held my hand up and met invisible resistance.

"Good evening, Mr. Matt. I trust you will find tonight's meal to your liking," Jefferey said as he stepped into the room completely uninhibited.

What. The. Hell?

I tried to force my hand through the opening, and again, met a perfect wall of resistance despite the lack of anything I could see. I slammed my fist against the barrier with enough force to crack wood and still nothing.

"If you are quite finished, your dinner is getting cold, and we have other matters to attend to."

"I already told her. I ate before." I turned to face Jefferey. How was it possible for him to get in while I couldn't get out?

"In that case, we'll skip right to our other task." The manager produced a thick yellow string and gestured for me to come closer. I took a tentative step forward and he draped the cord around my waist, pulling it tight.

"Get your hands off of me! What the hell do you think you're doing?"

"Mr. Duncan." I shot him daggers, and he held up a hand in apology. "Mr. Matt, I'm simply trying to obtain your measurements so that we can procure you an appropriate wardrobe."

I eyed the tape skeptically. Now that I was really paying attention, I could see the dashes marking inches and centimeters. "Oh."

"If you wouldn't mind?" He gestured to the center of the room. I dutifully walked over and held still. "Arms out," he commanded. I did as instructed.

The ribbon spanned the back of my shoulders and then was draped around my waist. This time, I was more prepared when he wrapped the cord around my middle. It didn't make me any more comfortable, but it wasn't nearly as bad as when he took the measurement for my inseam. I just barely didn't kick him in the face.

"See, that wasn't so bad. You will have a fresh set of clothes by morning. Though I imagine I should get you additional pants as well." He glanced at me and at the mark he had made on his notepad. "The new ones won't fit long."

I frowned, not following.

"At any rate, I trust you have found everything to your liking. If you should need anything, please ring. This room has a private line and the call will be answered almost instantly."

"I have not found everything to my liking," I snapped.

Jefferey's bushy eyebrows climbed toward his hairline. "Beg your pardon."

"Why can't I leave?" I gestured angrily to the still open door.

"Miss Scry made it very clear that you were to wait here until her return. Whatever holds you in this room is far beyond either myself or my staff."

"Who is Miss Scry, anyway?" Maybe he would give me the answers she had neglected.

He hesitated a moment. "A very respected and danger-ous woman. You would do well to appreciate her generosity. Not all have been so fortunate. Goodnight, Mr. Matt." The statement didn't leave any room for further questions and he walked out before I could even try, leaving me once again all alone in the massive suite.

Not really sure what to do with myself, I walked over to the silver dome that presumably held dinner. Despite what I'd told them both, I was ravenous. The mysterious meatloaf had barely scratched the surface of my hunger, and the fight after hadn't helped.

Cautiously, I lifted the lid. I wasn't sure I trusted food from someone who casually abducted and locked up people. Then my stomach growled as the scent wafted into the open air from the steam drifting off of the massive burger. Upon closer inspection, there was both bacon and cheese, not to mention a healthy side of fries. My mouth watered.

Did it really matter if it was poisoned? Vera'd already proved that I wasn't going anywhere. That decided, I tucked into the meal. As I ate, I began to feel a little bad for my treatment of Jeffery. The meal was absolutely to my liking. Sufficiently stuffed, I wandered over to the bedroom, where I spent time languishing in the shower.

Steam clouded the entire bathroom, and I had to wipe the mirror to even see myself. I looked slightly better clean, but I was still every inch an oversized ragamuffin, as an old matron used to say. I swiped the image angrily and went to flop on the bed. The whole thing sank beneath me until it felt like it was literally hugging my entire body.

How do people sleep on such squishy things?

Apparently easily, because I passed out, robe and all, on top of the patterned comforter.

In the morning, breakfast and the promised clothes were waiting for me. I tried on the simple jeans and t-shirts that had been provided. Much to my amazement, everything fit perfectly. Jeffrey really knew his stuff.

There wasn't much to do in the room beyond stare out the window and watch TV. Not fond of either, I went in search of better amusement. Eventually, I found some pens and a notepad. The day slipped by as I sketched. I began with the creatures I'd met at the orphanage and kept going until I ran out of paper. Before long, there was a knock at the door and another attendant came in bearing what I assumed to be lunch, followed, of course, by Jeffery.

"I'm pleased to see that the clothes are to your satisfaction. You struck me as a no-frills type of lad, so I kept the options fairly basic."

I hadn't really thought much of it. A shirt was a shirt. He glanced around, no doubt checking to see if anything was missing or broken. His eyes passed disinterestedly over the sketches that littered the floor.

"When can I leave?"

"When Miss Scry retrieves you," he replied calmly, and left once more.

We repeated the same routine every day. The only exception was that Jeffrey began checking on me at dinner instead of lunch, and on the third day, an entire supply of sketch tools appeared. Even then, as nice and accommodating as this place was proving to be, I still tried the door every time it was opened and well after they left, all with the same lack of results.

A whole week had gone by when Vera swanned into the room unannounced. I might not have even noticed her sudden appearance except I always sat facing the door, ready to try my luck again. The freaky part was that she didn't come through the door at all. She walked through the wall next to it.

"You're certainly looking better," she said as she inspected my overall appearance.

I jumped up from my seat. "How did you do that? Where have you been? You can't just lock people up, you know."

"I believe that's exactly what I did. And I've already told you, I had additional errands to run. Still do, as a matter of fact. I just wanted to see for myself that you were doing as well as Jeffery claimed. He tends to exaggerate, but I see he was not regarding your artistic ability. I never could draw," she mused to herself.

"Wait, you're leaving again?"

"Of course. Oh, and these are for you." She dropped a bag that thudded when it hit the ground. It instantly toppled over, allowing several pamphlets and brochures to pour out. "I thought you might like to know where you're going."

"The only place I want to go is out of here." I kicked the bag, and she rolled her eyes.

"You don't have to read them, but there is no reason to be rude. I'll try to be quick. I'd hoped to provide you with some company, but things are not going well. All of my other recruits seem to disappear before I can get to them." Concerned confusion flashed across her face, then it was gone. "Anyway, I'll see you later. Mind Jeffery." With that, she was gone. She didn't even bother using the door or the wall. Not even a poof, just gone.

CHAPTER 6

ARMINIUS

A

A rminius University.

Looking around, you'd never know that a full tilt battle had taken place at the pinnacle of the Rebellion when the Regency had dug into their last stronghold. The reports that had filtered out to our tiny supernatural community had said parts of the campus had been virtually obliterated. Not that you could tell. Guess that was a benefit of being a supernatural college. They probably had many spells to undo damage or roll back time.

I ran a hand over the side of the admissions building as we walked in. It even felt old, which shouldn't have been possible. I knew for a fact that it had been completely restructured. The pictures of this place made it seem like a bomb had gone off. Come to think of it, it was entirely possible that one had.

"Lexi, do you know where we're going?" My mother's voice snapped me out of my reverie.

"Yes, the letter said to check in at Admissions. They'll give me my schedule and further instructions." I confidently led the way to the main desk, but as I got closer, my nerves took hold. They'd know why I was here, what I was. How welcome was my kind, really?

The attendant smiled at me from behind the curving mahogany desk. Everything was pristine, from the perfectly stacked admission inquiries to his checkered polo buttoned all the way to the top. Even his dark skin was flawless, providing a striking contrast to his short-cut, golden hair.

I took a fateful step forward. "Hi."

"Good morning. I'm Marquis, Administrator of Freshman Affairs. How can I help?" His eyes looked like stars. It was both eerie and fascinating.

"I'm Alexi Roman." I took a deep breath and handed him the letter. Everything he needed to know would be in there.

"Ah, excellent. You're here for Vera's class. That should be interesting." He gave me a knowing smile, and I glanced at my mom.

She gave my shoulder a reassuring pat. "Why do you say that?" she asked conversationally.

Marquis laughed as he put together my welcome packet. "Don't get me wrong, she's wonderful. You'll love her. Patience just isn't one of her strengths. It will be interesting to see how she does as a teacher. I mean, she did put her own teacher through the ringer to hear him tell it." He rapped the stack on the desk, straightening it to perfection, then put it in a folder and passed it to me. "There, that should be everything." He slid a map around to face us and pointed. "This is where we are. You'll be going across the campus to this area here. It's the newer of the old sections." He chuckled like it was a joke. "Orientation is not for a couple more hours, so feel free to take your time getting over there. We're all really glad you're here."

"Why?" I asked as I accepted the itinerary.

"Honestly? We were really afraid no one would show. There have already been several dropouts. The class is about half the size that it was originally. If this year goes well though, I imagine they'll re-register in the spring."

"Oh." I wasn't sure if I should be alarmed or not. "Um, what do we do about luggage?"

"That, you'll leave with me. They're waiting to give room assignments until orientation to make sure everyone can room with a classmate."

"I'll be rooming with another Shadow Demon?" The question didn't sound more believable out loud. Another supernatural, sure, but another demon? And a classmate on top?

"Vera wants you to have as much opportunity as possible to spend time with your own kind, something you otherwise may never have had the chance to do." Sadness clouded his features. "There are so few of you left."

"She's really thought this out." Rooming with another Shadow Demon. I could've gone my whole life without meeting another one and now I'd be roommates with one for who knew how long.

"You have no idea. This has been her project since the rebuild started. It's not right that Shadow Demons have been forced into seclusion. You all are surprisingly social for notorious loners."

"Told you," my mom whispered in my ear. "Now, let's go explore before I officially have to send you to school," she added, then promptly led me out of the office.

All around us, kids wandered around the campus. For summer, the school was surprisingly busy. If it wasn't for some of the more blatant uses of magic or strange appearances, Arminius could have been any college campus, and it was hiding in plain sight. We'd seen no indication in the neighboring town that they were even remotely aware of who attended this ancient school. I couldn't help but wonder how many students took summer classes just to be somewhere it was safe to be themselves.

Right in front of us, a group of girls passed a levitated book back and forth. A Frisbee spun overhead to be snatched out of the air by a tiny point of light that turned into a guy in his early twenties. Suddenly, I was very grateful that my very human mom had exposed me to as much of the supernatural world as possible. I still wasn't entirely sure how she'd found the supernatural community in town.

"Thank you, mom," I croaked out, my emotions dangerously close to overwhelming me.

"For what, dear?"

I smiled at the woman who had sacrificed so much for me. "For making me come and making sure I had a well-rounded childhood."

"That's what mothers do." She gave me a good squeeze, and I didn't even care that it was in front of half the student body. They didn't seem to, either. "Are you going to show me some of these haunts or am I actually going to have to use this thing?" She waved the map.

I laughed and chose a direction at random. "Okay, okay, let's start this way."

The campus was massive, and even with a couple of hours to burn, we wouldn't want to wander too much. I tried to point out the structures I'd dedicated to memory and offer what history I could. All around us, buildings rose up in various colors of bricks and stone, each one seeming more ancient than the last as we worked our way to the heart of the campus. It was incredible to see firsthand the sweeping banisters on some and turrets on others. The Witch's College even looked like a full-blown medieval castle plopped right on the green.

It was as though we were walking through a life-size textbook on the History of Architecture. Literally, the only building even remotely modern, in as much that it had clear glass versus stained, was the commissary. We skirted around it, preferring to marvel like tourists at the ivy-covered structures. Eventually, we worked our way over to the building Marquis had circled. It wasn't until we were right up on it, though, that I realized what it was. When I did, I couldn't help but laugh.

"What's so funny?" My mother looked around for the source of my humor.

"Marquis' joke makes more sense now. This part of the university was established three hundred years ago, officially making it the youngest section on campus. And this is Mysterio College. It was rededicated about fifty years ago to cover the more obscure arts. Fitting that Shadow Demons would be here." My gaze traveled up the moss-covered stone. "I wonder if they'll end up changing the name again."

Mom kissed me on the cheek and rubbed my arms. "I guess it's that time."

"You're not coming in?"

She shook her head, a small smile on her lips. "I think this is something you can handle on your own, and should." She let out a sigh and her eyes turned sad. "When did you grow up?" She brushed the hair back from my face. "Call me once you're settled and let me know how it went." She wrapped me in another fierce hug.

I nodded and carefully squeezed her back, fighting back a sudden rush of tears. "I will. I love you, mom."

She released me and I found her eyes equally misty. "You've got this, Alexi. I'm so proud of you." She fanned her eyes. "Whoo! I better go before I make a scene. Right. You be good, stick to your studies, don't forget to call."

"I know, mom. I won't."

She blew me a kiss, turned, and made her way to the main entrance of the university. I watched her go until she was an indistinguishable blur, then looked back at the building. Now that everything was real, I was nervous again. It was easy to forget my anxiety when I was playing tour guide, but now the moment had finally come. I was officially a student at Arminius

University and was about to meet the most infamous Shadow Demon in the world.

I pushed the doors open into an empty foyer. Where I'd been expecting a welcoming committee or maybe a TA, there was only a nondescript sign that said to go down the hall to classroom forty-two. I followed the trail of signs around two curves before I found the room in question.

When I stepped inside, a woman behind a podium with a name tag that read Anne, Student Affairs, greeted me. She was petite, with a blonde bob and a friendly smile.

"Good afternoon. We're so pleased you could join us. Orientation will start in a few minutes. Could I get your name, please?"

Between the noise of too many people talking all at once and realizing they were all Shadow Demons, it took me a moment to realize she was talking to me. "Roman."

I'd heard about demons being able to sense each other, but this was a first for me. Disorienting was a mild way to put it. I could understand the insistence that we be made to bunk together. I was now absolutely sure I'd never run into another Shadow Demon before today.

"That's Alexi Roman?"

"Yes." My gaze continued to rove over the gathered crowd. The group was made up almost entirely of guys with only a few token girls.

"I've got you." Anne placed a decisive check on her clipboard. "Looks like you're the last."

"I'm sorry. I didn't mean to be late. We lost track of time while I was giving my mom a tour. I hope it hasn't been too much of an inconvenience."

"You're fine. I'll be surprised if Vera is on time herself. I mean, Miss Scry," Anne amended with a smile. "Don't worry, everyone has freaked a little. It's different being around someone of your own race, especially if you never have before."

It was mildly comforting to know I wasn't the only one who'd been taken aback.

"Honestly, only a couple of kids didn't react at all, including the first kid to get here. Poor thing. Vera dropped him off this morning, and he's been waiting all day. Anyway, take a seat or stand, whatever your preference." She scanned her list one more time, then set it down on the small podium and walked off.

I waited until the crowd obscured her, then scooted closer to her vacated post. A cursory glance showed over a dozen names. I double checked to make sure no one was watching me and gave the list a closer look. Beside many of the names were numbers, though not in any order I could discern, as well as a few question marks. My jaw might have actually dropped when I realized they were indications of possible power levels. I glanced around the room even more in awe. No one here was below a fifteen. There was enough power in this room to take out the entire building, if not a good portion of the campus.

I blanched at that and sought my name. The number nine stood out in bold. For a second, the entire room seemed to swim. I wasn't just strong; I was powerful.

I stepped away before someone could notice me snooping. I meandered closer to the crowd, still debating on whether to engage, when a couple of voices caught my attention. They stood off to the side and seemed to be looking at someone.

"Yeah, he was here when I arrived. Hasn't said two words to anyone." The comment belonged to a guy just shy of my height, with dull blond hair and an angular face. He sucked his teeth. "Probably thinks he's better than the rest of us."

His companion's face screwed into a scowl, highlighting his pronounced acne. "Wouldn't you if the most notorious Shadow Demon in history personally picked you up?"

The first guy smacked his sandy-haired friend's arm and pointed. "Look, George is going to get a piece of him." The two snickered. I looked around, but had no idea who George was or his intended victim. How was it they did? Had they met before coming to Arminius?

I was searching the vicinity the blond guy had pointed when a guy who I assumed was George stepped into my line of sight. His bulk was imposing, to say the least. He looked like one of those American football players you see in movies, and when he opened his mouth, he sounded like it, too.

"Hey, you. Who do you think you are?" George paused as if waiting for a response, though I still couldn't see who he was addressing. "Hey! I'm talking to you." His voice carried enough that it got most of everyone's attention, and several heads turned towards the commotion.

I slid around a few people to get a better look. Sadly, they moved as well. Now I could see George's profile, but not who he seemed to believe was slighting him.

"What was that? I didn't catch it." Another pause. "Are you dumb or something? I asked, who do you think you are?" He reached out and pushed whoever he was talking to, and the guy stumbled right into my line of sight.

My breath caught. He was gorgeous.

For a moment, my heart didn't even bother to beat. I swallowed, taking in every inch of him, from his dark, unkempt hair to the brilliant blue eyes that flashed with defiance. He was several inches shorter than me, and perfect in every way imaginable. My mouth went dry. Love at first sight was something for fairy tales, but I was two seconds away from being a full believer.

"I said, my name is Matt. I'm no one."

I seriously doubted that, considering my heart was still struggling to find a steady rhythm.

"That's right. You're no one." George pushed him again.

Matt scowled. "Do you have a problem with me?"

"Yeah, I do." George closed the distance he'd made. "Why did Vera bring you here herself? What makes you so special?"

"Nothing." Matt braced himself like he knew the guy was gonna take a swing at him.

George snarled. "Liar." George made to push him again, but Matt shifted and he missed. Wrong move.

I took a step forward, prepared to intervene, then paused. This wasn't like me. I didn't get into fights. Ever. Yet, even with all of my beliefs that violence wasn't the answer, there was no way I could just stand here and let this guy get pummeled.

"I am not," Matt insisted. "Leave. Me. Alone."

"Or what?" George countered.

Before George could actually hit him, I spoke up. "Cut it out. He didn't do anything to you."

They both turned to look at me. Matt appeared confused. George, however, realized almost instantly that Matt's focus had shifted. He took advantage of his distraction to give Matt another shove, this time hard enough to push the smaller guy off his feet.

I quickly closed the distance and barely caught Matt by the shoulders in time to prevent him from crashing to the ground. The second we touched, a current of electricity jumped between us, and I nearly dropped him.

Matt looked up at me, anger burning in his blue eyes. This close, I could make out more of his features. His face was surprisingly delicate. The rage that flashed in his eyes carried to his mouth to create the best pout I'd ever seen. In short, he was a damn work of art.

Eat your heart out, Daniel. Michelangelo has a new muse.

I stared down at him with a goofy grin. "Hi there."

Matt got his feet under him and pushed away from me. "Let go of me."

"I was just trying to help." My hands still tingled from where I'd touched him. I'd never felt anything like it before.

"I don't need your help." The words were sharp enough to cut, and my heart bled at the horrible thought that I might have just made an enemy of this stunning angel.

A woman's voice sliced through the babble of eager whispers, still curious if there would be a fight. "If we could please stop the juvenile behavior, I'd like to start."

I turned to find the source, hoping to glimpse the infamous teacher that had gathered us all here. To my disappointment, I didn't find some terrifying warrior, but a young woman with red hair pulled into a severe ponytail.

The woman continued her path across the room to the front. Instinctively, I gave way. Matt, however, did not. Instead, he watched her approach with an expression I could only describe as sour. After his reaction to George, I was beginning to think my angel might have a death wish.

She slowed as she got closer to where I was still standing beside the disgruntled Matt. "I swear, Matt, a couple hours, just a couple of hours," she hissed under her breath. His eyes narrowed, and she walked around him.

If I hadn't of been standing so close, I would've missed the whole exchange. I looked back at Matt, who was scowling even deeper now. My gaze flicked back to the woman making herself comfortable at the podium at the front of the room. This was Vera Scry? She certainly didn't look like a hardened murderer capable of wiping out whole towns. Night. She was barely older than the rest of us.

"Alright," she began, her voice filling the room. "I'm sorry I'm late. Apparently, nothing around here knows how to run without constant supervision." The undercurrent of resentment bordered on being an outright scathing rebuke. She stopped a moment, as if to check herself. Then, after a deep breath, she started again in a more professional tone.

"I would like to welcome you all to Arminius University. As many of you have either guessed or already know, I am Vera Scry. I'll be leading your classes for the most part. However, your curriculum will also include a variety of topics that go beyond just the study of your demonic powers. Your first semester will comprise Demonic History, Intro to Shadow Magic, as well as Battle Tactics." There were several high fives around the room.

I raised my hand.

"Yes?"

"Why? The others I understand. But why Battle Tactics? The Rebellion is over." I'd read it on the curriculum earlier and naturally assumed it was a mistake.

"I'm glad you asked. While we don't condone violence, we also recognize that each demon has their own strengths and weaknesses. As you'll learn, power levels with demons are broad with dramatic differences separating the levels, more so the closer you get to being an Original or level one. The priority of this semester is to determine where your strengths lie so that we can help them flourish. Understandably, some of you may excel in practical applications, whereas others might need more... structure."

It could have been my imagination, but it sounded like that last bit was for Matt. A glance at him proved he believed so as well.

"Now, can anyone tell me why we're here specifically?" She gestured to the room itself.

"To learn how to be total bad asses," someone offered, followed by snickers around the room.

Vera's jaw clenched. "Any other thoughts?"

I waited to give someone else a chance, then raised my hand again.

"Yes."

"Mysterio College is for the study of obscure magicks. Shadow Demon lore has been outdated and misrepresented for centuries. In addition, we're here to learn control and make sure our kind don't die out because of unfulfilled potential." I might have read the brochure... a few times.

"Very well said. To be clear, while the study of your powers may have been what brought you here, you will still be expected to maintain grades in all of your studies. This will include standard scholastic topics as well. Battle tactics may be fun, but you still need arithmetic and linguistics to succeed in this world." There was a collective groan. "Yeah, yeah. You'll live. Probably," she added as an afterthought.

I blinked. Surely, she wasn't suggesting that some of us might die.

"I'm going to give you the rest of the day to get settled. Sadly, I wasn't able to have you all housed in the same dormitory. Best I could swing was having each of you room with at least one of your classmates. Your schedules will coincide to ensure that, no matter what, you have someone readily available to rely on. As your powers develop, they may also become more volatile and unpredictable. It's paramount to have a safety-buddy, if you will." She chuckled. Personally, I didn't think the fact that we were all at risk of going violently insane was all that funny.

"Anne will provide your room assignments," Vera continued, as if our possible demise was par for the course. "Once you know your destination, you can make your way across the lawn to the set of dormitories on the other side. Be advised, the dorms are co-ed and not exclusively demonic. I expect all of you to behave yourselves." Snickers rippled through the room. Vera pointedly ignored them and went on. "Student Affairs will take care of placing your things in your rooms. They should be waiting for you by the time you arrive. Thank you all for being here. I'll see you next Monday," she finished, stepped aside, and vanished.

Her disappearance was met with muffled surprise that rippled across the room. However, the aforementioned Anne didn't seem the least bit phased as she stepped up to take Vera's place. Anne held up a tablet and began reading. "Duncan and Roman, you'll be in room 2708 in Starling Hall."

Surprised to hear my name listed first, I glanced around in search of "Duncan". Sadly, no one besides me seemed to react to the announcement. I glanced back towards the entrance, curious if the attendee list was still there.

I casually made my way over, trying not to draw attention. Anne continued to call out assignments behind me, but I didn't care. I was on a mission. As I approached the podium by the door, I only had one desperate thought—please be Matt, please be Matt. At last, the list was within reach. But with only fifteen of us to be paired, I was running out of time fast. I quickly scanned the names.

I finally found the "Duncan" scribbled in at the bottom like it had been a last-minute addition. Even scrawled, the name clearly read Matthew Duncan. I could have whooped for joy. Suddenly, I realized Anne had finished and people were shuffling toward the exit. I stole another quick glance to see if he had a power level listed. My curiosity was rewarded with nothing more than a question mark.

The sound of people getting closer brought me back to reality. As close as I already was to the door, I had no choice but to be the first one out. I looked over my shoulder, hoping Matt was nearby and we could leave together. No such luck. Reluctantly, I exited the room solo. Despite my determination to wait, after several minutes of milling around the front of Mysterio College, it seemed like Matt was intentionally hanging back. With a sigh, I walked across the lawn to Starling Hall.

After a short flight of stairs, I found myself on the second floor of the dormitory. At first glance, I was reminded of an old hotel my mom had taken us to once. Deep green carpet flowed down the walkway like a plush river. I reached out and touched wallpaper far more intricate and, frankly, ancient than befit a college dormitory. Further down the hall, a door opened. A resident with a tail as long as they were tall emerged, ran three doors down, then disappeared into another. The only sound to betray the commotion was the door slamming home.

I continued on, eying each entryway. As far as I could tell, all the rooms had locks. The farther I went, the more concerned I was that I'd missed Anne mentioning where to get our keys. Maybe that's why Matt had held back. He'd actually been paying attention.

I smiled to myself, still a little amazed at my good luck. Now all I had to do was make sure he didn't hate me for interfering with George. My mind called up those incredible blues he had for eyes, recalling with perfect clarity the fires that had danced within. An angry fire—at my intervention. I grimaced. We hadn't even been properly introduced, and I was already making a mess of things.

Like you do everything, a voice that sounded suspiciously like Daniel added without mercy. I shook my head and refocused on the room numbers. Finally, I found it. On the outside of a door that looked positively ancient were two envelopes with the names Roman and Duncan written on them, respectively.

I grabbed mine, dubious about the wisdom of leaving our keys where anyone could take them, though both looked untouched. There was just enough time to register the thick vellum before the entire envelope vanished. A heavy bronze key befitting the antique lock fell with a muffled thud to the floor. Curious, I touched the other envelope. Nothing happened. Spelled envelopes, of course.

I retrieved my key from the carpet and turned it in the lock. The door swung open on silent hinges to reveal an interior that did not match the aged door, or the rest of the dorm, for that matter. Where I'd expected to find a traditional, cramped dorm room with barely enough room for two beds, there was instead what amounted to a modern apartment, complete with open living space, a kitchen at the back, and even a small breakfast table. No beds, though. I stepped deeper into the living room and the door swung shut behind me, the lock automatically clicking in place.

Note to self: don't lose your key.

A quick inspection revealed that the place was fully furnished with a red fabric couch, plates, silverware, pots and pans, and even a TV. My excitement surged at the increasingly pleasant turn of events. I doubted my mother had anticipated my having so much independence my first semester.

I glanced around for beds or somewhere that might hide beds. What I found were doors on either side of the space that each led to a bedroom with its own bathroom. My things were set up in the room on the left. Which meant the other luggage had to belong to Matt. Bit of a bummer that we didn't actually get to share a bedroom, but I supposed the killer apartment sort of made up for that.

I was inspecting the kitchen when the door clicked again. Time for damage control. I stole a moment to gather myself, then turned around to greet my college roomie, mentally crossing my fingers that I wouldn't bugger this worse than I already had.

Matt stood, holding his key and looking a little out of sorts. His uncertainty was quickly replaced when he caught sight of me. "It would have to be you, wouldn't it?" he said, blander than dry giouvarlakia. He tossed his key on the coffee table. It clattered a moment, then went still with a hollow thud. "Today just keeps getting better and better."

I frowned at the obvious sarcasm. "What's wrong with me?"

He gave me an incredulous look. "For starters, you stick your nose where it doesn't belong. Not to mention, you're an arrogant suck up who probably thinks they're great at everything." The words were unnecessarily hostile and clearly chosen to get a rise out of me.

I refused to give in so easily. Daniel used to say way worse when he was in a mood. Matt, I could handle. "Maybe that's just because you don't know me."

"How long have you been here?"

"A while," I answered honestly.

He crossed his arms and basically glared at me. "I bet you know this whole campus like the back of your hand."

I shrugged. He wasn't wrong.

"Privilege." He shook his head in blatant scorn.

"For the record, all of us were recruited." Taking a gamble, I added, "I heard Vera picked you up herself."

He gave me a searching look, but rather than answer, he asked a question of his own. "What's your name?"

"Alexi."

He stared blankly back at me. "That's a weird name for a guy." He looked away, and it seemed like that would be the end of our very brief, unusual conversation.

In a moment of inspiration, I said, "Then call me Alex." No one in my entire life had ever called me Alex, but if it made Matt comfortable enough to talk to me, then I would learn to answer.

"Okay."

Finally, we were getting somewhere. "You're Matt, right?" His guard immediately went back up. At this rate, I would never make any headway.

"Yeah."

I walked closer, gliding around the couch. This whole interaction was reminding me of the time I'd tried to encourage the neighborhood stray cat to follow me home. "How long have you known about the school?" I prodded.

"Two weeks," he replied while he looked around the space.

Only a couple weeks? No wonder he'd been penciled onto the roster. If that was the case, it begged another question. Which could either go really well or really poorly. "Um... how long have you known you're a demon?"

"Two weeks," he responded in the same flat tone.

Ho-ly. Shit.

"Well, that explains a lot." The words were out of my mouth before I could rethink them.

Matt's eyes narrowed, cutting the ice blue down to shards of glass. "What's that supposed to mean?"

"Nothing." I smiled to help play it off. However, the response only seemed to unnerve him further. "Demons tend to be more aggressive when they don't regularly use their powers. Like they're pent up... or something..."

"Are you saying I'm aggressive?"

Yes. A thousand times yes, you gorgeous, angry angel of a man.

"No. I'm saying you should lighten up, not take everything so seriously. I mean, look at this place. Aren't you even the littlest bit excited?" I chanced another smile, but it didn't seem to help.

He blinked and looked around again. It was almost as if he was taking inventory, either that, or looking for another exit.

"Oh, your stuff is in that room." I gestured to his right, my left, then switched directions. "Mine is over there. It was already set up when I got here, but the rooms are identical, so I don't think it really matters. Unless you're into Feng Shui or something, in which case, I don't mind switching."

Stop. Talking. You're rambling like some kind of tongue-tied preteen.

Matt eyed me, then walked over to his room. He hesitated before opening the door, as if he didn't trust what might be on the other side, then walked in. After another minute of silence, the door closed, and that was that, leaving me right where I'd started: alone in the living room with my foot in my mouth.

CHAPTER 7

CHARYBDIS'S INFERNO

M

I flopped onto the bed. It wasn't as nice as the one from the hotel, but it was still better than nothing. My roommate seemed nice enough, if a little too friendly. He clearly wasn't from the states. His cool, olive complexion and black hair reminded me of something, but I couldn't quite put my finger on it, not to mention his accent. British maybe? But that didn't really fit his looks.

At least he wasn't some bug-eyed creep or covered in thorns. I gave an involuntary shiver. This whole place was crawling with creatures right out of a storybook. It just wasn't possible. Yet here I was, lying on a free bed with my own bathroom at a university full of make-believe. All because apparently, I was a freak, too. No. Not a freak. A Shadow Demon. Whatever the hell that was.

I suspected that my roommate probably knew a lot about Shadow Demons, but over my dead body was I going to ask. I still wasn't sure why I'd told him the truth about how long I'd known. That was a rookie mistake. I knew better. Even thinking back on it, I was sure if he asked again, I'd reply with the same level of honesty. It didn't make any sense, except that he didn't strike me as dangerous—at least not in the way I was used to—not in the way the jerk at orientation was.

Recalling how easily that guy had pushed me around prompted me to get up. Now that I wasn't running from authorities, back-alley creeps, or trying to stay out of the next "well-meaning" home, I could finally start working out again.

The door didn't even creak when I opened it. This place might look ancient from the outside, but the inside was practically brand new. I wasn't even surprised to find Alex still nosing about in the kitchen, clearly at home in this world. It seemed cruelly unfair since I wasn't at home in any.

"I don't suppose there's food in that fridge."

Alex straightened up to his rather impressive height and glanced around in confusion until he spied me lurking by my door. "In the what?" He glanced at the refrigerator. "Oh, the icebox. No, but I found these." He held up two cards. "I think they're for the dining hall."

I frowned. "What's the point of a fridge if we have to eat in a cafeteria?" It would have been nice to make my own food for a change.

He cocked his head to the side, making him resemble like a bird. "There's a grocery there, too."

I rolled my eyes, and he went back to his perusal of the kitchen. From what I could tell, the place appeared fully stocked. I caught glimpses of plates and glassware as Alex continued to open and close various cabinets. The sound of the wooden doors shutting filled the roomy space until I couldn't take it anymore.

"Hey, you know this place pretty well, right?"

He turned back around and gave me a look. "I have a name."

Really? I got stuck with this guy? "Alright, Alex, do you know if there is a gym around here?"

"Why?"

"Because that's where you go to work out." I bit my cheek to stop myself from snapping. At the very least I'd be stuck with this smart ass for a few months, last thing I needed was to make him an enemy.

"I know why one would go to a gym," he said with a laugh. "I'm asking why you want to go."

"Look, just answer the question." Aaand... there went all my attempts at being calm. "Is there or isn't there?"

"Yes, but you don't need it."

"I think I know what I need a lot better than you."

"That's not what I meant." He seemed to flounder a second before finally asking, "You're going for strength training, right?"

I just looked at him. I didn't appreciate the assumption, even if it was true.

"That won't do anything," he added.

"Like hell it won't." I took in his excessively tall, lean form and pretty face. He'd probably never so much as thrown a punch, let alone stepped foot in a gym. All he had to do was smile and the world would give him whatever he wanted on a silver platter.

Alex smiled as he shook his head, which only emphasized my assessment. "Demons don't need to work out to be strong, we just... are. All it really does is make you look intimidating, bulky. If that's what you're into, then you do you. But you don't need weights to be strong."

"If you didn't want to help, you could've just said so. I'll find it on my own." I turned to make my way to the door. This was why I didn't talk to people. Useless waste of time. Now I'd have to waste even more time and probably get lost trying to find the damn place on my own.

"No, wait! I'll prove it to you."

I glanced back at him, curious despite myself. "How?"

"Take me for example. Do I look intimidating?"

"No."

His mouth fell open, then he closed it. "I'm going to choose not to be offended at how quickly you answered that. Come here." He waved me over as he sat at the table.

I continued standing by the door.

He stared back at me. A hardness that contradicted his obviously amiable nature flashed in his eyes. "Matt, don't be stubborn. Let me show you. If you're not convinced, I'll tell you where the gym is." He paused a moment, as if reconsidering. "Fine, I'll tell you anyway, but only after you at least let me try to make a point."

Begrudgingly, I walked over and sat down across from him. It was a little unnerving how excited he was.

"Give me your arm." He rested his right elbow on the table and held up his hand like we were going to arm wrestle.

I eyed his waiting hand. "You're joking."

"Are you going to let me show you or not? What's the worst that could happen? You lose?" One raised brow accompanied the edge of challenge.

I caved and placed my elbow on the table. Before I could change my mind, he snatched my hand. A jolt went through me as if there was one of those hand buzzers in his palm. In the shock of it, my hand almost got to the table. The muscles in my arm tightened and our joined hands stopped perfectly an inch above the surface. It was clear he wasn't trying very hard to hold it there. I felt the resistance lessen even more. His eyes sparked with triumph.

"You haven't proved anything," I said, at a loss to explain his unusual reaction or lack of apparent effort.

He smiled. "I know."

"This is stupid." I moved to free my hand.

"If you try to let go, I will win." The spark in his eyes made them look like they were gemstones, momentarily distracting me... again.

I frowned at my lack of focus and his weird attitude. "Fine."

"Try not to break my arm, okay?"

I didn't even have a chance to ask what the hell he meant before he pressed. I tightened my grip and pushed back. To my infinite surprise, nothing happened. We were in a perfect stalemate. I pushed harder and so did he. His grin widened.

I tried harder. Still no difference. My jaw tightened as I really laid it on. There was no way this lanky guy could match me for arm strength. I didn't care if he was freaking six feet tall and secretly ripped beneath that shirt. No one had ever come close to besting me like this.

I glanced at him. He wasn't even focusing on our hands. He was watching me, a smile teasing his lips and shimmering in his absurdly green eyes.

He's enjoying this.

The revelation only pissed me off further. I pushed past reason and gave it all I had. Finally, his arm slowly descended until it gave a decisive smack against the thin wooden table. Alex laughed as he rubbed his arm.

"What's so funny? You lost." I huffed and fought the desire to give my arm the same treatment. That had been hard.

He continued laughing anyway. "I don't think I've ever met anyone who could do that." He pushed away from the table and stood. "I'm telling you, Matt, you don't need a gym to be strong, but if you insist, there's a student gym not far," he said, then promptly disappeared into his room. Rude.

Before I could call him out for being a lying jerk, he returned holding a map. Guilt wormed around in my chest. I should know better than most not to judge people on appearances. Just because Alex was put together and seemed to take all of this in stride, didn't automatically make him a privileged know-it-all.

He laid the map down on the table where my arm was still resting. "This is where we are." He pointed to a cluster of rectangles. "This is Mysterio College." His finger swept across a wide swatch of open space to circle another square. "If you go this way," I followed the path he traced, "you'll run into the main dining hall. To the left is the student gym. I confess, though, I know nothing about it past that."

I stared at the map, trying to commit it to memory.

He slid it closer. "Take it. You're right. I have this whole place memorized."

"Thanks," I said, now officially feeling like an asshole for my behavior earlier. I folded it and stuck it in my back pocket. Then I made my way to the door, scooping up my key from the table.

"Hey, Matt."

I turned back. He was smiling again. Shocker.

"Thanks for not breaking my arm. You may not know it yet, but it wouldn't have been hard."

I shrugged, not knowing what else to say, and left. Once the door closed behind me, I took the map back out and made my way outside. In the early twilight, the campus spread out before me, a daunting arrangement of shrouded buildings and infinite unknowns. A tiny amount of fear wriggled up.

Pull it together. If you can make it on the streets, then you can make it here.

Except the streets didn't have expectations, and food, and a roommate that looked at you funny. I shook off the feeling and walked over to the nearest lamppost. In the dim light, I mentally traced the path Alex had pointed out, then glanced around. I oriented myself with Starling Hall at my back and set off.

The gym was at once closer and farther than I expected. I found the cafeteria no problem, and finally understood what

Alex had meant when he said there was a grocery. Behind pristine glass doors were not only the expected food options, but at the back was what looked to be a small store. There was even a sign advertising fresh fruit.

In retrospect, I probably should have grabbed the dining card Alex had found. At any rate, I could always come back. Now that I wasn't locked in that hotel, I had all the freedom in the world.

I stopped in the middle of the sidewalk. I was free. Did the Nebraska age of majority apply over here? Even though Vera had failed to elaborate on where exactly here was, the brochures had mentioned Austria and a name with too many vowels and accent dots. I wasn't about to admit out loud that I didn't know where that was supposed to be, but it didn't take a genius to realize I definitely wasn't state-side anymore. Between the accents and languages I'd heard since I arrived, it seemed a safe guess that I was in Europe... somewhere.

I referenced the map again and looked around for the promised building. Now that I had found the cafeteria where Alex had said it was, I had faith that the gym would be as well. Except there was nothing. I spun around, searching the amber grounds for any kind of sign.

Finally, a discreet plaque far off to my right declared Campus and Recreation Center. I walked inside to the familiar sound of clanging metal and grunts of effort. At first glance, it looked like a typical gym, until you considered the odd assortment of patrons. Some appeared human enough, but others were decidedly not.

Lying on a bench was a rocky-looking creature, casually tossing up what looked to be hundreds of pounds in weights like they were nothing more than loaves of bread. In the corner, a man-sized lizard did flips up a Jacob's Ladder. And dead-center of it all was someone who looked human enough, except his legs were nothing more than a blur on the treadmill. Already these people were just as strange if not stranger than what I'd run into at Superno House.

How did this many types of beings exist and I'd never known? How was it even remotely possible that I was one of them? I didn't have horns, or wings, or a tail. Wasn't a demon supposed to? But then, Alex hadn't had any of those things either, and he was definitely... something. I thought about what he'd said as I walked the perimeter about demons being inherently strong. He seemed convinced that I could've broken his arm, but it felt like he'd held his own to me.

At a sudden shout, I tore my gaze away from a guy with static dancing in his hair to see a rail of a girl plummeting towards the padded floor. Horror rooted me to the spot as I realized she was totally going to splat. Why wasn't anyone doing anything?

Then, mere feet from the ground, she turned into a bright point of light that immediately zipped upwards. My eyes widened in alarm as I discovered another layer to this madhouse. Suspended forty feet in the air was a full gymnasium swarming with acrobats. These people were certifiable.

I shook my head and kept moving. As I skirted past a man with claws for hands, I caught sight of my reflection in the wall of mirrors and stopped dead. I barely even recognized myself. On the one hand, I was cleaner than I had probably ever consistently been and the weight I'd lost during my latest stint on the streets had come back. The hotel manager's comment that I would probably need new pants made more sense as I realized how much my body had changed. I may have been ragged and dirty before, but at least I had an edge. Now I looked... soft. Rage pounded through my veins.

Alex played me.

I glanced over at an unattended barbell. The last person had been lazy and hadn't removed the weights. I walked over, eager to see just how much strength I'd lost while I'd been kept like an overfed house cat. My hands were less than a foot from the textured bar when a thought occurred to me. Curious, I adjusted my stance and leaned down to pick it up one-handed, though it was substantially more weight than I'd ever lifted with two. But if Alex was right...

Still skeptical, my fingers wrapped around the cool metal. It rose effortlessly off the floor as if it weighed nothing. Shocked, I let go and gravity immediately reclaimed it. At the last second, I snatched it out of the air before it could crash. I looked around to see if anyone had noticed the scene I was making. Thankfully, no one seemed to care, being too busy with their own routines. I curled the bar up to get a better look at how much weight was supposed to be on it and quickly did the math. Ninety kilograms made it roughly two hundred pounds. Except that wasn't possible.

I carefully replaced the bar and shuffled off to test other weights, determined to prove that it was some sort of trick or faulty equipment. After going through pretty much every available weight, I started waiting for someone clearly struggling to finish before testing it myself. That earned me a few hateful glares. Once I'd pissed off the third meathead that was easily three times my size, I had to admit that maybe Alex really was right.

All of these years I'd struggled not to be the short, dumpy kid, to be strong enough to defend myself. And... none of it mattered. If what he said was true, then it was no wonder I'd thrown Scylla clear across a courtyard. I stared at my reflection as if seeing myself for the first time. Just what exactly did being a demon entail?

I immediately thought of two people I could ask. Neither struck me as appealing. If I asked Vera, then the entire class would hate me even more than they already did. All it had taken was the rumor that she'd picked me up to brand me as a teacher's pet. No doubt they all believed I had some secret "in" and was receiving special treatment. As far as I was concerned, getting abandoned in a mysteriously locked room for a few weeks did not magically make me her favorite. If they knew the truth—that I really was nobody—they probably wouldn't care at all. Strange part was, I didn't want them to know. Just once, I wanted people to like or hate me for no other reason than me.

The only other person I could think to ask was Alex. He'd already proved that he clearly knew a lot about being a demon, not to mention everything else in this wild place. But the thought of asking him was worse. The last thing I needed was the actual teacher's pet schooling me. And I certainly didn't want him to know that I was basically gutter trash, though I wasn't entirely sure why it mattered what he thought of me. Maybe it was because I'd have to see him every day.

I glanced up from my musings to see several offended gym junkies eying me unpleasantly, including the rock-freak. It seemed prudent to scoot out of there before one of them could decide to take my experiments personally. Outside, no one may have been giving me death stares, but there were still plenty of outrageously odd people. Everywhere I looked were wings, claws, teeth, scales or something I didn't even have a name for.

How am I ever going to survive this place?

"Hey kid," someone said behind me. It sounded suspiciously like one of the meatheads from earlier.

I turned around slowly to see the source and swallowed. Yep, definitely one of the guys from inside. He had to be pushing seven feet and looked like he ate linebackers for breakfast. I struggled to remember if I'd actually tested one of his weights.

"You look like you're looking for trouble." His voice tumbled and rolled like the beginnings of an avalanche.

I quickly shook my head. Enhanced strength or not, I had no desire to figure out how I would measure up against this behemoth of a guy. He laughed harshly, and I flinched.

"Nervous little thing, aren't you? I saw you back there." He pointed his thumb towards the gym entrance. "You must be new around here, but you look like you could handle yourself in a fight."

I eyed him. Given my new decidedly squishy appearance, it was a wonder he hadn't already clobbered me for no other reason than he could.

"It's clear what you're looking for isn't at a gym. I've got a better place for people like you."

I bristled. "What's that supposed to mean?"

His grating laugh set my already frayed nerves on edge. "Good, you've got some life in you, after all. Name's Otto. Follow me, I wanna show you something."

I refused to move. Big guys were usually slow. If I took off unexpectedly, I could probably outrun him.

"Here." He passed me a buck slip.

I squinted in the low light to make out what it said, then frowned. No way I was reading this right. I held up the small paper for a better look, but the words didn't change. It was clearly advertising an exclusive underground fight club. Who in their right mind fought on purpose?

"That's where we're going. We meet every Tuesday and Thursday. But we're having a kind of summer kick-off tonight."

"Show me." The outrageous demand flew out of my mouth unopposed. A downright menacing smile spread across his face. Then he turned and led the way across campus while I quietly followed in his wake, silently questioning my sanity every step of the way.

The red brick of the gym disappeared behind us, as well as several other buildings that I couldn't really make out in the growing dark. We walked in silence until he stopped unexpectedly on the perfectly manicured grass.

"This is the official boundary of the school. You see that door there?" I followed the path of his outstretched arm to see a small metal door that could have belonged to a warehouse and nodded. "That's where we're going. If we get caught fighting on school grounds, we could be suspended, expelled, or bound. Behind that door you won't find sympathy or healers. It's everyone for themselves. So don't expect your mama to come rescue you here. Got it?"

I didn't have a mom, and I had no idea what a healer was or what being bound meant, so I simply nodded again.

"Good. Now, we can't let just anyone in this place. What are you anyway?"

"A demon."

"I got that much at the gym. What kind? Some of you are a bit more trouble than you're worth. No offense." Otto shrugged, as if I should know what he was talking about. I didn't, so I answered honestly.

"Shadow Demon."

He gave a low whistle. "Neese is going to flip his shit. I heard y'all were getting your own class." He tightened his fist in triumph. "This year is going to be epic."

After a quick glance around that I echoed, and found what I suspected he had as well—a whole lotta nothing—he stepped toward the door. I followed a couple of paces behind, despite the fact that every logical bone in my body said I should run as far and as fast as I could in the other direction.

"By Tuesday, they'll have set up the gate key. That's when you'll need the password to get in."

I scoffed.

"Watch it, bub." Otto shoved a finger at my chest. "This place is no joke. I hope you're not suggesting it was a mistake I bring you here?" Even in the pitch dark, Otto looked intimidating.

When I failed to respond, he rapped on the door. Part of it phased out, and I heard someone ask for a password.

"Charybdis' inferno." Otto looked back at me. I gave a sharp nod to let him know I got it and we stepped in.

Noise hit me like a wall. There were people and things everywhere. Their shouts bounced off of dusty concrete floors and distant barren walls to create a bubble of sound that swallowed you whole. The collection here made what I'd seen thus far seem like a fluffy children's story. Where everyone before had been as normal as something with an extra set of arms can be considered normal. This group looked straight up like thugs and brutes. With dawning horror, it finally occurred to me why someone like Otto would invite nice, squishy me here—I was the bait brat.

"What do you have there, Otto?" The hissed question belonged to a guy with an iridescent bluish-green skin that seemed to ripple as he moved. I squinted in the uneven lighting and realized he had scales—like actual scales—covering his entire body. The only thing preventing him from looking like a human-sized snake was the fact that he was walking on two legs instead of slithering.

Otto grabbed me by the shoulders and squeezed. "This is our latest recruit. He's a Shadow Demon, Neese."

I shrugged off Otto's massive ham hands.

"No fucking way." Neese's slitted eyes turned on me. "You any good, kid? Ever been in a fight?" A forked tongue flicked out with each query. Maybe he was some kind of snake-thing. I frowned, and he laughed. "I'll take that as a yesss. You got a name?"

"Matt."

"Alright, Matt the Shadow Demon, let's see what you've got," he said, the S's dragging each time his tongue caught on the consonant. I repressed a shudder at the overall creepiness of it.

Without warning, he snagged my arm and flung me forward.

I stumbled through several people before stopping in what was clearly a ring. The circled crowd eyed me standing in the middle of the open space like an idiot. Logic finally caught up with me. I rushed to the edge of the informal ring as fast as I could.

"Oh, no, you don't," Neese hissed behind me. "Don't worry, the betting ssstarts next week. Tonight is just initiation." Snickers filled the room while wicked eyes seemed to pick me apart.

Fuck me.

"The kid's a little nervous," Otto called from the sideline. "Let's start him off easy. Is Granite here?"

What the hell kind of name was Granite?

I didn't have to wait long to find out. Less than five seconds later, the owner of the preposterous name stepped into the ring. He looked like he was made of solid rock. For a split second, I feared it was the guy from the gym. My gaze traveled up and up until I finally found what I hoped was his face. Not the guy from the gym. This one was definitely bigger. Looked meaner, too. Adrenaline shot icy cold down my spine as the reality of my situation sunk in.

I'm going to die here.

In a misguided attempt at self-preservation, I tried to backpedal, only to be hindered by Neese pushing me forward. I shook my head adamantly while my feet found no purchase on the grit-coated floor. There were no pads here, just unforgiving concrete. I didn't even care that the people gathered were jeering at my obvious unwillingness to face such an opponent. Despite my blatant refusal, Neese pushed me closer to the walking mountain.

At last, I found my voice. "You want me to fight that? What is he?"

"Oh, Granite? He's some kind of earth elemental or something like that." Neese shrugged like the answer was irrelevant. "Should be no problem for someone like you."

I did a double take. He hadn't advertised what I was. He'd said what he thought Granite was, but not what I claimed to be. He also said the betting started next Tuesday. Then it hit me. He didn't want people to know what I was. The only time you did that was when you were trying to get a jump on people, let them draw their own conclusions, make mistakes.

I reevaluated the gathered crowd as well as Neese's and Otto's reaction when they found out I was a Shadow Demon. Why were we so terrifying? Compared to the horned and thorned brutes here, I was a small fry. What did they know that I didn't?

"You just going to stand there, kid, or you going to come at me?" Granite looked behind me to Neese. "Really, man? I didn't come here so I could beat up little kids more likely to wet themselves than to throw a punch."

"Let's just see what he's got." Neese made to give me one last shove forward, only to fall on the ground for his trouble.

I'd had enough of being pushed around. If they thought I was some sort of terrifying creature, then maybe I was. At the very least, I could put up a good front. I walked closer to my opponent, who was literally made of rocks, without further prodding.

Neese looked up at me with anger seething in his eyes from where he was still lying in the dirt. "Give him hell, Granite."

I barely turned in time to see a fist that looked more like a boulder rushing towards my chest. Out of pure reflex, I twisted away, and the blow landed on my back. Pain radiated from the point of impact. By some miracle, I didn't fall beside Neese as all the air rushed out of my lungs.

The fist vacated my back, and I quickly dropped to the ground before Granite could take a swing at my head. When I came back up, I was behind him. He turned faster than anyone his size had a right to and started swinging. It took every ounce of concentration I had to stay ahead of the hits. But avoidance would only get me so far. Sure, I might eventually wear him out, but the longer we went like this, the better chance there was he'd get lucky, and I wouldn't survive a direct hit.

Right now, I couldn't feel my ribs thanks to the adrenaline, but that wouldn't last forever. I needed to knock him out first. How did you hit a rock, though? If I tried to use my fist, I'd just end up breaking my hand. I needed a weapon. Something small and light that could still break teeth.

I thought wistfully of the club I'd used on Rufus. Then, without explanation, it was in my hand. I grinned triumphantly and stopped side-stepping the attacks. My sudden shift in tactics made Granite hesitate. It was all the opening I needed.

The club landed with a resounding crack on the side of his face. The force of the impact traveled up my arm to jar my shoulder. Granite's eyes went wide as his head spun in slow motion. Then time caught up, and he fell to the ground in a mound of indistinguishable rubble.

A deafening cheer went up around me. Neese had regained his composure and was appraising me from the sidelines as

Otto held up my arm. I had no idea what had happened to my convenient club or even where it had come from. All I knew was that I'd never felt more alive.

Then Neese was once again at my side as I was being shuffled out of the way for the next fight. He dropped a small bag in my hand and I glanced at him in confusion.

"Consider it a taste of things to come."

I frowned harder and pried open the bag to take a peek. It took a hot second for what I was seeing to register, then I snapped the bag shut.

A knowing smirk curled on Neese's reptilian face. "I suppose you could always just watch, but fighters get paid."

Oh, I was definitely coming back.

CHAPTER 8

BENCHMARK

A

I shifted my pack higher up my shoulder and wound my way through the room to take a seat at an empty desk. The classroom itself was bigger than the number of students it contained. Still, there were more people than I would've expected for a summer class. Everyone from orientation was there, plus several others—most likely other demons.

I took a deep breath in a completely wasted attempt to temper my enthusiasm. Pen and paper found their way out of my bag and onto my desk. A quick glance around showed that I was one of maybe three who actually looked prepared. As I scanned my classmates, I noticed someone missing: Matt. I'd intended to suggest walking to class together since we'd already established he didn't know where anything was, but he'd already been gone.

There was a commotion by the door, and I turned, hoping it was my elusive roommate. To my disappointment, it was the teacher. Professor Hargrave was a bulk of a man that looked more like a dwarf than a demon. It just went to prove that we came in all shapes and sizes. I couldn't help but wonder if all earthen-type demons were like that.

"Good morn, class," Professor Hargrave said, his thick accent giving all the vowels a low rumble. He hobbled into the room, struggling to maneuver the hefty sack slung around his shoulders. "These be yer books for the term." He removed a leather-backed tome from his bag and passed it to the nearest student. Despite my concerns about being able to understand any of what he was saying during a lesson, I brightened.

I accepted my textbook as he walked past, making his way towards the front of the room. The book was weighty, with a faded blue cover and nearly indistinguishable lettering. My fingers coasted over the aged text reverently. This was it. History. Real demonic history.

I had a powerful urge to smell the worn pages, but promptly decided against it. Professor Hargrave was saying something at the front of the room, but I missed it, as I was too enraptured with my new treasure. I delicately opened the book as if it might crumble in my grasp at any moment. Instantly, my face fell.

Wait a minute.

Completely ignoring whatever instructions Professor Hargrave was giving, I reached down and dug through my pack until I found my red-backed demonic history. I sat it next to the one provided for the course and stared at them in disbelief. They were the same book. Unwilling to accept the truth, I flipped through, choosing a page at random. I quickly scanned the text. Aaand... they were exactly the same. I could have cried with disappointment.

A glance up showed the professor busy writing on the board. I slumped in my seat, my prior excitement thoroughly vanquished, and let my gaze wander. Picking out my fellow Shadow Demons was easy, not only because I recognized them from orientation, but because I could still sense them. Where I distinctly had a peculiar tickle of familiarity with them, I did not with others in the room. The guy sitting next to me was clearly a fire demon with those singed cuffs, but it was a pure guess, albeit an educated one. The brunette diagonal from me, however, I hadn't the faintest clue. Maybe something from the Carnal class? A succubus, or maybe a fastosus?

My gaze caught on a head of dark hair about three rows over, and I did a double take. When had Matt gotten here?

He turned around, as if sensing my stare. His crystal blue eyes held me captive.

All the moisture in my mouth evaporated and my attempt to swallow stuck in my throat. Damn, he was beautiful.

Matt glanced at my desk, blinked, and twisted back forward.

The break in eye contact snapped me back to my body. I dragged in a pained breath and turned to see what had snagged his attention. The only thing on my desk were the two books, a spiral notebook, and a couple pens. I hung my head in my hands. No wonder he thought I was an arrogant know-it-all. Could I be any more of a nerd? Had I been this much of an insufferable prat before?

What on earth did Daniel see in me?

A tiny voice in my head supplied the unpleasant answer. Nothing. That's why he cheated.

I angrily stuffed the redundant book along with the paper and pens back into my bag—I certainly wouldn't be needing them—and slumped in my seat. I cast a surreptitious glance back at where Matt was sitting. He had nothing to take notes with, but the book was open and he, at least, was paying attention. I let out an aggrieved sigh and turned to the appropriate page.

After class, I found myself once again attempting to catch Matt so we could walk to Battle Tactics together. In continuation of my disappointing day, I had zero luck. Whatever that guy did to get from place to place was making me think he might secretly be some kind of ninja. I shook my head at the preposterous thought and walked myself to class.

A guy that was maybe a year or two older than me was putting up a flier on the bulletin board in the hall a couple of meters away. He caught my glance and smiled. "Hey, you in Hargrave's class?"

"Yeah." I stuffed my hands in my pockets and ventured closer.

"I know that tone." The sandy-haired guy crossed his arms and rested his shoulder on the wall. "Let me guess, already read the book?"

I frowned. "How'd you know?"

He flapped a hand. "Eh, happens to a couple kids every semester. Those books have been reprinted a thousand times, but they haven't been updated in over a century." He held out a hand. "Name's Rubio. I'm a third year."

I accepted his hand and returned the smile, my funk momentarily lifted. "Alexi. And I'm pretty sure it's obvious I'm new here."

Rubio laughed and pinched his index finger and thumb together. "Only a little."

I tilted my chin at the bulletin board beside us. "What have you got there?"

"I run a tutoring business. The pay's not great, but it beats nothing." He shrugged, then glanced from the bulletin to me. "You're pretty familiar with the material. Would you be interested in being a tutor for the Demonic History classes?"

"Really? You'd trust me to teach other people?"

Rubio's eyebrows lifted, and he gave me a crooked smile. "Should I not?"

I chuckled and shook my head. "Okay, yeah, that was a weird question. I just didn't get... the best reception once my local supernatural community found out what I was."

"You're one of the Shadow Demons Vera scared up, right?"

I nodded and tensed as I waited for the inevitable rejection.

"That's pretty cool." Rubio straightened and pulled out a pen. "How about this?" He grabbed my hand and started scribbling on it. "Take some time to think about it and when you decide you'd be perfect for this gig, call me. Of course, you can call me for other things, too." He finished writing his name and number, even including a cute little heart over the "I," and gave me a wink. "See you around, Alexi."

"Uh, thanks. See you." I stared at my hand for a second, then reassessed him as he walked away. Rubio was maybe an inch or two shorter than me and had a pleasant face with dimples that popped when he smiled. His deeply bronze skin was intriguing, and he swayed a bit when he walked. Overall, he was pretty cute and friendly, which was a definite plus. I looked at my hand again, then at the flier advertising for affordable tutors. It couldn't hurt to have a little extra money while at uni, and it would certainly take some of the pressure off of my mom. Plus, I'd be able to put the hours I'd devoted to memorizing the textbook to good use.

Feeling a lot more hopeful, I tightened my hands around the straps of my backpack and set off for Battle Tactics class in Mysterio College. Despite my dalliance with Rubio, I still arrived with plenty of time to kill. Given this was the only Shadow Demon exclusive class, it wasn't like I had to wait for the room to be available, so I let myself in to wait.

With no chairs to choose from, I found a spot on the far side. My bag slid to the ground with an impressive thump. The wall was smooth against my back as I rested my head against the plaster and watched my classmates trickle into the room. I wondered if I would ever get used to sensing other demons like myself. Shadow Demons or not, though, some things never changed. Already I could make out the beginnings of cliques. There were your shy types, the gossips, and, of course, the bullies. My eyes narrowed as they fell on George and the two guys with him, the same two I'd eavesdropped on at orientation. I wasn't even surprised that those three had found each other.

On cue, Matt slipped into the room. Despite his unobtrusive appearance, George zeroed in on him like some kind of bloodhound. Cold caressed my back as it left the wall. My gaze flicked between the now advancing George and Matt.

Not again.

Matt glanced up, then back down to his backpack without acknowledging the pending threat.

I took a step toward him and hesitated, his rebuke from last Friday fresh in my mind. He hadn't said a word to me since that evening. With forced resignation, I stopped my advancement.

"Hey, pipsqueak," George said, now practically on top of Matt.

Matt's flinch was barely perceptible before he calmly straightened. Although George was taller than him, Matt met his gaze evenly, defiance written in every line of his body.

"Can I help you with something?" The question was eerily flat. Matt's presence seemed to swell, though he himself did nothing.

"Yeah. You still haven't answered my question. Who the fuck do you think you are?" George practically growled.

"I told you, I'm nobody. As for being special or the teacher's pet, I never met Vera before she showed up three weeks ago."

"I don't believe you." George pointed aggressively at Matt. "You're hiding something."

Matt's quiet calm evaporated in the blink of an eye. "How many times do I have to tell you..." Matt's words trailed off even as his fists clenched by his side.

George snickered at seeing Matt's reaction. "What are you gonna do? I'll tell you what. Nothing. Because you're a scared little chicken."

"Don't call me that," Matt gritted through clenched teeth.

"What? Chicken? Or Little?" George's snide response sent a wave of snickers rippling through the rest of the class.

Even from across the room, I could clearly see Matt's fury.

I have to stop this. I'll worry about him hating me later.

Just then, the door flung open and Vera herself waltzed into the room. She casually strode between the hostile pair, sparing Matt a disapproving glance. His furious gaze immediately switched from George to her.

Vera pointedly ignored his look and took a position in the center of the room. My classmates shuffled around her, thoroughly cowed now that a higher authority was here. "I have decided that in light of—certain circumstances," she began.

I frowned and glanced around at everyone else who seemed no more enlightened about these "circumstances".

"Rather than random assignments, each of you will pair with your roommate for training. I mean, class," Vera quickly amended. "Hopefully, the simple fact that you share living quarters will keep you from tearing apart your sparring partner."

My gaze slid to where Matt was still hovering by the door. He turned to look at me, and for the second time that day, our eyes met. Once again, my mouth went dry. Rubio was cute, but Matt was a dream. Maybe if he was forced to interact with me, I'd have a better chance at winning him over.

That's right. Forced. Because that's the only way a guy like that would ever talk to you. Daniel's voice was an unwelcome intrusion in my thoughts.

That's not true, I countered, doing my best to squash the insecurity. My efforts were met with a degrading chuckle that echoed in my head.

We both know it is, the voice insisted. You aren't worth his time. You were barely worth mine. The words stung, and I grimaced.

"What are you all standing around for?" Vera scolded when no one moved. "Pair up."

Mumbles rose as the cliques I'd been observing broke apart into room assignments. Vera walked through the class, pointing at where she wanted groups stationed from now on. Matt spared one final glare for George before rolling his shoulders and walking over to where I stood.

"Hey," I said in a greeting that he didn't return.

Instead, he crossed his arms and leaned against the wall in the same spot I'd been before.

"The nerve of that guy, right? I mean, is it really worth getting kicked out of school just to give you a hard time?" I laughed awkwardly.

Matt's gaze flicked to me, then refocused on a spot on the floor.

Vera clapped her hands, claiming my attention. "Good. Now that everyone is sorted, we will not be sparring today." A few disappointed murmurs greeted the declaration. "Quit your belly-aching. We'll get to that eventually. First, we need to figure out where all of you are developmentally."

I glanced at Matt out of the corner of my eye, fully aware that this would not help my case where he was concerned.

"We'll start simple enough. I want each of you to focus on the thing inside of you that is different. For some of you, it may feel like a still lake, or other body of water, others like the night sky. However, it appears to you, I want you to reach out and touch it. Nothing drastic, just like a get to know you hand shake."

Someone in the back made a rude comment, earning themselves a glare from Vera.

"The time to be juveniles is done. Whatever reasons brought you here, know this. Without this training, you will die." She scanned the suddenly pale faces, adding even more weight to the dire statement. "It may not be today or tomorrow, or hell, even in the next five years, but it will happen. Your powers, your potential, is raw and untapped. Without the proper guidance, they run the very real risk of taking over. Who here has heard fairytales of soulless demons?" She paused, giving the class a chance to respond.

A few hands, including mine, made their way into the air.

"That is what happens when your powers win. You become the monster everyone already assumes you are." Her gaze continued to travel the room. Eventually, she reached the part of the room where Matt and I were standing. "Don't let them decide who you are for you." The statement was clearly directed at Matt, but I felt it just as pointedly.

I glanced back at where he was still stubbornly resting with his arms crossed. He shifted his shoulders as if her words made him uncomfortable. She let the warning sit for a moment, then went back to addressing the class.

"Now, with a little more give-a-damn if you please. Failure is not an option here. This is your life. If you can't take your classes seriously, then you have no business being in them. Am I making myself clear?"

I blanched.

Her eyes narrowed at the lack of response from the class. "Let me be crystal. If you fail any of your classes—I mean any—then you will lose your scholarship and be expelled from the university. I will escort you from campus and you will become someone else's problem. Just remember who is still responsible for cleaning up supernatural messes."

The threat was clear. Fail and be sent home where one day our nature would consume us. When that day came, she would be there to take care of us. Permanently.

I raised a shaky hand.

She acknowledged me with a curt nod.

"Perhaps meditation would be helpful?"

She let out an aggrieved sigh and stared up at the ceiling. Just like that, her entire fierce demeanor changed. "Well, that's a bet I lost. Fine. Meditation it is. Everyone, take a seat."

The class did as ordered, with substantial sounds of complaint, but I was officially shaken. I'd known there were risks for all demons when it came to mastering our powers. But this... this was something else. What horrors had Vera seen during her tenure with the Regency to make her this way?

I glanced over at Matt, kind of dying to know what he thought about all of this, especially since he'd only recently learned he was a demon. Where I'd expected to be captivated by his piercing gaze yet again, I instead found his eyes closed and face completely relaxed. I spent a minute appreciating the smooth angles of his slightly pink cheeks, the fullness of his mouth, and the delicate curve of his nose. I let out a wistful sigh at the sheer innocent beauty that was Matthew Duncan.

His lips parted, and he seemed to sink into his meditation. Then it hit me. My angel was asleep.

CHAPTER 9

PLAY BALL

M

I braced myself on the bathroom counter and let out a breath. Two weeks and I still didn't have a fucking clue what I was doing. School had never exactly been my forte. I'd never once considered pursuing higher education, maybe a trade school or on-the-job program, but never college.

Not for the first time, I considered walking out the door and right off campus. I wasn't afraid of Vera finding me, or powers I supposedly had, but couldn't use, destroying me. I wasn't even afraid of ending up in the hospital from a fight gone south. What I was afraid of was an empty belly, of getting caught in an alley by some creep, of never being able to have a decent night's rest again.

I shook my head and plunged my hands under the faucet that I'd left running. It wouldn't matter what I was or wasn't afraid of if I couldn't get my shit together. I believed Vera when she said she'd give us the boot if we fell behind. Considering my education had been a long series of stops and starts, with more time spent in trouble than in class, it went without saying that I was behind.

The door to the public restroom swung open behind me. I glanced into the mirror to see Alex's startled expression. Like every time I looked at him, I couldn't help but pick out his features. His strong, perfectly straight nose. His pronounced cheekbones that paired perfectly with his angular jaw. His lips that always seemed to be moving, even when he wasn't talking.

"H-hey." Alex held up a hand in greeting. "Fancy running into you here."

I blinked and turned off the water, then grabbed a paper towel.

Alex cleared his throat and shifted his backpack. "What did you think of that quiz in Demon History the other day?"

My jaw clenched. "Total bullshit."

"Yeah. Total." He shifted his weight, drawing my attention to his absurdly long legs. It wasn't remotely fair. Height, looks, and good grades? I didn't have to ask to know he'd aced the quiz. Not like my failing grade shoved into a crumpled mess in my bag. His gaze darted to the side toward the urinals.

I pushed away from the counter and swung my bag over my shoulder. "Don't let me stop you."

"Right. Yeah." He crossed the room and disappeared into a stall.

Shrugging off yet another weird encounter with my awkward roommate, I wandered outside. I was still drinking from the nearby water fountain when Alex emerged from the restroom after what had to be the fastest piss ever. He glanced around as if looking for something, then stopped when he spotted me. For some reason, that made me feel good. I wasn't sure if I'd ever been anywhere people wanted to see me. Most of the time, they pretended like I was invisible.

"You up for walking to class together?"

I crossed my arms. "What if I was ditching?"

Alex's face fell, and it was like someone kicked me in the gut. Maybe that was why people were inclined to give him whatever he wanted, because seeing him disappointed was physically painful.

I uncrossed my arms and licked my lips. "I'm not. Was just asking, you know..."

"Hypothetically?" Alex filled in with the beginnings of a smile that instantly made me feel better.

"Yeah, that." I waited for him to join me by the exit, and we stepped into the bright afternoon together.

"Well, hypothetically, if you were skipping, then I'd hope it was for a good reason."

I seriously doubted Alex would agree with my list of good reasons. We fell into an easy silence as we made our way across the quad. All around us, other students hurried to and from classes, shouting to each other, but it didn't quite touch our quiet little bubble. It was kind of... nice? Was that what having a friend was like?

I glanced over at Alex, curious if I should say something. That's how socializing worked, right? He said something, then I said something, back and forth until we reached our destination or ran out of things to talk about. Except, what could I possibly say that was even remotely interesting to someone like Alex?

"I joined a tutoring program," he said, taking the decision out of my hands.

"Oh?"

He flashed me a grin that somehow made his green eyes brighter. "Yeah, ran into this guy—his name is Rubio, he's older than us—but he started this tutoring business and invited me to join, seeing as how I've already read the whole Demon History text." He gave me a quick glance. "Did I mention it was for Demon History? Anyway, turns out there's a tremendous demand for tutors on campus. I already have a couple of clients. Can you believe that?"

I could absolutely believe that.

"I know the uni stuff is covered, plus we got those dining cards, but it'll still be pretty cool to have some extra cash. Don't you think?"

I nodded, because of course having money was great. I already had a bit stashed away from the couple of fights I'd done. Granted, Neese took his cut, but it was easily more than I'd ever earned.

Alex switched to talking about the day's lesson with a passion I'd never seen anyone show history, not even the professor.

I debated asking how much the tutors went for. Surely I could spare some of my winnings for a few sessions. There would always be more fights. But the words stuck in my throat. Alex was smart, really smart. Would he be interested in being friends if he knew I was struggling so badly? Even if I got a different tutor, he was bound to find out eventually.

"Oh, hey. We're here."

I glanced up at the moss-covered bricks and groaned. If I was bad at regular school subjects, I was worse at Battle Tactics. Which didn't make a lick of sense to me, considering I was holding my own at the club.

Alex's forehead crinkled in a frown. "Don't worry. You're not the only one having a tough time figuring out this shadowing business."

Great, so he'd noticed that. I walked toward the doors and he pushed them open.

"Seriously, did you see when Elle lost Cara's backpack in a pool of shadow? It took Vera half the class to fish it out. The whole time Elle kept apologizing. Meanwhile the rest of the class couldn't even figure out how she'd done it. You'll get it."

I hiked my shoulder in a noncommittal response and made my way over to the section of the room we'd been assigned. Instructions were already on the board to spend fifteen minutes meditating and basically connecting with our inner demon, then to move on to summoning enough shadow to fill your hand. A handful of our classmates were already getting situated, but there was no sign of Vera. Not surprising really. Sometimes she showed, but most times it was a TA.

"Really?" Alex groaned. "When are we going to do something else?" Grumbling to himself, he folded his legs and sat on the ground. Within seconds, an inky substance began swirling in his upheld palm.

I couldn't help but envy him. He made it look so easy. Like all you had to do was want it and it would come. I wanted it plenty, but I didn't understand how it worked. Why it worked and no one had bothered to explain that. Vera kept talking about all of this stuff like I was supposed to just get it. Alex clearly did.

The dark fog-like substance swirled around his palm, then ventured to curl around his wrist and twist slowly up his arm. For a second, I thought he'd lost control of the stuff, then I realized he had a light smile on his face. The darkness continued to move, intimately gliding over his body. I swallowed as it reached his shoulders and he tilted his head back so it could sweep over his throat. With his eyes closed like that, his body perfectly relaxed, Alex looked comfortable and completely at ease. No tension in his shoulders. He sat with his back perfectly straight, highlighting his tapered waist, which the shadowy substance was now encircling.

"Hey, Matt! Think fast!"

I tore my gaze off of Alex and his effortless skill in time to see Vera hurl a ball of something at my head. But it was too large to catch and too late to get out of the way. I threw my arms up to shield my face, bracing myself for impact. Except, when it came, it was dull, like it was far away.

I cracked an eye open and found a black shield hovering before me. Beyond it, Alex's mouth was hanging open and Vera had a smug expression on her face. I dropped my arms to get a better look at the timely shield, only to have it vanish.

"What was that?" I looked at Alex in the hope he had some idea.

He stood and walked over, eying the area in front of me. "I don't know. She threw something, and you... stopped it. Whatever she threw hit your shield and shattered." He looked at me with wonder and I stared at the empty space in front of us.

"But how?"

He blinked a few times and shook his head. "You've got me. I can summon shadow and make it do a few things, but I've never sustained anything of that magnitude."

I frowned. "But I didn't do anything."

Alex looked at me. "You definitely did something. I... felt it. Both what she did and what you did. Didn't you?"

Short answer: no. Not short answer: maybe?

Vera whistled. "Alright, enough gawking. Yes, it was a very impressive counter attack." She smiled at me and a tiny ember of pride burned in my chest. Then she spun to address the rest of the class. "Three guesses what we're doing this week."

A girl whose name I was pretty sure was Colleen held up her hand.

Vera pointed at her. "Yes."

"Making shields?" possibly Colleen guessed.

"Nope, try again."

A guy who I knew for a fact was named Kyle by virtue of the fact that he ran with George raised his hand, but didn't wait to be called. "Trying to kill each other?" He and his buddy Travis snickered and elbowed each other while George leered at me.

"Not quite." Vera held her palms out by her sides. "Come on, no one else?" After another empty pause, she snorted. "Fine, y'all are no fun. Today, we're going to play ball." She held up her hand and a much more reasonably sized sphere appeared above it. Unlike when Alex summoned shadow, hers was always just there. "Right, so here's the new lesson plan. You're going to work on making grapefruit sized spheres, like this one. From there, I want you to work on keeping its shape. You'll need to exert more influence than you do when simply calling it up."

For once the statement didn't seem to be directed at me, but at Alex. I felt him stiffen beside me, confirming that he believed so, too.

"When you're confident that the ball won't wink out of existence and rejoin the shadow plane, I want you to practice tossing it. Nothing complicated. Something like this." She illustrated by bouncing the ball in her hand, then juggling it to her other. "After you've got that down, then comes the hard part. You're going to take turns throwing your manifested shadow with your partner. Right. Those are your marching orders. Get to it." Her sphere disappeared, and she waved her arms for us all to get started.

Alex spared me a glance before putting some distance between us. To my surprise, I was disheartened he'd felt the need to move. Maybe we weren't becoming friends. It was probably my fault. With a huff, I focused on my hands and willed with everything I had for shadow to show up between them. Though how Vera expected me to do this when I couldn't consistently summon shadow in my palm was beyond me.

A solid back sphere flashed between my palms. I barked out a triumphant laugh, and it promptly disappeared.

"Motherfucker," I growled under my breath. Of course, Vera would choose that moment to walk up beside me.

"Relax, Matt. The power is there. You don't have to wrangle it into submission."

I huffed and dropped my hands. "Are you trying to tell me I'm trying too hard or not hard enough?"

A half smile tilted her lips. "Both."

I glared at her back as she walked away. "Fat lot of help you are."

CHAPTER 10

SWEET DREAMS

A

I set my bag down and sank into the couch. As far as sofas went, it wasn't too bad. The whole place wasn't too bad. But none of it was what I'd spent the last few months looking forward to. Sure, the apartment-style set up was nice, but whatever happened to cramped dorms? Or arguing over who gets what bed? Or, well, anything. What about the college experience?

Arminius had always been the ultimate destination for me, a place where I'd finally be able to appreciate who and what I was. But while I was physically on campus and technically enrolled, I still didn't feel like an actual student. My entire curriculum was basically Demons for Dummies. At least the tutoring thing had panned out. So that was something. Rubio was a super nice guy and the team he'd put together were equally friendly. I could already see myself becoming great friends with most of them, even if they were older.

Then there was Battle Tactics. My fears about the class had clearly been unfounded, as we had yet to do anything remotely battle-like or even complicated. Despite that, several of my classmates couldn't seem to grasp the simple mechanics of using their innate abilities. Namely, Matt.

I sighed and fiddled with the hem of my shirt. It was clear to me, at least, that without help, Matt would likely fall behind and would more than likely be sent home. I really wanted to help him, but he'd made it abundantly clear that he wasn't interested. He barely said more than a few passing words to me each day, and that was if I was lucky. What did I have to do to get him to stick around long enough to get to know me?

The small voice in my head that sounded eerily like Daniel spoke up. You're not worth knowing.

I tried unsuccessfully to push the cruel words away. But maybe he was right, maybe it was me. I sighed again, sinking deeper into my misery. This was going to be a very long summer at this rate. There had to be something I could do to show him I wasn't his enemy.

My heart still skipped every time I saw him, and I was starting to think that my uncontrollable yammering was why he was avoiding me. I couldn't really blame him; it was probably annoying.

What I wouldn't give, just to get him to talk to me.

I wanted to know about him—was practically dying of curiosity. Talking to people had never been something I'd struggled with before. Even when Daniel had been in one of his moods, I could still get him to open up, laugh even.

Absently, I pulled out my phone. I'd called my mom a few times since she'd dropped me off and her number was the only one listed in recent calls. I switched over to contacts and went through my options. While I loved my mom, it didn't really compare to talking to someone my age. It was a testament to my level of my desperation that I was already a click away from calling Daniel. I stared at my finger as it hovered over the call button.

It'll be a mistake. If I call him, only one thing will happen—he'll win.

Oh, there were lots of different ways he could go about it, but the result would still be the same. He could refuse to take the call to punish me for not spending that last day with him, only to call me back when I was asleep or in the middle of class. Of course, he could also answer, in which case, he would play so nice it hurt. He'd do everything he could to make me regret my choice to end things, pouring on the charm, no doubt all the while lying next to whoever he was using to ease his ego.

Angry at myself, I closed the phone. I didn't actually want to talk to Daniel. Nothing he said could make things better.

Maybe I should have given him one last day or a chance to at least try to explain.

I shook off the traitorous thought. The whole point of coming here early was to get away from him. No, who I really wanted to talk to was Matt. I longed for him to show more interest beyond ghosting around the dorm. I wanted him to see me.

I let out a sigh and tossed my head back to stare up at the beige ceiling. Who was I kidding? He was probably straighter than a fucking arrow.

"What's up with you?"

My body came a full inch off the couch at the unexpected question. I craned my head farther back to find Matt standing right behind where I was sitting. "You scared the crap out of me. How long have you been there?"

He simply shrugged and returned to whatever he was doing in the kitchen. "A while," he finally said. "So, is something bothering you or what?" I couldn't believe it; he was actually initiating conversation.

"Why do you think something is bothering me?" I asked, trying to hide the surprise from my voice.

He shrugged again. "Because normally by now you've already re-told me the entire lecture from class, quoted some dead scholar, or have given me a history lesson on why this is called Starling Hall." He pulled down a glass and glanced over his shoulder. "You haven't said a word since you got in."

I straightened up and stared, flabbergasted, at the door to stop myself from gawking at him. He'd actually been listening to all of that? "No, nothing is wrong." I wracked my brain for any hint that I might have overlooked that would have indicated he was already here.

"You sure?" The light concern in his voice had my heart doing those obnoxious somersaults.

I shifted to a more comfortable position and begged my hormones to be reasonable. "A little home sick, maybe. These last couple of weeks haven't gone like I expected."

"That's the truth." The faucet turned on briefly. "Anyway, I'm going to turn in early." He finished drying whatever he'd been rinsing, then a door opened and closed.

I swiveled around to confirm he'd truly left, then settled back with a disbelieving huff. Sleep was probably a good idea, considering I was clearly losing my mind. I looked over at my door.

Now to just motivate myself to get up.

I turned my attention to his closed one. Then again? Why should I? This was a common space and he'd already shut in for the night. I had every right to stay right here if I wanted. I nodded my head sharply, as if I'd just won an argument. I'd doze here for a bit, then maybe I'd feel more like relocating later.

That settled, I closed my eyes and tried to relax, beginning with my regular breathing exercises. In no time at all, I slipped into slumber's embrace.

When I opened my eyes next, the room looked strange, like it couldn't decide what shape it was supposed to be. Then I saw Daniel walking towards me and I knew it was a dream. Even in real life, he didn't look that nice.

Dream Daniel walked forward until he was kneeling over me on the couch. This version of him was much more like when we'd first met, all smiles and quiet confidence. When he kissed me, I let it happen. It was just a dream, after all. I didn't really miss him; I knew that, but that didn't mean I couldn't appreciate the dream of making out. At least here he couldn't be his usual arrogant, manipulative self.

I closed my eyes, letting memories fuel the feeling. Like the time we'd sneaked out to see a late movie. Or the time he convinced me to make out in the janitor's closet. I smiled to myself, remembering how much fun we used to have. Daniel hadn't been all bad. It was over time that he'd acted like he owned me. That was when all of our problems had really started.

This line of thinking was ruining what I was indulgently trying to enjoy. I reopened my eyes to get a handle on it. Where I expected Daniel's brown eyes, however, I was greeted with Matt's brilliant blue. I stared into them, getting lost. They reminded me of the clear crystal you see in pictures of the arctic. They were so bright that for a split second, I feared I was actually awake. Then he, too, leaned down and kissed me.

This dream just got a thousand times better.

I kissed him back, thinking of his natural pout.

He's probably an amazing kisser.

Shame you suck at it. I blatantly ignored the cutting remark.

Dream Matt sighed as my arms wrapped around him. This was everything and more than I'd hoped for in being room-mates. The feel of him beneath my hands was pure extrapolation from the two very brief times we'd touched. He melted into me as only a figment could. I sank deeper into the fantasy. I had no doubt that Matt would be nothing like Daniel. Not that I had anything to base that on. I just knew.

My fingers tangled in his insubstantial hair, longing to feel the real thing. I felt a little guilty as I allowed myself to fantasize about what he would taste like. In the waking world, he was probably dead asleep less than twenty feet away.

It doesn't really matter.

I pulled the dream Matt closer.

It's not like he'll ever know.

I deepened the dream kiss and felt an echoing ache. How was it possible to want someone so much? A flicker of awareness said I definitely should not be having this kind of dream on the communal couch, but I was too far gone to care. I dug my fingers into my imaginary Matt's sides, desperately needing him closer.

There was a sudden sound outside of my wonderful bubble, as if something very large had hit the floor. I struggled to solidify the hazy illusion, unwilling to let him go. Not when it was getting good. A door slammed, and the dream shattered. I groaned in disappointment as the pieces fractured into the ether.

Finally, I cracked an eye to see what the commotion was about. What I found was not what I expected. Matt's face was a mask of panic as he stood outside his door, like he was trying to hold something back. I woke up a bit more when I realized he was only wearing pajama pants. After the dream I'd been having, it felt like the universe was finally taking pity on me. My fantasy didn't do him justice.

Perfectly smooth lines ran across his torso, creating a subtle definition. My hand twitched by my side, remembering how, only moments ago, we were dreaming about tracing the entire map of his skin. I swallowed hard. He was incredible. He also still hadn't seen me. Which meant I should probably stop ogling him before he noticed. It didn't take a genius to know I definitely should not be fantasizing about making out with my straight roommate.

"You alright?" I asked.

Matt looked up sharply, his eyes wild. At the question, his entire body seemed to simultaneously tense and relax. I did what I could not to gawk as the ripple made its way down his torso. Whatever was going on clearly had him strung out.

He looked around like he was searching for an answer. "I... I'm fine. I thought I heard something." Unexpectedly, he straightened up and walked over to sit beside me on the couch.

I quickly snatched a pillow that had fallen and moved it to my lap. He gave me a quizzical look, but didn't comment. Meanwhile, my hormones were painfully aware that if he was any closer, we'd be touching.

He sat in total silence, gazing off at nothing. I didn't trust myself to speak, so I held my peace as well. Mostly, I tried not to stare. His current state of dress, or lack thereof, was not helping my situation.

He abruptly stood and looked down at me. "Do you want a drink? Like a beer or something?"

"I don't really drink," I replied by rote, and could have immediately smacked myself. Was it possible for me to be any more of a dork?

"Don't really drink like you don't like the taste or don't really drink like you never drink?"

I thought about it for a moment, not wanting to squander the second chance to keep him talking. "Both I guess. Maybe a little more the second."

He nodded like this didn't surprise him, then turned to walk away. I couldn't help but let my eyes wander over his broad shoulders and where his back dipped in the middle. Then my gaze caught on something unexpected. The right side of his back boasted a mottled bruise that easily covered half his rib cage.

"What happened to you?" I asked without thinking.

He twisted in place to get a better look. "Oh that? Nothing," he replied nonchalantly, barely even looking back at me.

I desperately wanted to know the real story behind the bruise, but was not about to jeopardize our rapport by pressing my luck. If he said it was nothing, then it was nothing. But how the heck did you forget something like that?

"Do you ever drink?" Matt called from the kitchen.

"Occasionally, but I find I'm not keen on it."

"Keen," he repeated quietly to himself.

There was some additional shuffling and then quiet. When I looked back up to see where he'd gone, he was making his way back over with a beer in his hand. Sadly, he'd also put on a shirt. I just barely stopped myself from frowning.

"What have you tried?" He took a sip as he crossed his legs beneath him on the couch.

"A bit of this and that." I shrugged, at a loss for how to sound even remotely interesting at this point. "Maybe I'm just a picky drinker."

He held his beer out for me to try. "See what you think of this."

I stared at it obtusely while a bead of condensation trailed down the side of the bottle and splattered on the thin strip of couch separating us. Drinking from that was literally half a step away from an actual lip-lock.

"Don't tell me you're afraid of cooties." He wiggled the bottle and raised a speculative eyebrow.

"Cooties?" I echoed, not sure I'd heard him right.

He rolled his eyes. "You know, cooties, germs. Are you afraid of my germs?"

A laugh bubbled up and finally broke the spell, keeping me frozen. "I know what cooties are, and I'm definitely not afraid of yours, Matt." I accepted the proffered bottle and took a sip.

It wasn't nearly as bad as I feared it would be. A little fruity even.

"Well?"

"It's better than I expected," I said, passing it back to him.

I will not think about how his lips were just on that. I will not think about how his lips were just on that.

My hormones clearly didn't care. Which is why the pillow remained firmly in my lap.

He smiled as he produced another bottle from behind his back.

My heart stopped altogether, and I forgot to breathe. I hadn't seen him smile once since we'd met. He was a completely different person when he did that. His entire face lit up and the shroud of anger he seemed to carry around like armor faded away.

I heard a pop and blinked. Then numbly accepted the fresh bottle. Had he really brought me one just in case? Failing to grasp what was actually happening right now, I latched onto the first question that came to mind. "Where did you get these?" The commissary definitely didn't sell beer or any other alcohol that I'd noticed.

He shrugged, taking another drink. "It wasn't hard. Hell of a lot easier than where I'm from."

I took an absent drink, mimicking his own. "Where are you from?" Another shrug. I was getting the impression that was Matt's way of saying he didn't want to say.

"Around, not really any one place. I moved a lot."

"Sounds rough. I didn't. Born in Greece, but grew up in a small-town east of London."

He snapped his fingers, startling me so badly I nearly spilled the beer. I quickly drank some to reduce the level.

"That's what you remind me of," he said.

"What?" I was spinning.

CHAPTER 11

TUTOR 101

M

Alex rested his forearms on the breakfast table and looked at me. "Let's try a different approach. How about you tell me what you remember from class?"

We'd been at this for over an hour. It was clear he didn't know where to start, and I was starting to think this whole tutoring thing was a mistake.

"Hey, I can see you checking out over there. Focus. Here." He swiveled around a fat text book. "Demonic History. It's been a few weeks. What have you learned?"

I slumped in my chair while the sense of failure I'd been battling swelled. "I already told you, nothing."

"I don't believe that, Matt. You pay attention to everything."

"You're exaggerating." Alex was nice, but he was also overly optimistic about pretty much everything.

His eyebrow lifted in challenge. "You think so? Alright. What color is the dish towel?"

"Green."

"How many plates do we have?"

"Six." This was ridiculous. Why wouldn't I know how many dishes we had?

"How long does it take to get to the dining hall?"

"Seventeen minutes."

"Was the TA's hair up or down today?"

"Up."

"How many students were in class?"

"Of course, that's what friends are for." I'd meant to say roommates, but apparently my brain thought intentionally friend zoning myself was a better idea.

He gave a slow blink as he stared back at me.

Suddenly, I had a different fear. Had I just scared him off altogether by calling us friends?

"Yeah," he finally said, the corner of his mouth tilting up slightly. He continued to stare at me while a smile teased his lips, then he blinked and he was right back to being awkward. "So, um, I'm going to go back to sleep. I guess we'll talk later?" The lilt at the end barely made it a question, like he still wasn't sure.

"Sure thing. I'll see you in the morning." The comment earned me an actual smile, though not the megawatt one that had sent me reeling earlier. He stood, gave me a half wave, then vanished into his room.

The moment the door closed behind him, I clutched my chest.

I think I'm having a heart attack. Can eighteen-year-olds have a heart attack?

The damn thing was in danger of beating right out of my chest. Had he heard it?

I looked back towards his room, afraid that he'd re-materialized and was witnessing my total freak out. Mercifully, the door was still closed. I now had zero doubts—I was one hundred percent absolutely in love with Matt.

"You look like one of the people from a documentary my school made us watch. You know, with the wars and the gods causing all kinds of problems? Which god was it…" Matt mused to himself a moment, then his face brightened. "Apollo, that's the one." He gave me a considering look that I could feel. "Almost exactly like him. Except his hair was gold, and yours is black."

I choked on my latest sip, causing it to go up my nose. I leaned forward to prevent the liquid from getting anymore on me than it already was. He'd been thinking about what I look like? How long had he been trying to figure this out?

"Easy there. It's not air." Matt laughed. It was a rich sound, carefree and relaxed.

I looked over at him, still struggling with the breathing concept.

He tossed back the last of his beer, then his whole body turned blacker than night. In a blink, he was gone and back again. "Here." He passed me a dish towel, looking like himself again.

"How… how did you do that?" I asked as I began the embarrassing task of cleaning myself up. When had I become so damn awkward?

"Do what?" He cocked his head to the side and relieved me of my discarded beer. He finished it and set it aside.

"You shadowed," I finally managed, though it sounded more like a wheeze.

Pull it together, Alexi. You're going to blow this.

"Are you sure? I mean, all I did was go to the kitchen and come back."

I cleared my throat again. "Yeah, except really fast. I can't even do that yet."

He looked towards the kitchen and back at me. "How?" he asked, the picture of innocent curiosity.

I stared back. "You really don't know, do you?" The comment instantly made him bristle. "I don't mean anything," I rushed to explain. "It's just, most of the class can't do that on purpose and you just did it without even thinking. If anything, I should ask you how."

"I don't know. I wanted to be in the kitchen and you needed help. That's all there was to it."

"Well, thanks." I waved the towel and let it drop.

He settled back, but still looked uncomfortable, like he wasn't okay with the shift in topic.

"So... if you ever want, you know, a recap or something of the lessons, all you have to do is say so." I'd intentionally not used the word help. Something told me it was probably a trigger word.

Matt shifted around and brushed his hair back. Once again, my mouth went completely dry as I became enraptured by watching him move. He worried his bottom lip and seemed to debate whether he wanted to say something. It was positively maddening. I was now immensely grateful I'd had the foresight to snatch the pillow. If he was any cuter, I'd combust. He took a deep breath and had a couple of false starts.

What do you want to say and why is it so hard?

At last, he spit out, "Would you be willing to tutor me?"

"Yes," I replied a little too quickly, my enthusiasm clearly taking him aback. I forced myself to dial it down. He wasn't asking me on a date, he was asking for help with his homework. "Any subject in particular?"

"All of them," he mumbled.

"Okay."

He glanced up sharply, doubt swimming in his eyes. "Really?"

"Nine. Three didn't show and Ellie had to leave early."

"What color shirt did I wear yesterday?"

"Blue."

"How many level ones are left in the world?"

"Five active."

Alex leveled a look at me.

"What?" I asked.

"You see and hear everything, Matt. You just need to learn to focus it." He smiled gently. "For the record, I'm assuming most of those were right answers. You tell me what would help. Everyone learns differently. We just need to find your way. Is it quiet study?" He held up the book, and I wrinkled my nose. "Do we need to turn it into a game with flashcards? Or do I just need to re-give every lesson?" None of those options sounded great.

"How should I know?" I'd never excelled in school. I'd always been occupied trying not to get pummeled at every turn. When you were a product of the system, the only one looking out for you was you. But it wasn't like that here, well, mostly. At Arminius, I was just another student. No one cared where I came from or who I was before. The only problem was that the classes were hard, like really hard. I felt like I was drowning. In class, everything sounded like white noise. How was I supposed to pass when I couldn't even hear or understand the lecture? For the first time, I actually cared. Besides, what good was being free, if I was only going to end up back on the street?

It had taken a while to sink in, but it finally occurred to me that this was a real opportunity to do something with my life. Asking my roommate to help hadn't been easy. Just admitting I needed help felt like admitting weakness. And he'd agreed, which I still didn't understand. No extra conditions or motives, wouldn't even take payment. He'd called us friends. I'd never had one of those before, had never been in one place long enough to try. And what was more, was that he seemed to genuinely care.

"I think we need a break. I feel like we're going about this all wrong." His head flopped on the table. If Alex couldn't help, I didn't know what I was going to do.

"It's okay, if you don't want to, you know," I mumbled. It wasn't fair to hold him on the hook for something so impossible.

Alex looked up at me from the table. "Did I say that?" He straightened back up. "Fine. No break. I want to help, Matt, but you have to give me something to work with."

"No, I think you're right. We need a break. Let's go down to the dining hall." Maybe food would help me focus.

He frowned. "It's raining."

"So, it'll take nineteen minutes," I countered.

He chuckled to himself and put the books away. We walked down to the front of the building together and stood staring out the glass doors. It wasn't storming anymore per se, but the deluge could resume at any moment. The rain had been constant since the thunder had woken me early in the morning, and now lakes of water obscured the normally clear lawn.

Alex glanced over at me, trepidation clearly written on his face. "You know we're going to get soaked."

"Yep."

"And we're actually doing this?"

"Yep." I looked at him, but he still seemed uncertain. "Race you." He barely had a chance to look confused before I was out the door. I heard the door behind me and knew he was following.

We were drenched in seconds, but kept going, laughing as we went. Other students gave us strange looks from beneath their umbrellas as we flew past. Water splashed up from each step. Running in the rain felt like being a kid all over again, except this time there was no mean matron to complain about puddles on the floor.

The dining hall came into view and I realized a fresh problem. I couldn't stop. My shoes and the ground were both too wet. I crashed into the building, skidding and sliding until I finally came to a halt. Alex had the same realization half a second after I did and came careening in behind me. I braced myself to catch him and we almost cracked skulls. Between his momentum and my soggy shoes, even hanging onto each other for support, we could barely keep our feet beneath us.

"That. Was. Awesome." I panted.

"We almost died!" He laughed, almost slipping again. I tightened my grip on his arms to steady him, and he cleared his throat. "Thanks."

"You sure you got it?" I teased. For someone always so confident, he didn't look it now. He looked nervous and he had water dripping in his eyes. I debated pushing his hair off his face so he could see, then his bright eyes caught mine. Just as quickly, he glanced away.

"Yeah, I'm good. But we're a mess." He wrung out the bottom of his shirt, lifting it enough to reveal that he was, in fact, ripped.

Mentally scowling to myself, I pushed the image of his damn near perfect abdomen from my mind and followed suit. "So what? Worth it. When's the last time you ran in the rain?"

He gasped. "Never." Then a light smile danced in his eyes. "I don't want to get pneumonia," he added.

"Can demons get sick like that?" Despite the obvious tease, now I was curious. I pushed my hair back from my face to stop the water dripping in my eyes.

Alex looked at me for a long second. I wasn't sure if he was considering the question or going to tell me I was overdue for a haircut. Then he blinked. "We should get inside before we find out."

We shuffled inside and he immediately bolted to the back of the cafeteria where the food joints and grocery were located. Meanwhile, I wandered around the periphery of the round room in search of a means to dry off. The rain must have been keeping people away, since the normally bustling space only had a few clusters of students occupying the round tables. It was by the restrooms that I chanced upon some unattended towels. Quest accomplished, I searched for Alex and found him at a table on the far side.

I tossed him the terrycloth as I walked up. "Look what I found."

"Awesome." He vigorously toweled his hair and wiped his face.

I laughed.

He glanced at me, frowning. "What?"

"You look ridiculous."

"What do you mean?"

I held my hands out from my head and he immediately started smoothing his porcupine hair. While he worked to tame his hair, I sat beside him and noticed he'd found some things as well. "What do you have there?"

He held up two small containers. "Oh. Peanut butter? Or cookies and cream?"

"Peanut butter."

He passed me the pint of ice cream and cracked open the other one for himself.

"I thought you were worried about pneumonia," I said around a mouthful of ice cream.

He waved his spoon at me. "There is always an excuse for ice cream. And I don't actually know if demons can get pneumonia."

I raised my chin to where he was decimating his pint of pure sugar. "Cookies and cream your favorite or something?"

He glanced down at the carton with a confused expression. "No. Why do you ask?" Now it was my turn to be confused.

"Because you gave me a choice and didn't care that I took the peanut butter. I just assumed that meant one or both were your favorite."

"That would make sense," he mumbled, taking a smaller bite.

"If neither one is your favorite, then why did you get them?"

He hesitated, as if he was really having to think about the answer, though it wasn't a complicated question. "Out of habit, I guess," he finally said.

I raised both of my eyebrows. That didn't make a bit of sense.

He caught the look and elaborated. "My ex couldn't ever really make up their mind, but always preferred the sweeter candy varieties. I just always got two different kinds in the hope one would work."

"That's really messed up." Alex's ex was an asshole.

"Yeah... it is." He absently stared into the frozen cream, his next bite forgotten.

I nudged him. "So... what is your favorite, then?"

"Strawberry." I laughed at the way he said it, like it was as much news to him as it was to me. He gave his own nervous chuckle and added, "I don't even know the last time I had it."

Rather than pursue what was obviously a painful topic for him, I shifted gears. "What do you know? You obviously have been studying demonology since before you got here."

"I know we got here in fifteen minutes," he said with a smile.

"No way." I looked up at the clock. He was right, and that included our near-death episode at the main entrance. "Alright, so we're fast."

"There's that. You already know about the strength."

Yep, it had proved quite handy on Tuesday when I fought another rock demon. "Okay, that, explain that to me more."

He cocked his head to the side. "What do you mean?"

"I get that there are levels and only a few of the highest left, but what does a power level really mean? How do they work?"

"You know, the lower the number, the stronger you are." I nodded, taking another bite, and he continued. "It's not just strength like being able to move heavy things, though, it's strength like overall ability. Most of us can do the same things, but how strong we are determines how well and how effectively."

"Can you get stronger?" It seemed like a logical question to me, but he made a weird face.

"To an extent. Eventually, though, you'll max out no matter what you do. You might get better at doing what you already can, but you'll never exceed it."

"I'm not following."

"Think of it like height. You can eat right and exercise all you like to get to your maximum height, but you'll never be able to go past it."

I gasped in exaggerated horror. "So, you're telling me I'll be short forever?"

He just stared at me a moment, then fell out laughing. His eyes squeezed shut as he laughed hard enough to make a few tears spill out.

"The secret is commitment... and platform shoes," I added belatedly, which only made him laugh harder. I enjoyed having a friend. "Okay, okay, let's see, what else?" I thought aloud as he sobered up. "What about that thing you can do?"

"What thing?"

"You know, the thing with the stuff." I mimed controlling something in the air.

"It's called shadowing. Well, technically, all of it is called that. It's not hard. See this?" He held up a spoon. "This is one of the first things I learned to do. On purpose anyway," he amended with a crooked smile. "Watch closely." The spoon turned black, as did his eyes as he focused on it. "Just stay relaxed and don't lose your concentration." The spoon melted down into a ball. "Hold out your hand."

"But I can't do that."

"I didn't ask if you could. Now hold out your hand." I did as he said and he dropped it onto my palm. "Keeping it in a different shape is called maintaining. Now technically, the spoon is just pure shadow right now with no defined shape beyond the one I'm giving it." At his words, the spoon morphed into a square, a pyramid, and then another ball covered in spikes. "What does it feel like?"

It returned to the perfect sphere, and I wrapped my fingers around it. "It's smooth, soft." Was this what it felt like when it twined around Alex's body?

"What else?"

"It feels a bit like holding fog, but like really thick fog, you know?" I looked up to see if that was the right answer. The sphere had spread out in my hand as if mimicking my description.

He smiled knowingly.

"What are you smirking about?"

"I'm not doing that. You are." The sphere dropped through my hand to the table where it was once again an inky black ball. "You're the only one standing in your way. Now turn it back."

"I don't know how."

"Yes, you do." His green eyes were intense as they held my gaze. "Remember, relax and focus. You know what it was before. Tell it to go back."

"If you're telling me to order this back into the shape of a spoon, you're a nutter."

He laughed again. "Not with words, Matt, with your mind. Will it back."

"That doesn't make any sense." Where were the rules? The logic?

"What did you say to me the other night? You needed to be in the kitchen? That's how it works. Need it to be a real spoon again."

"But I don't need it to be a real spoon again. I already have one." I held up my spoon.

He reached over and plucked it right out of my hand. "Now you don't," he said, using the stolen spoon to scoop another bite. "Go on. I would hurry, though, or your ice cream will melt."

"That's just rude," I mumbled, and he chuckled, still eating his stupid ice cream.

Guess I do need a spoon.

I picked the sphere up and thought about what it had been like before. Nothing happened. I looked at Alex and contemplated stealing my spoon back. "This is stupid. We already know I can't."

"Look at your hand."

I did as he said. Somehow, the spoon was back. It was still entirely black, but decidedly spoon shaped. "How?"

"You're overthinking it. Until you learn better control, everything is basically need based. If you need it, it'll happen. That's the thing that makes us so dangerous."

I thought about the mysterious club that kept showing up. "What about creating things out of nothing? Can we do that?"

"Of course. You basically just use available shadow and shape it to your will." He said it so matter of fact, it was hard to doubt him.

"But what if you're in a place that's really bright and there aren't any?"

"There is always shadow. Where there is light, there is darkness."

Suddenly, I felt a similar sensation to when Vera had intimidated Administrator Smith at Superno House. Like all the surrounding darkness was pulling into one space. I even felt a tug on myself, kind of like that night I'd woken up on the floor. All the while, Alex sat there with black eyes. In his hand, drifts of shadow spiraled into a new sphere. The pull on me got stronger.

My breath shortened and my hands sweat despite the container of ice cream I was holding. There was a pain in my chest, like something was trying to get out. My panic ratcheted up another level as I recalled a movie where an alien creature had done just that.

How could I not see how dangerous he is?

The spoon in my hand shifted to a miniature version of the club I'd used only last Thursday. There was inky black everywhere. The entire cafeteria had dimmed. My heart raced as I tried to determine the best way to make it stop. Meanwhile, Alex sat immobile, surrounded by night, then he closed his hand and the feeling stopped. His eyes returned to normal, and he looked back at me.

"That's what we are at our core—pure darkness," he said, once more his amiable self. If he could do that in a brightly lit room, what else could he do?

I swallowed my lingering fear and asked the only question that seemed to matter. "What happens if it's dark everywhere?"

"Then, depending on your power level, you could potentially exert control over everything."

I shivered and hoped he would blame the reaction on the ice cream. "That sounds like a nightmare."

"That sounds like how an entire race got a reputation for being evil." He sank into his chair, his shoulders curling inward as he poked absently at his ice cream. Like that, my concerns about him vanished.

"Do you think we're evil?" I asked softly. Alex might be secretly terrifying, but there was no way he was evil. I'd met evil. It didn't have a conscience, and it certainly didn't help its roommate study.

"No, but I worry the rest of the world always will. The Rebellion didn't help things."

I tried to remember the lessons from the last couple of weeks in Demonic History. "Have we covered that yet?"

"No, it's more recent. The Rebellion only officially ended a few years ago." He scraped his spoon along the body of the empty container.

"What happened? How would that affect Shadow Demons? And how come I never heard of any war?"

Alex straightened up, abandoning his melancholy, and took on his lecturer tone. "There used to be a governing body called the Regency. They presided over the supernatural world and worked hard to make sure the human world remained oblivious to supernaturals. But for all they claimed to protect supernaturals, they also did some pretty awful stuff, too." Alex shivered. "The Regency had been in control for decades and rebellions were creeping up. In their desire for absolute control, they created a specialized task force to deal with insurgents. Ironically, that group called themselves the Shadows."

I laughed. "They come up with that all on their own?"

"They were younger than us." Alex's sharp gaze flicked up to capture mine and my face fell. "Vera was actually the only

Shadow Demon in the group. And truthfully, they didn't even know what she was when they recruited her."

"I'm confused. Did the Rebellion fail?" I asked, more lost than ever.

"No, they won. Eventually."

"But Vera is in charge of the class." None of this was adding up.

"They switched sides. The Shadows learned about the awful things the Regency had done, and was making them do in their name, and mutinied. They're why the Rebellion ultimately succeeded."

"How big was this group? They would need to be an army," I said, astounded at such a convoluted turn of events.

"Six people." He looked into his empty container.

I shook my head. "That's not possible."

"You don't understand, these people were better than the best of the best. And even after all the enemies they made, they held enough sway to get people to trust them." Alex didn't sound like he fully believed that.

"Is that why you hate Vera?" Granted, I wasn't too keen on her myself, but it was clear there was no love lost there.

He looked up, clearly surprised. "I don't hate her."

"It kind of seems like you do."

He shifted in his chair. "She just... she really messed things up for Shadow Demons. Before she came along and made such a mess, the world had all but forgotten we existed. You don't know what it's like to have people look at you and be afraid because of what you are." He was wrong about that, but I wasn't about to correct him.

"But if she hadn't, then we wouldn't be here." Alex seemed both surprised and pleased by my answer. "I certainly wouldn't be. Things weren't going well for me where I was. If she hadn't shown up when she did, who knows what would've happened."

I'd probably be a pile of ash.

Alex gave me a speculative look. "Are you ever going to tell me where you're from?"

I considered telling him now, but held back. Trust wasn't something that came easily to me and, as much as I liked Alex, I still wasn't ready for that. "Maybe someday." I looked around the table, unsure of where to go from there.

Alex glanced past me. "Sounds like the rain has stopped. We should probably head back before it starts again."

"We can take a stab at math," I added.

"I hope you don't literally mean stabbing the book."

"I won't lie. The thought did occur to me," I joked. "Oh, hey, will this thing ever go back to normal?" I held up the spoon, which was still darker than night, though it felt solid enough.

He laughed and reached out so that his hand was around mine and the spoon. A ripple of sensation went through my fingers and I watched as the spoon returned to its original silver.

"Eventually, it would have gone back on its own. But," he began, as he took the spoon from me once more and it faded back to black, "I would hate for it to get stuck somewhere." He calmly slid the shadowed spoon into the center of the table so that only the rounded bowl was sticking out, then returned it to normal. He spared me a mischievous grin. "We'll get it later."

"Wait," I said, as he turned to leave. He spun around, and I snatched his spoon. I leaned over the table and carefully added his beside mine so they were back-to-back. "I think that makes this our table."

Alex smiled. "I think you're right."

CHAPTER 12

STRANGE HOBBIES

A

Tutoring Matt had to be one of the most difficult things I'd ever done in my life, and it had nothing to do with how intelligent he was. Now that we were talking every day, it was obvious he was actually wicked smart. He was *also* incredibly funny, observant, and outrageously charming. And *that* was a big problem... for me. If I'd been crushing hard before, I was now irredeemably smitten. Every time he asked an insightful question about the lecture, overall supernaturals, or—night help me—*me*, my heart melted a little more. Pretty sure all that was left of it at this point was a goopy puddle that spelled "I heart Matt", and that wasn't even taking into account my dreams.

I thought again about last night's dream of seducing Matt. In the fantasy, he played coy, but of course, it felt like he did that in reality. His bright, curious eyes, his full mouth slightly parted as he sat way too close for standard friendship, leaning in with every word I said, as if he was waiting for something. In my dreams, I didn't have to be strong. I succumbed to his innocent invitation every time.

I hummed to myself and debated taking another shower. The first had been wonderfully liberating as I relived every delicious second of the dream, but clearly, it wasn't enough. I gave myself a good shake and pulled on a shirt. I'd have plenty of time to indulge my ill-conceived fantasies about Matt later.

As long as I didn't slip up and actually act on them, I'd be fine. Maybe. Probably.

Determined not to let my growing obsession with Matt ruin what was shaping up to be an incredible friendship, I walked into the common space. Matt glanced up from the workbook he was scowling at. I gave him a light smile and tried not to focus on how irresistibly adorable his pout was. "Good morning."

"It's about time you woke up. Sit down." He absently reached over and pulled out a chair.

I rolled my eyes and did as he bid. Matt could be bossy, yet it had nothing to do with wanting to be in charge. He was just blunt with his expectations. I examined what he was working on. "You're getting a jump start on the math, I see. You know this, you don't need me." I made to stand.

He sat up and caught me before I could get anywhere, then fidgeted like he did anytime he was anxious or unsure. Needless to say, that adorable habit had made it into my dreams.

My fingers itched to reach out and comb his hair back. He clearly hadn't brushed it yet. I mentally shook my head; this was not the place for that.

"I can concentrate better when you're here." He looked back at the vacant chair.

I suppressed an exasperated sigh.

It's like he really doesn't care how much he makes me suffer.

"Okay, if I promise to come right back, can I at least get some coffee and a book?"

He released my arm and went back to staring at the page where all that was clear were eraser marks.

I bustled about the kitchen in pursuit of caffeine. "How long have you been up, anyway?"

"Long enough to know you take excessive showers."

I almost dropped the porcelain mug. A glance over my shoulder revealed he was still focused on the blank page with single-minded intent.

"Are you going to get your book and sit down, or what?" He grumbled without looking up.

I set the coffee to start with the simple coffee maker and went to retrieve something to read. When I returned, the coffee was done. I fixed a cup, then made myself comfortable at the table, propping my feet up on a free chair. "There, are you happy now?"

"Are you really wearing house slippers?" Matt's face screwed up in obvious judgment.

I looked down at my feet. "I'm not defending my footwear to you. My toes are cold.

"They're probably always cold because of lack of blood flow," he deadpanned.

I took too big a drink and scalded my tongue. "I beg your pardon."

"Because you're so tall, Alex." He said it like it was the most obvious thing in the world.

He was going to be the end of me. No amount of caffeine could right this morning. "Shouldn't you be doing your homework?"

"No need to be so fussy about it."

I waited to glance over until I heard the steady scratch of pencil on paper. Matt hunkered over the table while he steadily scrawled out the solutions. We both knew he knew this, so why did he need me here? I shook it off and picked a spot at random in my book. I'd certainly read it enough times for it not to matter where I started.

Somewhere along the line, I must've dozed off. The book sliding down my chest startled me awake. I wasn't sure how long I'd been out or when Matt had finished his homework.

All I knew was that the sound of writing was noticeably absent. When I looked out of the corner of my eye to see what he was doing, I found him openly staring at me. I quickly refocused my attention on my neglected book.

"Did you know you snore? It's not a lot, barely even there, really."

"I can't say that it's been mentioned before." I reached out for my coffee. It was still mostly full and stone cold. I spit the chilled liquid back into the cup and set it down. At this point, the only mercy was that he hadn't said anything about me talking in my sleep. That would only lead to trouble.

"What're you reading?" Matt's head was suddenly right next to mine as he looked over my shoulder.

I swallowed. He was so near I could practically taste him. "N-nothing, just an old history."

"It doesn't look like a history." He reached forward to touch the book.

I couldn't resist, he was just so close. I arched my head up and stopped just shy of actually touching him, then took a deep breath. The soft scent of sage curled in my nose, both calming and invigorating. "You really don't believe in personal space, do you?" I whispered. Suddenly, the book was out of my hands. I scrambled in my chair, nearly falling over.

Matt took a step back to avoid my flailing and continued flipping through the pages. "Are you sure this is a history? It sounds more like a love story to me."

"What? Of course, it's a history. It was written in the twelve-hundreds which, by definition, that makes it a history."

"Something can be old and still be a romance. See?" He held out the book with the page turned to the image of the Shadow Demon and the knight.

I looked at him in disbelief.

The book swiveled back to face him as he leaned against the table. He crossed his ankles and read the page. "This guy really needs to sort out his priorities, though. What do you think he means by the light going out?" Matt asked, glancing up at me from the stolen book. He looked sexy as hell standing there like that and I was having trouble convincing myself I was awake. When I didn't answer, he flipped through a few more pages. "I suppose it could be considered a history, even if it is more of a memoir." He snapped the book shut and held it out for me. "Looks interesting."

I stared at him in mute wonder. Every time I thought I had Matt figured out, he peeled back another layer. Finally, I found my voice. "It's my favorite."

"I can tell."

"How?" I turned the recovered book over in my hands.

"For starters, it's really worn. Now I know what you are going to say. It's old, of course it's worn. But it also has your name on it and no bookmark. You literally just opened it and began reading, which means you know it well enough not to have to pick up at a certain point."

I was completely flabbergasted. He'd gotten all of that while doing math? I glanced down at the book again. "Why do you think it's a love story?"

His brow dipped in confusion. "You don't? Look, if you think I'm going to judge you because you're reading a romance, I won't. They have some great pointers in those." He flashed a devilish smile. Now, that you're masquerading it as a history book, that I will judge you for."

"You've read romance novels?"

"Hey, check the judgment. There weren't a lot of options where I was. I made due. Besides, some of them weren't half bad."

I smiled wistfully, rather enjoying this latest revelation. "You're just full of surprises."

"Yeah, yeah. What're you doing today?" he asked, in an obvious attempt to change the topic.

"I'm doing it." I gestured to my lazy attire.

"Seriously?" He made to dump me out of my chair.

I hurriedly got up before he could deposit me on the floor.

"We need to get out of here. What would you say to some more practice?"

I rolled my eyes. "You don't need any more practice."

"I didn't say I *needed* it." He shuffled his feet. "But the first exam is coming up and I really don't want to blow it."

"It's not really an exam. More like a make sure you're trying quiz."

"Same difference. Now go put on some real clothes so we can go." He pushed me towards my room.

I stubbornly dug in my heels, making him work for it. "You know, I actually have three *interesting* books if you wanted to read something."

"Shut up and get dressed."

He went to give me an extra shove and I let myself become one with the shadows, causing him to fall right through. I laughed, and he spun around to grab my leg.

"That's cheating!"

I moved it out of the way just in time and his hand closed on empty air, then squatted down to look him in the eye. He pouted back at me. Any other time, any other person, I knew exactly what I would have done. That mouth was practically begging to be kissed. Instead, I simply said, "I have to get my kicks where I can. Besides, I thought you wanted to practice."

He narrowed his eyes, then went all black and disappeared.

I quickly stood and scanned the room. He was already way better at shadowing out than I was. Almost immediately, something slammed into my back and I went crashing into the couch. I thought he'd thrown something at me, but it turned out to be Matt himself. I struggled and ended up flipping both of us over the furniture. We landed with an epic thud that knocked the wind out of me. As I regained my breath, I could hear him wheezing his own laugh.

"You're messed up." I snagged a fallen pillow and smacked him.

"Oh please, that was fun and you know it." There was a loud banging on the wall and we both fell into fits of laughter.

"Okay, you win. It was fun," I finally managed. "But maybe we should keep it to the training rooms."

"Then hurry up." He snatched the very pillow I'd just used in order to smack me back.

I scrambled to my feet to do as he asked. After changing quickly, I snagged the small stack of books I'd brought with me. Without thinking, I placed them on the counter and gathered my things so we could go. As we made our way over to the training rooms specifically set aside for our class, we continued to chat amicably.

"What exactly were you wanting to work on?" I glanced at Matt.

"I don't know. What do you think will be on the test?"

"Practicum," I corrected.

"Whatever. I just don't want to look like an idiot."

"You won't look like an idiot," I said, opening the door to an empty training space.

He flipped on the switch and tossed his things to the side. "You say that now, but I never do well in class. Working with you is one thing, but having to perform like some monkey in front of everyone..." He trailed off and ran his hands through his hair, oblivious to how hot he looked when he did that.

"I think you've been doing better during the lessons," I said, trying to school my renegade thoughts.

He spared me a glance full of earnest hope. "You really think so? You're not just saying that?"

"What are you really worried about?"

He hesitated before answering. "What if I mess it up and Vera decides I can't stay?" He stared down at his shuffling feet, looking more adorable than ever.

I snorted. "There's no way she'll ever send you packing."

His gaze rose to meet mine. "That's easy for you to say. You're great. You get all of this school stuff. I... I can't go back. This is the only real opportunity I've ever had. I can't afford to mess this up."

The sad statement hurt my heart. I really wished he'd tell me more about his past. It would be so much easier to comfort him if I only knew what he was so afraid of. But if he didn't want to tell me, then there was nothing I could do to make him. In lieu of real answers, I would just have to make sure he felt confident enough in his own abilities.

"Then I guess we should get to practicing." I tossed him a sphere of shadow.

He caught it with no problem and lobbed it back. "Catch, Alex? Really?"

"It still requires concentration and you're the one who wants more practice."

"Yeah, but I was hoping for something a little more intense."

I caught the sphere and juggled it between my hands. "Intense, huh? How about this? I'll make this more interesting if you help me shadow out better."

"What're you talking about? You did it just fine not half an hour ago."

"For the record, I had no idea that would work. It's still pretty hit or miss for me."

"Deal. But I don't know how you expect to make throwing a ball more interesting."

"Who said it was going to stay a ball?" I gathered more shadow material and willed the simple sphere into a large spiked morning star, sans handle. It would be a lot harder to catch if he couldn't touch it.

Matt's eyes widened as I sent it sailing over to him. Rather than even try to catch it, he dodged. "Are you out of your mind?"

"Who can really say? Now hold still and catch it."

He spun out of the way again as it veered straight for his head. "I can't catch that!"

"That's because you aren't even trying."

"You're insane."

"Just catch the damn thing."

Matt's back pressed into a corner of the room. He had three options left: he could shadow out of the way, take control and eliminate the spikes, or stop it. The sphere sailed towards him. He held out his hands defensively, and the ball stopped in midair. He cracked open an eye and let out a relieved breath.

"I wouldn't have let it hurt you, you know."

Matt looked between me and the floating weapon. "What? Did you stop it?"

"You tell me." I held up my hands. The sphere stayed put.

He reached out carefully to touch one of the spikes, then yanked his hand back and glared at me. "Those things are sharp."

"It had to be believable." The spikes instantly vanished into a perfectly smooth sphere.

He took hold of it, removing it from where it was hovering above the ground. His voice filled with wonder as he bounced the over-sized ball in his hands. "Never in a million years did I think I'd ever be able to do something like this."

My traitorous heart fluttered. Sometimes he really looked like some innocent kid eager to see the wonders of the world. I was too busy staring at him to realize the sphere was now hurtling right at me. I blinked in alarm and it blasted into streams of shadow. When the room cleared, Matt was almost right in front of me. Again, with the lack of personal space.

"You checked out a minute there," he commented.

I played at smoothing my hair to hide my blush. One of these days, I was going to get caught for real and my goose would really be cooked.

Matt shifted his weight. "So, how do you want to do this?"

"Do what?" I asked, still trying to pull myself together.

"Shadowing out. That was the deal."

"Right. I mean, however. You're the expert."

"I wouldn't say expert. Okay, let me think." He tapped a finger against his bottom lip thoughtfully, which did absolutely nothing for how I wasn't supposed to be thinking about how plump that lip was or how incredible it would feel between my teeth. "The way I do it is all instinct based. It's like what you told me before with the spoon trick. You just *need* to be somewhere else."

"But I'm not really motivated like that."

"Then I guess we'll need to motivate you." Without warning, he swung at my face.

I caught his hand before he could actually hit me. "What do you think you're doing?" I asked, incredulous.

He gave an evil grin. "Motivating you." His fist shifted in my grasp and suddenly he was holding my wrist.

I didn't even have a chance to react before he sent me flying. My feet barely got under me in time to spin around and catch another swing. He seemed genuinely surprised that I'd caught him and his smile grew. His leg swung out to kick me and I shadowed out before I could lose my stance. He struck again, and I dodged. Every move he made was lightning fast, without restraint. If he hit me, it was going to hurt like hell.

I shadowed out of the way just in time to avoid another smart punch and materialized a short distance away. I braced myself, expecting him to slam into my back like he had at the dorm, so was completely unprepared when he came at me with a frontal assault. He slammed into my chest and I grunted as we both went down.

When the stars cleared, I was staring up into ice-blue eyes. Laughter danced in their chilly depths and my hormones started doing their own jig at realizing Matt was on top of me. Mercifully, he rolled over to lie on the floor, where he chuckled to himself.

"See, you don't need practice." The back of his hand smacked my stomach and I let out an oof. "You've got it just fine."

"Sure thing, Matt," I wheezed, sitting up. I looked down at him.

He blinked back and smiled.

It would have been so easy to lie down beside him and pretend for just a moment that we were more than roommates, more than friends. Instead, I started getting to my feet. I was going to have to start a list of things we couldn't do together.

"Wanna go again?" Matt asked, still a tad breathless.

"I think I'm good on the near death for one day." I extended a hand to help him up. He took it and surged to his feet. I misjudged where he would land and his face stopped right in front of mine.

"I wouldn't have hurt you, Alex," he said, catching my eye.

Matt really didn't have any sense of personal space. He was inches away, if that, and my entire body was screaming at me to do something. But I couldn't seem to move. I was stuck in a trance, drowning in blue. I wasn't even sure if I was breathing anymore. My only saving grace was that I seemed to literally be frozen in place. Desire for Matt smashed violently against all of my control. Abruptly, I released his hand like I'd been burned and took a step back. Air finally found its way back into my lungs. I braced my hands on my knees. It felt like I'd run a marathon.

"Are you okay?" He sounded confused.

"I'm... I'm fine." I struggled with steady breaths. "Just got the wind knocked out of me, is all."

"I'm sorry, I didn't mean to..." He stepped closer.

I quickly held out a hand to stall him. If he got any closer, I was going to be in even more trouble than I already was, and I wasn't sure what I would do if he touched me again.

"You didn't. I just wasn't expecting it is all. It's been a while since I saw stars." I glanced at him. He didn't need to know that two of those stars were his eyes.

"I feel bad anyway. You know what you need?"

To get laid.

"Ice cream."

That could work, too.

CHAPTER 13

FIGHTING CHANCE

M

I didn't know how Alex did it. One day I was in danger of flunking out altogether, then a few later, I felt like I actually stood a chance of turning this around. My grades still weren't anywhere as good as his, but they were undeniably climbing. Turned out, I was actually good at math, and while Demonic History would probably never be my favorite subject, it was Alex's. He could go on for hours about ancient wars and demonic battles, and most of the time, I let him. I found it surprising, however, for someone who was so clearly a pacifist to revel in such violence.

Of course, I had no room to talk. I was getting in more than enough practice for Battle Tactics at the fight club. Though I wasn't using shadow nearly as much as I probably should have been able to. Alex naturally had theories about my inability to consistently control my powers. He still held that somehow, I was the one preventing me from using them. Either way, all of my frustrations from class went into the ring. Or, at least, I tried to take them all there.

Alex and I walked into Battle Tactics together, as we'd been doing since he'd started tutoring me. We automatically veered to our designated corner of the room to prepare for class.

"Look what the cat coughed up," George snickered to his cronies.

Alex tensed beside me, but kept his focus straight ahead. "Just ignore them."

"Easy for you to say. He doesn't give a shit about you," I hissed back.

"That's because I don't give him the satisfaction of a reaction."

"Hey, Matty, come on little guy. Don't worry, I won't bite. Unless you ask." The barb needled under my skin and my fists tightened of their own accord.

Alex gave me an anxious look out of the corner of his eye. "Don't do it, Matt. You know the rules."

I knew the rules probably better than he did. The real question was if it was worth potentially getting expelled to punch George in the face. Having my powers bound—which I finally understood meant basically taking them away—that I could handle. I'd lived this long without powers. What was the rest of my life?

"Does little Matty need permission from his keeper?"

Alex must have seen the look in my eye. "Matt, don't," he cautioned again.

"That's right. Heel." George laughed.

I threw my bag down. "Fuck the rules." I shadowed in front of George before he realized what was happening and gave him a good shove.

"You son of a bitch," he roared and swung at me. He may have been bigger, but I was faster and actually knew how to fight.

Up 'til now, the only other shadow demon I'd sparred with had been Alex. But for some reason I didn't understand, he wasn't interested in sparring outside of class. Right now, that kind of sucked. I could have used the practice. My assumption that George would be slow and awkward fell flat as he shadowed out, only to cuff me in the ear a moment later.

He was supposed to be bad at that. But he wasn't the only one hiding a few tricks. The club manifested in my hand.

"That the best you got? Bring it on, bottom feeder," he goaded.

I charged George, fully prepared to smash his face. I should have known better. How many hard lessons growing up had it taken for me to learn "never make the first move"? A thread of darkness came out of nowhere. Unlike when Alex used shadow on me, this hurt. The normally ephemeral substance coiled around my neck without forgiveness.

My club vanished as I clawed at the shockingly firm whip of shadow. Blood roared in my ears and my breath came in fitful gasps. Dark spots swam across my vision and my body shook violently as panic took hold. This was just like when I'd gotten cornered in an alley. It had been right before I'd gotten scooped up and hauled to Superno House. The rope had burned as it cut across me then, and this burned nearly as bad now.

"That's enough."

The cord winked out of existence, and air poured into my lungs. I looked over to find Vera standing a few feet away and Alex only a few paces behind her.

"Don't look at me like that. The rules are here for a reason. They keep us safe." She rubbed her forehead like the mere act of talking to me was giving her a headache. "And as for you, George Cartwright, this is not your first offense."

He sneered back at her and gave me a look that promised pain.

Just fucking great.

"That'll be private study for the both of you. Maybe next class you can keep your tempers long enough to learn something new." The entire room seemed to hold its breath, frozen in anticipation. "Move!"

I snatched my bag off of the floor and slunk out of the room, passing Alex along the way. I didn't know whether to thank him or hit him for interfering... again. One of these days, he was going to get me killed.

I was swinging away furiously at nothing in a secondary training room when the door slammed. I spun around, expecting to find Vera ready with a tongue lashing. What I got was a face full of shadow. I quickly cleared it away, only to be shoved backwards without getting a good look at my attacker. Before I could regain my bearings, there was another sharp shove behind me that made me stumble. I barely caught myself when that same someone ripped me back to my feet. That someone turned out to be a very angry-looking Alex.

I freed myself from his grip and rounded on him. "What the hell!"

"Yeah, what the hell, Matt? Are you out of your damn mind? Fighting in class? Are you trying to get expelled?" He shoved me again.

I shifted and spun out of his way as he continued to advance. "Cut it out, Alex."

"Do you know what they're going over right now?" He paused, but not long enough for me to guess. "The subject of the practicum. Newsflash, it's one of the few things you're not a natural at."

"What?" I shouldn't have stopped moving. He came at me full force. "What's your deal?" I asked, grappling with him.

"What's yours? You're stronger than George. Fucking act like it."

"He's twice my size."

"It has nothing to do with that. Why won't you believe me? You should have knocked out his entire attack, no problem, but you just stood there and let him beat you. It's ridiculous."

I took it back. I didn't want to spar with Alex. He was freaking me out. "I won't fight you, Alex."

"Why not?" He held out his arms like some demented invitation to take a swing at him. "You were going to fight George. We're about the same power-wise. If you can beat me, then you can beat him."

"You two are nothing alike," I insisted, trying to put more of the room between us.

"You're right. I'm much better at this." He spun a disk of shadow into his hand, then sent it shooting at my head. It looked like a damn razor blade and sliced cleanly through the chair I'd been standing behind.

My eyes widened in alarm. I scurried away from the destroyed chair, but when I looked up, Alex was gone. A quick scan of the room revealed nothing. Suddenly, I caught sight of the disk of death whizzing towards me. I ducked in time only to get gut-checked.

The next few moments were a flurry of trying not to get sliced in two while simultaneously avoiding Alex popping out of nowhere to smack me.

When did he get so good at this?

Finally, I sensed him before he could strike. The disk spun harmlessly past my ear and I just barely managed not to flinch. Right as Alex materialized, I caught him and forced him against the wall. He squirmed like the devil and I had to use my full weight to keep him there.

"Alex. Enough." I tightened my hold on his biceps; he was definitely going to have bruises.

At last, he stopped struggling and glared back at me. As close as we were, I was a little afraid that the fire in his eyes might actually set me alight. I gave him another small shake, still keeping him firmly trapped. The last of the fight went out of him and I relaxed my grip, but didn't completely let go. He'd been absolutely wild before, this could be a trick.

"Enough," I said again for emphasis.

"Matt," he panted, his breathing ragged.

When I looked at his eyes again, the green fire was gone, replaced by total darkness. For a moment, I was afraid the disk of death was going to return.

"I need you to get off of me," he said, absurdly calm.

"Right. Sorry." I released him and stepped back. A glance around the room showed that the disk had wrought some very real damage. "What was that about?" Alex stood there looking like he was trying to pull himself together.

I hope it wasn't a mistake to let him go.

He shook his head, an obvious look of disappointment on his face slicing through me more efficiently than the disk would have. "I'm tired of you always acting like you're not enough. You're more demon than half that room." When I said nothing, he stalked across the space towards the door.

"Alex. Alex, wait."

When he picked up his bag, I grabbed his arm. He turned to look at me and his eyes were still black. He blinked, and they returned to normal.

"Are you alright?"

"I'm fine," he said, refusing to meet my gaze.

I didn't know what to say about what had just happened, so I fell on something more familiar. "Are you gonna show me what the practicum is about or not?"

His eyes seemed to search mine for an answer. Then he closed them and dropped his bag. "Fine."

The following lesson was awkward, not the least of which because it turned out that the disk of death was the lesson. That I could deal with. What I couldn't handle was that something was clearly bothering Alex and he wouldn't tell me what. It didn't matter how I tried to approach it; I got the same stonewall every time. By the time we finally called it, I was immensely grateful it was Tuesday.

I excused myself after the painful lesson and made my way to the warehouse. Already, I could feel the now familiar sensation of excitement and trepidation. I provided the password to the gatekeeper—now chimera's revenge—and was admitted into the underground scene.

The place crawled with the usual oddities and terrifying creatures straight out of legend. I was proving to be a crowd favorite and Neese's golden boy, which afforded me at least a modicum of respect when I arrived.

Otto walked up and clapped me on the shoulder hard enough to make me stumble. "About time you showed up. I was beginning to think we were going to have to track you down." He gave a full belly laugh that grated on my nerves.

I shrugged him off. "What's on tonight's roster?"

"Let's see, we've got a Spiculo in the house, if you're interested."

"A what?"

He gestured over to some guy that was about my height and covered head to toe with barbs.

I flashed to the sinister Khima. "I'll pass. What else?"

"Picky, picky. Something certainly has you all fired up. Alright, if you aren't up for Andy, how about Singe?"

"You mean Carl? He's a fire demon, right?"

"You better believe it. And unless you want to end up with third-degree burns, I don't recommend using his day name."

"He'll do," I said, removing my shirt. Things got burned when you played with fire and I liked this shirt. I shoved it into my bag and dropped it to the side.

"Yo, Neese! Your boy is raring to go tonight!" Otto called out over the crowd.

Neese stepped into the ring as the current fight ended and hissed for me to join him. I cracked my neck and rolled my shoulders while Otto retrieved my opponent. Before coming here, I would've never dreamed of taking on anyone that looked like Carl. He may have only been five-foot-something, but he looked like he'd been forged in fire. Which, to be fair, was entirely possible. I had no idea how fire demons came about.

He walked into the ring and snickered. Most people here still didn't know what I really was besides fast and slipperier than the devil himself. It was hard to hold a shadow unless you actually were one. I smiled in anticipation and waited. He didn't keep me waiting long.

Almost as soon as Neese announced the fight and cleared the ring, fire shot from Carl's hands toward me. I shadowed out, only to reappear completely untouched in the same spot once the flames cleared. Fury clouded his face. Perfect.

I'd started doing research on the supernaturals I saw here after that first fight with Granite, who'd turned out to be a type of golem. Fire Demons were notorious for their temper and lack of control. The angrier he got, the more mistakes he was liable to make. Of course, it also made him infinitely more dangerous, because there was no telling which way the flames would go. While he focused his attacks mostly through his hands, the ability wasn't exclusively limited that way. Get him mad enough and he could literally blow.

I danced out of the way of another assault. I had to at least make it look like I was trying. This was going to be way too easy. Across the ring, I could see Neese and Otto's smug grins. Carl may be strong, but he was still no match for me. I stepped in closer, forcing him to use shorter blasts. It clearly wasn't his style, and he didn't appreciate being forced to do it.

"Come on, Carl, is that the best you've got?" I goaded him as I shadowed out of the way of yet another blast, except I cut it a little too close and the heat of it washed over me.

Flames shot from his head and he swung wildly, abandoning the flame-thrower attacks. One moment his fists were normal, the next, they were coated in orange fire.

"There, you go. Now you're getting warmer." The pun only infuriated him more.

The flames disappeared, and he reached for my neck. Too late. In a blink, I was behind him. Less than a second later, I drove my elbows into the back of his neck. He dropped like burnt out coal, his flames extinguishing as he hit the ground. A cheer went up and Neese walked forward to retrieve me.

"You could have made it last a little longer," he scolded under his breath, even as he raised my arm up as the victor.

"Is it my fault he lost his temper?"

"I wouldn't say he got away Scott-free. Looks like our little Matty got caught by some after burn," Otto said, thumping me in the chest. A pain very much like the fire I'd been avoiding spread across my torso.

"Shit." I hadn't even noticed. I'd been reckless. Distracted.

"At least it shows the crowd you're not completely untouchable. You keep fighting like that and no one will want to challenge." Neese squeezed the back of my neck to the point of pain. "We certainly wouldn't want that, would we?" He released me with a shove. "Put something on that. After-burns can get nasty and I want you in top shape for the next meeting."

I walked over to my things and then to the corner that held what constituted as medical. While they didn't have healers to take injuries away like they never happened, they couldn't afford wounds getting infected and bringing unwanted attention to the club.

The girl manning the table tilted her chin at me as I approached. "Not bad." She unscrewed a container filled with some kind of goo. Even from six feet away, I could tell it smelled foul. "Well, come here," she snapped impatiently and indicated for me to walk around the table.

I eyed her warily. She had dark liner on and magenta hair worn in a choppy style that paired with the rest of her obvious bad-girl look. Normally, the medic on duty gave you whatever it was and left you to fend for yourself.

"The name's Misty," she said as she smeared the affected area with the ointment. "Okay..." she added when I didn't respond. "Everyone knows you're Matt, but what are you?" Her hand slid smoothly along my torso. The salve was definitely working, and already the feeling of fire sitting on my chest was dissipating.

"Are you finished yet?"

"Yeah." She quickly removed her hand and wiped it off on a spare towel, then replaced the lid.

The salve had yet to soak in when I put my shirt back on. I probably should have waited, but I didn't like her questions or the way she'd gotten handsy. I slung my bag up and turned to go.

"Hey, you didn't answer my question."

"If Neese wanted you to know, then you would."

Her jaw dropped, and I left. I could've stayed and watched some of the other fights, normally I would have. Yet something about Misty made me nervous. She wanted something, and I didn't trust the way she'd eyed me like I was something to pick apart and eat. Besides, I still needed to figure out what was up with Alex.

CHAPTER 14

ASSUMPTIONS

A

"You've come a good ways, Ed." I smiled and handed him back the writing assignment we'd been working on.

His face crinkled, and I assumed he was smiling. Always difficult to tell with Jotunn. Even with an amulet to make the Ice Demon appear more human, it didn't quite meet the mark. "I had nice help," he said with a thick Swedish accent.

"Help, maybe, but you put in the work to make it happen." I turned to his polar opposite, sitting on my other side. "Same for you, Fiadh. I'm really impressed with how much both of you have progressed."

The Merrow smiled, revealing sharp teeth and illustrating that she was as deadly as she was beautiful. "You are very generous." She brushed long strands of moss green hair back from her face with an iridescent blue arm, freckled with darker spots of navy.

"Just giving credit where it's due."

Fiadh made a pleased humming sound deep in her throat that instantly captured Jotunn's attention. She flashed him a coy smile that she then switched to me. It was easy to understand how Merrows had developed a reputation for luring men to watery deaths. Though her charms didn't have quite the same effect on me.

I pushed back from the table to signal the end of our session. "Thank you both again for coming. I'll see you next week and we can review the course's weekend homework."

"Sounds lovely, Alexi." Fiadh slipped her paper between books and rose abruptly, as if she was used to having more resistance than air.

Ed scrambled to his feet. "Yes. Good things." He reached for Fiadh's books. "Help?"

She gave him another toothy smile that might as well have been made of honey for the way Ed beamed. "That would be nice. Thank you, Edzard."

I buried my smile and focused on packing my things while Ed followed Fiadh like a happy puppy. As much as I worried Fiadh would ultimately break the poor guy's heart, I envied her as well. At least she had options. Meanwhile, my one-sided pining was getting worse by the day.

"You've got quite a way with them." Rubio pushed off from the wall he'd been leaning against and moved to help me with the last of my books. "I gotta hand it to you. When you suggested group tutoring sessions, I was dubious, but it seems to be working out just fine."

"As long as you don't count the fact that I'm not sure whether Fiadh plans to eat Ed in a good way or in a bad way later, yeah, I guess I'm doing pretty good."

Laughter erupted out of Rubio. He shifted the books to one arm so he could wipe away tears with the side of his hand.

"Oh no, the new guy has gone and broken our fearless leader." Mariah clucked her tongue while the other tutors chuckled.

I walked up to her and rolled my eyes. "How was your session with Jahzara?"

She let out a heavy sigh and placed a hand on an ample hip. "I swear, she tries my patience more every time. I don't care if she is some kind of heiress or whatever, she's still flunking rudimentary spells."

I bumped her shoulder. "You'll figure it out. You're the best."

"From your lips to Jahzara's ears. If she tells me one more time about her social position, I'm gonna kill her."

"No, you won't," Rubio said as he stepped between us. He looked around at the gathered group that had quickly all become good friends. "Great job everyone. See you later. Oh, and a friendly reminder not to kill our paying customers."

Mariah grumbled under her breath, but followed suit with everyone in leaving the study space Rubio had acquired for general meetings and now my group tutoring sessions. I might only have two in the group now, but Rubio had confidence that would change as word about me got out, and he liked to plan ahead.

I shielded my eyes as we stepped outside. Our little cluster of study rooms was off the west side of the main library, and the evening sun was brutal. A few blinks put me back to rights. I waved goodbye as the others broke away, leaving me and Rubio alone on the sidewalk.

Suddenly, Rubio let out a low whistle and shoulder checked me. "Would you get a load of that beauty? Mmm... the things I'd like to do to him."

I searched the area he was not so subtly hinting at until my gaze fell on who he was undoubtedly talking about. "Oh, that's my roommate. Matt." I was tempted to add that I was right there with him, but Matt was already walking our way with that radiant smile that kept my heart in a constant state of upheaval.

Rubio's head snapped around to give me an incredulous look. "That's your roommate?" he hissed almost quietly.

I let out a sigh. "Yep."

"And you're not hitting that. Why?"

I tore my gaze away from the stunning masterpiece that was Matt's pouty face and divine eyes to scowl at Rubio. "One guess."

"Fuck." He nodded with knowing commiseration. "The straight ones, am I right?"

"You have no idea."

Rubio gave me a sidelong look before returning his attention to the ever-approaching Matt. "He know you're gay?"

"Nope."

He raised an eyebrow. "Gonna tell him?"

"Not planning on it."

Rubio shook his head and took a deep breath. "I don't envy you. That's gotta be torture."

"Eh." I shrugged. "It's not all bad. We're friends at least."

"Sure you are."

I scoffed. "Just friends. He's straight."

"You seem awful sure of that. Have you asked him? I mean, you haven't told him about you. Seems like you're assuming to me."

"Pretty sure I would have picked up on it by now if he wasn't."

Rubio tilted his head to the side and gave me a considering look. "Does he talk about other people—girls—bring any by the dorm?"

I shifted my weight. "Well, no. But he also seems kind of new? to all of this. Could be he's trying to get settled."

"You say so." Rubio stepped closer and passed me the books of mine he'd been holding. "Just saying, you miss a hundred percent of the chances you don't take."

"What are you, a feel-good poster now?"

He laughed. "Fair. But if you tire of chasing after the straight guy, my offer still stands. And my roommate is more than game to play. He's a wyvern, you see, and he's got this wicked long tongue and when he—"

"Whoa, I'm gonna stop you right there. That's more about your personal life than I need to know, boss."

"Pft. None of that 'boss' shit. We're a casual thing, nothing serious, and you're absolutely my guy's type." Rubio gave me a slow once over that gave me chills. For an outrageous second, I was actually tempted to take him up on the offer. Maybe not the threesome part, but at least the hooking up. It would be nice to kiss someone, to be touched, craved the way I craved Matt.

"Alex!" Matt picked up his pace, quickly eliminating our space for this conversation.

"Really," Rubio deadpanned.

I shot him a look and waved to Matt so he'd know I heard him. "Shut up. As for the other…" I hesitated.

Rubio squeezed my shoulder. "Hey, no pressure, really. I like you, but if you're not into it, you're not into it. Just know you've got options if you give up on your 'probably straight' roommate."

I relaxed and offered him a smile. "You're a good guy. Thanks. I appreciate it. That's just… not quite my speed."

"Understood. Good luck with your day, Alexi." Rubio gave me a warm smile before turning on his heel and walking off. I watched him go, biting the inside of my cheek while debating whether I'd made the right choice.

"Hey, who was that?"

I turned my focus to Matt, per usual, standing a little too close. Rubio's assessment that I might be jumping to conclusions about Matt's sexuality played in my mind. Would it be wrong to ask? Would it scare him away? Or bring him closer? Fully prepared to throw caution to the wind, I opened my mouth. "That was Rubio. He's in charge of the tutoring group I joined." And... totally chickened out.

"Huh." Matt stared after Rubio, then shifted his gaze to the books he'd handed me. "He seems... nice."

I pushed any lingering temptation to delve into Matt's preferences away. "He is. The whole crew is. There's about eight of us, including Rubio, though only five were here today. I confess, I'm really relieved we all mesh so well. I was kind of worried given I'm the newest member and the youngest. Not exactly vetted."

"They're all older?" Once more, Matt was staring off in the direction Rubio had vanished.

"Uh... yeah. I'm not exactly sure of their ages, but they're upperclassmen, at least."

Matt seemed to shake off whatever funk he'd fallen under. "That's cool, I guess. You done for the day?"

"Yep. Just need to drop these by the dorm, and I'm a free man. Why? Were you wanting to study together?"

"No. I figured we could grab dinner together."

Why was it every time Matt talked to me, it inevitably felt like he was asking me out? I was pretty sure it was an overwhelming dose of wishful thinking, but maybe Rubio had a point. "Dinner would be nice. Where were you thinking?"

"The cafeteria is not too far. I noticed you left your dining card on the counter, so I brought it." He held up the square of plastic with a grin. Then his gaze dropped to the books I was holding. "I can carry those if they're heavy," he said as he reached for the books, his hands encasing mine.

My heart thudded loud enough I was positive he could hear it, and my breath pointblank refused to come. His hands were warm and oddly gentle, despite their coarseness. Where I should have been formulating a response, all my traitorous mind could do was think of how nice it would be to have his touch on other parts of my body. I swallowed hard with exactly zero moisture in my mouth. "They're not heavy."

"Okay." He blinked those stunning eyes at me, but didn't move.

We stayed like that for a long minute, that might as well have been a panicked eternity. What was I supposed to do? I couldn't think clearly enough while his hands were on me and I wasn't exactly eager to make him move them.

"Alex?"

"Yeah?" I croaked.

"Are you gonna give me the books?" He shifted his hold, making his fingers slide along mine.

Irresistible longing shot down my spine. He was so close. All I had to do was lean forward and I could finally taste those full lips, show him that as much as I enjoyed being his friend, I wanted more.

A shrill whistle pierced the air and shattered the moment. Matt glanced around for the source of the sound while I tilted the books into his hold. "What were you thinking for dinner?" I asked, wiping my sweaty palms on my slacks.

He followed the movement, then adjusted his grip on the stack of literature. "I don't know. Whatever you're in the mood for, I guess."

I wasn't sure I would ever understand why Matt insisted on eating the same things I did when he could literally have anything. Surely, he had different tastes. Plus, most of the time, the dishes seemed to be entirely foreign to him, not that he ever complained. I chanced a smile. "What would you say to trying some Greek?"

"I've never had Greek before." He tilted his head while he seemed to consider something. "If I'm remembering right, I've seen a few dishes, though. Looks tasty." With that, he took off towards the cafeteria.

I sighed to myself and followed at a more sedate pace. If only he was talking about me and not food.

CHAPTER 15

BILLIARDS & BESTIES

M

The classroom immediately began buzzing with conversation the second Professor Whittle left. I glanced around the room and fiddled with my pencil. Typically, I'd occupy myself by drawing in my notebook, but frankly, I was running out of space. That, and I didn't really feel like it. Alex sat at the front of the class—naturally—and was animatedly chatting with a girl with pink hued skin that seemed to shimmer every time she moved. I frowned. Something still wasn't sitting right with me about his new tutoring group or this Rubio guy. I wasn't about to tell Alex, but I'd seen the way Rubio had looked at him and I didn't like it one bit.

The pencil snapped between my fingers. I stared down at the broken pieces like they were somehow symbolic of my unease. With a huff, I threw them into my bag and resolved not to relocate so I could chat with Alex instead of sitting here by myself. If Alex could have other friends, then so could I. Right?

I took stock of my options. No one nearby struck me as interesting. I'd never been good at making friends, at least none that stuck. Much easier to be on my own. I hadn't even cared about having friends before. I blamed Alex.

The conversation behind me caught my attention, and I swiveled in my seat to get a look at the people responsible. Two guys, maybe a little older than me, but definitely not as old as Rubio, were laughing so hard tears were streaming down their cheeks. The one on the left had dark hair that fell around his face in jagged sweeps to frame his square face. He shoved his companion, who was noticeably paler, his skin a subtle pink where he was a rich earthy color.

"You're making that up!" Pale blond guy smacked his friend's hand away.

Messy hair shook his head. "I shit you not. The cue ball bounced off the nipple, flew into the air and landed with a huge splash in a pitcher of beer. Worst part? It was our beer. I'm telling you, that's the last time I play pool with my cousins."

I finished turning all the way around, hanging half out of my chair. "You guys play pool?"

"Sure do." Messy hair tilted his dimpled chin at me. "You?"

"It's been a while. Didn't realize there was any place nearby."

Blond guy leaned forward on his elbows. "Not too far from campus, but it's a total dive."

I smiled, recalling the hole in the wall I'd learned to play at. "I find those tend to be the best places."

Messy hair gave me an approving nod. "Damn right they are. I'm Lucas." He gestured with his thumb at blond guy. "And this disaster is Sam."

"Matt."

"Nice to meet you," Sam said. "We're actually headed that way tonight if you'd like to join us." A mischievous smile curled his lips. "The staff is hella cute, too."

Lucas elbowed him in the ribs.

"What?"

"Not everyone goes to bars to hit on waitresses."

Sam scoffed. "You're just saying that because you can't get any of them to look at you twice. Me, on the other hand..." His features blurred a moment, then I was looking at someone straight out of a movie poster.

"Holy shit. How'd you do that?"

Sam's face did the blurry thing again, then he was back to himself. He rubbed his knuckles on his shirt. "Magic's the game, illusion the name."

Lucas scowled at him. "You're so full of yourself." He rolled his eyes and shifted his focus to me. "In short, he's a witch. I'm a werewolf. What about you? Haven't seen you in any of my other classes and there's not exactly a ton of them during the summer."

"Uh..." I floundered, still trying to wrap my head around the fact that I was talking with a legit werewolf. A million questions bubbled in my mind. Was he more like the Wolfman or did he do some weird hybrid thing like that vampire-werewolf movie I'd seen eons ago? Could he shift any time or just with the moon? What could he do? Holy fuck, werewolves were real.

"Matt?"

I blinked at Sam, who was wearing a curious expression. "Huh?"

"I asked what you are."

"Oh. I'm..." I waffled on how much to say. Neese didn't like people knowing what I was, but then again, it wasn't exactly a mystery to everyone. Anyone who actually took a minute could probably put it together. In the end, I opted for total honesty. "I'm a Shadow Demon."

"Cool." Lucas grinned. "So, what do you say, wanna hang with us later, shoot some pool?"

Was making friends really that easy? "Yeah, I'm game. Where should I meet y'all?"

"I'm in Dire Hall," Lucas said, like I had any idea where that was.

"I have a late class in the witch's college," Sam chimed.

My brow furrowed. "That's the castle looking place, right?"

"That's the one. How about we meet on the quad over by that cluster of benches around seven? Then we can head over together."

"Sounds good to me," I said, flabbergasted at how easy this was.

Lucas nodded his agreement as well right as Professor Whitlow returned. She passed out the next week's assignment and set us loose. By the time I made it out the door, after confirming the time again with Lucas and Sam, Alex was waiting for me.

I smiled at him as I adjusted my pack and wondered if he'd ever played pool before. "What are you up to later?"

Alex fell in step with me. "I have a joint tutoring session with Rubio. Will probably go pretty late."

My jaw clenched so fast I nearly bit my tongue. "Didn't you see him the other day?"

Alex frowned, confusion clearly stamped on his face. "Yeah, but that was for our weekly meeting. This is for an actual session with clients." He shook his head and let out a short laugh. "That still feels so weird to say."

"Oh." It was all I could manage while I grappled with what was proving to be an unreasonable amount of anger directed at Rubio.

Concern flashed in Alex's eyes, briefly darkening their bright green. "Why?"

I reminded myself that this was why I'd struck up a conversation with Sam and Lucas. Alex had other friends. It wasn't a betrayal of our friendship if I did, too. "Going out with some friends tonight. Thought you might like to come."

A giant smile split Alex's face. "That's great, Matt! Sorry, I can't join. Maybe next time?"

"Yeah, maybe," I echoed, though my heart wasn't in it.

"Where are you all going?"

I shrugged. "Some place in town."

"Well, I hope you have fun. You'll have to tell me all about it." He stepped to the side into an adjoining hallway. "Well, this is me. I have some prep work to take care of before the group tutoring tonight. I'll catch up with you later." He waved and turned away before I could say anything. Past him, Rubio stepped out of a classroom and greeted Alex with a huge smile.

Irritation prickled the back of my neck while I squeezed the straps of my backpack within an inch of their life. I spun sharply on my heel and stalked out of the building. Looked like I'd be grabbing dinner on my own tonight.

Seven o'clock rolled around, and I wandered over to the benches where Lucas was already waiting. His eyes caught the setting sun and flashed yellow.

"Hey, you made it. We're still waiting for Sam. I'm convinced that guy couldn't be on time if he was an actual clock." Lucas chuckled.

I shoved my hands in my pockets and leaned against a nearby tree. "How long have you two known each other?"

"A year or so. Met in Language Studies our first year and sort of hit it off. This your first semester at Arminius?"

I leaned my head back and gave him a crooked grin. "What gave it away?"

"Nothing. Just a guess. I heard a lot of the Shadow Demons had no idea what they were. Made sense."

I appreciated the way Lucas had a way of asking questions without it feeling like he was prying. "I'd never even heard of this place until Vera scooped me up."

Lucas let out a low whistle. "Damn. For real? She as scary as everyone says?"

"Not by half." Lucas's eyebrows shot up, and I reconsidered my answer. "Well, not as a person, anyway. Demon-wise, she's kind of terrifying, but if you tell anyone I said that, I'll deny it."

He crossed his heart and grinned. "Your secret's safe with me."

"What secret?" Sam asked as he popped up out of nowhere. For all I knew, he had.

Lucas tilted his head in my direction. "Just that Matt's new to the whole supes thing."

"That has got to be wild, man. I don't envy you. So glad I had a coven looking out for me. Right," Sam clapped his hands together, "what do you say we get this show on the road? I've got a pretty brunette waiting for me."

Lucas snickered and leaned over to whisper. "In his dreams."

I smothered a laugh as Sam spun around and eyeballed us. "Lead the way."

A twenty-minute walk later, we approached what could have been a condemned building if it wasn't for the flashing neon sign that said "Open". Trusting that my new friends weren't taking me somewhere to off me, I followed them inside. Luckily, the inside bore little resemblance to the crumbling exterior.

An oval bar sat in the middle of the large space, surrounded by bar-height tables and stools. On either side was an array of pool tables bustling with people. A quick count brought me maybe a dozen total. At the back of the joint was an assortment of vintage pinball machines and dartboards. Overall, I had to say; I was impressed.

"What do you think?" Sam asked over the ambient noise.

I swept the space once more, noting that all the patrons at least appeared human. "Not bad."

Beside us, Lucas took out his wallet to pay the host the cover, and I reached for the cash I'd shoved in mine earlier. He noticed the move and waved me off. "This one's on me. That way, if Sam chases you off, the night's not a total loss."

"Hey!" Sam shouted in outrage. "Why am I the one who's running him off? I'm not the one that smells like wet dog."

Lucas snorted as the host gave him his change and pointed at a table that had just opened up. "You sure about that? Because that new cologne you're so proud of is fucking awful."

"It is not." Despite his statement, Sam still pulled up his shirt and took a sniff. He frowned and turned to me. "What do you think?"

"I think it's weird you're asking me to smell you."

Sam's mouth fell open, and Lucas guffawed loud enough to grab a few people's attention. "Oh, I like you. You can stay." Lucas slung an arm around my shoulder and guided us to the table while Sam slunk off with a pout to secure three cue sticks.

I rubbed the back of my neck as Lucas adjusted the balls on the table. "Hey, uh, thanks for getting the cover."

"No big. It's nice to have someone else join besides that ham." Lucas crossed his arms and rested his hip on the table. "Don't get me wrong, he's a great guy and a better friend, but he can be... a lot." Lucas pointed subtly behind me.

I twisted around to find who I assumed was Sam, except now he had a deep bronze tan and dreadlocks that reached the middle of his back. He smiled broadly at a young woman with flushed cheeks and a high ponytail. Within seconds of me spotting him, her face morphed into blatant outrage and she stormed off. Sam sagged in defeat, then shrugged his shoulders and returned to himself.

When he rejoined us, Lucas gave him a level stare. "Striking out already?"

"Like you could do any better." Sam stuck out his tongue and bumped Lucas aside so he could break. "What do you say you and me take first round, Matt?"

I leaned against my cue stick. "Sure. Heads up, though, I'm rusty."

Sam smiled from his position laid over the table, ready to strike. "Don't worry, I'll take it easy on you." He took his shot, and the break was... less than impressive. He scowled at the balls, none of which had found a pocket. "My hand slipped."

"Sure, it did," Lucas teased as I assessed the table. "What about you, Matt? Any luck with the ladies since you came to Arminius?"

I shrugged and took my shot. "Eh, not really. But then I haven't exactly been trying either." I sank the nine, making me stripes, but missed my next shot.

Sam smacked Lucas in the chest. "What if he's not into that? Rude." He squared up with the four and sank it easily.

"Shit. Good point. Are you into girls?"

My face scrunched in confusion as I watched Sam sink two more shots before finally missing. "Why wouldn't I be?"

Sam and Lucas shared a look, but neither offered clarity. Sure, it had been a while—a long while—but I hadn't exactly had the time to pursue anything resembling a relationship lately. And if I was being honest, the interest, either.

Lucas cleared his throat. "No reason. Maybe we can hook you up. What's your type?"

"Not sure I have one."

Lucas chuckled. "So, you're like Sam."

Sam straightened from the shot he was never going to make. "What the hell is that supposed to mean?"

"I'm guessing he means anyone with a pulse." I kept a straight face for a couple of seconds, then cracked a smile.

Sam missed his shot by a mile and ended up sinking the eight ball instead. Meanwhile, Lucas was crying he was laughing so hard.

"I see how it is," Sam said as he fished out the black ball. "I'm totally kicking your ass next game and first round is on you."

"Fair." I flagged down a waitress in an obscenely short skirt with a few buttons missing from her top.

She bounced up to me and beamed. "What can I get you, fellas?"

I looked at the guys.

"Pale ale on draft," Lucas offered as he finished racking the balls, and Sam echoed him.

I turned back to the insufficiently dressed waitress and gave her my best smile. "Make that three." Color rose in her cheeks before she confirmed the order and ducked away. I waited 'til she was gone before looking back at the others, both of whom were staring at me. "What?"

"I already hate you," Sam stated without any real conviction.

Lucas shook his head and gestured for me to break. "I take it back. You do just fine with the ladies."

"Right..." I wasn't entirely sure what the hell they were talking about, but they were nice and this was fun. Honestly, the only thing that could make it better was if Alex had tagged along instead of hanging with Rubio... again. I pictured the guy's face on the cue ball and cracked the stick into it. Balls rolled in every direction with three solids sinking into separate pockets.

"Fuck. He's a hustler."

I smiled up at Sam and sank the two.

CHAPTER 16

AN INNOCENT MISTAKE

A

"**W**e should celebrate," Matt insisted as we entered the dorm.

I laughed as I closed the door behind us. He'd been on like this since Battle Tactics had let out early.

"We survived our first practicum. We have to do something!"

I endeavored not to laugh at his comically wide eyes and pleading expression. "It wasn't really a big deal." But it was kind of adorable how excited he was.

"For you maybe. Come on, don't leave me hanging. We don't have class tomorrow and we got an entire afternoon back." He gave me that puppy dog face I couldn't say no to, even if I wanted.

I held up my hands in surrender. "Fine, fine. What did you have in mind?"

"Yes!" he shouted triumphantly, and punched the air. Then he disappeared and reappeared in the kitchen.

I shook my head and started relocating the texts and papers strewn across the coffee table to our bags beside the door. I'd given up pointing out whenever he shadowed in the dorm. He never believed me anyway. "You didn't answer the question. What're we doing?"

"You'll see."

"That doesn't sound like I'm going to like whatever it is."

"Don't be so negative." He returned with a glass of yellow liquid. It was too dark to be lemonade and something told me it had alcohol.

"I told you, I don't really drink," I said, accepting it anyway.

Matt rolled his eyes. "Would you at least try it before you decide you don't like it? Besides, we're celebrating. You can suck it up and drink with me for one night.," he concluded with a wry twist of his mouth.

"I still don't know where you get all of this stuff." I took a sip.

"I have my ways. So, what do you think?" A grin stretched across his face like he already knew the answer.

I stared at the cold glass, already coated with condensation in surprise. "It's actually quite good." I glanced over at him to discover he had a matching glass and a pitcher full of the concoction. How much did he expect us to drink tonight?

"No beer for you?"

"And let you have all the good stuff? As if."

"What's in this, anyway?" I took another sip and smacked my lips at the sweetness. "Tastes like fruit."

He shrugged as he set down the full pitcher. "This and that."

I squinted at him and took another drink. "I see what you did there."

He smirked and grabbed my wrist, pulling us both to the floor between the couch and the table. "Sit down, you're making me nervous."

"Why can't we sit on the couch?" I asked, even as I leaned against the furniture in question. The deceptively strong drink coated my tongue with sweetness edged with just enough tart to make it palatable. I reached for the pitcher to top off my dwindling glass. Something told me Matt's idea of celebrating would entail getting absolutely smashed. I leaned back and relaxed. "Why aren't we sitting on the couch again?"

"Because I said we're sitting on the floor." He took a drink, and I mirrored him.

"You're such an odd duck."

"And you're not?" He laughed, bumping his shoulder into mine, and I barely prevented the liquid from sloshing out of the glass. "None of that this time, got it?" Matt gave me a serious look that belied the humor dancing in his eyes. "And no snorting it up your nose, either."

I licked off the little liquid that had escaped. "Got it. So, now what?"

"Now? We hang out." He flopped dramatically against the couch as if to emphasize his declaration.

"And do what?"

"We're doing it. Not everything has to be about school. Or studying. It's possible to just chill, you know."

My eyebrows lifted. "Are you really giving me friendship lessons?"

"Sounds like you need them." He winked and gave me another infectious grin.

My heart stuttered at that beautiful smile, the one that seemed uniquely reserved for me. I smiled into my glass and stretched out my legs beneath the table, getting comfortable, then we both took another drink.

"Mm," he began around a mouthful of liquid. "Did you see George almost pop a blood vessel trying to control his disk?"

I laughed as the image of George's stricken face resurfaced. "Yeah, but it was nothing compared to when Marcie's zipped off and smacked Thomas. If she wasn't such a petite woman, I'm pretty sure he would've throttled her."

"It can't be easy being one of only three girls in the class," Matt commented as he leaned forward to reach the pitcher. He promptly topped off his glass and mine. "Why do you think that is?"

"Maybe females of our kind are rare? I heard Vera searched everywhere, but couldn't find more."

Matt cocked his head to the side and stared off pensively. "Do you think it's a genetics thing?"

I took another drink and shook my head. "I can't believe we're sitting here talking about the genetic heritage of our kind."

Matt returned his full attention to me. "Would you rather talk about girls?" It was hard to tell if he was being facetious or serious.

"Not really," I said, sitting up straighter. "The problem is, there's no way to tell. We're kind of rare, anyway. And it's not like it takes two demons to make a demon."

His forehead crinkled. "What do you mean?"

"Most demons—any demons, really—hookup with other species. We're kind of notorious for it," I added, wiggling my eyebrows. We both laughed, and a lightness filled my chest. I refilled my glass.

This is awesome.

"Really? So, both of your parents aren't demons?" Matt stared at me in wonder.

I shook my head. "Nope, my mom is decidedly human. Were yours?"

He darkened a bit at the question. "I don't know."

Determined not to lose this good mood, I powered on. "Neither of Vera's parents were."

His eyes widened, and his beautiful mouth fell open. "No."

"Nope," I echoed.

"Then how is she a demon at all, let alone one of the strongest?"

"Genetics are weird like that. Apparently, there was enough latent potential on both sides and... viola, super powerful Shadow Demon. To be fair, she did kind of shock the supernatural community. And that's not talking about all the horrible things she's done." I took a sizable gulp as I continued to work myself up. "She can do stuff that no one's ever seen or heard of, at least not anyone who's still around can remember. She even taught her teacher a few things, and he's a level two as well. Which is absolutely wild, since he's like outrageously old."

"She said something about that before. Just how old is he?"

"I don't know. Over a thousand for sure."

Matt snorted, almost spilling his drink.

"Hey, I thought you said none of that?"

He waved away the scorn and pulled himself back together. "How's that even possible?"

"Demons, or at least Shadow Demons, live a really long time. The more we use our powers, the more our aging slows down. Probably has something to do with being part of a plane of existence that doesn't observe the passage of time. So, the good news is I'll probably look this good forever." I did my best to maintain a stoic expression, but laughter won out.

Matt quirked a half smile at me. "A little full of yourself, aren't you?"

"Eh, beauty may be a curse, but that doesn't mean I can't enjoy it."

"Let me make sure I have this right." He shifted around and put on a super serious expression that I couldn't help but chuckle at. "You're saying that because you've been using your powers for years, that you'll look sixteen forever."

I pressed my free hand to my chest and gasped in exaggerated insult. "Excuse you, I will be nineteen in a few months."

"No way!" Matt's face lit up with a joy that did a better job of intoxicating me than whatever alcohol he was plying us with. "When's your birthday?"

"Yes, way. It's in November. When's yours?"

"I can't believe you're older than me. Mine is in February. The thirteenth."

"Dang. So close." I chuckled and gave him a crooked smile. "Still, I bet you're a regular Casanova."

He tilted his head to the side before taking another drink. "A what?"

"Casanova, Matt. Notorious guy who slept with like half of France."

He scoffed. "I don't know about that."

I shrugged. "Honestly, it wouldn't surprise me if he was some kind of supernatural in real life. Maybe one of the Fae. Those guys can get around."

Matt looked at me with those absurdly full lips and high color on his cheeks. "How do you know all of this stuff?"

"Because, Matt, I want to." I finished my drink and poured another, not sure how many that made. Judging by Matt's slurring words, he'd had as many, if not more than me already.

"You seem like the kind of guy who usually gets what he wants." He finished his latest drink, then rolled the empty glass between his hands. Night, he was cute.

"Not always," I replied, casually setting my glass down next to the empty pitcher. I did a double take. When had we finished it?

"Oh really?" He laughed. "And when do you not?" he asked, turning to me.

I was waiting for him, though. When he turned, his lips met mine. I giggled to myself and sat back. I'd literally caught his laugh. Another giggle bubbled up, but he just sat there, staring blankly back.

Maybe I should give it back.

"Why are you looking at me like that? It was just-" My chest constricted.

Oh shit.

He blinked and turned to look straight ahead.

What have I done? I knew drinking with Matt was a bad idea.

He looked around at the room as if trying to figure out what to do.

"I didn't mean to do that." No response. "Matt," I tried again.

The sound of his name seemed to break whatever spell he was under. He set his glass down on the coffee table and glanced at me out of the corner of his eye. "So..." The question trailed off.

This was my worst nightmare. He could barely even look at me. I swallowed. "It was an accident."

"I'm getting that."

"Matt, please." I didn't know what else to say.

"I... I need to... Yeah." He got up none too steadily, then walked to his room. The door closed quietly behind him.

I could have screamed.

What have I done? I've ruined everything.

My breathing came in short, shallow gasps while my heart seemed determined to beat itself out.

He's never going to talk to me again. He'll hate me forever.

The thoughts tumbled over each other, each bringing a fresh wave of despair. Suddenly, his door opened, and he stepped out. I swiveled around to face him, and he looked over at me. I'd have given anything to appear calm and collected right then, but there was no hiding the panic that had to be clearly stamped across my face.

"So, you... you're..." His gaze slid away from me, much like his words.

"Matt, I can explain."

He nodded to himself, still looking lost. "How drunk are you?" he asked unexpectedly.

"Pretty drunk," I admitted.

"How drunk am I?"

"Also, pretty drunk."

"Okay. Right. And..." He didn't finish, just walked back into his room.

He couldn't even say it. There was no way I could undo this. I grabbed a pillow and yelled all of my frustration into it. What was I going to do? We were really starting to get along and I fucked it all up.

"Right, let's try this again."

I looked up to see that Matt had reemerged once again. Only this time, instead of confused, he looked determined. I got up and walked around to face him. I had no idea what I was going to say, but I had to try something. "Matt, I'm sorry, I..."

He held up his hand, cutting off my string of apologies. My mouth closed with an audible snap. He searched my face like he was trying to decide something. "Let's try this again," he repeated.

"Try what?" I asked dubiously.

"Kiss me."

Immediately, I was wary. "You're messing with me."

"No, I'm not. I'm perfectly serious."

"I don't think that's a good idea," I hedged, still clinging to the faint hope that I could come up with an adequate excuse for the first kiss.

"Alex, would you just do it already? I'm trying to figure something out." He looked at me expectantly.

I hung back, filled with trepidation, but his face clearly said he wasn't backing down. Maybe if I did something super small, it'd meet his demand and get me off the hook without making things much worse. He obviously wouldn't let me out of it.

I took a deep breath and leaned forward. In all of my dreams, this was not how I'd seen this moment going. This time, when our lips touched, I made a conscious effort to keep it minimal. Even then, my heart gave a traitorous skip. I was kissing Matt. On purpose.

It was probably the liquor that made me believe he was pressing back. I stubbornly fought the urge to slip into the easy fantasy. That wouldn't help anything. Then I felt his tongue glide along my lip. Alcohol-addled brain or not, it was all the encouragement I needed. I dropped all pretense of restraint and pulled his face closer. Then I kissed him like I'd wanted to do for weeks, claiming his mouth with mine. And it was incredible, so much better than I could have ever dreamed. Fireworks, sparklers, electric current, all of it and then some.

A distant part of me screamed that this was not the right answer. But as I felt his lips move against mine, I couldn't have stopped if my life depended on it. I wanted this, needed it like I needed air to breathe. He was every bit the amazing kisser I'd imagined, and I wanted more. I drew him closer, deepening the kiss, and he let me. The whole world teetered on its axis and I fell infinitely into Matt.

Abruptly, he pulled away, the suction of separation making an awful sound. Still in a daze, I drifted to follow him, more than willing to drown for an eternity, but stopped myself short. My heart beat like it was going to come right out of my chest. We were only inches apart, and I could still taste him on my tongue.

He pressed his lips together, and I longed to tease them free, to kiss them 'til they were cherry red and his breathing was as ragged as mine. Suddenly, I realized my hand was still cupping his face and snatched it down. He'd yet to look at me, and I could practically see his mind turning as he tried to absorb what had happened. It didn't look to be going in my favor.

He nodded as if to himself. "That's what I thought. So, you're definitely...?" His eyes were clouded crystal when they snared my own.

"Yes." The admission felt like it was being dragged from the depths of my soul. I could have lied, should have lied, but I couldn't, not to Matt, not after that.

He nodded again. "Right." He turned on his heel and vanished into his room yet again.

I stood there waiting to see if he would make a repeat appearance like he had before. After a while, though, it became clear that he wouldn't be coming back. I hung my head in my hands while the room continued to spin around me. Now, whether it was because I was exceptionally drunk, high off of kissing Matt, or because I was liable to pass out at any moment from mortification, was anyone's guess.

I stumbled over to the kitchen and fixed myself a glass of water. I downed it and two more. As inebriated as I was, all I wanted was to lie down and forget this whole thing had happened. Maybe I'd wake up on the floor having dreamed the whole evening. I recognized the empty hope for what it was. I knew this was real, and I'd pay dearly for it in the morning.

The empty pitcher sat defiantly on the table. Miserable thing had gotten me into more trouble than seemed possible. I walked over and snatched it up along with the empty glasses. I was far too strung out to go to sleep, no matter how much I wanted to. For want of a distraction, I stayed up and cleaned the entire living space, kitchen included. By morning, the place was spotless, and I was exhausted. Even then, I couldn't bring myself to retire. I wanted to be awake when Matt got up to at least attempt damage control. However, despite spending the entire night thinking about what to do, I was still coming up empty.

A faint shuffling came from his side of the dorm.

Instantly, anxiety laced with dread flooded through my veins. I quickly poured a glass of water, orange juice, and blue sports drink. I wasn't sure what his preference would be and wanted him to have options.

The shuffling got louder until, at last, Matt's door finally opened and he staggered out. His hair was a sleep-tangled nest, gray smudges sat beneath tired eyes, and his shoulders slumped forward as if trying to shield him from the light. In short, he looked rough. Somehow, though, he'd had the wherewithal to change into pajamas and stood leaning against the frame in his usual lounge pants and tee. It was a measure of how stressed I was that I didn't bother to appreciate the view.

He looked up at me bleary-eyed, then saw the glasses and walked over. He downed the water and blue sports drink in quick succession before taking the orange juice over to the couch. A miserable groan rose out of him as he sat down.

I refilled the water and brought it over to sit it on the coffee table. When I sat down, I made sure there was still plenty of distance between us.

He didn't react except to drink half of the glass and lay his head back. "You look awful," he said with his eyes closed.

"So do you," I countered.

"I feel worse. Just how much did I drink?" It sounded like a rhetorical question, so I didn't respond. He finished the OJ and the extra water before leaning back again.

"What do you remember?" I asked cautiously.

"Shh, not so loud," he admonished. He sat still for a moment before continuing. "Most of the night is a blur," he moaned, rubbing his temples.

I let out the breath I'd been holding. He didn't remember.

He cracked an eye. "Don't look so relieved. I wasn't that drunk."

Cold washed over me as all the blood drained from my face. "Matt, I..."

He held up his hand, much like he had the night before. "It's okay, Alex."

"But, Matt..." I tried again.

He opened both eyes and looked at me. There was no confusion or doubt this time. They were perfectly clear. I felt speared in place. "You're gay, Alex. It's fine." I opened my mouth to try once again to offer some desperate defense, but he beat me to it. "You were drunk. I was drunk. Shit happens." He glanced at the table. "I don't suppose I could get some more water and something for this?" he asked, rubbing his head again.

I was gone and back again in record time. My mind struggled to accept what he'd said. He obviously remembered the night before and was... okay with everything?

"Please stop staring at me. I can practically hear you freaking out over there. It's very loud."

I shifted my position so I wouldn't be looking directly at him, but it did nothing to quiet my mind.

He let out an exasperated sigh and sat up. "We're still friends, if that's what you're worried about."

I looked over at him. It wasn't quite what I'd been thinking, but it was close enough. "It won't be the same."

"Why not?" He leaned back again, the absolute picture of hungover ease. This was not at all the person I'd expected to see this morning after his reaction last night.

"Because... because..." I floundered.

"Because you kissed me?" It seemed prudent not to point out that he'd technically kissed me too.

I know I didn't imagine that. I know I didn't.

When I didn't respond, he officially turned to face me. "You're still my best friend, Alex."

I was completely caught off guard. The vulnerability on his face took my breath away.

"I... I've never had one of those before and I'm not about to give it up because of one drunken night." He kept his head down as he fidgeted with the hem of his nightshirt. "Is that alright with you?"

There were still a thousand things I wanted to ask. Were we really not going to talk about this? How was he okay with what had happened? I'd practically admitted that I was into him and he still wanted to be friends? I didn't voice any of them, instead I nodded numbly.

"Good, now can we please turn off all the lights? It's way too bright in here." Before I could get up, I heard all the switches click, and the room went dark. "Never mind, I got it. Try to take a nap, Alex. You really do look like hell."

CHAPTER 17

KNIGHTS OF CONFUSION

M

Alex was gay. The best friend I'd ever had in my life was gay, and I was pretty sure he was into me. Everything he'd ever done since we met took on a new meaning. His sudden bouts of awkwardness, why he didn't want to spar outside of class, his weird insistence on personal space, his mini freak outs he didn't think I noticed. All of it came together to paint the picture I should have seen all along. I couldn't believe I'd missed it.

Did I not want to see what was right in front of me?

It didn't matter, not really. I'd never had a friend like Alex and over my dead body was I going to give him up. So, what if he was gay? People got crushes on their friends every day, then they moved on. That was a thing. Right?

I finished changing into pajamas and was about to put on a shirt to go into the living space so Alex and I could hang out like we did practically every night. I got all the way to my door, then stalled. The shirt fell uselessly to the floor and I crawled back into bed instead. I just needed a little more time to get my head clear before I tried to be normal again.

While I lay there waiting for sleep to take me, I stared up at the ceiling and replayed every awkward moment I'd ever seen Alex have. There weren't that many, but the ones that made the list certainly stood out. Deep down, I was a little disturbed at how not disturbed I was. That I'd totally missed it and been taken off guard was what had me spinning, not the actual information.

I reached up to touch my mouth tentatively. If I thought about it, I could still feel the slight buzz of his lips against mine. I felt horrible for tricking him like that, but I also knew Alex. If I hadn't, he would've found some way to explain it all away. It would've been easy. After all, we were both exceptionally drunk.

As I trailed my finger along my bottom lip, I let the guilt sink in. I'd intentionally baited him so that he couldn't hide behind some noncommittal peck, but I hadn't been prepared at all for what I would get. No one had ever kissed me like that. It was... different. I thought about that. Why was it different? Ironically, I didn't think it had anything to do with the fact that I'd been kissing another man. No, it was different for some other reason. Even completely shit-faced, I could tell that, but I still didn't know why.

I let my hand drop and rolled over, like I could roll away from the thoughts. A good night's sleep would help me sort things out. I'd already told Alex that nothing would change. I just had to figure out how.

I should have known sleep wouldn't be a refuge. It was strange enough that I seemed to dream about Alex all the time, so I wasn't surprised to see him. Except, this wasn't like the other dreams. We didn't sit around and talk or hang out like we normally did. Instead, it was like my brain was re-writing my memory.

We were running in the rain and getting absolutely soaked. It didn't matter that people were judging us; we were having fun. The dining hall swam into sight. I already knew we wouldn't be able to stop. In the dream, I slid to a stop against the outside wall and waited to catch Alex. He immediately began laughing when he crashed into me and couldn't seem to hold his balance. His green eyes danced with humor as he struggled to get his feet under him. Something else flashed in them. You could see every thought he had in those outrageously green things.

Kiss me.

The thought was an echo of what I'd said the other night. I wasn't sure if I said it aloud in the dream or not. Either way, he leaned forward, water dripping into his eyes. When his lips met mine, it wasn't the first accidental kiss; it was absolutely the very intentional, all-consuming second one. Like that night, I kissed him back. I didn't know why, past that's just what you did when someone kissed you. In the dream, we stood pressed together, rain falling all around us and let go, drowning in water and each other.

Thunder cracked, and I bolted upright.

Trying to shake it off was pointless; there was no way I'd be able to get back to sleep with a storm rolling overhead. As I grabbed my discarded shirt from the floor, I told myself the reason my heart was hammering so hard was because the thunder had startled me, not because of the dream. I pulled open my door, then had to fight my disappointment at seeing the living room empty.

Probably best that Alex is still asleep, considering.

My gaze rebelliously sought his door anyway in the hope that he'd miraculously appear. The mere thought of seeing him had my heart rate kicking up. I strangled the sudden urge to march over there and get him. Perhaps a more sober experiment would help clear things up. I flashed to the less-than sober attempt at clarity, the way Alex had held me close, his hand on my face as he conquered my mouth in a way that instantly set my blood on fire.

A hollow crack of thunder shook the dorm and me out of the fog. I needed something to distract my thoughts, otherwise I'd just end up in the same spiral that had led to the dream. The television would certainly offer that, but I wasn't really a fan of mindlessly vegging, and I didn't want to risk waking Alex up. I glanced at his door again. It was still firmly closed. I ignored the second, sharp sting of disappointment and wandered around the kitchen, opening and closing cabinet doors as quietly as I could.

I was about to despair when I caught sight of a stack of books on the counter. The tiny pendant light flicked on with a soft click and an even softer glow. All the covers were worn with age. These had to be the books Alex was talking about. I smiled to myself as I picked each one up and examined it. They did all look interesting, though none struck me as a romance novel like he'd implied.

He must've been messing with me.

I set them back down and looked back toward the couch.

I wonder.

I searched through the mess of papers on the coffee table, then shifted to the side table. At last, I spied the worn cover beneath a notepad. I knew I'd seen it in here.

The couch groaned in protest as I took a seat. I spared a quick glance toward Alex's still closed door before settling back and opening the book. It fell automatically to the page with the drawing I'd asked about before. I ran my fingers over the illustration. A faint whiff of something tickled my nose. I inspected the tips of my fingers, then lifted the book. Soft tendrils of lavender curled in my nose and I let out a relaxed sigh. It was strange, though, that it didn't hold the typical "book" smell, given how old it was. I couldn't help but wonder why.

With a shrug, I let the mystery go and considered the virtually ancient book. Alex might be able to pick up wherever he wanted, but I actually wanted to see what this thing was about.

I flipped back to the front of the book. Alex's name greeted me in his perfectly swirled letters. Before I could succumb to the temptation to trace the elegant curves, I turned the page and started reading.

My family had been fighting the darkness for as long as I could remember. Since the day the night had taken form, we had struggled to beat it back. But the darkness was all-consuming and the battle fraught with temptation. What was one soldier in an infinite war against evil? Against Darkness?

I 'twas but seven when I met my first shade. The creature stepped from the void onto our family's land. The shock of being so brazenly approached blazed through my young body, an insult to life itself. Even at such a tender age, I knew what my response should have been. This thing was a monstrosity and yet my hand was stayed. Mayhaps the creature had spelled me to forestall its demise. It mattered not. The torches came, and it fled back to the depths that had spawned it.

Thus began my crusade to ultimately capture and destroy darkness defined. I was a man obsessed. The night itself had touched me and I would not be at peace until I hunted it down once and for all. This was my destiny.

"Storm, wake you up too?"

My entire body jerked. I looked up from the book, hoping like hell guilt wasn't plastered on my face. Alex stood just outside his room, the door open behind him, looking all kinds of disheveled. "Yeah," I replied noncommittally.

He scrubbed his hands through his hair, causing it to stick up in every direction. There was another roll of thunder and suddenly he was standing there soaked from head to toe, water dripping from his hair to puddle on the carpet.

I blinked, and the vision was gone. "What?"

"I said, do you want anything?"

I shook my head, not trusting words, then swallowed and returned to my stolen reading material. In the kitchen, I heard the faucet as he fixed something to drink. When I glanced back up, it looked like he was trying to figure out where to sit. I scooted over and gestured at the couch.

"Just sit down, Alex. It's only weird if you make it weird," I said, keeping my nose firmly in the book. I squeezed my eyes shut. Ugh, I was such a hypocrite. I was making it weird.

He didn't say anything as he sat down with his water and another book.

I'd seen him notice my reading choice, but he'd yet to comment on it. Despite my dedicated effort to resume reading, the words blurred together. I couldn't focus. Alex certainly qualified as a distraction, although maybe not the best one, considering. It didn't matter. If Alex was here, I wanted to talk to him. That he actually seemed interested in what I had to say was one of my favorite things about our friendship. It was nice to feel like I had a valid opinion.

"Do you think he knows he's in love?"

Alex looked up from his own reading with a completely neutral expression.

"In the diary," I elaborated, holding up the book with my finger in it to hold my place. "Do you think he knows?"

His face relaxed, and he set his book down. "You tell me."

"What do you mean?"

"Well, someone put notes in the margins about what they thought. It could've been the author or someone else who knew the situation.".

"I haven't seen anything." I reopened the book, and he leaned over to get a better look at where I was.

"Oh, that's because you haven't gone far enough. It starts showing up everywhere." He made to turn the pages.

"Wait, I don't want to lose my place."

He frowned, then leaned across me to grab the notebook that was still lying there. The distinct aroma of lavender floated up to curl in my nose. He tore out a page and handed it to me before sitting back. I stared at him and he got fidgety. He cleared his throat. "Sorry, I—"

"You smell like lavender."

He blinked, clearly not expecting the comment, then scooted back to his corner to retrieve his own book. "Yeah... I had trouble sleeping when we moved to England, so my mom started putting sachets of lavender under my pillow. I guess I just kept it going. Anyway, you'll eventually see handwritten notes. Full warning, I don't agree with most of them." His smile felt a little forced, but I wasn't really paying attention. If the book smelled like lavender because Alex did, that meant he probably slept with it... regularly.

I looked down at my hands curled possessively around the book. The thin piece of paper sticking out was a stark white in contrast to the aged binding. With a force of will, I loosened my grip. "This is about a Shadow Demon. That's why it's your favorite."

His mouth twitched with the start of a smile that didn't fully form, then he looked away. "I suppose you're right."

"Does he kill her?" I didn't want to read any book where that was the outcome, especially one that read like a love story.

He lifted an eyebrow. "That would ruin the ending, now, wouldn't it?"

I scowled, and he returned to his own reading material.

Such a typical bookie answer.

"Do you think it's true?"

"Do I think what is true?" he asked, once again putting his book down.

"That there was a family dedicated to wiping out Shadow Demons."

He sighed and rested against the back of the couch, his dark hair a stark contrast to the red fabric. "Honestly, it wouldn't surprise me. Fear is a really powerful motivator. Back in those days, we were more common, and like any demon race, making a mess of everything." This time, his smile felt more genuine.

The tightness in my chest eased, and I returned the smile. It was nice to see my friend again. "How many times have you read this, anyway?"

He looked sheepish. "A few."

"You know, some of this doesn't make a damn bit of sense." I waved the book around. He laughed like I hoped he would. See, we could be normal.

"Well, it was written a very long time ago."

My smile widened as he shifted to face me more squarely. "And I bet you've looked up every arcane reference."

"Maybe," he smirked.

I smiled back, feeling lighter than I had in days. "You really are a know-it-all."

"Are you going to ask me to explain parts of it or just wait for me to volunteer?" he asked, then promptly smacked me with his book.

"Watch it. I will come over there."

"Empty threat." He made to smack me again, and I snatched the book right out of his hand. His mouth fell open with an indignant cry. "Come on, Matt, you've already stolen one."

I tossed it back. "Then stop hitting me with it. And for your information, I have a better idea than swallowing my pride and asking for more help than I already have." I picked up the notebook still lying on the side table. "I'll just write my own theories and you can correct me later."

"That's also not yours."

I gave him a pointed look. "Do you have anything important in here?"

"Not really."

"Then I guess you won't mind if I borrow it."

He rolled his eyes, but kept smiling. "Maybe one of these days you'll check to see if someone else's name is on something before you decide to commandeer it."

Before he could stop me, I snatched a pen from the table and opened the small notebook to the front. Sure enough, Alexi Roman was written on the cover in his perfect penmanship.

He leaned slightly toward me to get a better look. "What are you doing?"

"You'll see." I added '& Matt' then held it out for him to see. "There, now it's communal property."

"You're a regular artist."

"You're just jealous you didn't think of it first."

He shrugged and looked around. "I haven't heard any thunder for a while. Maybe the storm is finally over. I never imagined there would be so much rain when I came out here. Everything is going to be soaked tomorrow."

At the mention of the rain, I flashed to him laughing, drenched from head to toe while trying to keep water out of his eyes. It wasn't from the dream, though; it was an actual memory, complete with every tiny detail, including the soft look in his eyes as he stared back at me.

"Hello. Matt. Are you listening?"

"What?" I asked, returning to earth.

"I said, I'm going to try to go back to sleep. Maybe you should too if you're falling asleep with your eyes open."

"You're probably right." I yawned wide enough to crack my jaw. "I'll see you later."

I waited until he'd retreated to his room. While I didn't relish trying to sleep again, he had a point. I confirmed the bookmark was in place before setting the book down and marching into my room.

CHAPTER 18

DEMON'S ADVICE

A

I went through class in a daze. Thank goodness I already had a solid grasp of the material, because not so much as an iota of the lecture pierced my fog. All my thoughts circled on replaying that night over and over again. What should I have done differently? Had it been a mistake to admit the truth? It wasn't like I was ashamed of being gay; my mother had given me all the support any kid could want. Why should it matter that Matt knew?

Of course, knowing or not knowing the answers didn't change a damn thing. Matt did know and now nothing would ever be the same again. I wasn't even sure which one of us was being more awkward. Personally, I believed Matt was acting especially weird. While he wasn't outright avoiding me, he also wasn't exactly lingering in shared spaces.

But I couldn't lay all the blame for our suddenly strained friendship on him. It was me who'd kissed him first. And if I was being honest, my behavior had altered as well. I'd stopped yammering his ear off. I didn't initiate studying sessions. Whether that was helping or hurting, though, was anyone's guess. Maybe if I—

A hand landed on my shoulder. I yelped and lurched straight into the air, briefly shadowing.

"Whoa there. Didn't mean to startle you." Rubio chuckled and dropped his hand.

I glanced around, surprised to find myself in an unfamiliar hallway.

A crease formed between Rubio's golden brows. "You okay? I called to you twice, but you didn't seem to hear me."

"Um... yeah, I'm fine." I cleared my throat and adjusted my backpack.

He gave me a curious look, but didn't pursue the lackluster answer. "What brings you around here? Meeting a tutoring client?"

"Uh, no. I actually have no idea where 'here' is," I replied, a little abashed.

Rubio's eyebrows lifted. "You sure you're alright?"

"Totally. Just distracted lately." I chose a direction at random and started walking, secretly hoping it would lead to an exit, or at least somewhere familiar.

"Uh-huh." Rubio fell in step beside me. "I haven't been loading you with too many clients, have I? Don't want to burn you out. Especially it being your first semester and all."

I shook my head, only half listening. "No, of course not. The clients are great. Really making progress."

"What about your private tutoring lessons?"

My steps faltered, and I shot Rubio a look. "My what?"

"The private lessons. The ones with your roommate." He held his hand up to nose level. "About yay tall, really hot. You know, the lessons you're not charging for."

I scrambled for words, anything that could vaguely sound like a response, but like the broken record it had apparently become, my brain stalled out.

"Ah-ha! There is something wrong."

"No, there's not. I just... just..." No matter how much I wanted the lie to come, it remained elusive.

Rubio's face took on a more profound concern. "Hey, flirting aside, you can still talk to me. I get it, you're not interested. No worries, no hard feelings. We're friends."

"It's not that. I appreciate the offer—both of them—but I..." But I felt like someone had plopped me on a possessed merry-go-round or maybe a rocket spinning out of orbit. My thoughts were a mess and my emotional state worse.

"Alexi, talk to me, man. Let me help."

The worry in Rubio's voice officially broke me. I scanned the hallway until I found what looked like an empty room. Much as I wanted to respect Matt's right to privately discover things on his own, I needed help. "Okay, but not out here." I took off for the room, with what I expected was a very confused Rubio. The room turned out to be barely more than an oversized closet, but it was mercifully devoid of people. I waited for Rubio to clear the door, then slammed it shut. Before he could say a word, I blurted, "I kissed Matt. My roommate. Whose name is Matt."

Rubio stared at me, frozen mid word. He blinked and moved his mouth, but no sound came out.

As I flopped against the wall, I groaned and fisted my hands over my eyes. "I don't know what I was thinking. I knew fantasizing about him would get me in trouble. We'd been drinking—like a lot. We were laughing and having a good time, then I had to bugger it all up by kissing him." I dropped my hands and looked at Rubio, who still seemed to be struggling to put a whole word together.

He cleared his throat and held up a finger, then paused, as if still working to wrap his head around my haphazard explanation. "So... he knows you're gay."

I rested my head against the wall and stared up at the ceiling. "He certainly does now."

"Okay, let's break this down."

I glanced back at Rubio, simultaneously relieved to have finally told someone and even more anxious because now that it was out in the world, I couldn't pretend it hadn't happened. Not that I'd been doing such a great job of that before. "What's there to break down?"

His mouth twisted to the side in a scowl. "Seriously? What's there not to break down? You kissed your supposedly straight roommate."

"He's straight, Rubio."

He snorted. "Most people aren't half as straight as they think. They simply never take the chance to consider anything else. What did he do when you kissed him?"

"Freaked."

Rubio scowled harder. "Care to be more specific?"

I sighed hard enough to stir up some dust and straightened up. "He went all quiet, gave me a funny look, eventually said he needed a minute, then went to his room."

"Ouch." Rubio winced. "Harsh."

"It gets worse. After a few minutes, he came back, floundered trying to say I was gay, then went back to his room again."

Rubio shook his head. "Yikes, man, no wonder you're in a state."

"Not done yet."

His eyes widened.

"After another few minutes, he came back out and demanded I kiss him again."

"Did you?"

I took a deep breath and let it out. "You don't know Matt. He can be really insistent. So, yeah, I did. Except..."

"Except?" Rubio leaned forward, anticipation written clearly across his face.

"He kissed me back? At least, I think he did."

Rubio smacked me on the arm. "See, not so straight after all."

"Please, the last thing I need is more confusion. And it's not like he stuck around afterward to chat about our feelings."

"Have you talked at all about what happened?" Rubio crossed his arms and leaned against the wall opposite me.

"Not beyond him saying it doesn't matter that I'm gay." The bitter sting of tears burned my eyes. "Besides, if that was true, then why is he avoiding me? He can barely be in the same room with me long enough to review his notes.".

"Hey, hey, things will be alright." He held out his arms, and I didn't think twice about stepping into the hug. "Give him time. Sounds like this might be his first experience outside of hetero-normative expectations." Suddenly, Rubio leaned back and gave me a stern look. "Unless he said or did something hurtful that you're not telling me about, because if that's the case, I'll kick his ass."

"No, nothing like that."

Rubio gave a curt nod before enfolding me back in his embrace, backpack and all. "Good."

I relaxed and rested my head on his shoulder. It really was a shame I wasn't attracted to Rubio as more than a friend. I soaked up the comfort for a few more seconds, then pushed away. "Thanks. I guess I needed that more than I realized." I wiped at my nose with the back of my hand and hoped I hadn't gotten snot on him.

He hiked a shoulder and smiled. "That's what friends are for. But now you have to tell me what I really want to know."

"Oh? What's that?"

"How was the kiss?" He wiggled his eyebrows, and I barked out a laugh.

"Sweet night, it was incredible. Beyond incredible. Straight or not, Matt can kiss." I sighed a swoon and returned Rubio's grin.

"What are the chances of getting him to do it again?"

I snorted and rolled my eyes. "Nil. I'll count it as a miracle if we stay friends."

A crease formed on Rubio's brow. "But you do want it to happen again."

"I want a lot of things with Matt. Doesn't mean they'll ever happen."

"Doesn't mean they won't, either. Tell me how I can help." He smirked. "Besides stealing a chance to feel you up."

I couldn't help but laugh. "You're ridiculous." I sobered and let out a sigh. "In all seriousness, I do appreciate the offer, though I'm not sure what you could do. Unless you have some pearls of wisdom about how I can help us move past all of this awkwardness."

"I wish. Sadly, I think it will simply take time. Try to give him space. I hate to pitch the cliche, but it's possible that you've turned his world upside down and he's working through it. That being said, if he starts acting like a homophobic wang, don't put up with that shit."

I chuckled at Rubio's colorful word choice.

"Go ahead and laugh, but I expect you to say something if he gets out of line. You've got the whole tutoring team at your back. None of us want to see you get hurt."

"Damn it, you're going to make me tear up again." I sniffled and Rubio placed a hand on my shoulder. He gave it a good squeeze, then met my gaze.

"I know you're really hung up on this guy, but don't let that give him a free pass to be an asshole. No one deserves that."

"Who says I'm really hung up on him?" I asked, even as his words warmed my heart.

Rubio scoffed. "Pretty sure the only one it's not blatantly obvious to is your oblivious roommate."

I opened my mouth to argue that Matt wasn't oblivious, then I recalled his genuine shock at realizing I was gay, and promptly shut it.

"That's what I thought. Now what do you say we skip our next classes and grab some coffee in town or something?" He immediately held up his hands. "Promise I'm not asking you out. Just think it'd be a good idea to get off campus for a bit."

I smiled and felt myself truly relax for the first time in what felt like days. "Yeah, I'm not the skipping sort." Rubio's face fell into an exaggerated pout and I bit the inside of my cheek to keep from laughing. "You're in luck. My next class isn't for another couple of hours." Normally, I'd meet up with Matt for lunch, but given how he'd conveniently already eaten or not been hungry the last couple of days, this seemed a better alternative than eating by myself.

"Sweet. Let's sneak out of this closet like we've been up to no good and head for the main entrance of the campus."

"Really? You had to go there?" I snickered as he pushed open the door and glanced around, looking sketchy as hell.

"And miss this beautiful opportunity? Never." He held the door for me and I slipped into the hallway. "Besides, it could have been worse. I could have made a dozen different closeted jokes."

I laughed loud enough to catch someone at the far end of hall's attention and clamped a hand over my mouth. "You're the worst," I hissed as I let him take the lead.

"I think you mean the best." He slung an arm around my shoulders and dragged me even with him. "You're going to love the place I have in mind. Not only do they have amazing coffee, but rumor has it that's where your notorious teacher met her mentor."

I gasped and nearly gave myself whiplash turning to look at him. "No way."

"Yep. Not that anyone in town realizes the significance of the quaint spot, everyone being human and all."

"That's true, then. The town really doesn't know that it's sitting next to an ancient university for supernaturals? How is that even possible?"

"One word, my friend." Rubio waved his hand and wiggled his fingers. "Magic." He pushed open a set of doors and we stepped out into a cloudy afternoon. "That, and people have a tendency to see only what they expect to see. Long as we don't do anything extra supernaturally, then no one pays us any mind."

"But don't they think it's odd that none of their residents are ever accepted at the university?"

Rubio gave me a sidelong look. "Who says they're not? You should know as well as anyone that supernaturals are everywhere. Not to mention you don't have to look like a supernatural to be one. Unless, of course, you took one look at me and knew I was an incubus." He lifted an eyebrow and my jaw fell.

"You're taking the piss."

"Nope. Granted, I'm not exactly a high-level Carnal class, but I'm one hundred percent sex demon."

I laughed so hard my shoulder shook, which in no way encouraged him to let go.

"What's so funny? I'm serious."

"No, no, I believe you. But that explains sooo much."

"Not sure what the hell that's supposed to mean," he grumbled to himself.

I looped an arm around his waist and squeezed lightly. "It means you're incredibly charismatic and clearly have a way with people. You're also a pretty great friend, though now I'm a little worried I've wounded your Incubus pride by not being interested in being more than friends."

"Don't be. I'm all about the casual, and I strongly suspect you are not."

"You would be correct. It might sound a little silly, but I really do believe in true love and soul mates and all that other mushy stuff."

Rubio graced me with a soft smile, gave my shoulders a last squeeze, and released me. "Not at all."

CHAPTER 19

ROOMMATE TROUBLE

M

For a supposed hole in the wall, the still unnamed pool hall Lucas and Sam frequented was incredibly well kept. Everything was clean. No one was abnormally surly. Even the food was decent. I shoved my hands in my pockets and brought my attention back to where Lucas was currently beating Sam's ass in a game of Nine Ball. He missed the seven and waved for a scowling Sam to take his shot.

Lucas glanced over at me, not remotely concerned about whether Sam could make the shot—we both knew he couldn't, not with the nine so perfectly boxed. "You've been awful quiet tonight. Not that you're much of a chatter. Is something up?"

I flashed to the image of Rubio's arm thrown around Alex's shoulders and Alex's wrapped around his waist. The anger I'd been fighting all day seethed in my stomach. Sure, I'd fucked up. Maybe I should have made more of an effort to talk about the drunken kiss, but actively blowing me off for that guy? And it wasn't like I could look at it any other way either. When class let out, I'd made a beeline to grab Alex for lunch, eager to regain some normalcy in our friendship, but he'd been nowhere to be found. It had taken thirty minutes of wandering around the building and getting lost—twice—before I'd stumbled across the pair of them.

"Matt. You still with us?"

I blinked away the memory to find Lucas and Sam both staring at me with concern. "Huh?"

They glanced at each other, then Sam spoke up. "Lucas was asking if you were alright, and you sort of... spaced."

"Shit." I wiped a hand over my face like it could somehow scrub away any of the millions of thoughts that refused to leave me alone. "Sorry, guys. My head's not really in it."

Lucas shrugged and rested his cue stick against the high-top to grab his beer. "Anything you want to talk about?"

"Not really, just roommate trouble."

Sam slammed into a chair, nearly toppling it and himself to the ground. "Tell me about it. Mine is a total slob, and he eats all my food. Never replaces any of it either. Does yours do that?"

"Uh, no... Alex and I share pretty much everything and take turns replenishing the fridge. Though we eat at the dining hall more often than not." Now that I said it out loud, I couldn't help but wonder if that was normal.

Lucas downed the last of his beer and wiped the froth from his mouth. "Lucky bastard. I'm like eighty-five percent positive my roommate is a supe of the aquatic variety."

"Like a mermaid?" I frowned as I tried to make sense of that.

"Maybe, but there are a lot more aquatic supernaturals than merfolk. Could be any of them. But whatever they are, they clearly prefer their air more wet than not. I swear the humidity in our dorm room gets so bad, it's like walking through soup. And it's murder on my hair. I have to keep an extra fan in my room just so I can sleep."

Sam rolled his eyes. "You could try talking to them. I don't know, ask what they are. Maybe if you knew, you could find better middle ground."

Lucas snorted. "Last time I tried to hint around, they stared at me while a film covered their eyes before sliding back in a weird double-blink." He shuddered, and I was right there with him. Neese did something like that and that was on top of his long tongue and hissed consonants. "I know supes come in all shapes, sizes, colors, and what have you, but you gotta understand. They didn't say a word. And I could hear the film move across their eyes. As much as I love being a werewolf, there are some perks I could do without."

Sam leaned forward on the table. "I'm guessing your roommate doesn't do that."

"Definitely not." I chuckled, feeling slightly easier. "We're both Shadow Demons, though he clearly knows more about that than I do."

"So, what's the deal? He a snob or something?" Sam tilted his chin.

I shrugged a shoulder and shifted to relax my stance. "I thought he was at first, but that doesn't seem to be the case. He's actually really nice, even been helping me with some of my classes."

Sam's lips twitched in an almost smile. "Sounds like he's a really great guy."

Lucas shot him a glare. "Did something happen?"

My heart rate quickened like it did right before a fight or when I was about to snatch and run. Did I dare tell them about what had happened? I certainly could use some solid advice, like if either of them had ever kissed a guy and what it felt like. Was it different to kissing other people? Was it all the same? Why did I feel like it was different? And why did I want to try it again?

"You don't have to talk about it if you don't want to." Lucas squeezed my shoulder and there was no way he could miss how tense I was.

Problem was, I did want to talk about it... with Alex. Then there was the whole hang up of appearing weak in front of my new friends. What would they think when they realized I clearly didn't have my shit together? Not to mention I didn't know whether or not Alex was out. But now I was going too long without talking again and I had to say something. "We got drunk together the other day."

Lucas and Sam frowned, but it was Lucas who spoke. "Okay... Someone puke or something?"

"No, no," I repeated with a forced laugh, "nothing like that. It's just now things are... weird. We may have gotten a little too honest."

"That'd do it." Sam leaned back in his chair, clearly believing he had one up on gravity. Given he was a witch, heck, maybe he did. "I can think of a few drunk truth-spells I wish I could undo. Never," he angled his hand at me, "I mean never tell a girl her dress makes her look like a cow. Even if it is cattle print."

I snorted into my drink and subsequently choked laughing. "You didn't."

"Oh, he definitely did. But he hasn't even told you the best part," Lucas said with a smirk.

"You're never going to let me live that down, are you?"

"Not on your life."

I set the remnants of my beer aside. "What's the best part?"

"This dumbass," Lucas pointed his thumb at Sam, "proceeds to create an illusion of himself as a cow-person."

Sam groaned and dropped his head to the table. "It really sucks, because I was pretty sure that was going somewhere until I went all drunk magic."

"Is that a thing?" I asked at the same time Lucas said, "That's not a thing."

"Well, it should be. I shouldn't be held liable for what my magic does when I'm shit faced," Sam huffed.

"You're ridiculous." I shook my head and straightened up. Maybe my current conundrum with Alex wasn't so bad in the grand scheme of things. "Thanks for listening, but I think I'm gonna call it a night. Hopefully next time I'll be in a better frame of mind."

"Anytime." Lucas smacked me on the back, not bothering to check his werewolf strength. I coughed out air in a big gust.

"Geez, man, what are you trying to do, kill the guy?" Sam asked.

"It's cool, I'm fine. Trust me when I say that's nothing. Caught me off guard is all." I glanced between the two of them. "You sure y'all are okay if I bounce?"

Lucas shrugged. "To be honest, I have a paper I should be writing, but I didn't want to miss a chance to hang. And someone has to make sure Sam doesn't get us all banned from here."

Sam stuck out his tongue and hopped free of his chair. It tilted alarmingly before coming to rest miraculously without falling over. Magic. That was the only word for it. "If you two are bailing, then I'm hitting up the witch bar."

I glanced at Lucas, who shook his head. "Trust me, it's better not to ask. You think he's a handful? Imagine an entire bar filled with people three times as bad." We waved to Sam as he headed deeper into town, then angled toward the university.

"I get the impression you're not too keen on witches."

"Eh, they're not all bad. Sam is one of the good ones. But they've done their fair share of harm to the supernatural community, to demons in particular." Lucas gave me a wary look. "So, you know, be careful if one seems to take an unusual interest in you."

I thought back to Misty, the goth witch from the fight club. Maybe that was why she'd given me the creeps. "Noted. Thanks for the heads-up."

"No problem." We paused at where the sidewalk diverged to the different dormitories. "And, you know, if you ever want to talk about anything, Sam and I are pretty good listeners. I mean, obviously me more than him, but you get the gist."

I laughed. "Thanks. See you around."

"See you." Lucas waved and wandered off.

With a sigh, I trudged toward Starling Hall. I opened the door to our dorm and my shoulders immediately sagged when I found no trace of Alex. So much for trying to talk to him. I flung my key on the coffee table. It settled with a loud clatter that chased me into my room. It wasn't until I finished changing into a pair of loose sweats and a relaxed shirt I realized Alex was likely with Rubio at one of their joint "tutoring" sessions.

I flopped onto the bed with a creak of springs and an irritated grumble. So much for going out to get my mind off of things. I stared up at the ceiling as silence settled around me, my thoughts already orbiting around Alex. Was he in a relationship with Rubio and that's why he was avoiding me? Because he'd never meant to kiss me in the first place? Did Alex kiss Rubio the way he'd kissed me?

I swallowed hard and licked my lips. I'd certainly never kissed anyone the way I'd kissed Alex, but it had been kind of hard not to. The way his lips had perfectly fit mine wasn't anything I'd experienced before. My eyes fluttered shut as I remembered what he'd tasted like—sweet, rich mango from the tangaroa cocktail we'd been drinking. It had kind of been like an Amaretto Sour, but I'd wanted something sweeter in the hope Alex would like it. There were plenty of other things in the drink that should have been there, but on Alex's lips there was only sweetness.

My thoughts took on a life of their own as I stopped remembering the way his tongue had curled around mine in a delicate invitation to explore and imagined doing it again... on purpose. I wasn't alone in the dorm, moping in my room. I was with Alex, leaning over him to taste his smiling lips. My breath hitched as his long fingers curled in my hair and pulled me closer. A distant part of me wished I'd had the courage to touch him back that night, then I'd know what he felt like beneath my fingers, too.

Between one heartbeat and the next, I was suddenly the one on their back with Alex hovering over me. His grin was confident as he closed the distance to capture my mouth once more. Everything Alex did was confident, it was intoxicating. I couldn't help but wonder if he knew that, even as the fantasy kiss deepened and stole my breath. But it wasn't enough. I wanted more, wanted to know.

Thankfully, this was all in my head and my imagination was more than happy to supply me with exactly that. Alex's lips abandoned mine to trail along my neck. All I had to pull from were past make-out sessions with other people for what it might feel like to have his lips pressing against the tender skin, and I suspected the experiences would pale to the real thing. That didn't stop me from indulging, though. As if sensing my wavering focus, fantasy-Alex shifted to look down at me. An apology was already on my tongue—I shouldn't be doing this. It was wrong—then I saw the wicked gleam in his emerald eyes.

He lowered his mouth once more to capture mine with a kiss that had my fingers and toes curling in the sheets. Aching want pumped through every vein so hard it was a wonder I didn't explode. Then Alex's hand slipped beneath the band of my sweatpants. I gasped as I mirrored the movement and nearly came undone. He teased my lips, but didn't relent. Release danced closer and closer with each stroke, making my extremities tingle and my mind fuzzy—everything except Alex. His name became a needy chant in my mind as he—I—we, kept going.

"Hey, Matt, did you call?" My bedroom door opened to reveal a confused Alex.

I squeaked out a yelp and yanked a pillow over my crotch so fast it was a wonder I didn't break something important. "What the hell!"

Alex echoed my squeak at realizing what he'd interrupted. "Shit." He tried to back out and ran into the doorjamb. "Fuck. Sorry. I could have sworn you called my name." He attempted unsuccessfully to leave again and muttered more curses. "Clearly, I was, uh, wrong. I'll just... leave you to it." Finally, he righted himself enough to leave, and the door slammed shut.

For one insane moment, I contemplated calling him back. Maybe if I could see the fantasy all the way through, I could finally get the answers that eluded me. Like was this something I really wanted? Why now? Why Alex?

I smacked the spare pillow beside me so hard it made my palm sting and flopped back, forgetting that my main pillow was now sitting on my lap. My head bounced uncomfortably. I covered my face with the pillow and screamed as hard as I could. People said letting it all out could help make you feel better. But I didn't feel better. I felt as lost as ever. I dropped the pillow back and stared up at the ceiling, almost exactly like I had when this horrible night had started.

"What the hell is wrong with me?"

TALKING IN YOUR SLEEP

A

I was at a complete loss for what to do with Matt. The first few days had been beyond awkward. Then I walked in on him. Where I'd expected the weirdness hovering between us to get infinitely worse, he acted as if nothing had happened at all. It wasn't like he acted like he didn't know I was gay, more like he was going out of his way to show that nothing was different, nothing had changed. But it had, everything had. Try as he might, there was no way to put the genie back in the bottle.

I looked up at him across the library. The light filtering through tall stained-glass windows fell in dappled patches on the cluster of deep mahogany tables. Within the cathedral-like building, Matt looked more like an angel than ever. He was sitting with a group of people that seemed vaguely familiar. He'd talked to them before and I was pretty sure he'd hung out with them beyond class as well. Which was great. I loved he was making friends; he needed more friends. The trouble was, I was almost positive he was only branching out to give me space.

Even from half a room away, I could tell he didn't want to be talking to them. I knew Matt. Any normal day, he would've been right next to me, making jokes and getting us endless rebukes to be quiet. I hated that I'd taken that from him. My heart ached with guilt, and I refocused my attention on my own work. I'd caught him glancing over here enough times to be sure that if he saw me looking, he'd come over.

Only the muffled sound of distant voices disturbed the bubble of silence I'd cocooned myself in. I turned another page of the text I was perusing, still undecided on whether I wanted to use it for the Demonic History research project. At the muted scrape of a chair, I glanced up to find Matt sitting less than two feet away, watching me.

"You know, we are allowed to do the project in groups." He rested his head on crossed arms. The move put him squarely within arms' reach, his head practically in the book I was currently eliminating.

I checked the impulse to run my hand through his hair. That I had such a strong desire to do that even after everything that had happened, was exactly why everything was so strained, whether he wanted to admit it or not. "It looks like you have a group," I said as casually as I could, moving the book farther away from his face and temptation.

He scoffed and leaned back. "Them? They still think they can get away with the class text. You and I both know there's a perfect book sitting in the dorm." He wanted to use my book. For some reason, that hurt.

"Then use it, Matt. I'm still looking."

"Alex."

I scanned the next page. I'd lost count how many times I'd read it since he'd pulled up.

"Alex, look at me."

I took a deep breath and did as he asked. Ice-blue eyes snared me, just like they always did. I felt like a fly caught on a web and I didn't even have the luxury of pretending that he didn't notice anymore.

"I won't use the book without you."

"Matt, I don't think-"

"You know what I think?" he cut me off. "I think you need to get your head out of your ass and start acting like my friend."

I was completely taken aback. "Why do you want to do a project with me, anyway?"

"Because you're my friend and you're the only one worth doing a project with. Now get off your ass." He hooked my arm and hoisted me out of my chair. "If we're going to use that book, then we're going to need some reference materials," he declared, then commenced dragging me over to the stacks.

His grip was like a vise, as if he was worried I'd bolt if he let go. Truthfully, I might have given the opportunity, but by the time towering shelves of books surrounded us, I'd given up fighting him. He finally released me and started thumbing through spines.

"You're more familiar with the memoir. What sort of references do you think we'll need?" He pulled out a dusty tome and flipped through it. "Translators for sure. Maybe even genealogy texts." When I didn't move or respond, he glanced over at me out of the corner of his eye. "Are you going to help or just stand there? Come on, what do we need?"

"You know, you can be really demanding."

"Are you saying you don't want to be my partner?"

I hesitated. That was a loaded question if I'd ever heard one. "No," I replied awkwardly.

"Good, then get to work."

I rolled my eyes and started perusing the options. At least we were in the right section of the library. "We'll definitely need an old English translator and Latin, of course. I'm a little rusty," I added.

"Of course, you know Latin," he mumbled.

"I didn't say I know Latin. It's just been a while since I looked up some of those passages."

"Whatever you say, Alex."

I scowled at his blatant sarcasm, which he pointedly ignored. "You know what," I looked around at the faded titles, "I think we're in the wrong aisle. These are translations. We need translators."

He swiveled around and began marching down the aisle. At the end, he hooked a right to go to another row.

"Wrong way," I called after him. Almost immediately, he crossed back the other way. "You are absolutely ridiculous," I said when I caught up to him.

He spun to face me, his blue eyes holding a touch of heat. "Look, we both know that Demonic History will never be my best class. It is, however, yours. So, if you could stop being selfish for one minute and give me a hand, I would really appreciate it."

I was thoroughly ashamed of myself. Here I was, being so stuck in my own head that I couldn't even be there for my friend. He wasn't exaggerating that history wasn't his best subject. He'd need a stellar project if he had a hope of doing anything more than scraping by with a pass.

"You're right. I'm sorry." I glanced around at the books surrounding us. "This seems more promising. Now, if I'm looking at this right, the old English should be on this side." I indicated the shelves closest to Matt. "See if you can find one that has old English and middle English. I'm going to go a little further down to see if I can scare up a decent Latin one that's not overly convoluted."

"Okay." He instantly turned to inspect the bindings for a relevant title.

I left him to it and walked away to see if I could accomplish my task. After about half an hour, I had a couple of hopefuls, but the sounds of Matt's frustration were only increasing.

"What's the matter?" I asked in too loud a whisper. The noise earned me a shush from someone sitting at a nearby table. I grabbed my small assortment and walked back to where he was. Knowing Matt, he would shout and get us both scolded, or worse, kicked out.

"Are you sure we need middle English?"

"I feel like it would be prudent."

"Prudent or not, I don't think it's here." He huffed.

I stepped up behind him to get a better look and started scanning titles. "This is the only place it would be." I adjusted my focus to search the next shelf up.

"I'm telling you, I've checked like three times. It's not here."

I smiled and reached over him to grab a book that claimed to have both translations. "You're such a dork. It's right here."

"It's not my fault I'm short," he grumbled. "You're just freakishly..." He turned around and trailed off.

I hadn't considered how close I was, and the move brought us face to face. He looked up at me and then immediately down. From a distance, I probably looked like I had him caged, with my arm still extended for the book. The smell of sage enveloped me. I'd kissed him before and the desire to do so again was overwhelming. I was pretty sure he'd kiss me back. That was, if I hadn't imagined it the other day. It wouldn't take much, maybe another half inch.

The roaring in my ears was so loud, I thought for sure it was going to draw another reprisal to be quiet. It looked like he was breathing hard, but I couldn't hear over the noise, only feel his breath on my lips. "This is a bad idea," I whispered.

His lips parted, and I wanted more than anything to taste them again. He wet them and swallowed before responding. "It'll be fine." He shadowed out, materializing behind me.

My hand not holding the book fisted by my side. It just wasn't possible to be friends with someone you were in love with, but Matt was refusing to take no for an answer.

"Do you think we'll need all of these?"

I took a deep breath to steady myself before facing him. "Let me see what you've got."

He passed me his stack. After a quick look, I put three back on the shelf and gave him the one I'd retrieved and one other he'd found.

"That should be good for now. If we need something else, you can come back." I ran my hand through my hair absently.

I don't know how I'm going to make this work.

There wasn't really anything else to say, so I grabbed my stack and headed for the checkout.

"Alex."

I stopped, but didn't turn around. It was bad enough he couldn't even look me in the eye a minute ago. Why was he so damned determined? "Yeah?"

Suddenly, he was in front of me, the reference books tucked beneath his arm. "We're still doing this together, right? Partners?" He held out his hand.

I looked at it skeptically, not sure I trusted myself to touch him.

At least he didn't spit in it.

"Partners," I finally said, accepting the hand. When I went to let go, though, he refused to release it, tightening his grip instead. I looked at him, a little alarmed. The blue of his eyes was like glass and sharp enough to cut.

"And friends. Best friends. I'm not going anywhere, Alex, so you might as well get used to it."

The rush of cold air on my hand said that he'd finally dropped it. I stood rooted to the spot as I watched him go down to the end of the aisle. He looked back to see why I wasn't following, and I quickly hurried to catch up.

The walk back to the dorm was relatively quiet. We made a pit stop at the dining hall for snacks and immediately got started when we got in. I set up things on the breakfast table while he plopped on the couch. He could say things were normal all he wanted, but his position did not invite company. His legs stretched all the way across, barring anyone from joining him. I sat down at the breakfast table, expecting to work in silence. I should have known better.

"What should our topic be?" he asked.

I fought back a groan. "You mean you didn't already have something in mind?"

"Well... no. I figured you would."

I rubbed my forehead. He was going to be the death of me. "Let me get this straight. You bullied me into doing this project with you and you don't even have a thesis?"

"When you say it like that, it sounds awful. And I didn't bully you. You agreed."

I scoffed. "After you dragged me across the length of the library and made me feel like a selfish prat."

"I don't recall doing any of those things."

"That's because you have a selective memory," I mumbled to myself.

"I heard that."

"And hearing," I added louder.

"Okay, what if we did the research project on the knight?"

"I don't follow. It needs to be a history project. We can't do it off of one person. Especially when we don't really know anything about them... like their name."

"No, but we could do it on a whole family. It's the first thing he says. 'My family had been fighting the darkness for as long as I could remember'. I could be wrong, but that sounds like it's an entire family that's been doing this for generations."

Okay, that idea held water. "You're not wrong, but how do we prove it?"

"First, we'll have to translate all the odd bits, and of course, I need to finish reading it. That would probably help."

"You have got to be kidding me. You haven't even finished it yet?" I stared at the back of the couch in disbelief.

Judging by the shuffling sounds, he was fidgeting. "I've been a little distracted, okay? I'll work on it now."

"And what am I supposed to do while you have the book?"

He snorted. "I know you're not going to pretend that you don't have this thing virtually memorized."

I made a face at his back. "Cheater."

He didn't respond except to turn another page. I saw him pick up a pencil and heard the telltale scratch of graphite against paper. At least he was taking this seriously and taking notes.

I pulled over an empty notebook and started making notes about the things I could remember needing translation. It was rough going, but I was confident that I was getting at least a good chunk. I'd never tried to see how much I could recall on my own before and was intrigued by how many pages I filled.

Suddenly, I realized I couldn't hear the scratch of writing anymore.

I swear.

I extricated myself from the table and walked around the side of the couch to see his head resting on his chest. The bugger was out cold. I let out a sigh. He may be hell-on-wheels awake, but asleep? All the innocence he didn't want the world to know about was plain to see.

My fingers itched to comb through his hair, but I really didn't want to risk waking him. I reined in the impulse and looked at the book propped against his knee. If he wasn't using it, then I certainly could. I leaned over, careful not to disturb him. One episode was enough for today. By some miracle, the pencil was still in his hand. I squinted at the paper in the book.

Cheeky bastard hadn't been taking notes at all, he'd been sketching on the bookmark.

I leaned a little further to get a better look. The image was still mostly unformed, but I had a sneaking suspicion it was a Shadow Demon. Even unfinished, I could still tell he was quite good.

Surprises everyday Matthew Duncan.

I shook my head and ever so slowly reached for the book. I was debating whether to pull it up in one swift motion or try to ease it from his grasp when he shifted in his sleep. He took a deep breath that brought him alarmingly close to where I was hovering just overhead.

"Alex." My name was barely even a whisper.

I looked down at him, not sure if I'd heard right, to find his eyes still squeezed tightly shut.

He shifted again, his face taking on an anxious expression. "Don't."

With one word, my heart broke to pieces.

I straightened up, abandoning my quest for the book and tried not to lose my shit right there in the living room. Matt might not say anything to my face, but it was clear he was struggling. I wanted to run to the safety of my room, to escape this unfolding nightmare, yet my feet stayed rooted. There wouldn't be any comfort for me there, just more misery when he eventually woke up and demanded my presence yet again, despite everything.

His face took on additional levels of anxiety. "I'm sorry."

I blinked.

What?

He shifted restlessly. The dream seemed to go from bad to worse. Seriously questioning my life choices, I squatted next to him. My hand hovered above his arm. Did I really want to do this?

He groaned and his face twisted in what could only be pain. Strained as our friendship had become, I couldn't sit here and watch him suffer. In a moment of bravery, I reached out and touched his shoulder. When he didn't react, I gave him a light shake.

"Matt. Matt." Another shake.

Stubborn even in your sleep.

"Matt, it's okay. Wake up." At the next shake, he startled up, eyes wild and nearly stabbing me with the pencil clutched tightly in his fist. "Easy, it's alright. You were just dreaming."

Finally, his alarmed gaze focused on me. I was surprised to see the fear almost instantly be replaced by relief. "What happened?" He broke the contact and pushed himself up.

"You fell asleep reading." I gestured to the still open book.

He looked over at it, confused, then snapped it shut, hiding his sketch.

I ignored the unusual behavior. "Maybe you should go to bed."

He nodded his head. "You're probably right. I haven't been sleeping well. Should have known it would eventually catch up with me."

A sharp pain lanced through my chest. I couldn't help but feel responsible. He was lying about coping, that much I could tell. I got out of the way as he swiveled his legs around to get up.

He set the book on the side table and scrubbed at his face. If I hadn't been such a mess myself, I might have laughed. He didn't say another word, just stood and shuffled off to his room, looking very much like a zombie.

I eyed the discarded book. After seeing his reaction, I was now keen to get a better look at that drawing. I was just about to pick it up when he shuffled back into the room substantially faster than he'd left.

He looked around like he'd already forgotten what he was searching for, then stepped over to retrieve the book. Again, in perfect silence, he disappeared into his room, closing the door firmly behind him. So much for me doing more research.

CHAPTER 21

BACK TO NORMAL

M

The dreams were steadily driving me insane. Gone were the days of reliving our day. Now it was always Alex kissing me. Alex kissing me in the rain, in the stacks, on the couch, in the kitchen, on the floor, in the training room. Anywhere we'd had a close call, my sleeping mind followed through with the natural conclusion. No interaction was spared. And it didn't matter what I did or how I acted when awake.

If I pretended nothing was wrong, that nothing had changed, we inevitably ended up too close. I was starting to think that was actually my fault. But if I tried to give us each some space, I was absolutely miserable, and he got sullen, not that he'd never admit it. I continued hanging out with the guys from our math class. They were cool, albeit a little preoccupied with picking up chicks. I'd tried that too, but hadn't shared their single-minded focus.

As confusing as the dreams were, they were better than the nightmares. Without fail, if I didn't spend at least a good part of the day talking with Alex, then horrible visions of him leaving, of never getting to see or laugh with him again, plagued my nights. I needed to figure this out. Preferably before my nightmares became self-fulfilling prophecies. Why was I having any of these dreams in the first place? I'd never dreamed before I came here, not with any level of detail anyway. But even that first night in the dorm, I'd been accosted with vivid dream after vivid dream. And now they'd all escalated. For fuck's sake, he'd walked in on me rubbing one out thinking about him.

I shook my head and finished packing my bag. Was it me? I could always get Alex to kiss me again. But there was no way he'd do it on his own. He was already tiptoeing around me like I'd turn on him any minute. That made me sad. I'd never hurt him, at least not intentionally. I walked into the living room with the bag slung over my shoulder. Alex, of course, was already ready, though I was a little surprised he'd waited for me.

"Good morning," I said, trying to sound cheerful.

"Morning," he replied without looking up from the research book.

I sagged. He wouldn't even look at me. I'd hoped that getting him to do the class project with me would help to resume some normalcy, but that wasn't looking to be the case. "You ready to go?" I shifted my pack.

"Of course." He shut the book and stood up in one fluid motion. I couldn't help but notice the grace with which he moved. I certainly wasn't graceful like that.

"Alex."

He looked over at me. Did I have the same circles under my eyes as he did? "What?"

I stalled out. What could I say? That I missed my friend? How things used to be? That I was having terrible nightmares about him disappearing? Or even better, that I was dreaming of making out with him and it was confusing as hell? All of these things I should have been able to talk to my best friend about and yet, I couldn't seem to say anything. "Nothing, we should get going. Don't want to be late."

He opened the door. "Since when do you care about being late?"

I caught a faint hint of teasing and glanced at him hopefully. "Since we have an actual test coming up."

"After class today, do you want to go to the dining hall and compare notes?"

I smiled. He was actually acting like his usual self. "Is that when you'll point out that I've been taking notes on all the wrong things?"

"Probably." He gave me a crooked grin.

The tension coiled inside of my chest loosened ever so slightly.

"Of course, this assumes that there are actual notes in your workbook and not just a bunch of doodles."

My grin faltered. It had been stupid to hope he hadn't seen the bookmark. I wasn't even sure why I'd started sketching him, and now he knew. I scrambled to come up with some kind of explanation that wouldn't dig me in any deeper than I already was.

"I didn't realize you were such an artist. It's a Shadow Demon, right? Self-portrait?"

My feet froze. He didn't know. He must not have seen the whole thing. Sure, it was nowhere near being done, but I'd thought for sure he'd seen both sides of the folded page. "Um, yeah..." He could assume whatever he liked.

"Have you always been a drawer?"

"I don't know, maybe? I've scribbled forever, though all it's ever done is get me into trouble."

"I can imagine, especially after you've tricked your friend into doing all the hard work." He bumped me with his elbow.

He'd made it a point not to touch me at all for days and my entire body was viscerally aware of the contact. My heart beat a little faster and my palms instantly started to sweat. I scanned him for any sign that the touch was anything more than a friendly nudge, but there was nothing. He was the same

Alex he always was. The bitter taste of disappointment filled my mouth. I swallowed it down and forced a laugh.

"I'll try to be a little more focused." Which would be a lot easier after I could figure out what was going on with me. I was even getting sloppy at the fight club. Neese didn't appreciate that his golden goose suddenly couldn't perform as advertised.

"It might also help if you weren't holding the book hostage. I could use it for those translations, you know."

"Right." Of course, the book. That was why he was looking at me funny. Not because I was acting weird. "I'm almost done." There was no way I was letting him get his hands on that book with the bookmark still inside.

The day's lessons were a blur. Most of the classes focused on review since the most weighted exams were coming up. Alex said that was normal, but I thought he was fibbing. Granted, I didn't exactly have stellar attendance where school was concerned, so maybe it was? It didn't really seem possible to have already gone through an entire semester. Though I supposed summer semesters were a little shorter. At any rate, it was more difficult to focus than usual since all I could think about was studying with Alex afterwards.

"Do you know what classes you'll sign up for in the fall?" Alex asked when we settled in the cafeteria. Unsurprisingly, the oval building was bustling with students.

I shrugged. I hadn't really thought about it. Honestly, I'd assumed we'd just take all the same again.

He gave me a considering look. "You should sign up for Advanced Spells."

"Why?" I asked, pulling out my notes, which mercifully were without too many sketches.

"I think you have a knack for it. And it's one of the few classes where you didn't really need any help."

"Yeah, but intro is basic and advanced..."

"Is not?" he finished for me.

I rolled my shoulders. I supposed it was a little excessive to take all the same classes together.

"I can't believe Vera is making everyone continue taking Battle Tactics," Alex continued in the wake of my silence. "She didn't even make it optional."

I let out a sigh, grateful for the topic change. I didn't want to take different classes than Alex. While it was nice that he'd be able to tutor me if we had the same course load, I knew the real reason had nothing to do with school and everything to do with the dreams keeping me up half the night. I pushed that line of thought away and cleared my throat. "I'm pretty sure she knows you don't like her. Maybe if you weren't so focused on that, you'd like the class more."

"I told you, it's not that I don't like her or that I don't like the class. I just don't see the point. The Rebellion is over. Why do we need battle training?"

I plucked at the frayed edge of a notebook and thought about all the ways a class like Battle Tactics could have helped me over the years. "Battle Tactics is more than training. It teaches you to trust your instincts. You never know when you might need to defend yourself, and if you do, you need to have confidence in your powers and your reactions." Which I currently did not.

"Wow, Matt, that was really enlightened." He stared at me for a minute that felt like an hour, his green eyes looking into me as if they could see every wayward thought I'd had over the last few weeks. When he finally blinked, it was as though a tether had been snapped. "Fine, I guess I can try to be a little more open-minded about it. Besides, it's not like I can do anything about it, anyway. Now show me what you've got."

I maneuvered my notes around the spoons stuck in the table. It was kind of awesome that this had become our spot, a place that was purely ours.

"Let's see," he mused aloud as he scanned through them.

I watched as his emerald eyes roved over each page, patiently waiting for him to make a pronouncement of deficiency. Suddenly, I realized he was on a page with no notes at all, just a picture that took up most of the space.

His fingers brushing lightly over the penciled sketch. "This is really impressive. Did you do this from memory?" He lifted his head to look at me and I got a better view of what he was referencing. It was a replica of the illustration from the book we were doing our research project on.

"What do you think about the extension of the report?" I asked, trying to shift the conversation back. The last thing I needed was him recognizing the similarities between the illustration and the bookmark sketch.

He turned to the next page and held back a relieved sigh. "I suspect it's because no one's taking it seriously. I overheard the TA say that they might just turn it into a rollover assignment."

"That wouldn't be too bad. I had no idea how difficult it was going to be to find information about that family."

"Same here, but I wouldn't get too excited. That would mean they expect a full-on research thesis. As in, not a few pages."

I didn't bother stifling my groan.

"It'll be fine, Matt. Trust me, the paper will be epic."

"I hope you're right. But that also means that I'm going to have to dominate this final."

Alex sat back and laced his fingers behind his head, his usual picture of self-confidence. The position made him look absurdly tall and relaxed. I envied him that, not just the height, but that it seemed like he'd had an easier life. "That's what you've got me for," he said with a smile.

It was nice to see him acting normal. Which made what I had in mind to figure my shit out that much worse. I tried not to think about it too much as we resumed studying. Apparently, my notes weren't as abysmal as I feared, and we made some good headway. Still, I wasn't taking any chances. I actually liked it here and wasn't ready to get booted. Plus, I still had to figure out my deal with Alex.

The week of finals, I stayed up every night studying until I went cross-eyed. I even skipped the fight club Tuesday and Thursday—I was too distracted to be any good. By the time I actually sat down to take the test, I was positive I was going to blow it. Alex naturally wasn't concerned and kept trying to convince me not to be as well, but I couldn't help it. True or not, it felt like a lot was riding on this one grade. Rather than join him back at the dorm, I lurked outside the classroom and waited for the grades to be posted. Alex had tried to explain that it could take days, if not weeks, to get the grades; mercifully, Vera had announced she'd be getting them to us by the end of the day of our last exam. No one wanted to talk about why she would do that, but her threat about failing loomed heavy on my mind.

I feared I'd put a groove in the ground as I paced the short stretch of hall. The door across from our Battle Tactics classroom opened and Vera walked out. I caught sight of someone in the room behind her, and for a moment, I thought it was Alex. Except it couldn't be: he hated her, and I knew for a fact he'd gone back to the dorm. The door swung shut with a thud and she walked over.

"I'm impressed, Matt."

I scowled at her. Just because I was here didn't mean I'd forgiven her for locking me up. I'd like to see how funny she thought it was if I warded her in a room for two weeks.

She let out an aggrieved sigh. "Let it go already. You were a flight risk. I'd already lost so many others. I couldn't take the chance that you'd bolt before I could get you here. Especially since you're doing so well." She held up a stack of papers and shuffled through them. "Here we are. It looks like you've brought up all of your grades across the board. Math and literature seem to be doing well. I'm a little surprised you didn't do better in Battle Tactics. I would have thought that was right up your alley."

She peered closer at the page with unmasked surprise. "Yet you are doing spectacularly well in Shadow Magic. I hope you consider enrolling in Advanced Spells." She winked. "Don't worry, I won't tell anyone. But I imagine you don't want to hear me prattle on about your classes."

I shuffled from foot to foot, eying the stack of papers, curious if anyone would be sent home.

"Here, this one is yours and I imagine Alexi won't mind you bringing him his." She held out the papers.

I snatched them and surveyed the page for the only grade I was worried about. I couldn't believe my eyes when I saw the 'B' next to Demonic History.

She glanced back at the room she'd left before saying, "History wasn't my best subject either, though I hear you have a killer thesis for Demonic History II next semester." She gave me a warm smile, I was tempted to return. "Congratulations, Matt. What are you going to do now?"

"Celebrate." I couldn't believe it; all of our hard work had paid off. I'd get to stay. Alex would be pleased.

Alex.

I switched the pages to see how he'd done. All As, no surprise there. Even then, I knew he'd want the paper.

"Any plans in particular?"

I narrowed my eyes at Vera. "Why?"

"There's no need to be defensive. I was just asking." She shook her head. "Go celebrate with your friend, Matt."

I took that as my dismissal and ran. When I opened the door to our room, Alex was sitting upside down on the couch with his feet over the top. Man, he was weird, but he was mine.

CHAPTER 22

TRUTH OR DARE

A

S itting upside down on the couch was undoubtedly odd, but it was what I usually did when left to my own devices. Plus, it made for some pretty hilarious views. Like Matt standing on the ceiling when he was actually standing in the doorway. I smiled at him, echoing the grin on his face. "I take it you got the grades?"

"Yep." He waltzed into the room with a box under one arm and a couple of papers poking out.

"Well, how did you do?"

He pulled out the papers, and they floated down onto my stomach. "See for yourself."

I picked them up and read over the first page. "These are mine." I wasn't too surprised at the final grades, though I certainly hadn't expected to get an 'A' in Battle Tactics.

"The other one, Alex."

I switched the pages and immediately spun so I was right side up again. The move was far too fast, and my head swam for a moment. "Matt, this is amazing! I knew you could do it. I told you'd knock out the Demonic History final."

He zipped around the couch holding a bottle and two glasses, as well as a few beers. "Which is why we're celebrating." He set the items down and started filling the shot glasses.

All of my happy, relaxed feelings vanished. "This didn't go so well last time."

He passed me the shot anyway. "Drink," he ordered.

"But, Matt..."

"Drink."

I did as I was told, and he refilled the short glass. "I'm serious, Matt, we can't just sit around and drink," I argued even as I knocked back what turned out to be tequila.

"You're right." He passed me a third shot. He held up his glass, and we downed them at the same time. "We'll just have to make sure we're doing something this time."

"Like what?" I scoffed, accepting the beer he passed me.

"We could play a game," he suggested before taking an additional shot and sitting on the couch.

"What sort of game? I swear if you say drinking, then I'm out."

"Okay, fine." He laughed. "What would you prefer?" He leaned into the cushions, looking completely relaxed, his dark hair fanning over his eyes.

"How should I know? It's not exactly like we have anything lying around." I scanned the room for the games we definitely didn't have. "I'm not really a fan of cards, not that I have any. That doesn't really leave much. I suppose there's always truth or dare." I chuckled, because no way were we playing that.

Matt leaned forward with a gleam in his eye. "Okay."

I did a double take. "Wait. What?"

"I said, okay. We can play truth or dare. You can go first."

My mouth opened and closed uselessly. He was serious. I noticed another shot sitting patiently on the coffee table. I tossed it back and shook off the burn. "All right, but rules." My tongue was already feeling a little fuzzy. There was also a noticeable lack of snacks by the alcohol, which was odd, considering Matt seemed perpetually hungry. If I didn't know any better, I'd swear he was intentionally trying to get me drunk.

"Rules," he mimicked, giggling.

Great, he's already tipsy.

Then I realized I was giggling, too.

"Enough. Focus, Matt." He put on an air of intense concentration and it took me a moment to pull it together enough to continue. "Okay, we can play, but you can't choose the same thing more than twice in a row. The third automatically has to be the other."

"What do you mean?" His face squished in confusion. It was adorable.

"I mean, you can't just choose dare. I know you, Matt."

He frowned. "That also means you can't just choose truth."

I stuck out my tongue, earning a cheeky grin.

"You go first."

"Does that mean I ask first or I pick first?" I took a sip of the beer he passed me.

He rolled his eyes. "Truth or dare."

"Truth." I laughed when he gave an even more exaggerated eye roll.

"What is the dorkiest thing in your room?"

I shrugged and swirled the half empty bottle. "I guess that depends on who you ask."

"I'm asking you."

"Um, I don't know." I went through a mental inventory of the things in my room for something he would deem dorky. "Oh! I have a poster of the university from when I was like seven."

He snorted. "You do not."

"I totally do. Okay, you: truth or dare."

"Dare"

"Of course." I fought the urge to roll my eyes right back at him. Maybe I could dissuade him from constantly choosing a dare by making the first one awful. I noticed he'd already kicked off his socks and shoes. I shifted and looked him dead in the eye with as straight a face as I could muster. "I dare you to lick the bottom of your foot."

He didn't even hesitate, just grabbed his ankle and dragged his tongue from heel to toe.

I cringed and gave a full body shake. "That's disgusting."

He coughed through a grimace. "No kidding." He washed away the taste with another shot of tequila and a swallow of beer. "Another?"

I accepted the fresh beer but declined the shot. "Truth."

"You didn't even let me ask. Fine, you want to play like that." He gave me a serious look, his eyes squinted and his luscious mouth pursed with intensity. "When was your first kiss?"

"Oh, goodness," I gasped and sat back. "I don't even remember."

"Liar."

"Busted. Alright, my first technical kiss would be Carla Rushing when I was ten." I ducked my head at the confession.

Matt spit out some of his beer. "No shit."

"But, the one that I would consider my first was Brandon later that year. For the record, I never saw it coming. What about you?" I asked.

He scowled behind his beer. "Hey, I didn't choose anything."

"You're choosing truth." I poured him a shot. "Come on, cough it up."

"Fine. I was twelve. Shut up," he added when I snickered. "It was Michelle Carter, and she told me I was terrible."

"You are definitely not terrible."

"Thank you," he said, clinking his bottle against mine. "I believe you are up for a dare."

I groaned. "Please have mercy."

"I don't know. You look pretty hungry."

I cocked my head to the side, dubious about where this might be heading.

"Go into the kitchen and pick whatever snack you want."

If feeding myself was the dare, then I wasn't going to complain. I vacated the couch, grabbed a bag of crisps from the cupboard, then plopped back down.

"Now, open it without your hands or feet."

I gaped at him. "How am I supposed to do that?"

"I don't know, it's your dare. Get creative."

I thought about it a moment and then tried to use my teeth, but the damn thing wouldn't hold still.

"Ah-ah. No hands."

"Curse you, Matt. I actually am really hungry." In a stroke of inspiration, I dropped the bag and caught it with my arm, then used the air already in the bag to force it open. The bag made a loud pop and crisps went everywhere.

Matt fell off of the couch he was laughing so hard.

"Shut up," I said through my own laughter. "Go get me another bag while I clean up this mess."

He returned with a couple as well as a few other snack items, which were a little more substantial. "I believe I'm up, and since you hijacked my last one, I'm going with dare."

"Alright, Mr. Daredevil, I dare you to do a body shot," I challenged, waving the half full bag of broken crisps.

He looked genuinely surprised. "Did you really just... Okay." He walked to the kitchen then returned with the salt shaker and some limes I didn't know we had. "Lift your shirt."

I clutched the bag to my chest. "What? Why?"

"So, I can do the body shot."

"Yeah, so? What do I need to lift my shirt for?" He reached out to lift it for me and I forced it back down. "Cut it out."

He gave me a scornful look. "You can't dare me to do something and then refuse to let me do it." He pointed at me. "That's cheating."

I dusted crumbs off, glad I hadn't sat back down yet. "I still don't see what my shirt has to do with this."

He stopped trying to move the article and looked back at me. "You have no idea what a body shot is, do you?"

I shifted uncomfortably. "No."

He shook his head, laughing to himself. "Well, you're about to learn. Quit being such a prude."

Stunned, I stopped holding the fabric down and let him lift the shirt to reveal my stomach.

"Damn," he whistled. "This just isn't even right. I mean, come on." His hand glided warmly over my exposed skin, and I flushed from head to toe.

"Matt," I tried to admonish, though I sounded more strangled than anything.

"I'm sorry, but it's not fair. Some of us have to actually try if we want to look like this." His finger traced along my abdomen while my breathing devolved into shaky panting.

"You look fine, Matt."

"Not like this, I don't." If he didn't stop touching me, we were going to have bigger problems than his lack of self-esteem.

"Would you just get on with it?"

"Alright." The flash in his eye was positively wicked. He grabbed a lime and squeezed it enough to get the juice out, then rubbed it on my abdomen. It seemed unnecessarily low to me, but then I didn't really know what this was supposed to entail. "Lean back a bit," he ordered.

"Why?"

"So, the salt doesn't just go on the floor." Curious about what he meant, I did it. He sprinkled salt where he had rubbed the lime and reached back to grab the shot he'd already poured.

Oh, no. Please don't do what I think you're going to do. Please no.

It was all wishful thinking. In one expert move, Matt tossed back the shot and then licked the salt right off of me. My eyes rolled into the back of my head and I prayed my knees wouldn't buckle.

Of all the things to dare him to do...

When I wasn't afraid I'd simply fall over, I looked down at him. He was sitting, just finishing the lime, and he still had that look in his eye. "You did that on purpose," I accused.

"You're the one who chose the dare. If it's any consolation, you would've liked the other version even less." The cushions puffed out air as he flung himself back, clearly unconcerned about what he'd put me through. "Truth or dare," he asked.

"Truth," I said by rote, almost instantly regretting the choice.

Please don't ask me what that was like.

"Have you ever cheated on anyone?"

"Absolutely not," I replied heatedly, then promptly knocked back another shot to settle my nerves.

"Have you ever been cheated on?" he followed up, no doubt registering my anger.

"That is technically a different question, but I'll give it to you. Yes, my ex cheated on me. It's one of the many reasons we broke up... again," I added belatedly. "Your turn. Truth or dare."

"Truth." He was definitely throwing me a bone.

"Where are you from?"

He only hesitated a moment. "Nebraska mostly. Ask another, it's only fair."

I thought for a moment. The answer didn't really give me what I'd hoped for, but I wasn't about to waste another question on it. "Tell me something you don't want me to know."

"The drawing isn't a self-portrait. Truth or dare?"

My head spun. If it wasn't a picture of him, then who was it supposed to be? He smacked my leg. "Fine, dare, since I technically had two truths."

There was nothing remotely sweet or innocent about the grin he gave me. "I dare you to do a body shot."

"You can't be serious. Choose something else." I scrambled for any way to stop this. "Isn't daring someone to repeat a previous dare against the rules or something?"

He shook his head. "Nope. A dare is a dare. Let's see if you were paying attention."

I snatched a lime off of the table and the salt shaker while he poured the shot. "You're one sick pup. Give me your arm." He looked skeptical, but did it. Faster than he could stop me, I repeated the process on his forearm. The lime was worse than the tequila. "There, happy?"

"That's not how you do it." To his credit, he looked properly scandalized.

"Body, by definition, includes the arm."

"There is a spirit of intent that you've violated. You can either do it right or your next dare is going to be worse. And don't think you can avoid it altogether by just choosing truth. By your own rules, you'll eventually have to choose dare."

I had zero desire to find out what his obviously demented mind could come up with that was worse than what he'd already dared me to do. "Matt, I can't," I pleaded.

"I could lie down if that would help."

I had a very clear picture of me licking his stomach and then just not stopping until I'd licked every part of him. I vigorously shook my head. "That won't help."

He gave me a small mercy by lifting his own shirt, which helped stave off my desire to do exactly as he'd done. I wanted to get it over and done with like I had with his arm, but I couldn't seem to force myself to go any faster. The smooth lines of his stomach and the way it moved as he breathed captivated me.

He flinched when the lime touched his skin. I added the salt and took the shot. His abdomen shivered as I tasted the crystals. It was only through an active force of will that I stopped at that. I ached to keep tasting him, to feel his soft down on my face, to kiss every inch of him, to...

"You're supposed to do the lime next." He sounded breathless.

I tossed the wedge straight up, and he caught it. "You do the lime." I sat back on the couch and rubbed my face. I knew this evening would end up being a mistake. The temptation, the want, was just too great.

He passed me a new beer and sat back down as well. "Dare."

"Tell me a joke." I was in some serious need of levity.

He chuckled. "Have you heard the one about the broken pencil?"

I looked up at him from behind my hand.

"It was pointless."

The awful joke was so unexpected I couldn't help but giggle. The harder I tried not to laugh, the more I did. "That was absolutely terrible. Where did you find that? A cereal box?"

"Actually, it was a piece of candy. Now you, Truth or Dare?"

"Truth." Maybe I could trick him into forgetting I'd eventually be due a dare.

"Of course." He tapped his bottom lip, and I couldn't help but envy his finger. "Okay, what's your greatest fear?"

"That no one will ever love me for all of who I am," I responded without really thinking.

"What do you mean?"

I sighed into the cushions. "Shadow Demons have a terrible rap, Matt. Sometimes I think the world will never be able to see us as anything more than monsters."

His face clouded over. "You can't think like that. It'll all get sorted eventually. Stop being so melancholy."

"You asked about fears," I reminded him.

"Yeah, but I didn't think you were going to get all sullen on me. Now snap out of it. We're having fun, remember? Dare."

"Fun, you said?" I raised an eyebrow at him. "Do the worm for twenty seconds. And don't pretend like you don't know what I'm talking about, everyone knows the worm."

He shook his head; the sun shining once more in his smile. "I don't know if I've ever actually done this before. Here goes nothing." His attempt at the worm was even worse than his joke, but he tried it. When he was done, he was laughing every bit as hard as I was. "Please, let's never talk of that again," he said as he resumed his seat. He poured us each another shot and leaned back.

I had to scoot closer to the middle in order to get it, though, because he'd overfilled it. We chinked glasses, making an even bigger mess, and drank together. "Dare."

"Balance what's left of the bottle on your head for ten seconds in a row." He snagged the half empty bottle and handed it to me.

It took three tries, but I finally got it positioned so it didn't immediately topple back over. Even then, I almost didn't make it because I started laughing. I removed the bottle and let it slide to the ground, then rolled my head to face him. He was curled up beside me, still smiling from my pathetic attempts at balance. I loved looking at him. I loved everything about him, even his stubborn nature and the way he seemed to constantly torture me.

"I guess it will be truth," he sighed, looking at me with those perfectly blue eyes.

"What do you want, Matt?"

"For you to kiss me."

I shifted so that I was fully facing him. I couldn't have heard that right. "What? Why?"

"It's not your turn. Truth or dare."

"Truth," I replied quickly. I wanted to get back to the other thing.

"Ugh," he gave an exasperated sigh. "Why does it matter?"

"Because I want to know. Now answer the question. Why?"

"Except I choose dare," he replied maliciously.

I knew exactly where he wanted me to go with that and I refused to give him the satisfaction. "Then I dare you to tell me the truth."

"That's cheating," he argued.

"The truth, Matt."

"Because I liked it, okay? Are you ha—"

My mouth was on his before he could finish. He felt even better than I remembered, and I easily fell into the desire I'd been avoiding for the last few weeks. None of this is real, I thought distantly. I'm actually passed out drunk on the floor and having a really good dream. He tasted amazing.

"Definitely not a terrible kisser," I said between kisses as I shifted to get a better angle. I didn't care if this was a dream. Or if I woke up and had to explain myself. I kissed my imaginary Matt deeper.

Then his fingers curled in my hair. He pulled and, at the sharp pain, I realized I was still awake, but he didn't pull me away. He pulled me closer.

"Matt." His name was scarcely more than a gasp. My heart beat frantically as it tried desperately to keep up with what was happening right now. He arched into me and I pulled him tighter. Kissing Matt was like kissing fire and the burn was so good.

"Alex."

I moaned at hearing him say my name. He was still giving as good as he got, his tongue dancing with mine and addling whatever was left of my senses. I couldn't get enough of him. I abandoned his mouth to kiss along his neck. The smell of him was driving me mad.

"Alex." This time, it was more of a groan.

I recaptured his mouth, and he fiercely returned the kiss.

His hand released my hair and drifted down to my chest. He gave a solid push and forced me back a few inches. "Alex, wait." He swallowed, his lips a delectable cherry from the fervor.

"What?" I felt delirious. The world was fuzzy and intangible. The only real thing in it was Matt.

"I need a minute." His breathing came in shallow pants, every bit as labored as mine.

I so wasn't done with him, not after a confession like that. I leaned forward, still completely lost to desire. How long was a minute?

"Alex, wait," he said, his voice stronger, less of a whisper. "I think... I think... Shit." He scrambled back, failed to get up, and shadowed through the couch to land with a solid thud on the ground. I watched as he staggered out of the couch, solidified, then raced to his room. He flung the door open and vanished inside, leaving me with nothing but my confusion.

Fog continued to cloud my mind as I followed him. With his door hanging open, it was practically an invitation. I flicked on the bedroom light. I'd never been in his room beyond that first day, and not much differed from then. Where mine had books and posters, his was bare walls. The only book was the one we were using for the research project, and it was sitting on the nightstand. Other than that, there was nothing, not even Matt.

Then I heard someone being sick. I looked towards the source. The bathroom door was cracked enough to show a strip of white light. I opened it the rest of the way in time to see him retch again. He saw me come in and rolled his head on his arm, which was propped against the seat.

"How you doin'?" I grabbed a towel and wet it with cold water.

"You mean besides being absolutely mortified?" He accepted the towel, and I shrugged. "I feel like I'm dying." He laid on the cold tile floor while I sat on the rim of the tub and watched him. He looked up at me, his blue eyes swimming. "Why don't you look as miserable as I feel?"

"I'm pretty sure you had twice as many shots as me."

"That would do it. Well, I've made a complete ass of myself. Thank Nyx we don't have class tomorrow."

"Can I get you anything?"

"Water would be great."

I left to get him a cup of cold water, but when I got back, he was out. Wasn't that just perfect? Now my drunk ass had to figure out how to get his drunk ass off of the floor. The good news was, it didn't matter how awkward I was, no amount of anything was likely to wake him up.

It was far from graceful, but eventually I got him on the bed. I briefly contemplated stripping him down and putting him under the covers, but dismissed it as an exceptionally bad idea. Instead, I grabbed the other side of the comforter and rolled him up like a burrito. I was having a good laugh at myself tucking him in when he grabbed my wrist. A look at his face said he was still sound asleep.

I tried to extricate myself, but he wasn't letting go. The harder I tried to get away, the tighter his grip got. On a whim,

I leaned down and planted a kiss on his forehead, lingering a moment. Instantly, he relaxed, releasing me.

What I wouldn't give to understand your secrets, Matt.

Finally freed, I made my way out, quietly closing the door behind me. The event had sobered me but, I still wasn't ready for bed. The dreams would never compare, anyway.

I looked around the dorm. The room was a total disaster. With a sigh, I set to putting it right again. When it resembled its usual state of disarray, I sat down on the couch to take stock.

How had any of this evening happened? Despite the truths I'd accumulated, I felt like I had infinitely more questions to the riddle that was Matt. But I knew one thing for certain—he'd absolutely kissed me back.

CHAPTER 23

GRANITE

M

My head pounded so hard I felt it in my eyeballs and my mouth tasted like something had died in there while I slept. Groaning, I shifted to get up and met resistance. I struggled to free myself from the constricting cocoon and toppled out of the bed fully clothed, followed by a mountain of comforter.

Alex.

Just thinking his name brought back memories from the night before. The game had been hilarious and fun, but the kiss had been absolutely epic. I was officially convinced that my dreams weren't some weird manifestations of finding out my best friend was gay. No, I wanted Alex to kiss me. I still wanted it. And I'd made a total and complete ass of myself.

I groaned again to the agony of my throbbing headache. How could I ever apologize for my behavior? My only saving grace was that I hadn't actually thrown up on him. Still, what I did do was bad enough. I'd cut that far too close, but I couldn't stop myself. I wanted more. Even now, I could feel it like a hunger growing inside. It was right next to the actual hunger that said my dumb ass hadn't eaten anything substantial last night.

I quickly changed and went out to the living room. All evidence of the night before was completely gone. The glasses, the bottle, even the chip remnants. Nothing remained. Then I saw Alex asleep on the couch. I walked over to see that he was still in the same deep purple shirt and gray pants as the day before.

He must've stayed up to get this place looking normal again.

What did that say? Was he upset? I felt cruel now for the body shot fiasco. It wasn't his fault he didn't know what it was, and it was wrong to force him to do it. I was a terrible friend. A terrible friend that dreamed about making out with their best friend and tricked them into kissing them.

Shame kept my feet moving. Rather than wait for Alex to wake, I quietly fixed myself a cup of water and set one out for him as well. My gaze lingered on his relaxed face. He seemed so peaceful with his quiet snore and messy hair. Then my focus dipped to his mouth. I licked my lips and fought the impulse to kiss him awake. With a soft sigh, I let the fantasy go. After one last glance back at his sleeping form, I slipped out, barely remembering to grab my key before quietly shutting the door.

Alone in the hall, I was just as lost. The only thing I was absolutely sure of was that I liked Alex kissing me. I liked it a lot. None of it made sense though. I'd never been even vaguely interested in any other guy before. But that was it, he wasn't any other guy. He was Alex, my Alex. Determined to find clarity before facing him again, I wandered off.

What I really needed was a way to clear my head so all of my thoughts weren't on top of each other. The way his hair had felt between my fingers. How his mouth molded to mine. The overwhelming mortification of puking after the most intense kiss of my entire life. I'd have gone straight to the fight club—fighting always gave me a single-minded focus—but given it was Saturday and they only met Tuesday and Thursday, that wasn't really an option.

Eventually, I found myself in the library. The massive building reminded me of a tomb some days, but now that summer semester was officially over, it was mercifully empty... and quiet. I weaved past several heavy tables until I found one that was nestled up by some shelves about halfway through the room. The chair didn't even squeak when I pulled it out and flopped down. I took a deep breath and let it out slowly. Distraction. Maybe I could make some headway on the Demonic History report for the fall class.

I took out our research book—Alex's book—and ran my fingers over the worn cover. The rough edges of the corners contrasted with the front and back, smoothed from years of loving hands. I knew now why Alex didn't want to tell me if the knight killed the demon. He didn't know. There were pages missing and everything before that was too vague to be certain.

The bookmark fell to the table. Without enough pages at the end, there was nothing to hold it. Alex was right about the image—it was a shadow demon. In fact, it was practically a modern adaptation of the illustration in the book. I unfolded the page to reveal the half that he apparently hadn't seen. Technically speaking, this part of the drawing was a self-portrait. I'd never been all that great at drawing myself, but there was no denying the figure across from the shadowed demon was me. He certainly looked every bit as lost as I felt.

With a frustrated growl, I replaced the bookmark and shoved the book back into my bookbag, angry at myself for being too much of a coward to be honest with Alex and basically sneaking out. He deserved better. Finding information about his favorite book wasn't much in the way of an apology, but it was a start.

The cavernous room seemed to swallow what little noise my footfalls made as I wandered through the stacks in search of answers. I walked past several daunting displays of books until I found the genealogy section. Surely, a family dedicated to hunting down an entire supernatural race would be mentioned somewhere.

After an hour of searching, all I had to show for my efforts was an absurd stack of ancient families and hands so coated in dust they looked gray. I flopped onto the floor and began methodically going through each one. Names like Guerreros del Sol seemed promising, but their order didn't start until the fifteen-hundreds. Then there was the Danai family, which seemed to have been around since the dawn of time. They were a twisted bunch, but they were necromancers, or at least I thought that's what the text meant. I couldn't imagine anyone being able to bring the dead back to life. But then I couldn't imagine a lot of what had happened in the last few months.

I let out a huff as I surveyed my collection. None of these had what I was looking for. But how did you find an obscure family that kept to the shadows? I was sliding the last book onto the return cart when I had an epiphany. If we were right and it was a love story, maybe something came of it—marriage, kids, something. I raced back to the genealogies with an eye for family trees on the Shadow Demon side this time. There wasn't much in the way of Shadow Demon lineage, so I grabbed them all and returned to my table. The librarian on duty eyed my haphazard collection skeptically, but didn't intervene or comment.

I stayed there well into the night, searching the books. It was rough going. The first couple of layers were full of countless demons, but as the timeline progressed, more and more holes showed up. I wasn't sure if that was because of deaths or because literally no one knew. I traced each line from an Original, careful not to skip lines or pages. It would have been much easier if the lineage behaved anything like a normal family tree. That would have been too easy. Across time, demons skipped in and out of relevance. Some disappearing for decades only to show up again in a different branch of the history.

I was getting a headache from reading the tiny script, and I desperately wanted a shower. Then I saw something that didn't quite fit with the rest. Next to some demon's name I didn't have a prayer of pronouncing was a very simple Matthias. No last name or descriptor. Just a name and a symbol. Except I'd seen that symbol before.

I slid open books aside until I found the only one I cared about—Alex's book. There on the cover was the same symbol: a torch topped by the sun, surrounded by what appeared to be black flames. I knew better though, those weren't flames, they were shadow.

My eyes sought the link again. There had to be more. I scanned the page repeatedly until, at last, I found a reference for the symbol in a footnote. The chair almost toppled to the ground as I launched out of it to go find the matching reference, earning me a reprising look from the librarian. I was pretty sure if the library had hours, she would've kicked me out by now. Yet I was the only one there and it was pointless to exact wrath on one lowly student. I gave her my best smile and continued on my way.

Quest accomplished, I took the book back to my ridiculous display of notes. The chair screeched against the floor and I flinched at the harsh sound. It felt like days since I'd heard anything above a whisper. But no way could I leave now. I was on the verge of a breakthrough. I could feel it. The matching reference book turned out to be a compilation of symbols and coats of arms. I scoured images until I found the one I was looking for.

If I'd thought the Denai family was old, these guys put them to shame. There was no family name listed though, just a translation of the coat and their creed. The Order of Light:

Where there is darkness, there is light, and the light will prevail. It sounded similar to what Alex had said to me at the start of school, except it was all backwards. There is always shadow: where there is light, there is darkness.

It was fitting, really. The light that battles the darkness, the darkness that tempts the light. Which reminded me of my earlier thought. If there was a connection listed between a Shadow Demon and a supposed knight of this order, had anything come of it?

Like so much of demon genealogy, it was difficult to determine the path, but at last I found what I was searching for—they had a child. I gasped so loud it echoed back at me. The librarian appeared around a corner and gave me a scathing look. I offered her a sheepish smile and sank into my seat, my gaze once more fixed on my miraculous discovery. Alex was going to lose his shit.

At the thought of seeing him again, my chest tightened. I couldn't face him, not after what I'd done. Mortified didn't even come close. I needed more time. Now that I'd got my mind off of things for a little while, I could tackle how to go about apologizing to Alex and making sense of why I wanted to kiss him until I passed out.

I scrawled down the information from each book, including relevant passages and page numbers. He'd kill me if we couldn't ever find the information again. Then I set about putting them all back on their appropriate return carts.

When I was done, I glanced out the large window. Bright rays of morning light pierced the tall windows to create a stunning rainbow of color. Was it possible I'd only been here twenty-four hours? It felt like so much longer. I considered asking the librarian exactly how much time had passed, but dismissed it. I'd caused enough ruckus in her domain already. Besides, it couldn't possibly be all that long, right?

The cheery chirps of birds and the soft babble of morning people replaced the quiet hush of the library. Besides the fact that I wasn't sure how much time had passed since I'd last slept, I definitely did not qualify as a morning person. Upside, at least my head had stopped hurting. I made a beeline for the cafeteria, grateful that I'd remembered to pack my dining card. However, no one had ever mentioned how much was on it or if it expired with the summer semester.

I held my breath as the cashier slid the card and eyed my outrageous pile of food. To be fair, it was a lot. I thought I'd gotten better over the last few months about not eating like it might be the last thing I'd have in a while, but once I'd started grabbing things, I hadn't been able to stop. It could have been because I was legit ravenous... or it could have been another excuse to put off returning to the dorm. Either way, I wasn't leaving until every bite of my meal was gone.

It was well past noon by the time I popped my last bite and ventured back outside. Even after all the stalling though, I still couldn't figure out what to say to Alex. I'm sorry didn't really seem like enough. I tightened the straps of my bookbag with all its treasures. Maybe distracting him with my mind-blowing discovery would help soften him up.

Or... I could kiss him.

Like karma for the renegade thought, something hooked my book bag and yanked me backward. "Hey! What the—" The angry retort died as my gaze fell on the blue iridescent scales shining in the sunlight.

Neese gave me a toothy smile. "Otto said I might find you here. You sure eat a lot for a scrawny thing."

"Who are you calling scrawny?" I snarled, jerking my back-pack to no avail.

"Easy there, runt." He scowled and lowered his voice to a sinister hiss that made my spine crawl. "There's a fight tonight. You in?"

Judging by his tone and the scary look he was giving me, it wasn't so much a request as a demand. Suddenly, I regretted wasting so much time. If I hadn't of been such a coward, I would've already been in the dorm. Now I'd have to wait even longer to see Alex, to tell him what I found... to tell him how sorry I was for everything.

I nodded, and Neese finally released my backpack. He stepped to the side so we could walk next to each other. Clearly, he didn't trust that I wouldn't make a break for it. If I had any measure of faith in my shadow walking abilities, I wouldn't have hesitated. But I wasn't Alex. Guilt stabbed at me. Just how long had I been gone? My optimistic belief that it had only been a full day and night seemed unlikely now.

I cleared my throat and glanced at Neese out of the corner of my eye. He may have had two legs, but it still looked like he was slithering. "I thought the fights weren't starting until next week."

He stopped and stared at me. "What day do you think it is?"

I frowned, but kept my peace.

Neese shook his head and let out a hissing laugh. "You must've raged pretty hard after finals to lose a whole day."

I let out a breath of relief. I'd been right. Only a day. Well, two now.

"Today is just for members. Thursday we'll bring in the fresh meat." He waved a dismissive taloned hand and resumed walking.

My steps faltered. "What? I thought you said it was only Saturday."

"Saturday? Oh man, you did hit it hard. I've done a lot of wild shit, but I can't ever say I lost three days." He gave me a skeptical look, but didn't stop.

I groaned. Alex was going to be pissed. I didn't know how to explain one night. How the hell was I supposed to explain three days?

"I hope you enjoyed your siesta, because you're in it now." Neese opened the door to the warehouse without a password. Then he pulled me through.

The club was absolute chaos. Otto must have been riling everyone up while Neese tracked down renegade members. Noise buffeted my ears, a stark contrast to the quiet I'd apparently been living in for the past few days. My thoughts from before about needing a fight to clear my head vanished. I didn't want to be here, and I didn't want to do this. I needed to talk to Alex.

"Yeah, Neese, this is great and all," I took a tentative step back toward the exit, "but I really gotta get going."

"What, you got a hot date or something?"

"No." I had a roommate that was probably gonna tan my hide for making out with him, then disappearing without so much as a note.

"Then you can fight." Neese grabbed the front of my shirt and jerked me deeper into the warehouse.

I tried to pull his hand off, but only managed to put holes in my shirt. "I have other things I have to do."

"Like what?" he asked, dragging me towards the ring.

Digging in my heels wasn't helping in the least. I thought about trying to shadow, but that wasn't as consistent as I let Alex think it was. Someone ripped my backpack off. Panic spiked through me, and I fought harder to get free. I couldn't stay here. I had to get back to Alex. Why had I ever joined this club in the first place?

"Alright, you little shit. What's the deal? Where do you have to be that's so important?"

"I... I..." I couldn't say it. My issues with Alex were none of his damn business.

"That's what I thought. Give you a few days' reprieve and you go soft on us. Just for that, you get to go first."

I shouldn't have swung at Neese. I knew better. He easily avoided the assault, and I fell forward. The people I bumped into were more than eager to help me the rest of the way until I landed in a heap of limbs in the open space and left to my fate.

"Hey Granite, you ready for a rematch?" Neese called, his voice rising over the jeers from the crowd.

"You bet your scaly ass I am."

The distinct rumble of knuckles made of stone cracking came from behind me. I spun around and cursed. Granite looked more imposing than ever as he stepped into the ring with a leering smile. This was so not going to be my night.

"I've been waiting for you, you little brat." He walked around me and I kept turning to keep him in sight. "Let's see how you do when I actually know what I'm up against."

Double—no—quadruple shit. He'd finally figured it out. I spied the metal door behind him, having gone full circle, and my pack beside it. The only way out was through Granite and I needed out. I walked to the edge of the ring and Granite's rumbling laughter followed me. At the edge, I heard Neese's own hissing chuckle. I ignored both of them and reached out to push people out of the way.

Inches from the nearest person, my fingers met resistance and the air between us flashed a brilliant blue. Mind-numbing electricity ripped through my arm. I yanked back the appendage and cradled it against my chest while Neese, Otto, and pretty much everyone roared with laughter.

"What the hell?" I flexed my hand and winced against the pain. This definitely hadn't been here before.

Neese ran his long tongue over his pointed teeth and smirked. "We had a feeling you might run, especially after you no-showed on Thursday. So, we invested in a witch." He glanced over his shoulder at a girl dressed in spiked boots with black lipstick. "The spell may not be demon-specific, but it'll hold just about anything. Even you."

I swallowed back the bile crawling up my throat and hoped like hell terror wasn't written all over my face. The last time I'd been this scared, I'd been trapped in an alley with a bunch of masked guys wearing white, military-like jackets. "Please, Neese. Let me go." Despite my best efforts, my voice still shook.

Neese rewarded my desperate plea with a grin straight from the deepest depths of hell. "You can leave after the fight."

I stared at him for a long second in which neither of us blinked. He might as well have issued a death sentence. Granite knew I was a Shadow Demon. Whatever advantage I had before was nonexistent now. Braced for defeat, I turned toward Granite and a fist like an avalanche plowed into my face. The hit sent me reeling into the electric boundary so hard I bounced back and fell to the ground. I struggled to my feet and intentionally did not touch my face. The cheap shot had definitely broken my nose.

Angry, I raced towards him. He easily danced out of the way, and his fist crushed into my side. The bile I'd swallowed earlier threatened to return with a vengeance as pain washed through me and a disturbing crack filled the air. I grunted and stumbled, clutching my aching side and swinging wildly with my free hand.

If I could focus, get my head in the game, I might stand a chance, but with every hit, all I could think about was Alex.

The way he smiled when I got a question right. How he always had an encouraging word no matter how down I was feeling. The hint of lavender that infused his skin. How his hair always did whatever it wanted. The soft press of his lips as he kissed me in a way I'd never known I needed.

Granite grabbed me by the ruff and threw me into the barrier again. The electric charge surged through my body and I curled into a ball as I hit the ground. Without focus, I was nothing but a rag doll. Small, inconsequential. Nothing. All the things I'd been before Alex.

Ringing filled my ears as I pushed up from the grit covered floor. No sooner was I upright, then yet another solid wall of rock knocked me back down. I shadowed out before he could kick me in the ribs. When I re-materialized, though, it was in exactly the same spot and just in time for the second attempt.

Pain ripped through my side yet again and I fell to my hands. I wanted to tell him to stop, that he'd won, I just wanted to leave. But I could barely breathe, let alone beg. I tried once again to stand, only to have an elbow crack into the back of my neck. The world went dark as I slammed into the ground.

When I came to, someone had dragged me over by the door. Feeling like a giant bruise, I pulled my backpack closer and carefully slipped it on. I eased my way up the wall while waves of pain threatened to make me vomit right there on the floor. I forced the nausea down and staggered out of the warehouse. If I could've shadowed to the dorm, I would've, but that was substantially beyond me at the moment. So, I walked. It was slow going, but one way or another, I'd get back to Alex.

TEQUILA STRAIGHT

A

One of these days, I was going to learn not to drink with Matt. All it did was make sure I made a fool of myself. I still wasn't sure how much of the night had been real and how much imagined. Had he really said he wanted me to kiss him, or had that just been a product of wishful thinking on an uninhibited mind? That I hadn't seen hide nor hair of him in days suggested the latter. He could be pretty bad with avoiding things he didn't want to talk about, but this was taking it to a new level. At least when he was avoiding me before, he was still coming back to the dorm.

Whatever his issues or reasons, though, I needed to talk to him. We couldn't go on like this. It had been hard enough pining for him in secret. That was gone now. He knew I was interested in him beyond friendship and we'd kissed... passionately. Just thinking about how he'd pulled me closer made me uncomfortable in all the best ways. We were definitely overdue for a conversation.

There was one glaring problem, however. I couldn't find him. After I'd woken up Saturday, the only sign of Matt was the rinsed glass by the sink and the fresh cup of water he'd left on the coffee table. I searched everywhere, but he was nowhere to be found. Not in his room. Not at the cafeteria. Not in the training rooms. I'd even bumped into a few classmates that hadn't gone home after finals, but they hadn't seen him either.

Apparently, wherever he'd holed up didn't have prying eyes, or at least none of the places I thought he might be hiding.

Exhausted after yet another fruitless day of searching, it was time to face the truth I'd been avoiding with every cell in my body. Matt was gone. He wasn't coming back. And it was my fault. There was always a chance that I was wrong, that this time when I returned to the dorm, it wouldn't be empty. Despite the hopeful thought, I wasn't really optimistic. A couple of days I could understand, but four was decidedly intentional. Honestly, I wasn't sure why I was so determined to find him. He clearly wanted nothing to do with me. Maybe Daniel had been right all this time, and I was the problem. I swallowed past the sudden lump in my throat and realized I was staring at the lush green carpet outside our... my dorm room.

The door opened as silent as ever. My gaze instantly fell on Matt's pack sitting by the couch like it did every other day. It looked like it had been slung there and some of the contents had spilled out. I frantically sought his door. It was closed. I didn't care about respecting his privacy, I just wanted to see him. I was halfway there when the door slammed shut behind me.

"Alex? It's about fucking time."

I froze and looked around. At last, I found him stretched out between two of the kitchen chairs. His head was tilted back so I couldn't make out his face. However, I could clearly see the almost empty bottle of tequila on the table beside him.

"Where have you been? I need your help," he grumbled.

"Me? Where have you been? I've been worried sick." It was only when the words were out that I realized how true they were. I'd practically been beside myself when no one seemed to have a clue where he'd vanished. I walked over as he casually dismissed my concern with a wave of his hand.

"'Mere. Need you to make sure my nose is straight."

"What?" I stepped close and stifled a gasp at seeing the state of his face.

He rolled his head slightly to look at me, but his blue eyes were murky and lacked focus. "Make sure the damn thing is straight. I've gone this long and I'm not about to let one cheap shot land me with a crooked nose."

I battled with my shock and floundered for words that wouldn't come. Who had done this to him? Why was his nose broken? What did he expect me to do about it?

"Are you just going to stand there? Isn't it bad enough that I had to set the damn thing myself? Which hurt like hell if you were wondering."

"What even happened?" I asked, still perplexed about how we'd gotten here.

He scoffed. "Someone hit me in the face, obviously. Just look at the blasted thing."

"I don't even know what I'm looking for." I leaned over to get a closer look. Whoever had done it had not been small. The bruise around his nose looked like it would cover half of his face at least once it set.

"All you have to do is see if it is smooth. You know what my nose is supposed to look like. Make sure it does."

I leaned in more, stopping just shy of actually touching him, and squinted to inspect the damage. I could see where the break must have happened by the thin red line. As far as I could tell, it looked just as straight as ever.

"Matt I..."

His lips brush against mine and the words drifted off. I looked down at him just in time for him to crane his neck and steal another. After all of my anxiety over the last few days, I couldn't help but kiss him back. I hadn't imagined it, he really wanted to kiss me. The kiss grew more aggressive, and I pulled back.

"Matt, I don't want to hurt you." There was no way kissing was pleasant with an injury like that.

"Alex, I haven't been able to feel my face for the last twenty minutes." His hand slid through my hair and he pulled me back down so our lips could meet once more. Michelle Carter was a fucking idiot. Matt was an incredible kisser.

Every cell in my body was hyper aware that this was the first time Matt had initiated a kiss. It didn't even matter that he was drunk yet again. Alright, it mattered a little, but I was too busy drowning to properly care. I loved kissing Matt. There was a whole other world there waiting to be discovered. Would there ever be a day that I wasn't totally lost in him?

The chair screeched as it threatened to slide out from under him. I wrapped an arm around his waist to make sure he wouldn't fall. At the contact, though, he let out a pained hiss.

My worry returned tenfold. "What?"

"It's nothing," he mumbled, "just my side."

"Your side?"

"Yeah, but really, it's nothing. Don't worry about it." He dropped his propped legs to the floor and shifted to get up.

I forced him back down and lifted his shirt. His side was a mass of bruises, black, blue, yellow, purple, pretty much every color but normal skin. "What the hell happened?"

"I lost. It's not a big deal." This time, he succeeded in straightening, but remained seated. He snatched the tequila from the table and took a swig directly from the bottle. Small wonder he was three sheets to the wind.

"Lost what? A fight? When were you in a fight? How many fights have you been in? That doesn't look like one fight, Matt. How often are you getting into fights?" And how many times could I say fight in ten seconds?

He squinted at me, confusion evident on his bruised face. "Where did you think I went every Tuesday and Thursday?"

"I don't know." I threw up my hands. "Hanging out with your friends. WHy the hell would I think you were fighting?"

His gaze dropped to the floor. "I do hang out with friends... sometimes... after."

Anger that rivaled how furious I'd been when I'd discovered Daniel had cheated on me burned in my veins. I'd been literally sick with worry and he was voluntarily traipsing off to get his ass handed to him?

Matt must've recognized the mounting rage on my face, because he rose to his feet, holding onto the back of the chair for balance. "Look, can we talk about this later?" He took a shaky step and stopped when I blocked the way. "Unless you're planning on joining me while I pretend to take a shower, you'll have to excuse me."

I quietly fumed as he slowly made his way around me and hobbled towards his room. No matter how I felt, there was no point in trying to talk to him in his current state. Days of worrying about what was going on and this is what I came back to? If he wasn't already such a disaster, I'd have throttled him myself. I glared at what remained of the tequila. Without a second thought, I dumped it out and trashed the bottle. Then I yanked the chair Matt had been sitting on around so I could watch his door. I didn't know how long he'd be gone, but I'd be damned if I wouldn't be ready to give him an earful when he reemerged.

I stopped watching the clock as yet another hour crawled by. Three cups of coffee in and I was wired. There wasn't a chance I'd fall asleep this time and miss him. Even after several hours of waiting, I wasn't sure what I wanted to say to him. All of my rehearsed conversations from Friday night were distant compared to the anger that refused to abate. Fighting regularly? I couldn't fucking believe it. And I hadn't had so much as a clue until now. Livid didn't come close, and I didn't even know which part made me the angriest.

Matt's door slowly swung inward, and he made his way into the living room. His eyes sought me out right away, and while decidedly uncertain, at least they were clear now.

"How are you feeling?" I asked, doing what I could to maintain some level of calm.

He swallowed and darted an anxious look at me, like he'd caught the edge I was trying to hide. "Better."

"Still drunk?" I didn't bother to temper my clipped tone.

He winced. "No. Alex, I—"

"Are you out of your damn mind! Fighting on campus? Do you have any idea what the school would do to you if they found out?"

"It wasn't on campus. It's not for that reason."

That he already knew about the consequences somehow infuriated me more. "You can't be serious. So, this is like a real thing? You just traipse off every Tuesday and Thursday to some... some... bruiser club."

"I don't understand why you're so upset. It's not like you got your ass beat to a pulp," he snapped.

I gawped at him. "Upset? I'm not upset, Matt. I'm way past upset. How could you not tell me?"

"Why would I? It had nothing to do with you."

"Because I'm supposed to be your best friend! That's the sort of thing you share."

His face crumpled. "I didn't think."

His obvious hurt pained me, but I pushed it aside. I was hurt too, and I felt used, something I'd never expected to feel from Matt. "Of course not. You're just off in your own world and I'm collateral to use whenever it's convenient."

He took a step toward me. "That's not true."

"Where have you been the last few days? Have you been fighting the whole time?"

He shook his head, then seemed to regret the move. "No. I was in the library."

"Why?" I didn't bother to hide my disbelief.

"I needed somewhere to figure things out, and I lost track of time."

"For four days? You can't expect me to believe that." I crossed my arms and fought the urge to clench my jaw. "Did you at least figure out whatever apparently required absolute solitude?"

He shuffled his feet like he did any time he was anxious. "Sort of. I found something about the research project. I was coming back to show you when—" He took a step towards his discarded bag.

"Would you forget the damn book!" I couldn't remember the last time I'd yelled so much. I hadn't even yelled when I found out Daniel was cheating.

Matt stood there looking like some lost, injured puppy.

I couldn't do this. I hated seeing that I was hurting him. I hated knowing he was already in pain. And I hated how much he'd hurt me. I dropped my arms. "I'm not having this conversation anymore. You can do whatever you want. Get kicked out of school for all I care."

"Alex."

I ignored the plea in his voice. There was nothing he could say that would make this better. "Don't." I turned to go to my room. I needed space. I couldn't breathe. Then a fresh wave of anger flashed through me and I spun back around, startling him. "And another thing, try not getting totally smashed the next time you want to kiss me." With that, I slammed my door and finally lost whatever composure I had left.

No amount of deep breathing could alleviate the tightness in my chest. The whole episode smarted of a breakup, except we weren't dating. We weren't even anything close to resembling a couple. My deep breaths turned shaky. I couldn't do this. I'd never been in love with my best friend before, and it was proving impossible.

That brought me up short. When had I started thinking of Matt as my best friend? I knew I was completely head over heels since day one, but this was an entirely new level. Was that why the betrayal hurt so much? The worst part of all of it was that there was no one to talk to about it with. Who could understand? Lacking any better option, I called my mom. She picked up, eager as ever to hear how things were going.

"It's so good to hear from you, Lexi." Just hearing her voice helped relieve some of the pain that had taken up residence in my chest. She knew how I felt about Matt, though I hadn't shared any of the recent fails. "Tell me about finals. Surely, you're done by now. Have you gotten your results?"

I struggled to keep my tone light. "Um yeah. Finals were fine. All As."

"I'm so proud of you, honey."

"Thanks, mom. I admit I didn't expect to get one in Battle Tactics though."

She tsked. "I still don't understand why you need that class. I thought you said the war was over."

"It is. Think of it like a just-in-case class. Plus, it teaches us to trust our instincts and our powers." I almost choked. The words were nearly identical to what Matt had said to me.

"Alexi, are you alright?"

I was too busy holding back the beginnings of a sob to answer. Why did it hurt so much? I'd known nothing would ever come of my hopeless infatuation, and yet, some deep part of me had foolishly dared to dream.

"How did Matt do? Was he able to pull up his grades?"

I hadn't even made it five minutes. A sob that sounded like it'd been torn from the depths of my soul broke free.

"Alexi, honey, what's the matter?" Between heartbreaking sobs, I told her everything—from Matt finding out I was gay, to him disappearing for half a week and our horrible fight.

"I just don't know what to do, Mama," I blubbered.

"Shh, shh. It'll be okay, sweetheart. I know this is hard. It sounds like you have some tough choices ahead of you. Like you both do."

"And what choice is Matt making? He's not gay. If anything, he's too drunk half of the time to even be confused."

"You don't know that."

I scoffed, bitterness filling the hollow space left by my tears. "Please don't. Wishing it won't make it true."

"Then I guess you'll be deciding for yourself."

"I don't know if I can." I glanced toward the closed door I was positive he was hovering on the other side of. "He... he... doesn't take no for an answer." I dropped my voice and added in a whisper, "And I don't know if I can live in a world without him in it." I expected her to say I was being melodramatic. What I didn't expect were the options she laid at my feet.

"Ultimately, it's your choice, Alexi. You can stay and be miserable just so you can be near him or you can leave and try to find happiness again. But don't decide now, you're too worked up. Give it a few days, see if things settle down. Just putting it out there, but you could try actually talking to him."

"I yelled at him. Does that count?"

"Alexi Roman, you did not."

I flinched at the scandalized rebuke. "But-"

"No buts, that does not count. I mean a reasonable, level-headed conversation where you both lay all your cards on the table."

"Except Matt doesn't talk about things," I argued, "at least not personal things. He keeps everything bottled up. Mama, I don't even know where he's from. The most I got him to admit is 'Nebraska mostly'."

"What does that even mean?"

"That's what I'm talking about. Anything else and he's a bloody open book with the words written right on his face. But when he shuts down, a crowbar couldn't get in there."

My mother let out a heavy sigh. "I'm sorry you're going through this, Alexi. It breaks my heart to hear you're hurting. I wish I could be there for you, or better, we could afford for you to come home for a little while, get some space before the fall semester."

My shoulders caved inward. "I didn't mean to make you feel bad, Mama."

"You're not, Lexi, I promise. I'm just worrying and wishing I could do more like any mother would."

"Thanks for listening."

"Always. You know I love you and I'll always be here for you. I'm sorry I don't have more guidance to offer. But I really do believe you need to have a genuine talk with Matt. Try not to assume it will go as bad as you think. He might surprise you," she said, infusing her voice with more blind optimism than any voice had a right to have.

Surprising me was one thing that Matt was very good at. They just weren't always good surprises.

ICE CREAM FORGIVENESS

M

Alex was mad, like really mad. In the months since I'd known him, he'd never raised his voice like that, and that included when I'd gotten kicked out of class. But as much as the shouting had shaken me, it didn't compare to hearing him sobbing in his room. And it was all my fault. I hadn't even gotten a chance to show him what I'd found about our knight—which really felt like a half-baked apology now. To top it off, my body hurt like hell. I was tempted to seek out the healers on campus, but couldn't bring myself to follow through. I deserved every agonizing second it took to heal for what I'd done to Alex.

Everything he'd said played over and over in an endless loop. I'd been so preoccupied trying to figure out my issues that I never stopped to consider how it would affect him. He was absolutely right—I'd betrayed our friendship. Why hadn't I told him about the fight club?

It took me days to admit it to myself, and the answer only solidified how horribly I'd messed up. I hadn't told him, be-cause I didn't want him to know. I knew he'd disapprove, and I didn't want to feel guilty. The joke was on me though. I felt guilty anyway.

I dragged my backpack into the kitchen and flopped into a chair, where I fingered the torn strap. It wouldn't last much longer thanks to whatever asshole had taken it from me at the club. Thankfully, everything inside had escaped the rough treatment unscathed. I pulled out Alex's book. My vision blurred as I caressed the worn cover. I swallowed thickly and blinked back the sting of tears. Since he'd blown up at me—justifiably—I'd barely caught so much as a passing glance of him. Forget whether I could come up with an adequate apology. How was I supposed to give it to him if he was avoiding me?

Considering I hadn't actually come up with a way to atone and I wasn't much for talking, I opted to use being physically present as my mode of communication. I'd told him before that I wasn't going anywhere and now I felt like I had to prove it. But the silence was driving me mad. I missed Alex's constant chatter, his physical presence. It didn't take much to realize his persistent absence from my days was why all of my dreams had taken a hard right. Gone were the toe-tingling intense dreams with the power to make me squirm. Now there were only nightmares of Alex leaving... forever. I couldn't bear it if he left. Everyone always left. And though I tried not to think about it, beneath all of my fear and guilt was still the overwhelming desire to kiss him again.

I thought hard about what he'd said about my always being drunk. He was right. I was too scared to admit what I wanted and had used alcohol to get it without taking any responsibility. So, I was not only was I a terrible friend but also a total coward.

My grip tightened on the pages of notes I'd pulled out of my bag. The crinkle of paper filled the oppressively quiet room. I let out a sigh and set them down, determined to organize the jumbled mess into something that actually made sense. I'd just finished straightening them back out when I heard the soft snick of a door opening.

I glanced up from my carefully chosen seat at the breakfast table. By some miracle, I caught Alex's eye, but he immediately looked away to gaze aimlessly around the room. Without school papers everywhere, the dorm was disturbingly clean. While he was distracted, I took stock of his overall appearance.

Smudges of gray darkened his normally bright eyes, making his face appear gaunt and sunken. Even without the massive bruise on my face, I could tell they matched the circles under mine. His shoulders sagged like he'd somehow shrunk, which seemed an impossible feat for someone so tall. And yet, he seemed smaller, more fragile. The sound of his broken sobs haunted my dreams and were definitely taking their toll on him. Clearly, neither one of us was sleeping.

I wanted to say something, but was afraid that talking might scare him back into his room. So far, this was the longest we'd been in the same general space in a week. He sighed and tilted his head back to stare at the ceiling. He was always fantastically lean, but it looked like he might be even thinner than normal. I was afraid he wasn't eating, though of course, I wasn't really, either.

Alex rolled his head to the side to look into the kitchen, and I quickly resumed my study of the papers in front of me. I heard him grab a glass from the cabinet and fill it with water. Then, to my infinite surprise, he pulled up a chair. I glanced up, daring to hope that today might actually involve words. Time stretched on, filled only with the sound of pen on paper as I continued to transfer the notes to a clean page.

"I'm still mad at you," Alex said, breaking the silence.

I glanced at him. He only caught my eye for a moment, but it was enough to feel yet another stab of guilt. What had I done to my friend? "Okay."

I was debating whether to say something else when he let out a sigh that caused his shoulders to fall even more. He stood without another word and returned to his room, leaving the empty glass. It wasn't much, but it was progress. There was hope. I could still fix this. What I needed was a peace offering. Something totally neutral that wasn't likely to get me into even more trouble. Normally, the research I'd gathered probably would've been perfect, yet after his callous comment about the book, it seemed best not to press my luck. No, I needed something totally mundane and not remotely supernatural.

I packed up my notes and went in search of my nameless item. All I could hope was that I would know it when I saw it. There were plenty of possibilities to choose from that might have worked. But I didn't want mights and maybes. I needed a ringer.

After what had happened the last time I ventured out, I was substantially more cautious. The last thing I needed was to get snatched again. My ribs had mostly recovered, and I wasn't eager for any other rematches. Accelerated healing was great and all, but it didn't make the process any more comfortable. After all of my years trying to avoid fights, I still wasn't sure what had possessed me to keep going back to that damn club. Sure, earning money was nice, but I didn't actually like fighting for my life.

I wasted the better part of the day wracking my brain for something to show Alex how sorry I was. Then I remembered Alex believed ice cream fixed everything. I swung by the dining hall and loaded up with our favorites—including every carton of strawberry they had—then headed back to the dorm as fast as I could before they all could melt. It wasn't until I was in the hall leading to our room that I wondered if it would all fit in the freezer.

A few doors away from ours, I had to stop when a guy stepped out of his room carrying a precarious stack of metal and cables. He squatted down to sit them on the floor and I shifted to go around. A thin plastic case tumbled free as he straightened up to close the door.

I squinted to make out a title. "What do you have there?"

"Oh this?" The guy pointed to the heap of electronics. "It's my old gaming unit. My grams just sent me a new one. Why?"

It was perfect. Neutral. Normal. Distracting.

"What do you want for it?"

He checked out the bag I was carrying. "What do you got?"

"Ice cream."

"Sold. Here, there are even some games."

I traded him half of the ice cream and accepted the console. He probably would have given it to me for free, but it didn't matter, it was mine now. Now all I had to do was get Alex to play it.

Inside our dorm, there was no clear sign of Alex. I successfully put away the frozen goods and install the unit before he emerged from his cave again. He ghosted around a few minutes before finally settling on the couch. It was the first time he'd done that in days, so I chose to see that as yet another sign of hope. I quickly retrieved two pints from the freezer.

"Hey," I called. As he turned, I tossed him the strawberry. He wasn't expecting something to be thrown at him and almost dropped it. For a couple of shimmering seconds, it was like nothing was wrong. He was his usual self. I walked over and sat on the back of the couch, cracking open my container.

"You know a spoon would be—"

I held out a spoon for him, and he looked from it to me before accepting it.

He scooped up a bite and paused without taking it. "Matt—"

"It's fine, Alex. You have a right to be angry. I should have told you about the fight club." I stared into my frozen treat and mustered up the courage to be honest. "I... I didn't tell you, because I didn't want you to know."

He narrowed his eyes and slowly took a bite.

I rushed to elaborate, realizing too late how that must sound. "Because I didn't want you to think less of me. I don't even know why I kept going. I guess it was just nice for people to be afraid of me for a change." I bit into a frozen chunk.

He sighed, looking pensive as he scooped another spoonful. As apologies went, it wasn't the worst one I'd ever done, but there was really no way to make it right. It was already done. All that was left was to be honest about it.

Alex gestured with his spoon at my recent acquisition. "What's that?"

"Some kid down the hall was getting rid of it because he has a new one."

"That's wasteful."

"Agreed. He said nothing's wrong with it. Even gave me the controllers and some games."

"Should we see if it works?"

I diligently schooled my face from erupting into a grin. It was working. "I'm game if you are."

He hesitated a moment, then gave a small laugh under his breath. Joy surged inside of me at yet another sign I was making progress. While he inspected the selection, I put away what was left of the ice cream, then joined him on the floor. The cords for the controllers stretched over the coffee table, which he'd pushed out to give us more room.

"So, what are we playing?" I asked, sitting close enough to be present without crowding him.

He gave me a crooked grin that made my heart stutter. "Since we're apparently doing puns today, I went with Demon Crusader. It says it can have two players, though I'm not really sure how that will work."

"One way to find out." The console fired up no problem, and before long, the sounds of the game filled the room.

We played in silence, though it was substantially more companionable than the quiet I'd endured over the last week. The mechanics of the game were fairly simple, and after a while, I was confident enough to glance at Alex. He looked like he was actually having fun. That made me happy. Maybe I could fix this mess I'd made after all. Of course, there was still one more thing I had to take care of: I had to prove to Alex that I didn't have to be totally smashed to want to kiss him.

We paused at a checkpoint. While the game saved our progress, Alex excused himself and I grabbed a beer. I popped it open and sat it on the coffee table.

"What do you think of the game?" he asked, giving the beer a sidelong look as he resumed his seat. I wasn't even sure why I'd grabbed it. I didn't really want it, and it completely contradicted what I was trying to prove. My nerves were getting the better of me.

"It's not too bad. Though you would think someone would tell the creators that's not what demons look like. I mean, we don't have horns or wings and none of the other demons I've met do either."

Alex shrugged. "I don't know. Every myth has its roots in the truth somewhere. Maybe there was a time we did." He picked up the controller, and we resumed playing. He continued to glance at the neglected bottle throughout the game. Maybe grabbing it wasn't such a bad idea after all, he could clearly see that I wasn't drinking it.

I watched him, waiting for some comment or opening. There was only one thing I could think of to do to show him I didn't just want to kiss him with alcohol eliminating my inhibitions. Except I was so nervous, I could've really used that drink. Even nervous, though, the desire to kiss him was overwhelming. As much as I'd fought it before, there was absolutely no denying that it was exactly what I wanted.

I need to quit being such a chicken and just go for it.

"Alex." I shifted to face him.

"What's up?" he asked, turning to me.

I caught him in a kiss before he could say anything else. There was a moment when I thought he wouldn't kiss me back. Then there it was. I cupped the side of his face and kissed him deeper. He needed to know this was intentional, not some half-assed accident. At the feel of my hand, he relaxed into it a little more. I fought to hold myself back from completely drowning in the sensation. This needed to be as different as possible from all the other times.

The sound of something suffering on the screen invaded my concentration. I pulled away and leaned back against the couch. Alex sat there a moment looking a bit dumbfounded. I could have giggled with delight. I'd done it. I'd actually done it. And not a drop of alcohol. "You're dying," I said absently as I tried to regain control of my own character.

He turned blankly back to the game and rescued his demon before he could be fully minced.

I felt incredible. Kissing Alex sober was a thousand times better than I would have expected. It hadn't been nearly enough, but it was a start. I was probably grinning like a fool, and I couldn't have cared less. I'd done it. Suddenly, Alex's character abandoned the current mission and raced towards the next glimmering check point.

I frowned. "What are you doing?"

"Damn it, Matt." He vehemently threw down the controller.

Alarm shot through me. Somehow, I'd still made things worse. I set aside my controller and immediately started trying to apologize. "Alex, please don't be mad. I—"

He cut me off with a kiss I felt all the way in my toes. I gave in completely, melting into the soft press of his lips, his tongue confidently twirling with mine, the warmth of his hand on my cheek.

Kissing Alex sober really was like falling into a world of color I'd never even known existed. It was a drug, and I was absolutely addicted. My body reacted on its own, leaning into him, craving more, always more. His fingers slid through my hair as he pulled me closer. I moaned. This was everything I'd been dreaming about for weeks. Even more than his forgiveness, I'd wanted this, wanted it to the point it physically hurt. And now, I felt like I was spiraling out of control in a world of sensation.

I slipped and braced myself against the ground. Alex's free hand drifted down my side until it found bare skin where my shirt had ridden up. I hadn't been expecting that and broke off with a muffled gasp.

"What? What's the matter?"

What is wrong with me?

He looked me over frantically, concern clouding his face. "Are you still hurt? I would have thought by now..."

"It's not that." My heart hammered so hard I thought it might burst right out of my chest like one of the minions in the game.

His emerald gaze caught mine and I could clearly see my panic shining back. Fear flashed in his eyes to quickly be replaced by anger and then, worst of all, hurt. "Oh." He sat back, putting distance between us.

I could have screamed with frustration, but I couldn't seem to force my tongue to make words.

"Of course." He barked a laugh that sounded forced and bitter.

No, no, no.

He pushed himself to his feet, shaking his head. I leaned forward, but he refused to look at me. "I'm such a fucking idiot." He raked both of his hands through his hair while his gaze stayed firmly focused on the ground. "I can't do this." Without another word or even a glance in my general direction, he grabbed his key and left.

I stared at the door long after it had closed behind him. What did I do? Why did I freak out? It wasn't like I didn't want him to touch me, so why did I react like I didn't?

I snatched the bottle from the table with the full intent of chugging it. Instead, it flew across the room to smash against the wall by the door, sending glass and beer flying everywhere. I hung my head in my hands and let out a miserable groan. I'd ruined everything. Alex would never forgive me now.

CHAPTER 26

BLACK EYES

A

I wandered around the dorm, not really sure where to go. My shoes were still in my room, so it wasn't like I could go far. Classes would start back up again soon, and already I could see the campus milling with activity beyond the dorm windows. I wished I could've taken the opportunity to go home, at least for a couple of days. My mom was right, the distance would have been good for me. Maybe if I'd taken on a few more tutoring sessions, I'd have been able to save enough. But should-of's and could-of's wouldn't help me now.

Now... now I was stuck in yet another impossible situation with Matt. I'd been a fool to believe that he could ever want me the way I wanted him. Seeing the doubt and panic in his eyes had hurt more than I'd ever imagined was possible. Even hours later, the ache was still there, right beside my excruciating love for him. If the last few weeks had taught me anything, it was that I'd never be able to stop loving Matt.

The longer I roved the halls, the more I felt like there was really only one option left. I couldn't live like this. I'd tried. Maybe someday I'd be able to just be friends with Matt, but not now. Something told me that would never happen, though. It wouldn't be enough to tell him we couldn't hang out anymore—he'd never let it be—I'd have to leave.

My chest tightened at the mere thought of not seeing him every day. It hadn't exactly been easy when I'd left Daniel, but by the end, I'd felt liberated, like I was finally free to be me. This was different. The pain went way deeper. This wasn't some band aid I could rip off. It felt more like giving up a part of myself than trying to move on with my life. But that didn't change what needed to be done.

I took a deep breath to steel my resolve and made my way back to the dorm. Whatever happened, I couldn't let Matt steamroll me. I would be strong... for both of us.

When I opened the door, it was to an empty room. There was no sign of Matt or anything else. For a moment, I was a little put out. He wasn't even waiting for me to come back? I checked my disappointment and forced myself to see this as a mercy. I'd get farther along in packing my things if he wasn't around to stop me.

As I walked past the table, I saw my book was there, along with several notes and the bookmark. It looked like the sketch he'd been working on was almost done and, contrary to what I'd originally thought, it took up the whole page. I resisted the urge to take a closer look. It would just be one more thing trying to keep me here. Without really paying attention to the other things on the table, I grabbed the book from amidst the clutter and the others I'd left on the counter. A few more feet and I'd be safe in my room.

"You came back."

I gave an involuntary flinch. He sounded so relieved. Now that I'd been spotted, it was pointless to ignore him. He'd bulldoze his way into my room if he had to. I couldn't take that, so I turned to him.

"Alex, please. I'm sorry. I-"

"No, Matt." Even saying his name was painful. Damn it, I would make it through this without falling apart. "I can't do this anymore. I won't do this anymore."

His mouth fell open, and it seemed to take him a second to recover. "What are you saying?"

"I'm saying I can't be your friend. It's too hard. I'm going to pack my stuff up and request to switch dorms in the morning." I had no idea if it was even possible, but I sure as hell was going to try.

Panic that bordered on terror exploded across his face. "You can't. You're my best friend."

"Well, I can't very well stay here. Can I?" I snapped. At least if I was angry, I wasn't a teary mess. "You won't have to worry about anything. I'll go see Marquis in the morning and get the room assignment changed. Maybe you'll luck out and have the whole place to yourself for a semester."

"Alex, wait. Just tell me what to do." He took a half step forward. "How can I make this right?"

"There's nothing you can do. It's... it's not you." That was only partially true, but it got his ire up.

"I swear, if you try to pull some it's not you, it's me bullshit..." The threat hung unfinished. "There has to be a way to make this right. We can go back to the way it was. We won't drink together anymore and... and..." he floundered, clearly not sure what he could do to fix this.

"Just stop. I know you want to keep being friends, Matt, but I just... can't. It's too difficult for me."

"I don't understand why. What's the big deal?"

"Because I'm in love with you," I replied with a little too much force. I hadn't meant to tell him that, but I felt better now that it was out. Despite his obvious surprise, he still didn't back down.

"I can fix this. You just have to tell me how."

"How? This isn't something you can fix. I've already tried. I can't do both. It hurts too much."

"But I can't lose you." He might as well have plunged a knife in my gut and twisted. "There has to be something. We... I...

There has to be some way I can fix this." His voice threatened to break.

"There's nothing you can do."

He shook his head like it could somehow dispel what I was saying, a stubborn set to his mouth. "I don't believe that. There has to be a way to make this better. I won't let you go. I can't." His beseeching plea only made me angry. This was hard enough without him being selfish.

"What's it going to take for you to understand? These aren't just words, Matt. What can I do to prove that to you?" I set the books down hard enough on the counter that he jumped. I needed him to understand why I couldn't do this, why this was impossible for me.

Without warning, I stalked over to where he was standing. I grabbed his face with both hands and kissed him. He seemed unsure of what to do, but I didn't stop. I needed him to understand that loving him wasn't some passing fancy, or college crush; it had completely eaten me up so that I couldn't even breathe. I poured everything into the kiss, all the heartache, all the wishful thinking, even my desperate hope that someday he might love me back. This was probably the last time I'd ever get to do this, and I'd be damned if I wasn't going to make it count.

The longer I kissed him, the more I was in danger of losing what remained of my resolve. I loved kissing Matt; it was unlike anything else. I tried to rein it in, but he was still kissing me back.

"Matt, I've been completely wrapped up in you since the first time I saw you." I rubbed my thumb over his swollen lips. Perfectly kissable. I needed to stop.

I placed a lingering kiss, reveling in how his mouth molded to mine. I needed to go. Even having decided hours before, the decision felt like agony. I didn't want to leave Matt. I had to. I resisted the urge to steal one last kiss and released him. Already I could feel the ache spreading painfully across my chest. I quickly turned to retrieve the stack of discarded books.

"Like I said, don't worry about anything."

"Alex."

"I'll take care of everything. Student affairs will be open tomorrow pretty early and I should be able to get this sorted."

"Alex." I couldn't let him stop me. If I stopped, I'd never leave. I kept talking to drown him out.

"If I end up leaving something by accident, don't worry about getting it back to me. You can keep it."

"Alex," he said with enough force to pull me up short.

"What?" I looked at him. I knew I shouldn't have, but this was part of the problem: I couldn't seem to tell him no.

He swallowed. It looked like he was going to shuffle his feet. He didn't. He stared firmly back. "Let's try this."

I let out an exasperated sigh. "What are you talking about?" I already felt drained, and I hadn't even made it to my room yet. What was it going to be like getting my things out?

"This." He gestured between the two of us.

I crushed the stubborn hope that blossomed in my chest. "Don't. We both know you'll say or do just about anything to keep me. It's not funny, it's cruel." My voice cracked. I paused to gather myself. "I'm going to finish getting my things. I'll stay mostly out of the way."

"For crying out loud! Would you stop talking and listen?" He glared defiantly at me, heat shimmering in his eyes. "You're right, I would do pretty much anything, but I'm serious. I... I want to do this."

I shook my head, determined not to fall for it, no matter how much my heart wanted to believe. "You don't know what you're saying."

"Would you shut up? You don't understand, Alex." He paused as if not sure how to go on.

I waited patiently; he'd made it abundantly clear I wasn't getting into my room without him saying his piece.

He took a deep breath and let it out slowly. "I don't dream, not ever. Before I came here, I couldn't tell you the last time I so much as had a daydream. But I dream about you every night. Every single night without exception. And ever since... ever since that night, they haven't been the same."

This was news to me, but it didn't mean anything. We spent a lot of time together. It was bound to happen. I mean, I dreamed about him all the time too, but that didn't make them equivalent. I opened my mouth to stall him. This was only making things harder for both of us, but he beat me to it.

"And that kiss," he began with a lopsided smile. His eyes went black, catching me off guard. It didn't look like he was shadowing anything, but they were perfectly midnight just the same. "That kiss is certainly going to keep me up." He blinked, and they were back to their usual ethereal blue.

Shaken by both his words and what I'd witnessed, I didn't really know what to say.

"At least let me try." Matt stepped forward, and I danced backwards.

None of this was going at all like I'd expected. Of all the things I thought he'd say, this hadn't even made the list. Finally, I found my voice. "I need time. Can you give me that?"

He looked unsure, but nodded anyway.

Feeling out of sorts, I retreated to my room. Even with the door closed between us, I could still feel him on the other side. I pinched myself and was rewarded with a very sharp, very real pain. Not a dream then. I wanted to believe his proposal was genuine, but I couldn't bring myself to trust it. Not that I thought Matt would lie. It was that I knew he really would do anything not to lose me as a friend. Though I never dreamed he'd go so far.

My mind struggled to make logic out of the whirlwind of doubt and hope. Where did I even start processing what had happened? And his eyes. What was that about? Nothing had been shadowed, not even him. I was sure of it. It was as if he'd checked out, but I was at a loss for a time I'd ever seen him more intense.

Answers. I needed answers. There had to be an explanation for why his eyes would do that. Something I was missing. Something I didn't know. Deep down, I recognized that hyper focusing on the mysterious detail was really a way to avoid making a decision or thinking about what his suggestion. But that didn't prevent me from obsessing. But where could I go to get answers? Who would possibly know what that might mean? One name came to mind: Vera Scry. If anyone could tell me what or if his eyes turning black without evidence of shadowing was even a thing, she could.

I checked the time. It was definitely getting late, but there was a chance she'd either be in her office or in the classroom getting ready for the new semester. I glanced at the closed door where Matt's presence continued to hover. There was no way I was getting out of the dorm that way without him at least saying something.

I considered my bedroom wall. In theory, the hall was at worst twenty centimeters away. That wasn't far, right? Except, I'd never shadowed through anything before. Then again, Matt did it all the time... by accident. How hard could it be?

I slipped on my shoes and stepped up to the plaster where I let out a slow breath. The important part was not to overthink it. I just had to make sure I remained in a shadow state until I was positive I'd cleared the wall or risk getting stuck. My heart rate ticked up while I stared intently at my chosen point of passage. This absolutely qualified as advanced shadowing, and we hadn't really covered more than the concept. I shook off my mounting nerves. I could do this.

I let out another steadying breath and let my body become one with the shadow realm. The world appeared muted, both in color and sensation, but was more unnerving was the way my awareness expanded. I could easily sense even the smallest shadow in my room and Matt was basically a pulsing beacon of Shadow energy. That energy shifted as if he was aware of me too and fear that he would storm in here before I was ready to face him again got my feet moving. In two steps, I was on the other side. I made sure all of me was actually in the hall before returning to my physical form. My sensory perception of Matt shifted, betraying his realization that I was no longer in my room. I sprinted down the hall before he could investigate.

The sun sat like a molten ball on the horizon, its amber glow flooding the campus. I almost turned back at realizing it was even later than I'd thought, but that would mean going back to the dorm, which I wasn't ready to do. All the way to Mysterio College, I kept telling myself how ridiculous my fixation was. His eyes changing like that was probably nothing. Maybe he had shadowed something, and I'd been too distracted to notice. Besides, odds were that Vera wouldn't be there at all. She hardly ever was anyway. Why did I think she would be in her office now? Because I needed her to be?

When the oversized doors swung open, I gained a bit of optimism that at least someone was here. My footsteps echoed in the empty corridor as I made my way to Vera's office. To my dismay, her door was closed and the opaque window dark. I glanced around at a loss. Then I realized the classroom door was cracked open and noise was coming from inside.

I slipped inside, expecting to find one of the TAs. Much to my surprise, Vera looked up at my entrance and her face lit with surprise.

"Roman, what are you doing here? Is everything alright?" She put down the posters she was organizing, giving me her undivided attention.

"No, I mean yes, everything is fine. I... I have a question and I couldn't think of who else to ask," I stumbled.

She smiled and waved me over. "Why don't you give me a hand with these and I'll see what I can do about answering your question?"

I gently closed the door behind me. She noticed the move, but didn't comment. I plucked up the next poster and held it where she indicated while she pinned it down. "Why are you using push pins? Wouldn't a spell be easier?"

She shrugged. "Probably. But just because we have powers, doesn't mean we should use them for everything. Sometimes it's nice to do things the long way." She pressed in another pin and passed me the next poster. "So, what did you want to ask?"

"It's... uh... kind of personal."

"Oh? Is it about Matt?"

I looked at her in shock, but she didn't turn from her task of righting the poster. "Why would you assume that? Never mind, it is about another shadow demon. They did something I've never seen before. I mean, I've seen it, but not like this."

She finally stopped what she was doing to look at me. "Let's hear it then." She put her hands on her hips.

I swallowed, suddenly anxious about what I wanted to ask, not the least of which, because it was about Matt. "Have you ever heard of our eyes going black without us doing anything? Wait. That doesn't make any sense. Let me try again. Like, we aren't actually shadowing, but our eyes are black like we are. It's nothing, right?"

Her light curiosity vanished behind a cloud of dark seriousness. "Who did you see do this? Did someone say something to you?"

"What? No! No one has said anything to me about it. I just, I was just wanting to know. It kind of freaked me out." I glanced between the fresh poster in my hands and her, not at all liking her reaction. "So, you're saying this is a real thing? What does it mean?"

Her intensity slipped to be replaced by what looked oddly like embarrassment, but that couldn't be right. Vera had conquered nations, had helped overthrow an entire supernatural government. She was fearless. What in Nyx's name could have her looking so....awkward? "Well... it's... I mean..." she fumbled, which only ratcheted up my anxiety. "Good grief, of all the questions for a student to ask. I'm not old enough for this shit." She gave me a sidelong look, her mouth turned down in a resigned frown.

"I take it this is actually a really personal thing?"

"You could say that. So," she paused, taking a deep breath, "you know how Fire Demons can have flare-ups? Like when they get too worked up or emotional?"

I nodded, though I failed to see how that related.

"Consider this the Shadow Demon equivalent."

My face scrunched as I tried to make sense of what she way saying and came up empty. "I'm not following."

"I can't believe I'm saying this out loud." She ran her hands through her red hair, causing it to frizz. "Alright, here goes. Black eyes are a manifestation of a Shadow Demon's true nature and their true desires. It's not contingent upon manipulating shadow. It usually happens when we're exceptionally worked up and in the moment."

I shook my head, still confused. "Like angry? I've seen that plenty of times. This was different."

"Think other extreme emotion." Her face turned red, and she looked away.

"What? Like...." I trailed off. I thought about what had happened and what Matt had said about the kiss keeping him up tonight. "Oh." High emotion, and he'd given me that grin like... "Oh!" I repeated, the information settling. "Well, um..." I cleared my throat. "Alright then."

"Yeah, so be careful with that. Having a poker face doesn't do much good when it's literally stamped in your eyes."

I nodded numbly. Well, at least I knew I could trust what Matt had said about wanting to try. Now, to figure out what I was going to do about it. But not tonight. I'd had enough life-altering revelations for one day.

CHAPTER 27

RESTRICTED

M

Alex had fled the coop... again. I sank into one of the kitchen chairs, feeling absolutely miserable.

He'll come back. He did last time.

But the last time he hadn't said he couldn't stand to be here with me. I wasn't sure why I'd said we should try things his way. I didn't even know if I could. Yet, as I thought back, I'd say the same again, and it was more than just wanting him to stay. Some part of me wanted to see what would happen. Alex was unequivocally my best friend, and I'd do anything to keep him, but what if he was actually more? That would certainly explain the dreams. Maybe being... a couple was exactly the fix we needed. Except he'd left. Again.

Not left-left, though, or at least that's the hope I was clinging to. He'd asked for space and I'd do my best to give it to him. Yet, here I was, staking out both doors. If he'd gone through the wall, though, there was really no point in sitting here. I tried to think of something to do while I waited to see if he really would come back. Distantly, I considered heading to the fight club, but quickly dismissed the fleeting thought. It wasn't worth it, especially not if I was concerned about whether Alex would even agree to my outrageous idea.

I looked at the table covered with notes and realized his book was gone. Pain lanced through my chest as I shuffled through the papers in a panic. Nothing had been disturbed aside from the missing book. He'd taken it. No way I'd lost it.

He wasn't coming back.

I launched out of my chair, and it clattered to the ground. I spun in a circle, taking in the empty space. The dorm felt hollow without him there. I didn't want a new roommate or no roommate at all. I wanted Alex. Except I'd messed everything up so badly. He was never going to come back. He'd slip quietly out of my life without so much as a goodbye, and I'd be left alone. Again.

My chest tightened. I couldn't seem to catch my breath. I struggled for air, but only managed quick gasps. I couldn't do it, not again. Everyone always left. Even my bright, shining Alex, who saved me from the darkness. That's all there was, all there ever would be for me—darkness.

It felt like the lights in the room were dimming, like the hollowness of the space had been given life and was coming for me. Air refused to stay in my lungs and black spots swam across my vision. I'd be consumed by it. No one would ever care enough to rescue me, to keep me in the light. The room was closing in around me, crushing me with the overwhelming weight of emptiness.

This had happened before. The memory was distant and insubstantial, yet I knew with certainty this was not the first time this had happened. I needed to escape, to run, to hide. I needed Alex. I was drowning in darkness. It was going to swallow me whole.

Alex wanted space.

Alex wasn't coming back.

The room only got darker.

I begged my feet to move. Rather than to the door, they took me to the sink. I turned on the cold water and stuck my head under the frigid stream. Gradually, I regained my breathing and the oppressive darkness receded. I stayed beneath the spray for a few minutes more, letting the icy water run over the back of my head. Then I reached up and turned it off. It wasn't until I was drying my hair with a dish towel it occurred to me what I'd done.

I blinked and looked around the room. Everything appeared normal enough now, but I'd felt that sensation of darkness moving before: Vera had done it, and so had Alex. In my panic attack, I'd shadowed the entire room... and targeted myself. I swallowed hard. Yes, Shadow Demons were very dangerous and not just to other people.

Now that I was properly terrified of myself and everything else in the room, I couldn't stay here. It was getting late, and my options were limited. Wherever I went, I didn't feel safe enough to be on my own. What if next time I didn't snap out of it? The darkness was something that couldn't be escaped. What happened if the very darkness a Shadow Demon summoned consumed them? Could we come back from that? Or did we just become darkness?

I shook myself, fearing that the morbid thoughts would trigger another episode. I scraped the notes into my bag, not caring that half of them got crumpled yet again. My gaze fell on Alex's forgotten key as I went to grab mine. Darkness crept along the edges of my vision. I quickly exited the dorm and made a bee-line for the library. It was slim that there would be other students there this soon before classes or this late at night, but there was at least one guaranteed soul—the librarian.

I got there so fast that I couldn't help but wonder if I'd shadowed part of the way. It didn't matter. I was here now. I dropped my things on my usual table with an audible thud, earning me a reproachful glare from the librarian, who seemed to materialize out of nowhere. I'd been secretly toying with the idea that she was actually a ghost. However, I wasn't brave enough to test the theory, and couldn't think of anyone

I wanted to talk to enough to ask. Her appearance was timely though, because I had a question for her.

Quickly, before she could disappear to some other part of the library, I pulled out one of the pages. Thankfully, it was the one I needed. I smoothed it out and presented it to her. She eyed me and the page skeptically.

"I need to find this guy's last name." I pointed to where I had notated the reference books I'd found and their connection, as well as my copy of his sigil. "How can I do that?"

She contemplated the page without touching it, then silently walked away.

"Hey wait!" I called after.

She spun and gave me a stern look, holding up a finger to her lips. When it was clear I got the message, she waved me to join her. I followed a few paces behind as she quietly considered each row we passed. After what felt like an eternity of wandering, she turned down an aisle.

I'd never been in this part of the library. A glance at a dusty plaque said that it was restricted. Considering how much of her ire I'd earned over the last few months, not to mention weeks, I was impressed she was allowing me anywhere near this section.

She walked down the tight row and paused several feet away while I lingered in the opening.

I eyed the tall stacks of shelves situated practically on top of each other that seemed to reach toward the top of the vaulted ceiling. Dusty tomes lined the shelves, giving me an idea of the last time they'd been touched—a solid never. The more I stared at the imposing display of forbidden knowledge, the less I wanted to follow her. As it was, she seemed to be encased in shadow, the narrow space getting even darker farther on. Rather than urge me to hurry, she waited patiently for me to conquer my fear.

I thought about how close the darkness had come a short while ago. Did I dare risk walking into its embrace willingly? I took a deep breath and stepped forward. Almost instantly, my trepidation doubled.

This was a mistake. I'll never escape.

I took another deep breath. I could do this. It was only ten feet.

Ten months.

The thought came unbidden. Did I even care anymore? The only thing I really cared about was Alex. And if he didn't come back, ten months—seven now—meant nothing. Alone on the street or alone in the dorm, it wouldn't matter. I'd never live long enough to find out.

The sensation of darkness pulling at me got stronger, yet the librarian remained completely unfazed. Eight feet.

I did this to myself. I let all of my issues and hang-ups ruin the only friendship I'll ever have.

Five feet.

Slipping into the night might not be so bad.

The pull got stronger. Three feet. I was close enough now that I could see what the librarian was pointing to.

Two.

It won't matter what I find out about this mysterious knight whose family had decimated my kind. I'll never get to tell Alex.

One.

My hand shook as I reached up to grab a tome easily the size of my head. Like all the others, it looked like it hadn't been disturbed in decades. The gray leather binding felt like it might flake away in my hands. I carefully opened the book. Right at the beginning was a list of crests and sigils, and there among them, my knight's. The Latin beside it I knew said the name of his order, but past that, I had nothing. Everything was in Latin. Not a single word was in anything I could read or even pretend to understand.

I glanced at the librarian, who gave me a knowing smile. She walked past me towards the exit and I followed quickly, eager to leave this ominous place of darkness behind. She hadn't mentioned anything about replacing the book, so I took it with me.

As we left the confined space, the feeling of despair lifted. Maybe this book would have the answers we needed. Maybe Alex could forgive me long enough for me to share. Knowing more about his favorite story would mean the world to him.

I continued to follow my strangely silent guide to an old table with a lamp attached to it. She gestured for me to sit. I did so, placing the fragile book before me. When the binding touched the table, the lamp blossomed to life, creating a perfect pool of yellow light in which to read.

"This is great," I said, "but I already have a table."

She raised an eyebrow and looked at the book. I mimicked her and watched in amazement as the scrolling Latin transformed into a language I could actually read.

"Holy shit! It's a magic lamp."

She frowned at me.

"Oh, language, sorry."

Unfortunately, the cover was far too faded and abused to make out the title. I could only hope the inside was in better shape. I carefully turned the page. Slowly, the letters shifted and moved until I could understand them. Demon Wars: Volume Six 1100-1350. This was a history spanning two hundred and fifty years, and my knight's story fell right smack in the middle. This was everything we'd been searching for and then some. I glanced at the librarian and fought back the sudden stinging in my eyes. Even if Alex couldn't forgive me, I could still give him this.

"Thank you."

She shrugged, offering a small smile.

"Can I...?" I wasn't really sure she'd let me leave the library or even this section with the book, but I doubted I'd make it back down that aisle.

She gave the barest nod and turned to leave.

"Wait." I didn't know what possessed me, but I had to know. "Are you a ghost?"

She smiled again and gave me a wink before gliding silently away.

I shook my head and returned to the ancient volume, handling each page like it might actually crumble at the touch. The material was surprisingly thick, though, and resilient. Perhaps, like the light, the book had also been spelled. I'd read of spells that could make items resistant to time. At last, I found a page that looked like the start.

The war on Darkness was led by the Wardes, Guardians of Light. They alone held the power to harness light itself and burn the Shadow Horde.

In two sentences, I'd learned more than I could have hoped. I'd never heard of a war against darkness or even demon wars like the title suggested. I knew from Demonic History there had been plenty of "demonic wars", but nothing like this suggested. This seemed to imply that this war had been going on for ages. I couldn't help but wonder if it still was.

I gently touched the elegant letters that proudly proclaimed the Wardes as the destroyers of night. This was the first time I'd ever seen the name mentioned. The crest I'd found a few times, but never any names. Most of the time, the sigil wasn't even labeled. And here, on one page, I had an entire list of names and coats of arms, listing the families responsible for culling the demon race.

I closed the book, and the light went out. It was a shame there wasn't a way to take that with me. We'd have to come back. Assuming, of course, Alex was willing. I clutched my prize tightly to my chest and made my way back to my original table. Fortunately, no one had bothered my things, and I could add the book to my pack. I still couldn't believe the librarian was going to let me leave with it. Maybe she also didn't want to venture down that awful aisle.

I shuddered, then swung my noticeably heavier bag onto my shoulder. With exaggerated care, I made my way across campus, very aware that the last time I'd made a similar journey, I'd gotten grabbed. Luck was with me, though, and I didn't run into any unwanted faces.

I stopped in front of the door to our dorm and hesitated before opening it. What if Alex was on the other side with an answer? What if he wasn't?

I took a deep breath and stepped inside. The room was a soft dark that reached out Like a gentle caress. The door closed behind me without a sound. Subconsciously, I pushed my awareness into the darkness. It didn't feel threatening like it had in the library or like it had earlier in the day. It was warm, like a friend, and there, back in his room, I sensed Alex. I let out a breath I hadn't realized I was holding.

He came back.

I was tired from the exhausting day and my draining experience in the library, but I was just as afraid that if I went to sleep, I'd wake up to a world without Alex. For a moment, I debated sleeping on the couch. Except that wouldn't do any good. He'd already proved he didn't need the front door to come and go. Besides, it wouldn't bode well for agreeing to give him space.

I shrugged off my pack and walked to my room. Once inside, I changed and lay on the bed. I had no idea how I'd ever sleep with so much anxiety clamoring in my mind. Yet it seemed in hardly any time at all that I fell into a deep slumber and dreamed about being swallowed whole by the night. The only thing that prevented me from waking up in terror was that I knew Alex was in the darkness, waiting for me.

CHAPTER 28

LAVENDER & SAGE

A

I dallied in my room. While I had a better idea of Matt's sincerity, I still couldn't bring myself to trust it. A subconscious response just wasn't the same as someone telling you outright that they wanted to be with you. Even more than my distrust of Matt's motives—subconscious or otherwise—was my distrust of myself.

I wanted it to be true so bad I was afraid I might be deluding myself. There was no way this could end in anything but disaster, and yet, I desperately wanted to hope, to believe that this could work. That we could work. Before I could, though, I needed Matt to answer a few questions. When I walked into the living room, I wasn't surprised to find him sitting on the couch.

"I wasn't sure you'd come back," he said without looking up, confirming my suspicion the other night that he'd known when I left.

"I would never leave without saying goodbye, Matt. You should know me better than that." No matter how much doing so would hurt. I walked over to join him. The cushion shifted beneath me, but everything else remained perfectly still, including Matt. "Where did you go yesterday?" If he said the fight club, I was done.

He glanced at me out of the corner of his eye, but didn't turn. "The library." It was looking like that was his go-to place to think.

"Find anything?"

"Yes." His gaze flicked to his pack. I expected him to reach for it, but he stayed still, like he was waiting for something. Then it hit me.

He's resigned himself that I'm leaving.

I studied him closer. He looked like a child lost in the woods that had given up trying to be found. My heart ached. I took a deep breath. Here went nothing. "Tell me about these dreams of yours."

Matt still didn't face me. He did, however, turn bright red. Well, that was something. Whatever they were, they weren't innocent.

I didn't prompt him. If this was going to be a thing, then I needed him to volunteer information without me dragging it out of him.

He twiddled his thumbs as if trying to decide how to start. "They began simple enough. Aside from the fact that I was dreaming at all, there was nothing particularly unusual about them. You were just there, something permanent that never changed." He almost looked at me and let out a heavy breath. "That's a really big deal for me." He paused, like admitting that out loud was especially hard.

"After the practicum, that changed. It wasn't just memories of our time together, they were... different. Do you remember that day we ran in the rain?" He looked over briefly and I nodded. How could I forget? I'd almost kissed him right in front of the dining hall. "The night of the practicum, I dreamed of that again. Except this time, when I caught you, we didn't laugh about it and go inside. Instead, we stayed outside and kissed in the rain." He plucked at the hem of his shirt, worrying a thread loose. "It was like my mind was trying to show me how that moment should have gone. Looking back, I realize that it's right. Then all of my memories of us changed. Every time we were too close, anytime I thought you were being awkward, all of them." He took a shaky breath.

I had so many questions, but it seemed best not to interrupt. This was the most personal information he'd ever shared at one time.

"As it went on, I had to admit that they weren't happening because I found out you were gay. I think I actually knew the whole time and was willfully ignoring it. That doesn't matter though. The bottom line was that I kept dreaming about us kissing because... I wanted to." His face flushed a deep pink again. "And it's not just in the dreams. No matter what we're doing, that want is there, and I don't know what to do about any of it." He let out a frustrated huff, then regathered himself. "All I'm asking is that you let me try. I'm not promising I'll be perfect. I'll need patience, but... I do want this."

I felt like the entire world had been suspended. Through his speech, he'd yet to face me. Meanwhile, my heart was somewhere between wanting to race and being too afraid to beat at all. "Okay." The word popped free, and it was like someone had finally pushed play on the world around me.

Matt turned and really looked at me. Doubt shone in his blue eyes like he was searching for the other shoe. So I gave him the clarity he needed.

"We'll do this."

A spark of hope brightened his worried gaze. "Are you sure? I know I've already made a real mess. I don't expect you to forgive me for what I've done."

I sighed and gave him a small smile. "I've already forgiven you, Matt. But I need to know that you understand I love you, that I'm in love with you. It's not some teenage crush on my roommate. Is that going to be okay?"

His eyes were wide, but he nodded. He licked his lips. "I'll make mistakes. This is very... different for me."

"I know." I leaned forward to caress his face. He didn't flinch or pull away. He simply stared back and waited. How was it possible to love one person so much? "We'll just have to take it slow." I closed the distance and gave him a soft kiss.

He let out a faint sigh, and his lips pressed back against mine. The pure intimacy of the moment shattered every romantic notion I'd ever had. This was everything our first kiss should have been. I rubbed a thumb over his bottom lip. "You have a fantastic mouth by the way." I felt him smile against my finger and kissed him again. There was a lingering heat that felt like it was clearly being held in check. I thought about his eyes the night before and what that apparently meant.

I wonder if I could make him do that on purpose.

I pulled back slightly to get a better look at him. They were still decidedly blue, albeit a bit dazed. "Also, you smell like sage."

He blinked. "What?"

"You once told me I smell like lavender. I thought you might like to know what you smell like."

"Oh. Is that okay?" He frowned.

I leaned forward until my nose brushed the sensitive skin beneath his ear, then inhaled deeply, appreciating the pure scent that was Matt. "I like it," I whispered before leaning back again.

It took a moment for me to shake off my fog. When I opened my eyes, I was rewarded with two perfectly midnight ones looking back at me. My lips twitched. I'd never been the seducer before and already I could tell I liked it immensely. I stole a more chaste kiss.

He blinked, and the blue returned.

"Now, are you going to show me what you found in the library or not?"

He blinked a few more times, then glanced around like he was trying to regain his bearings. "What? Right. The library." Without standing, he used shadow to bring his bag over.

I shook my head. He really was impossible, but he hadn't run away yet, so we were already off to a better start. When he pulled out a dusty tome and a handful of papers, I stared in shock. The book looked older than the university.

"Here," he said, passing it to me. "Almost all of it's in Latin, but there's a special lamp in the library we can use to translate."

What he was saying didn't make a bit of sense. I accepted the book, terrified it would crumble in my hands. "Where did you get this?"

"It was in the restricted section."

I looked up at him sharply.

He shrugged as if it was nothing. "The librarian showed me."

I didn't know what was more surprising, that the librarian, who never said a word to anyone, had helped him or that she'd let him take the book out of the library. "Matt, the restricted section is spelled. How did you get in?"

His brow furrowed. "What kind of spell?"

"It's an avoidance spell that makes you face all of your greatest fears." His eyebrows shot up. I'd only heard about it, but it was apparently pretty potent stuff. You had to get special permission and everything. No one simply walked into the restricted section.

Matt gulped. "No wonder I almost didn't make it."

I carefully opened the ancient book. "How did you?"

"I wanted to get it for you."

I glanced at him. "Beg your pardon?"

"I asked the librarian where I could find what we were missing and she took me there. Pointed it right out. Here, look at this." He reached over and began turning the pages.

I thought about telling him to be careful, but I was too busy staring at him in disbelief. He'd faced down his greatest fears, just to get me a book?

He stopped fussing with the pages and started riffling through the crumpled notes in his backpack. "That book, plus this, gives us our knight." He pushed a piece of paper at me. "This goes way deeper than we ever thought. I think your romance might actually be a forbidden affair."

I finally looked at what he was showing me. In the miraculously whole book was a page with a family crest and a name. I recognized the staff encircled with shadowed flames from my book. On the handwritten sheet Matt had given me were reference notes to yet another book, only this one was a Shadow Demonology.

He pointed at the page. Beside two names was the symbol once again. "Meet your knight—Matthias Warde of the Order of Light."

I gasped and nearly dropped the relic. "Mother of Night, Matt. I could kiss you."

"No one's stopping you," he quipped.

I ignored the invitation. He was right about the old book. Every scrap of it was in Latin. "Do you have any idea what this says?" I turned to the title. He looked a little put out, but produced another page. "Demon Wars: Volume Six 1100-1350." I squinted at it, not sure if I was reading it right. "Demon Wars? The only demon wars I know about are the original Wars of Power, but that was way before any of this. And was demon against demon."

"I know. Same here. I haven't read of anything about people and demons fighting. There's more, though. This book specifically references a war against darkness. This was how our kind almost became extinct."

I suddenly felt like I was holding the Holy Grail of Shadow Demons. "Why does no one know about this?" This was definitely something that should have been covered in Demon History.

"I don't know. I thought the same thing. But, Alex, there's another thing."

"How can there possibly be more?" I looked around at his pages full of notes now scattered everywhere.

"The missing pages."

My head snapped up. "You found them?"

"No, I found something else." He drew my attention back to the page with the two names. There was a line connecting them and another that went down to make a 'T'. "They had a child, Alex."

The page swam before me and I feared I might have fainted. "This, this... it's incredible. How did you ever...?" I looked up at him. Per usual, he was watching me. "This is what you were doing for four days." I didn't even need his nod of confirmation. "And..."

"I got snatched on my way back to show you. They wouldn't let me leave without going at least one round. I tried to anyway, but... you saw how that worked out."

I searched his face. I was the reason he'd gotten beaten to a pulp. He didn't have to say it, I knew it. "I'm sorry."

He averted his eyes, his shoulders hunched inward as he studied the carpet.

"Matt, there's one condition to us trying this dating thing." He looked back at me and I saw the fear in his eyes. "No more bruiser club. I can't do this if I know you're fighting all the time."

"Done," he replied faster than I would have expected. "I doubt they want me back anyway after my last performance."

"Have you healed up alright?" Concern colored my words. I'd been so worried, even while I was beside myself with anger.

He raised his eyebrows. "Do you need to check?"

I laughed. Cheeky bastard. "Slow, remember?"

"I remember." He swiped a kiss before I could react, then bounded off to the kitchen, leaving me speechless.

That little devil. Oh, this is going to be fun.

When Matt returned, he had an ice cream in each hand. He held out a carton of strawberry with a smile that warmed me despite the cold now suffusing my hand.

I popped the lid free to discover it was a fresh carton. "Just how much of this stuff did you buy?"

"Enough to be prepared." He extended me a spoon. "You were really mad."

"Who says I'm not anymore?"

He leveled a look at me.

"Alright, alright. I'm clearly not. No need to be smug about it." I shifted to a more comfortable position on the couch. "Now, show me everything you've found. Walk me through this."

He flashed me a dazzling smile and discarded his ice cream to reach for the pages. Then he folded his leg under him and joined me on the couch. He began by laying out each of the pages so he could straighten them and then sorted each into its own stack. The leather-bound monstrosity he left where it was at the edge of the coffee table. I didn't know why, but that book made me nervous.

As Matt bustled about, I couldn't help but think he was every inch his usual, carefree self. I'd known that finding out I was gay had affected him. I just hadn't realized how much until now. Without thinking, I reached out and brushed his hair with my fingertips.

He turned to look at me, his gaze curious yet unconcerned. "What's the matter?"

"I'm sorry."

Instantly, anxiety flashed across his face. He was so sensitive and would never admit it. I'd missed him.

"You weren't the only one so wrapped up in their own thoughts they couldn't see what was happening right in front of them."

His gaze shifted back to the papers, and he seemed to shy away.

I gave him a gentle push on the shoulder, prompting him to meet my gaze again. "I missed my friend, too." His smile started nervous and grew to a brilliant one that shone in his eyes. "I knew you were struggling, and I assumed I knew why."

"Alex, I'm not sure there's anything you could do that would ever make me not want to be your friend anymore." Despite all his protests to the contrary, Matt really had a way with words... when he used them. He squinted at me. "What?"

I shook my head, mirroring his smile. "Just you."

"What about me?" A shadow of the fear I'd caught earlier darted behind his eyes.

I couldn't very well have him doubting his conviction now, not after he'd finally admitted to being interested in pursuing something between us. So I set my ice cream aside and waved him over. "Come here."

His breath caught, and for a split second, his eyes turned solid black. Then I blinked and the distance between us was gone. I refused to let my joy at his instant reaction get the better of me and leaned forward to capture his mouth once more. He melted against me, making my heart soar. I cupped the side of his face and kissed him deeper, slipping my tongue past his parted lips. I'd gotten the sweet first kiss we deserved. Now I wanted the all-consuming ones that had driven me to torment.

Matt sucked in air through his nose, pressing back just as fiercely, but refusing to break away. His fingers scraped against the fabric of his jeans as he clenched and unclenched his fingers.

Smiling against his mouth, I reached down with my free hand to grab his wrist, then moved his hand to the small of my back. I didn't restrain my hum of contentment as his fingers unfurled and warmth seeped past my shirt. No sooner did the sound leave my throat than his hand clenched once more, bunching the fabric.

Matt kissed me harder, like he was starving. If I hadn't been so concerned that he'd freak out like he had before, I would have pushed him back and taken this make-out session to another level. With a restraint I didn't even know I possessed, I pulled away. His tongue flicked out to taste his swollen lips, and I smothered a groan.

There was a decidedly wicked gleam in his stunning blue eyes as they met mine. And said, "You have an interesting definition of slow."

I took a deep breath and let it out slowly, then scooted away from him enough to see the red fabric of the couch between us. "I may have gotten a little carried away."

He shrugged. "Don't hear me complaining."

I laughed and smiled back at him. "You're going to be nothing but trouble."

"So, I've been told."

"Now about these notes of yours..." I arched an eyebrow at him.

Matt's face fell. "For real? But... what about... we..."

I placed a hand on his knee and gave it a gentle squeeze. Instantly, his fumbling ceased. "There's no need to rush. We have time."

He grumbled incoherently to himself and reached for his forgotten papers. When he sat back up, though, an air of excitement had replaced his obvious disappointment.

I left my hand where it was, absently rubbing my thumb on his leg, while he regaled me with his discoveries. Everything about this moment was perfect. My lips still tingled from our fevered—albeit brief—make out. Matt was letting me touch him. We had more information about a story I'd treasured growing up. There was no obnoxious voice in my head belittling me. If this was how incredible being with Matt was in one afternoon, I couldn't wait for an entire semester.

ACNOWLEDGEMENTS

From the day I sat down to write Matt and Alexi's story, I knew they would always be one of my favorite couples. They helped bring a part of me to life that I didn't know was hiding in the shadows. I've poured so much love into writing War on Darkness, and hope it brings others a modicum of the joy it has brought me.

While I'd love to regale the world with an exhaustive list of all the people who've helped me on this journey, there a few that I'd like to extend a special thank you. M. L. Eaden was the first person to show me that my stories could be read with the kind of passion I'd only dreamt about. It's because of her I knew I had something worth sharing with the world.

To my Beta readers, Teri, Lara, and Brandon, I couldn't have done it without you. Your kindness, encouraging words, and helpful feedback led to some of the most amazing scenes and character interactions. Thank you for pushing me and for pushing my characters.

Last, but never least, thank you, Chloe, for loving these two as much as I do.

ABOUT THE AUTHOR

S Bolanos (she/they) is a genderqueer author and the founder of Chaotic Neutral Press LLC. They believe in love, equality, and the Oxford comma. As a member of the Inclusive Romance Project, S can support and connect with other creative minds.

She is proud of their Cuban heritage, and currently lives in Texas, a startling eight miles from everything, as the saying goes. Their two Labradors, Mr. Darcy & Lizzie, along with their Boxer-mix, Elinor (Dashwood), keep them plenty busy with cuddles, kisses, and never-ending demands for more walkies. S adores their supportive husband who's invaluable when it comes to working out sticky plot points. When not playing with her three dogs or spending time with her incredible husband, she's probably agonizing over edits or escaping into her latest fantasy.

She enjoys creating worlds that feel as real as they are fantastical, and doesn't shy away from the darkness that makes the light so much brighter. Readers can look forward to many stories within the same universe that reach into the past and stretch all the way to the future.

WEBSITE: BOOKSBYSBOLANOS.COM
TWITTER: @BOOKSBYSBOLANOS
INSTAGRAM: @SBOLANOSBOOKS

Special Treat

Scan or click the image below for the Darkness Defined playlist at Spotify!

Want to stay in the loop with all the latest and greatest? Sign up for the newsletter and an opportunity to become an ARC reader! Booksbysbolanos.com/newsletter

Keep reading for a sneak peek at the second installment of War on Darkness!

UBI UMBRA
MORTIS LUX LUCIS ET
OBTINEBET

A NEW SCHEDULE

MATT

I already didn't like the new class schedule. Demon History II was first thing in the morning, which was an obscene time to expect anyone to function. The only plus was that Battle Tactics was right after. Of course that meant you were also a sweaty mess for the rest of your classes. But the worst part was that they were the only two classes Alex, and I shared. Half of the time we couldn't even have lunch together because one of us was running off. The bottom line was it sucked. It was a good thing that I stopped going to the 'bruiser club' as Alex called it too; there just wasn't enough time or energy for it. My only concern was that they would eventually track me down, anyway. It was a constant fear anytime I stepped out of the dorm and was on my own, but thus far, there hadn't been a single sign of either Otto or Neese.

The campus was a blaze of amber as I trudged toward Starling Hall. It had only been a week of fall semester and my back already ached from all the books I was carrying. Part of me couldn't help but wonder if my back really was sore or if it was purely psychological because I was so grumpy about the extra class. Not that I had a right to be grumpy, considering I'd voluntarily signed up for it. By the time I made it to the dorm, I was more than a little tempted to shadow inside rather than climb the stairs, but I didn't trust the backpack to make the trip. My shadowing skills may have improved, but they were still inconsistent.

I walked into our dorm and dropped my bag unceremoniously to the floor. It made a heavy thump before toppling to its side, reinforcing my belief that it really was getting heavier by the day. Maybe a witch had put a curse on it. There were more than a few in my classes. That would be just my luck.

Unsurprisingly, Alex was already there and working on some assignment at the table. His dark hair swept across his forehead in stunning contrast to his flawless cool olive complexion. He looked up and smiled. "Hey, you," he said, the greeting touched by a slight British accent. The way his emerald eyes lit up made my stomach flutter.

I still wasn't sure what to make of the feelings. I'd never been attracted to a man before, but then, I'd also never had the liberty to be attracted to anyone. As uncertain as I was, there was no denying I was into Alex—*really* into Alex. Truth be told, not much had really changed since he'd agreed to date me, except he was noticeably more relaxed... and I was getting in fewer fights.

"I'm going to say it again. This totally stinks. Why do you get to be out of classes before me? It's not fair."

"Might have something to do with the fact that they also start before yours," he said, setting down his work.

"They wouldn't if we were taking the same classes," I griped under my breath. In all fairness, I *had* opted to take different courses from him.

"Oh, I don't know. I kind of like it."

I narrowed my eyes at him.

He laughed as he walked toward me, making my stomach flutter again and my skin tingle in anticipation. "It certainly makes that I get to this more special." His fingers slid around my neck and my breath caught. He hesitated only a moment before he leaned down to press his lips against mine.

All the tension in my shoulders loosened. Even my back stopped aching. Much as I hated my schedule, this was probably the best part of it, even though I had to wait all day for it. I kissed him back, tasting his lips like they were the sweetest treat I'd ever had. Yes, this was definitely the best part of my day, though his fixation on taking it easy was borderline making me manic. I had no idea when I'd become addicted to Alexi Roman, but he always left me craving more.

Alex pressed harder, and I took a reflexive step back to keep my balance, gasping when the wall brought me up short. He took advantage of my surprise to kiss me deeper, his tongue teasing past my lips, his wonderfully soft mouth holding me entranced. It always amazed me how confident he was. I, however, still didn't know what to do with my hands. They opened and closed by my side. I wanted more, *needed* it. I just wasn't sure how to go about it.

Fuck it all.

Throwing my doubts right out the window, I slid my hands around his waist. The rightness of it settled into my bones, making me lightheaded. I pulled him closer, pressing his lithe, muscular frame against me, and deepened the kiss without waiting for an invitation. There was a soft moan, though I wasn't sure who from. It didn't matter. I could do this forever. I tugged on his lip and slipped into the heat that sprung to life anytime we kissed.

He pulled back slightly and looked at me with a grin that made me want to pull him close again.

"What?" I asked, pretending to be equally confident. Thinking about what I was doing usually ruined everything.

"Nothing," he said, his smile growing. He looped his arms around my neck and claimed my mouth again.

I completely melted into it. This was more than he'd given me since this whole thing started, and I hungrily ate it up.

I tightened my arms around him, determined to keep him close where I could savor how amazing he tasted. This was incredible, perfect—and it still wasn't enough. I needed more.

He sighed into me, heightening the buzz already clouding my head. Then he leaned back again and released a soft laugh. "Easy there. Slow, remember?"

Yeah, I was too far down the rabbit hole for that. "I can do slow," I responded, my voice low. I slipped my hand beneath his shirt and trailed my fingers across his lower back. His breath caught and heat flashed in his eyes. Maybe I wasn't the only one desperate for more.

"Night, Matt," he said breathlessly as he reached around to place my hand far from its wandering. "Anyone ever tell you you're nothing but trouble?"

"It might have been mentioned a few times." I gave him a crooked grin. It was definitely more than a couple.

"I bet it has." He brushed his lips against mine in a chaste kiss, then pulled away before I could steal more. "What would you say to hanging out this Friday? We could stay in, watch a movie?"

I couldn't contain my smile. "Alex, are you asking me out?"

"If I am?" He teased me with the possibility of another kiss.

"Then I only have one question."

He quirked an eyebrow.

"Are we getting Chinese or pizza?"

He laughed, stepping back and venturing towards his abandoned homework on the breakfast table. I could have groaned with frustration. He was an insufferable tease. "What would you prefer?" he asked as he resumed his seat.

"Chinese, definitely."

"Done." He pointed at the chair pulled out beside him. "Now get over here so you can actually have free time on Friday."

I rolled my eyes. "Everything is always school with you."

"School is important. What kind of homework have you accumulated?"

"You say that like you assume I haven't done any of it," I scoffed as I dragged my ridiculously heavy bag to the round table.

"Have you?" He had me there.

I plopped down and pulled out my books.

"Are the classes going well?"

"Eh." I shrugged. "Math is easy enough. I can't believe you didn't have to take the next course, though."

"It's not my fault I tested out."

"If I'd known that was an option, I might have tried harder," I complained, not for the first time.

"And now you see why it's important to pay attention during class and not just doodle the whole time," he teased.

I thought about the sketch I'd started during the summer semester—our first semester together at Arminius—when I'd started having weird feelings about my awkward roommate. It was almost done, but there were still a few details I was working on. I wanted it to be perfect. It had to be the longest I'd ever worked on any project.

"What else?" he prompted as I took out a few notebooks.

"They aren't all sketches," I said, belatedly defending myself.

He snagged probably the only folder that was predominantly drawings and gave me a look as he flipped through. "Oh, really?"

"One class." I snatched it back.

He let me have it and grabbed another one. "What's this class?" He gazed at the page curiously.

I shifted to get a better look. "That's Advanced Spells."

"You took the class?"

I rolled my shoulders uncomfortably. "Of course. You said I should."

He looked just as surprised by the admission as finding out I was taking the class. "How's it going?"

"Well, I guess. Most of the stuff so far is pretty basic in concept, though the execution seems far more complicated than necessary. I suspect it's one of those things that it's easier done than explained."

"What do you mean? What kind of magic are you learning?"

"It's still all shadow magic, kind of like our version of things that other people can do. Like manifesting something out of shadow and getting it to hold its form without constant concentration or creating a portal. Hiding a portal," I added as an afterthought.

"That all sounds really complicated."

"But it isn't. You just have to know what you're doing." I shrugged again. The irony, of course, was that I rarely felt like I knew what I was doing, especially where Alex was concerned. "What?" I asked when I realized he was staring.

"You never cease to amaze me. I can't get you to admit to being able to shadow half the time, and here you are, telling me that shadow spells are easy. Matt, only higher levels can even hope to master shadow spells. I bet you're top of your class."

I squirmed beneath his intense gaze. Alex was the smart one, not me. "Why do you say that?"

"Because, aside from Vera, I'm pretty sure you are the strongest shadow demon on campus."

I barked a laugh. "That's preposterous. There are plenty of others better than I am. I mean, look at you. Besides, the entire class isn't demonic. I think some are just there for research."

He shook his head, clearly exasperated. "I don't know how many times I'm going to have to tell you before you finally believe me. You are a more powerful demon than I am."

"You don't know that," I insisted.

"Yes, I do. I can sense it." He dropped his gaze to where he was playing with the edge of some papers. "Turns out that might actually be my specialty."

"Specialty? We have those?"

Like flipping a switch, Alex brightened, momentarily stealing my breath with the passion shining in his eyes. "Yeah, I learned about it in my Powers class. Like witches, some demons have areas they excel in. So, like a witch might have a gift for scrying or weather magic, a demon could be sensitive to power levels or exceptionally good at shadow walking. The higher up you go in levels, the more likely that you have more than one specialty."

"If you say so. If yours is sensing power levels, then what's mine? Besides getting into trouble," I added.

He chuckled. "That's definitely one of them. Who knows? Personally, I also think you're fantastic at shadowing. You seem to do it without thinking most of the time. But maybe you're also a natural at shadow magic."

"I don't shadow *all* the time."

"Maybe not in class, but when we're alone, you do. It's almost instinctive. That day I left; you said you knew. How?"

"That's obvious, because you weren't here anymore." I didn't enjoy having to think about that day. I'd been terrified my insecurities around my attraction to him had royally screwed everything up. That not only would I never get to understand these feelings, but that I'd also sabotaged the best and only friendship I'd ever had. Even a couple weeks later, I was still nervous he'd change his mind and disappear altogether without a word, no matter what he said to the contrary.

"But how did you *know?*" he pressed. "It's not like you saw me leave. The only way you would have known was by sensing the shift in my shadow presence. Instead of seeing me leave the dorm, you *felt* it."

"That still doesn't make sense. I'm not doing anything special."

"You've got to be the most stubborn person. Alright, homework can wait for a minute. I'm going to prove my point." He pushed away from the table and stood with his hands on his hips.

"We're not going to arm wrestle again, are we?" Not that I would object to getting to touch him again, even if it was for a silly game. He laughed like I figured he would. Strange to think that first interaction was only a few months ago.

"No, we're not going to wrestle. I'm pretty sure at least one of us wouldn't survive that," he replied with a smirk. "I'm going to shadow out and I want you to find me."

"Alex, really? Hide and seek? Always the kid games with you," I teased, though some of those "kid games," were my favorite memories.

"Shut up and just try it." In the blink of an eye, he faded all to black and was gone.

Damn it.

I looked around anxiously, expecting him to pop out at any moment and say boo. "Alex, this is stupid. Come on, cut it out," I said into the seemingly vacant space.

He walked out of the cabinets still the color of midnight. "Not until you actually try. Quit being so bullheaded." Once more, he vanished.

I ground my teeth.

Why can't we sit here and do homework like normal people?

I blew out a frustrated breath and attempted to focus. He hadn't gone far before. Maybe I could guess where he'd be and get lucky. I stood and walked toward the fridge. But the closer I got, the more wrong it felt. I frowned. Maybe he'd spirited away to his room. That was definitely something I could get behind. I eagerly adjusted my course, but as I got closer to his door, that also felt wrong.

What the hell?

I stopped halfway to his door and considered what I could sense. The shared living/dining/kitchen area was quiet beyond the sound of my breathing. Beyond our sanctuary, I could hear the muffled steps of someone walking down the hall. There, in the back of my mind, I could just make out the strange sensation of someone else. Close. The more I focused on it, the more it *felt* like Alex. I zeroed in on the source. I walked towards the center of the living room, then halted by the coffee table. Before I could second guess myself, I reached into the couch and pulled Alex out by his arm.

He grinned ear to ear as he returned to normal. "I told you, you could do it."

"But I didn't..."

"Now do it again." He disappeared.

"I thought we were supposed to be doing homework?" No response.

He's absolutely insufferable when he wants to prove he's right about something.

I tried to relax and get back to the state that I'd just been in, but the focus wouldn't come.

This is ridiculous. I just want to sit down and be with my friend. That's all. Why does he always have to make things so damn difficult? Isn't it bad enough that he gets to start chilling out for the day early? I knew I shouldn't have signed up for that extra class. If he's going to be pulling stunts like this, I'll never get to spend any real time with him.

My exasperation was only getting in the way. He said that this was no different from Shadow Magic. You just had to know what you were doing. But I didn't. I didn't know how any of this worked. Spells were easy. They came with instructions and rules. This was more like making it up as you went. I felt something move to my right by the front door and dismissed it. No way it was Alex. He was in the kitchen.

My eyes widened, and I turned in place. Alex was in the kitchen. Why was I so sure that he wasn't by the front door? Because I could sense him, just like the night he left.

"You can come out now. I know you're in there," I said, staring at the corner where the fridge stuck out. Sure enough, out he stepped.

"You really should have more faith in yourself. It's almost like you're intentionally ignoring all the things that make you a Shadow Demon."

I shook my head again, almost as discouraged as when we'd started this weird game. "I just don't understand how any of this works."

"Do you have to understand how your arm bends in order to catch something?" He tossed an apple from the bowl on the counter at me.

I snatched it out of the air. "Of course not."

"Or how your feet grip the ground in order to walk?" He took an exaggerated step toward me.

I placed the apple on the table. "You're being silly now."

He smiled in response and walked closer still. "What about this?" He was officially way too close.

I watched him warily. Alex had a unique ability to unsettle me. I never seemed to know what he was going to do next.

"Do you have to know how your lips work in order to kiss?" He didn't wait for another flippant response. His mouth closed on mine and I forgot what I was going to say. I wanted to wrap my arms around him like I had before, but he didn't give me the chance. After a single brief kiss, he was back at the table, looking exceptionally smug.

Insufferable tease.

"If this is how homework is always going to go with you, we're never going to get anything done," I griped, taking out the last of my notes and joining him. He laughed and picked up his pen to keep working. I shook my head and followed suit.